Murder
in the
Tower of
Happiness

Murder
in the
Tower of
Happiness

M.M. Tawfik

ARABIA BOOKS
LONDON

First published in Great Britain in 2009 by
Arabia Books
70 Cadogan Place
London SW1X 9AH
www.arabia-books.co.uk

This edition published by arrangment with
The American University in Cairo Press
113 Sharia Kasr el Aini, Cairo, Egypt
420 Fifth Avenue, New York, NY 10018
www.aucpress.com

ISBN 978-1-906697-14-3

Printed in the UK by J F Print Ltd., Sparkford, Somerset
Cover design: Arabia Books
Page design: AUC Design Centre
Cover image: Getty Images

The First Page

One of these days I'll write a poem
about the sky, a rose pinned on a bosom,
my kitten, the vagabond violin,
two palms soaring in happy heights,
bread crumbling in a faraway room,
a paper fan,
a sultry black girl;
about sponges,
grapes, new clothes,
the kites of Shoubra;
about chess
a bridge to the gallows,
a jar of sleeping pills,
a foal leaping over a rail
as the iron pierces his belly,
about a child in a nightshirt,
a rainbow after Eid prayers,
the splashes of the sea . . .
I'll write one day,
I'll write a poem,
I'll write it, and if I don't, so what . . .
Birds are not obliged to sing.

Salah Jahin

Sergeant Ashmouni

When the first armchair smashed into the asphalt, Sergeant Ashmouni was at his usual spot in the middle of the Nile Corniche, trapped by the road's twin currents turbulently flowing forth to Maadi and back to Old Cairo. He was wiping the sweat away from his eyes with the worn-out sleeve of his white traffic-police uniform — adding a new stain in the process — when surprise from the thunderous impact catapulted him into the fast lane of the riverside road.

The shocked policeman landed in front of a speeding cab whose driver managed, in intoxicated spontaneity, to avoid him, but at the cost of losing control over his loose-braked Fiat 128, which henceforth became liberated from mankind's hysterical rule. The cab's fate had been taken over by the complex laws of aerodynamics, which caused it to spark a chain reaction that, in a split second, had engulfed a public transport bus, a van taking a shift of workers to the steel plant, five private cars, three taxis, a tricycle, and a handcart carrying a pile of lupine beans.

Thus, without prior warning, Ashmouni found himself at the center of an animated carnival that had sprung up in an instant and quickly spread to the other side of the road. This was the side of the road nearest to the towers that have proliferated along the Nile's bank, the side on which the armchair had fallen in the first place.

The incident lasted no more than a few seconds, yet to the policeman, it seemed like an eternity. An open-ended interval during which, in a succession of confused leaps, he tackled buses, passenger cars, and cabs, narrowly avoiding the vehicles hurtling in every direction. Then he achieved that moment of silence he had always longed for. A moment of security—of the sort that, for years, he had scarcely enjoyed. Ashmouni suddenly found himself washed up on an island of calm and serenity amid Cairo's loud, aggressive ocean. He realized he was lying on his back on the ragged grass in the middle of the broad sidewalk along the Nile.

At that moment—at precisely two-fifteen p.m. on the second of August 1999—as the sergeant lay on the grass catching his breath and trying to collect the fragments of the past few moments, as his fingertips gingerly checked his chest and bare head to make sure he was unhurt, the plates and glasses, the forks and knives, started to pour like rain. He instinctively rolled his body and wrapped his arms around his head, preparing himself for the impact of the incoming projectiles.

A few seconds later, when the ax had spared his neck, he opened his eyes and cautiously looked upward, just in time to observe the cushions and tablecloths fluttering coquettishly down. So he asked himself the delayed questions:

'What's happening? Has doomsday erupted? Have people gone even crazier than they already were?' Gradually, he regained his composure, and started to contemplate the falling books and drifting sheets of paper. Then he raised his head while supporting his body on his elbows, and started to curse those spoiled brats and their parents who thought that money could compensate for bad behavior. But no sooner had the piano's edge emerged from one of the balconies near the top of the building, than the swearing froze in his throat.

Like an angry cloud, the piano's blackness blocked the disc of the sun. It was a fancy piano. He was familiar with its likes from watching Abdelhalim and Farid Alatrash movies. But from his current perspective, the piano lacked any poetic or musical allure. It was menacing, ghost-like, as it floated out of the balcony held by a firm but invisible hand. Its

4

straight, wide edge appeared first, then its silhouette narrowed and ended in the shape of the tip of a roasted sweet potato.

After it had completely cleared the balcony, the piano remained for a few seconds suspended in mid-air. Then suddenly, it plunged. The invisible hand had abandoned it to its fate, rendered it to the force of gravity that makes no exemptions. So, like a bomb, it dropped on the unsuspecting Nile Corniche.

The sergeant followed the piano's fall to the ground as if he were watching a movie in slow motion. A movie that remained silent, only to regain sound the moment the piano crashed into a Mercedes parked at the foot of the tower. The sound-bomb was followed by a series of musical groans: materials of diverse densities colliding, springs tinkling, echoes reverberating—in short, the groans of a dying piano. Then there was silence: a tense alert silence.

When an eternity had passed and nothing else fell, the voices started to come in waves. Intermittent whispers at first, then shrill calls: the shouts of those who suddenly remembered a child who had strayed out of sight, or a spouse lost in the commotion. Then, like long-range artillery, came the honks of cars kept away from the center of events, expressing a temporary displeasure at this unexplained delay and a more profound anger at being left out of the limelight.

At a glance, Ashmouni grasped that it was Shaker Pasha's new car the piano had flattened and turned into mincemeat. A luxurious silver Mercedes of the model nicknamed 'powder' as only drug-dealers can afford one. The millionaire would be angry today and buy a new one tomorrow. These people have mountains of cash from which they shovel without counting. As the famous belly dancer says: if she were to pile her money up and stand on top of it, she'd see as far as Timbuktu.

As if Ashmouni's troubles were not enough, just then the officer arrived on his official motorbike with the shiny nickel parts. His expression revealed it had been no small feat to negotiate passage through the impregnable flesh-and-metal wall of interlocked vehicles and people

5

rushing about in confusion. The officer doled out blame at drivers and passengers alike. Nothing was spared the curse of his frigid eyes: buses turned over on their sides, cars that had crashed into lampposts and tree trunks, the 128 taxi that had ended up on top of the lupine bean handcart on the sidewalk next to the Nile.

The officer found Ashmouni shuffling from where the remains of a piano lay squarely atop the squashed roof of a Mercedes to the location of a broken armchair on the asphalt. The sergeant looked helplessly about him and kept picking up torn books and tattered cushions whose feathers were dispersed on the ground. He had lost all touch with reality as the distinguished officer knew it.

The sergeant's anxiety started to ease when he reassured himself he'd survived the ordeal unhurt, and even more so, when he understood from the exchanged calls between bus drivers and garage attendants that, due to divine intervention, no one was hurt. The incident had ensnared all these unsuspecting victims in its nets then left them alone as if nothing had happened. So, when Ashmouni, at last, noticed the officer, he saluted the man as if a simple accident had occurred or a commonplace quarrel had erupted between two drivers.

The officer took his helmet off, held it under his arm, and looked around him in disbelief. Then he came back to the sergeant, eyes bursting with accusation, and muttered through clenched teeth:

"Damn you, Ashmouni."

✖

The following morning, Ashmouni accompanied the police recruit sent by the investigator to summon him. The sergeant mentally cursed his fate. Here he was, condemned to spend his days among the rabid cars, his shoes sinking in the melting asphalt, with nothing to shelter him from the August sun. A trainer of beasts, protected by neither whip nor moral authority, only separated from the predators' fangs by destiny's delayed hand, yet united with them by the inevitability of his fall. And to make things worse, he had to contend with these mighty officers, who neither showed mercy nor allowed God's mercy to prevail.

The two men crossed the road, walking away from the sergeant's median and approaching the tower's sumptuous entrance with heavy steps. The sergeant fell two or three steps behind the police recruit, trying hard to conceal his anxiety. On this side of the road, there was not a trace to be found of the previous day's events. The Pasha's car had been towed away before the day broke. As for the remains of the piano, armchairs, china, and pillows, these had all been piled into a small pyramid on the pavement next to the Nile and left for the government to deal with.

A young woman suddenly blocked the sergeant's path and shoved a microphone in his face. The foreigner had black, silky hair and slanted eyes. Despite her unintelligible language it was not difficult for Ashmouni to classify her as Japanese. A man behind her carried a camera on his shoulder, which was also pointed at him.

The sergeant instinctively pushed aside the microphone and redoubled his pace to catch up with the police recruit. He signaled to the woman, by raising his shoulders and pursing his lips, that he did not understand a word she was saying.

As he followed the police recruit up the polished granite steps that led to the tower's entrance, he stole a look backward. The young woman was on the sidewalk talking into the camera and pointing to the pile of broken furniture on the other side of the road.

Then the sergeant entered the Tower of Happiness.

Ashmouni voiced customary greetings as he passed the security clerk, but the other did not bother to respond. The sergeant cursed him under his breath in the vilest of terms. The man had barely been here a few months and he was already looking down on him. He missed Abdelaty, the previous security clerk and a good man. Alas, some powerful figures had wanted him out of the way.

The police recruit pressed a button and a musical bell rang. The electric door rolled sideways and the two men stepped into the elevator. Their ghosts stared back at them through the tinted mirrors that covered the elevator's three walls. They felt embarrassed just being here amid all this opulence. The elevator sped toward the thirteenth floor, carrying them across barriers of time and space neither of them had dreamt they would ever traverse.

Since the previous day, Ashmouni had been unable to free himself of the piano's ghost-like image. Its specter had disturbed his waking hours and disrupted his sleep. He even started to suspect that Souma the Owl had cast a magic spell on him. Ever since he took a second wife, he had anticipated her rage and almost expected her to find a way to dampen his fire for Zuzu, the young lass with the bold eyes and the thighs like sculpted marble.

Zuzu would faint at the sight of these lights that glowed with every floor the elevator crossed. And, if her cracked feet were to tread the red marble floor of the tower's foyer, the Owl would surely lose the remaining quarter of her rusty mind.

A grin took shape on the sergeant's face as the thoughts raced inside his head. He is still here in the elevator, but all alone with Zuzu. The tip of her pink nightgown is showing beneath the edge of her loose cotton gelabia. She has nothing on underneath her nightgown. The sight of only a few inches of her see-through nightgown is enough to set his loins on fire. He presses the red button and the elevator stops between floors. With eager shaking hands, he raises her gelabia, then her nightgown. Her silken skin feels like warm cream. True, he married her in accordance with the laws of Allah and his prophet, yet he cannot escape the feeling that he's enjoying her in sin. At the peak of his arousal, the elevator door opens with a metallic ring. He pulls up his trousers and turns around to find the Owl staring at him with a smile that exposes her missing teeth. She sings in her coarse voice:

'Let him take another wife, sister . . . .

We'll see who'll come out on top, me or her.'

With the same metallic ring, the elevator door slides shut. Ashmouni turns to his young wife. She is lying on the floor with her body rolled to one side, naked as the day she came into this world, silent. There is no trace of her clothes or of her plastic slippers. Her black hair fans over her back and across part of the elevator floor. Her small body is fully rounded, its frozen whiteness starting to turn blue.

But this woman is not Zuzu. It strikes him like lightning that this is the corpse of Ahlam Shawarby, the deceased movie star. Fear's uncompromising fist grips Ashmouni, as though he were the accused murderer. He wants to cry out, 'I'm innocent. As God is my witness, I'm innocent.' But his voice is held back, incapable of finding its way to existence. He gasps for breath as if the air is about to run out . . . .

"Don't look so worried, sergeant! The investigator will just ask you a couple of questions then you'll be free to go." The police recruit was already on the landing, holding the elevator door from sliding shut before Ashmouni had come out.

It took him a few seconds to pull himself together and gingerly step onto the thirteenth floor. Then he followed the recruit into apartment 1301, whose door had been left ajar. But no sooner had he crossed the threshold than he froze in his shoes.

Books, sheets of paper, music discs, broken liquor bottles, and torn-up curtains were strewn all over. Gilt chairs, missing seats and some legs, were knocked over. The sofas had been overturned with cushions, springs, and tufts of straw pouring out, as if a giant hand had pulled out their entrails, like women do to birds before cooking them. Video jackets were scattered everywhere: some of well-known movies, others showing naked women in obscene positions. Shattered tables, an eviscerated VCR with cogs spilling out and electronic circuits exposed, a TV with a smashed screen; everything bore the brunt of indescribable rage. Jagged shards of glass from the windows and mirrors and fluffy pillow-feathers equally defied all boundaries and were sprinkled in every corner, adding a dreamlike element to the destruction that inhabited the large apartment.

Were it not for two intersecting passages cleared of debris, one to allow the investigators to cross the wide hall from the entrance—where Ashmouni was standing—to the terrace straight ahead, and the other running sideways between the dining room to the left and the corridor leading to the bedrooms to the right, it would have been impossible for him to tell that the floor was a glistening marble. A pistachio-green marble that imparted a sense of depth and transparency as if one were walking on water, the sensation he'd often imagined of floating across the canal that separated his village from the Abaida farm. This was a floor whose extravagance he'd never seen the likes of, nor imagined in his wildest dreams.

"Wait here."

The police recruit left him and, with measured steps, crossed the green passage to the left side of the hall where another recruit stood under an archway draped in a thick curtain of olive-green velvet. The two young men exchanged whispers with the gravity of generals whose deliberations could alter the course of history.

The sergeant took a few steps along the marble passage. He stopped to contemplate a life-sized statue of a scantily clad woman. The brass figure was leaning on a sofa that had prevented it from falling to the floor. But the woman's head was not visible from the sergeant's vantage point, as it had gone cleanly through a large oil painting that had evidently been smashed against it. The sergeant's eyes toured the hall for the hundredth time but he could still not believe them. It was as though a raging tempest had been trapped in this apartment, and did not rest until it had left it in ruins.

A scene from hell. This was devastation on a scale the sergeant had never witnessed, and he was by no means a stranger to squalor; he had grown up with poverty as a friend and hunger a companion. The stench of sewage overflowing in the alleyways hardly disturbed him, nor was he moved by the sight of a child foraging for food in a heap of garbage.

10

All these were situations that people had no choice but to live with. But what surrounded him in this apartment was deliberate destruction. All this affluence had been shattered on purpose.

The sergeant had witnessed people's anger in the alleys. But it was an anger generated by overcrowding and need. It came in instantaneous outbursts, understandable and soon dispelled. People's smiles would soon return and the music would resume. As for these rich people, he had never imagined that they experienced anything but joy and merriment.

He never imagined this pure loathing that today he could almost touch with his fingertips, this absolute evil that screamed from every corner. It could only be the devil's work.

The sergeant's attention was drawn to a corner of the hall next to the terrace overlooking the Nile. Closer scrutiny only increased his bewilderment. The corner housed a small circular side table with a spotless varnished surface. On a delicate white tablecloth, a porcelain vase with dainty floral designs held a vibrantly fresh white rose. The section of the balcony's windowpane next to the table, clean, intact, and partly covered with a white chiffon curtain, stood in stark contrast with the rest of the room's shattered glass and ripped curtains. Beneath the table also, the pistachio marble floor was crystal clear. This corner had, by some miracle, escaped the devastation that covered every inch of the large hall.

But how and why?

Searching for a clue to explain this mystery, the sergeant noticed a slim copybook on the table next to the vase. But he could not prevent his eyes from drifting back to the rose, which seemed to call out to him, as if saying, 'Come! Here you'll find all explanations, in my perfumed nectar, in my magic touch, in my pristine beauty, here away from the madness that surrounds you.'

Ashmouni invoked the name of God in a loud voice. If it were not for his fear that the police recruits would make fun of him, he would most certainly have unbuttoned his vest and spat inside his undershirt to dispel the devil.

"Boo!"

A shrill cry accompanied by a sudden movement from the statue's direction took him by surprise. The sergeant recoiled backwards with hands raised to protect his face from the small body that approached him. Was this a ghost or a jinn? Ashmouni froze for a few seconds until he realized it was only a child who had been hiding beneath the painting that hung around the statue's neck.

"Yay! I got you I got you I got you!"

The little devil had wide black eyes, spongy disheveled hair, and two matchstick legs protruding from his shorts. Worn-out sandals exposing his dirt-blackened toes appeared and disappeared as he jumped in the midst of the diverse shrapnel that covered the floor. The boy—no older than six or seven—beamed with pride over his outrageous behavior.

"Yesss! One for me, one for me, one for me!"

"Shame on you, son. Like I don't have enough to deal with."

"But it was a good one, right? Right? Ri—"

"Antar! What are you doing there, you little devil?"

Before the sergeant could respond to the boy, a sonorous voice assailed him from behind. Its owner, a bulky man in a safari suit and leather sandals, with not a single hair on his head, was a teacher at university. The sergeant remembered him because of his broken-down Russian-made Lada. Of all the tenants, he alone did not drive a luxury car. The garage attendants called him doctor, though he was no doctor, not even a nurse.

"Hello sergeant, where have you been hiding? You never drop by, that's not right. "

The sergeant could not grasp what the man was saying. He wondered if he had mistaken him for someone he knew well. The man glanced behind his back at the two police recruits then whispered in the croak of one who has swallowed a frog, "How rude! They keep me waiting for an hour in this dump . . . just to ask me a couple of pointless questions! Seriously, this country has no respect for people's intelligence or their time."

He went on in his thunderous voice: "I'll be waiting for you, as soon as the good investigator is finished with you. It's important. Remember, sixth floor, apartment 61."

Then he turned his narrow eyes and hooked nose to the child. "Come on, you little devil."

Antar was busy tearing yellowing pages from a thick book with a worn leather cover. It crossed the sergeant's mind that a book like this would fetch a hefty sum at the second-hand bookstalls of Asbakia. The boy dropped the tome, leaving it to its fate amid the accumulated trash on the floor, and rushed to the door. But the doctor was quicker and caught him by the nape of his neck. He maneuvered the child, like a doll in his steel grip, out of the door. The child's eyes were ablaze with defiance.

The man's voice came to the sergeant's ears after both of them were out of sight. "You've been molded in devil's water."

⁙

The investigator's face seemed paler than the last time Ashmouni had seen him. Ashmouni stood before him, attentive to his every tense move. The investigator, on the other hand, turned over his papers without giving any indication that he was aware of the sergeant's presence. Ashmouni considered the tapping of the investigator's fingers on the table and the periodic grating of his teeth as crucial signals to be overlooked only at one's peril.

At the head of the long table sat the investigator's assistant, silent behind his shabby official register. It was the same assistant who had taken notes last time, except that the interrogation for the actress's murder took place in the tower's foyer. Then, the investigator had stood with his hands in his pockets while the assistant leaned on the security clerk's desk to take notes. Now they both sat behind this great table, which until recently had been the site of banquets—that is, until doom struck without warning.

Ashmouni's left foot started to go numb. With a slight motion, he shifted his weight to the other foot. The investigator raised his eyes and gave him a stern look then went back to his papers, showing for the first time that he was aware of the sergeant's presence. The sergeant's discomfort deepened with every tick of his watch—gigantic ticks that he not only heard, but felt pulsing inside his head.

"We have summoned the abovementioned witness, today, the 3rd of August 1999, at exactly. . . ." The investigator looked at his wristwatch, then the questions followed like a torrent tumbling down on the sergeant's head.

Where had he been at the time of the events of August 2nd? What exactly happened? What did he have to say about the furniture thrown into the middle of the road—had he witnessed anyone tossing it from the building? The cabs, the buses, the tricycle, the truck with its trailer, the handcart with its pile of lupine beans, and the sundry objects that had fallen from the sky . . . how could he describe all this and what did he have to say about it?

"Try to be specific, sergeant." The investigator's fingers tapped on the table.

"Everything happened in the same second, Pasha."

"You are required to recount all that you witnessed. Or are you going to say this time—*again*—that you didn't see anything?" The investigator's anger was muted but palpable.

An extended silence. The sergeant felt a cold drop of sweat meandering down his neck then along his spine. He wished the man would forget the past and focus his questions on traffic accidents.

The investigator banged on the table. Ashmouni was about to explain that there was no reason for him to get all upset since the harm this time— praise be to God—had been limited to material damage, and that in any case, these were people who lost no sleep over a few thousand pounds or even a few million. Instead, the sergeant chose to keep his silence. He was puzzled by the investigator's excessive stress, especially since he

14

had been calmer during the previous interrogation, despite the fact that it had involved the murder of a famous movie star. This observation only heightened the sergeant's anxiety.

"Can you determine the floor and the apartment out of which all the furniture was thrown?"

"This one, of course." The sergeant looked around the dining room for a trace of the outer hall's destruction to prove his point, instead he found the dining room to be clean and in perfect order, as if nothing had happened.

"Are you stating that you witnessed the furniture as it came out of the balcony?" The officer pursed his thick lips. His thin moustache reminded the sergeant of Emmad Hamdi, the classic actor.

"No, Pasha. I didn't see anything. Nothing."

The investigator leapt up, shouting, "You idiot! Then how did you know that the furniture fell out of this apartment?"

"The piano . . . I only saw the piano."

With his arms behind his back, the investigator took a few strides to the end of the table. His crew-cut head looked like an olive on top of his well-built torso. He pursed his lips in concentration. "According to what you *actually* saw, how did the piano get out of the balcony?" His black eyes were menacing.

The sergeant pouted his lips and shrugged his shoulders.

"It would take four men just to move a piano like that a few inches. Who do you think flung it out of the balcony, the spirits?" The investigator's pale face brightened momentarily in a childish smile before giving way again to his customary frown. Then he added in a tone laden with accusation: "Do you have any information or suspicion that there may be a link between the events of August 2nd, 1999 and the murder of the actress Ahlam Shawarby on May 17th of the same year?" The investigator's voice, piercing to start with, was now as incisive as a surgeon's scalpel.

"No, Pasha. I told you everything I know."

15

"Naturally, you're aware of the grave consequences of concealing information in an official investigation." Without giving him a chance to respond, the investigator pressed on: "Now, do you have anything further to add?"

⁘

The sergeant rushed out of the elevator and headed for the tower's entrance. The security clerk stopped him, and tersely said that Dr. Mahgoub needed to see him about an urgent matter. All Ashmouni wanted was to get out of this damned place. Besides, no benefit could possibly come from the doctor who, alone among the tenants, had never given him a tip. He was the only one accustomed to shopping for vegetables and fruit in person, and was notorious for bargaining and giving the vendors a hard time. So it was with a sense of satisfaction that the sergeant flatly rejected the self-important security clerk's request.

But no sooner had he escaped into the open air than a painful sting shot through the back of his neck, a sneaky bee or a vicious wasp's punishment. He turned around to find the young devil Antar cackling. "Yesss! Got you! Got you! Got you!"

The sergeant rubbed his neck and gave the child a look that embodied all the anger he'd accumulated over the past two days, a fleeting glance that betrayed a volcano awakened by fear and guilt. What if the investigator were to uncover what he had done? What if yesterday's incident—which he would never have believed had he not witnessed it with those very eyes the maggots would devour one day—was a sign of heaven's wrath?

"But it was a good one, right? Right? Right?" Antar cackled, swinging his catapult in his hand, unconcerned by the state of the sergeant's neck. "Daddy wants you. Now, now, now!"

The sergeant's anger began to subside before the child's sparkle and vivacity. "But the intersection is on its own, my son. Somebody has to take care of it."

Antar looked up and down the road, trying to figure out what the sergeant was referring to, then his little eyes lit up. "That's okay. You go see daddy and I'll take your place, I'll take care of the cars." Antar gesticulated to prove he knew how to direct traffic, then added quickly, "Can I just borrow your whistle?"

"I guess the intersection can take care of itself for another five minutes. I'll see your daddy and come back straightaway." In his exhausted state, the sergeant found no alternative but to surrender to the child's insistence; he did not doubt that if he wanted to, Antar would gladly hound him for the rest of the day.

"But why? We don't want the cars to crash into each other." The boy's disappointment was evident, then the clouds dissipated and he regained his smile. "Okay let's race! You take the elevator I'll take the stairs!"

Alone in the elevator, Ashmouni watched the numbers flicker past. Who knew, he might yet skim a pound or two off the doctor, since he was so desperate to see him. 'Will you sweeten my mouth tonight?' was young Zuzu's daily greeting. If he happened to go home empty-handed, she'd curl her lip, wrap herself in the blanket, and pretend to go to sleep. And if he persisted and pressed his body against her, she'd push him away, screaming, 'What's wrong with you man . . . can't you see it's that time of the month?' But on those days when he brought home a quarter kilo of basboussa or a roll of baklava from the confectioner's, or even a pack of sunflower seeds and salted peanuts from the roastery, she'd open up to him like a blossom and give him a taste of her honey. Only Zuzu could bring back the years of his youth that—mistakenly—he'd assumed had slipped away.

Ashmouni's eyes lit up with every floor the elevator crossed. Three months had passed since his marriage to Zuzu, yet a normal marital relationship had never developed between them. He treated her like a seductive mistress and she reciprocated by demanding gifts. He lived with her as if in sin and she did not seem to mind—in fact, she astonished him day after day by her brazen pursuit of pleasure. Who would have thought the innocent chick he had wed was capable of all this?

17

The elevator door opened and Antar shouted, "Boo." The sergeant knew he was on the right floor.

Dr. Mahgoub sat in an armchair not so different from the one that had been dropped from the thirteenth floor and started all this mayhem. Wearing striped pajama bottoms and only a sleeveless undershirt on top, he crossed his legs, bringing into view his enormous toes that protruded from a pair of plastic slippers. He held a sports tabloid in the air. The colored photographs of soccer players and beautiful girls sparked Ashmouni's curiosity. The doctor set aside his paper when Antar alerted him to the sergeant's arrival.

"Antar, be a good boy and ask them to bring the sergeant a glass of iced lemonade . . . and tell them to fix it really well." He turned to the sergeant. "Welcome."

After an awkward silence the doctor picked up a thick pile of paper from the side table. As he waved the papers in the air he said brightly, "I'm doing a study on the psychological roots of Egypt's traffic problems. What do you think of the idea?"

Ashmouni started to doubt that he would ever manage to wheedle a pound or two off the doctor who—if the garage attendants were to be believed—had used up his savings from years of work in the oil-rich Arabian Gulf to buy this apartment.

The doctor scrutinized the sergeant's face, but when he found no reaction, his smile faded away and he went on, "Anyway, I would appreciate it if you'd share with me some of the experience you've acquired through daily contact with traffic."

The doctor paused, waiting for the sergeant to react.

Feeling the sweat trickle down his forehead, Ashmouni took off his official beret and started to toy with it. Finally, he was saved by Soad, the maid, who carried in a small tray with a glass of lemonade. She leaned forward with the tray, allowing him a sensational view of her full breasts. As she turned to go, Soad gave the sergeant a quick look from under her long lashes. He found it impossible to resist staring at her departing behind.

The doctor, no longer able to bear the delay, started reading the first page in his pile, in his strong, monotonous voice.

"It is a fact that the traffic problem reflects a civilizational crisis, the product of stress and the psychological imbalances that affect the Egyptian people. . . ."

The taxi driver who blows his horn for no reason, the self-important yuppy who gesticulates to the traffic sergeant to speed up a green light, the drivers who crawl past a red light half a meter by half a meter until they've blocked half the intersecting street: all forms of behavior that— despite their everyday familiarity to the sergeant—sounded strange in the doctor's manicured language.

Then, elated by his own words, the doctor sprang to his feet. His head closely missed the crystal chandelier and his body blocked a considerable section of the Nile view afforded by the open window. The man's enormous mass dominated the hall.

The sergeant felt compelled to say something. "That's big talk, Pasha." He put his beret on the side table, then raised the glass to his parched lips and took a long slow sip of lemonade.

The doctor settled down and went on reading, wagging his large toe in time with his voice, as though he was Maestro Mohamed Abdelwahab waving his baton to his orchestra.

The smooth flow of lemonade down his throat stopped unexpectedly. The sergeant tilted his glass until the ice cubes rolled down against his nose. He discovered the glass was full of ice, which left almost no room for lemonade.

"You like melonade?" Antar sprang suddenly from behind the sergeant's armchair, but by the time he turned around the boy had vanished.

"I found my whistle . . . look . . . better than yours, right? Right?" the child whispered in the sergeant's ear before disappearing again.

The doctor's stern look caught Ashmouni searching around him for the mischievous imp. The sergeant felt it prudent to express renewed interest in what the big man was saying. "Or a trailer carrying steel rods

19

without a sign, sometimes without even lights in the middle of the night," he quickly said.

The doctor's features relaxed and he went on without actually reading from his papers, "And then there's the big squares with five or six police-men, each one doing whatever the hell he feels like—one signals to the cars to stop and the other gives them the go-ahead and the next stops them again, no attempt at all at coordination. Who do they think they are, ministers? Actually, they're not very different from ministers when it comes to the lack of coordination. . . ."

The sergeant interrupted him for the first time. "Oh no sir. You can't compare policemen with pasha ministers. Please don't say things we might regret."

"Well, take another example: the corteges of high officials."

The sergeant jumped up and decisively cut the man short. "The inter-section has been on its own for more than an hour," he said on his way to the door.

"Wait! The heavy stuff is still to come, like when a driver gives a right signal then makes a left turn. . . ."

The sergeant had already pressed the elevator button. The doctor fol-lowed but stopped in his doorway.

"But you haven't finished your lemonade!" The doctor's words reached the sergeant as the elevator door slammed shut.

✖

Ashmouni pressed the ground floor button as soon as he stepped into the elevator, yet the elevator raced upward. He put his finger on the button but to no avail, so he surrendered to the whims of the steel beast that carries people in its belly and watched the small numbers light up in succes-sion. Suddenly, he remembered he'd forgotten his beret on the doctor's table. Should he go back to fetch it and face the man whose talk he mostly didn't understand, and the little of which he got could land him in a load

20

of trouble? Or should he simply send one of the garage attendants for it? They wouldn't object, all good boys who respected him for his age.

At the height of his indecision, the electrical numbers stopped at 13. The issue of the beret faded from his mind as the sergeant was overtaken by the sour taste he had felt in his throat as he'd followed the recruit to this landing. It seemed like an eternity although it was no more than an hour ago.

As the door slid open, he found himself face to face with Mr. Kasseb. He was accompanied by a young man in jeans and blue canvas shoes holding an electrical appliance—a radio or a tape recorder—and in his other hand, a black Samsonite briefcase. An electrician, probably.

"Good man! We were just talking about you," Mr. Kasseb said to Ashmouni, deepening his discomfort.

He had suddenly become the focus of everyone's interest. But what did they all want? These very same people would once have passed him by without noticing he was even alive, that he was a human being with feelings and needs. Sometimes, they would show him charity without looking him in the eyes. When they gave, it was not out of the goodness of their hearts but to relieve their consciences of their own philandering and immorality. They thought they could buy divine blessing, and some-times his silence, too.

If Mr. Kasseb had mentioned him in his conversation, then he must expect him to be of some service to this technician. But how?

Mr. Kasseb held the elevator door open with a small delicate hand that contrasted with his chubby forearm, whose black hair added a shade to the darkness of his skin. A thick gold bracelet dangled on his wrist. He turned to the technician. "This is Sergeant Ashmouni in the flesh, the only person who witnessed the whole thing from beginning to end. You'll need a session or two with him." The elevator door struggled to slide shut, but Mr Kasseb's experienced hand prevented it.

As was his custom in the summer, Mr. Kasseb wore a short-sleeved silk shirt with a colorful floral design. He left his top four buttons open, exposing

21

an enormous belly under a thick blanket of dark hair, a black forest in which a gold pharaonic cartouche swung from a chain. His white trousers were transparent and exposed his shirttail covering his privates and part of his thighs. He wore his white shoes—made of delicate leather—with no socks.

The sergeant's first impulse was to deny what the short fat man had said, but he found it prudent not to make the man look like a liar before this stranger. After all, Mr. Kasseb was the landlord's agent, and the man with the final word on all matters, since Sheikh Wahdan, who owned the tower, rarely visited Cairo.

"Nice to meet you," the young technician muttered as he stepped into the elevator.

"Some other day I mean, when you've had the chance to check out the tower and meet the tenants," Mr. Kasseb's full bluish lips added.

He held the elevator door for another moment, while sweat oozed from his forehead and cheeks. He cleared from his eyes locks of long soft hair that the garage attendants swore was either a wig or extensions. The man seemed to expect the technician to say something, but when it became apparent he wouldn't speak, Mr. Kasseb freed the door to slam shut with a metallic ring that was muted by its rubber encasing.

Unable to control his curiosity, the sergeant released a torrent of questions as the elevator started its descent. The young man responded at first with obscure and tentative answers, but finally admitted, "I specialize in the paranormal."

Ashmouni had heard that the owner of the ruined apartment had decided to enlist the help of a spiritual medium, but he could not believe that this tall skinny youth, probably in his mid-thirties, was the psychic sheikh upon which all hopes hung. The sergeant was not too shy to stare. The lad's jeans and T-shirt were clean but not really respectable. His short kinky hair, broad forehead, dark delicate features, and hazel eyes with an attractive glint only indicated normality.

The sergeant rushed out of the elevator in dismay. Did this guy think he could conjure up the spirits with a transistor radio or a tape recorder?

Whoever said these matters required technicians and appliances? All you really need for a séance is a straw basket, a piece of string, and a pen. These days the poor were being kicked out of all professions, even quackery. But what shocked the sergeant most of all was the young man's bare head. With neither hat, wizard's cone, tarbush, nor even an emma, how could he sit in the masters' presence? Did he expect to converse with the spirits bareheaded?

What had these arrogant people done to the world? Had they no respect for anything anymore?

The sergeant was surprised to find the investigator in the foyer facing the doorway. He was talking to a woman who scribbled in a notepad, zealous to catch every word he said. Alert yet motionless, the two recruits waited a few meters behind. Ashmouni ducked to one side of the hall where he hoped he wouldn't be noticed, and waited for the investigator to leave. He could only see the investigator's backside but had the opportunity to study the woman. Her grass-green suit covered her small body like cellophane wrapped around quality chocolate. His focus moved quickly away from her slender arms to feast on the shapely thighs beneath her trousers.

The investigator was trying to leave, but the journalist kept blocking his escape and encircling him with a torrent of questions. She bit the end of her pencil, then glanced sideways at the sergeant, as though his gaze had burnt her skin. With a quick motion, she removed the pencil from her mouth and gave him a fiery glare, silently accusing him of invading her privacy.

Taking advantage of her momentary lapse in concentration, the investigator stepped around her and out of the doorway. The first recruit rushed ahead of him, while the second followed a few steps behind, carrying the man's briefcase with exaggerated respect. The journalist pushed a strand of her coal-black hair away from her eyes and took a few steps down the front stairs. The recruit opened the back door of the navy-blue Peugeot but the investigator froze before getting into the car. Something in the direction of the sergeant's intersection had captured his attention. Unable, from his vantage point, to see what was happening, Ashmouni's heart fell. Hadn't the damned intersection witnessed enough catastrophes?

While the journalist stood on the stairs shaking with laughter, the recruit shut the car door behind the investigator, then hurried into the driver's seat. The second recruit sat down next to him with the investigator's briefcase on his lap.

The sergeant waited for the car to move, then he rushed outside. He had barely cleared the doorway when he came to a complete stop next to the laughing journalist. His bewildered eyes wandered from the Japanese cameraman to the small foreign journalist speaking into the camera and pointing at the intersection behind her: his own intersection that he had abandoned for barely an hour. Then his eyes fell on the child who stood in the middle of the road, impervious to the speeding vehicles, whistling intermittently and waving his skinny arms. But what really incensed the sergeant was that these frenzied Cairo cars, accustomed to ignoring the pleas of the most experienced traffic policemen, responded like peaceful lambs to Antar's slapstick gesticulations, and showed every respect for the stolen beret the boy kept lifting above his eyes to be able to see the world.

"Son of a jinn!" the sergeant muttered with bile.

The Second Page

The future came into my room
covered in the dust of his eternal wandering . . .
withered, slim-shouldered,
his nails a distasteful sight,
his shoes in tatters.
His short cane condemns him to a stoop.
He poised it against my chest.
How painful, his jab!
How imposing, his tone:
What are you doing here, man?
Stand up.
And he challenged me to a duel.

Mourid Barghouti

Abd al-Malak

In the waiting room, Abd al-Malak was absorbed by a fly meandering across the windowpane. It paused, rubbed its head between its forelimbs, continued its stroll, then flew to another corner of the fingerprint-stained glass. The fly took to the air, circled a few times, then returned to the same spot. But what were its motives? Surely it possessed a special kind of consciousness, a particular vision of the surrounding world. Otherwise its movements would be no more than random applications of the laws of probability.

Creation: how complex it must be. Mankind's understanding is shrinking just as the information available to us mushrooms at a breathtaking pace. What if humans — like flies — are directed by random laws they can never understand? Their consciousness — both humans and flies — would be merely an attempt to rationalize the absurd, to justify their existence: unconvincing, futile.

Outside the window, Cairo's buildings stood bleak and lonely. The sky above them was a dull red. Dust, humidity, and exhaust had fused into a thick cloud that, in the July heat, enveloped everything. But people were used to this and all but ignored its corrosive effects on their eyes and lungs. Only on rare occasions did the pollution surface into somebody's awareness: at times like this, when one had the opportunity to observe reality from an artificial air-conditioned environment, from behind a golden aluminum-framed window in a modern building in downtown Cairo.

Abd al-Malak sank into an orange leather armchair by the window. Although his physical migration had come to an end, in spirit he was still a migrant. Alone among the multitude of young men who filled the waiting room, he did not don a suit and tie. Even the women were dressed in gray or navy-blue suits with short skirts that, in a peculiar collusion between the solemn and the frivolous, showed off their shaved legs. With such splendid legs around, all was well under the Egyptian sun.

'Who among these showoffs has one tenth of my qualifications?' Abd al-Malak kept repeating to himself, except his words did not sound convincing and instead redoubled his malaise. He started to wish the earth would split open and swallow him.

Helplessly, he hung on. It crossed his mind that there was an odd similarity between himself, waiting here in this trendy office, and the people who packed the stairs of his house in the crowded neighborhood of Elsayeda Zeinab, seeking an audience with the clairvoyant. In both cases, people were soliciting help to achieve improbable goals. People trapped by their pressing needs, hordes of the imprudent—because to be in need is to be reckless. And in both cases, there were those who were only too happy to capitalize on people's needs.

He smiled sarcastically but quickly got hold of himself. There was no room for such negative thoughts now. Besides, there was certainly nothing in common between Abd al-Malak and the characters on the stairs. After all, he was a modern man who adhered to scientific discipline, while they were ignorant fools who allowed charlatans to take advantage of them.

Since he first walked through the building's front entrance, Abd al-Malak's admiration for this place had grown. It was one of the modern office buildings of Suleiman Pasha Street. The foyer's floor was covered in black-and-white marble tiles and its walls were clad in tinted mirrors. With his first step, he became aware that he was crossing a dual barrier in time and space. And as he stood on the doorstep of this particular office on the sixth floor, he almost evoked the familiar feeling that accompanied an airplane's landing in one of the airports of the developed world. He would have certainly felt again that mixture of freedom, fascination, and awe, were it not for a rotten odor that whiffed for a fleeting moment before blending with the artificial air fresheners, or the harsh look the receptionist with the loud makeup slapped him with.

More than an hour had passed since the girl verified through the intercom that he indeed had an appointment and pressed the buzzer to open the glass door. She was dark with dyed blond hair and scrutinized him from his unkempt head all the way to his canvas shoes. When he placed the consultation fee on her desk, she picked up the five ten-pound notes one by one, with a finger and thumb whose nails were painted blood red. She curled her lips in disgust. But beneath their sensuous coating, what luscious feminine lips they were.

He had initially attributed the girl's cold behavior to his modest attire. Then he noticed that a number of newcomers left her an extra five or ten pounds over and above the fee. It had been eight years since he'd last given a tip. Now he'd returned to these shady customs. In any case, the fifty-pound fee was already more than he could afford, and it was only a taste of what was to come. The fifty pounds merely gave him the opportunity to meet the agent. If the office succeeded in finding him a job, they'd be entitled to ten percent of his total earnings for the first year. Still, these young people were leaving ten-pound tips. And he'd come back to all this of his own free will: to the flies, trash, and pollution; to poverty and ill-treatment. All this, he'd chosen to return to.

The gray ceramic floor glittered with confidence, except for small pockets of dust that had gathered around the legs of the lavish leather furniture. But more conspicuous still, in the corner facing him where there was a gap of ten to fifteen centimeters between the sofa and the wall, were cigarette butts, a crumpled Chiclets pack, and a small dark heap at the deepest point. Just then, that smell whiffed past him again. As if his eyesight had provided support to his sense of smell and enabled him to hone in on the source of discomfort, he became convinced that the

29

rotten odor emanated from that small heap in the corner. Quickly, the two senses determined in tandem that the object was the corpse of a small rat. Now his earlier uncertainty evaporated and the picture became clear. He allowed himself a cynical smile. Things are never what they seem.

"Mr. Abd al-Malak. The agent will see you now. You may proceed." The girl's voice came loud and clear, adding a new dimension to his sense of revelation.

Abd al-Malak was surprised to be greeted by a man in his early thirties. He wore a blue short-sleeved shirt and a yellow tie with red circles. He had expected an older person. The man's desk, even the legs, was made of thick glass; a desk of pure crystal. Abd al-Malak had never seen anything like it, not even in America. The indirect lighting and soft background music were designed to soothe, yet a sudden rage took hold of Abd al-Malak to the point that he noticed his fist tremble as he shook the man's hand. Here he was: still struggling to launch his career, while this guy had already achieved everything—money, social status, self-fulfillment.

"Welcome, Dr. Abd al-Malak. This is the first time we meet but, from reading your file, I feel I know you well." The man smiled mechanically after each sentence.

This was the American way Abd al-Malak knew so well. Everything in a business meeting is studied: tone of voice, hand movements, seating postures, even smiles are reduced to a tool for buying and selling. The buying and selling of people.

"First of all, I would like to express how much we appreciate your decision to come back home. I am fully aware that someone like you, with a PhD in genetic engineering from MIT, would find no difficulty in landing a good position with a major US corporation." The agent spoke with a contrived foreign accent, while his eyes studied Abd al-Malak's reactions.

The MIT graduate felt it was his turn to keep the conversation going. So he simply said what he was thinking. "I see you also did your degree in the US."

"Georgetown." The agent flashed one of his mechanical smiles. "But my studies were not as specialized as yours. I understand you've published some important research."

"My research proves the possibility of doubling Egypt's agricultural production. That's why I came back, to serve my country."

Abd al-Malak's response was immediate, almost rehearsed. But he was no better than a barefaced liar. Maybe he was just trying to justify things to himself. Naturally, what he said was partly true. Egypt, after all, had given him an education and made a scientist out of him. The son of a simple postman in the backwaters of the world's richest country would never be able to achieve what he had achieved. It was a debt he would always shoulder and now that the knowledge he possessed was worth millions, repaying it was a solemn duty. This was an obligation to the people of his village, to his mother who had passed away while he was abroad, a debt he owed his father who had died when he was still a child. Still, he was no better than a barefaced liar. He had not really returned out of patriotism. He had come back for himself. He had left when he was beaten, and could not bear to remain a loser. He had run away and could not keep on running for the rest of his life.

What troubled Abd al-Malak the most was that by lying about his motives, he had come to resemble the charlatan who sat before him.

"Unfortunately, Dr. Abd al-Malak, we live in country that worships academic degrees but doesn't value knowledge."

"What do you mean? I was led to believe that you've already found a suitable position for me."

"Of course. Of course. After a lot of effort we were indeed successful. Thanks be to God. Congratulations, doctor. A position that perfectly suits your requirements. And the package is excellent, something to make you feel valued."

Abd al-Malak barely stopped himself from enquiring about the salary. He was curious about the money, not just because of his swelling debt and the creditors' nags and threats, but mainly to figure out how much the agent would make from the deal. If he added the cut he'd get from him and the fee the employer must pay, Abd al-Malak could calculate how much this man would profit from his hard work.

"There's only one small problem . . . not really a problem, may God never bring problems . . . I mean there is a new element you should be aware of . . . to make a long story short, there's an element of distance involved."

"You mean the position is in one of the land reclamation projects in the desert? Well that's no problem. As a matter of fact, that's my preference." Initially taken aback by the man's insinuations, Abd al-Malak started to relax. At least he'd get away from the crowds and the pollution. In any case, it would be easy to travel to Cairo whenever he needed to for recreation or business.

"No, nothing like that, it's actually in a beautiful city. But it's outside our borders . . . Don't worry, not as far away as America."

"You mean in an Arab country?"

"Arab countries have no need for advanced sciences."

So the man meant Europe. But Abd al-Malak had not abandoned America only to be estranged in Europe.

The man responded as though he had read his mind, "A very close country. In the region, I mean. But highly developed in your field, with the capacity to make full use of your expertise. And let me assure you that their technology will bring prosperity to the entire region."

Abd al-Malak's tongue froze. Things are never what they seem. He found himself unable to respond.

The man took his silence as acceptance and proceeded with the details. "Some procedural matters will, however, need to be taken care of. I mean you'll have to travel via Europe, just to avoid anyone giving you any trouble. As you know, we have people over here who love to complicate things. But no need to worry, we're experienced in these matters."

The chill of the air-conditioned atmosphere gripped Abd al-Malak's body like a tight steel glove. He was unable to move or articulate one syllable. His chest contracted and he could scarcely breathe. He needed to break free of this sudden cold that was squeezing the life out of him in the heat of July. He stumbled to the door. Running away had always been his reaction. Leaving the agent's door wide open behind him, he passed the secretary, who was spraying a thick cloud of air freshener in the waiting room. The echoes of his own voice were acute and frightening, loaded with a desperation that, alas, had become part of his very existence.

"It stinks in here! How long are you going to keep spraying perfume?"

✖

'When does a drowning man's despair reach the point where he's forced to cling to a straw?' he often asked himself when he'd brush past people queuing on the stairs and landing that led to the clairvoyant's apartment. All the tenants cursed the day the man set up his 'practice' among them. But Abd al-Malak felt a certain empathy toward the confused seekers. Whenever he passed their brooding faces, he'd remind himself that if not for their dire need, these people would not be here.

Ever since Abd al-Malak had returned from America and rented a room in the fishmonger's apartment on the fifth and last story of this run-down house, he had barely enjoyed a single moment of calm and quiet. Day and night, the clairvoyant's customers lined up on the stairs. Rich and poor alike, they came in hordes to this narrow alley in Elsayeda Zeinab to lay their needs at the bearded man's feet. But could the ugly soothsayer resolve their intractable problems? Or was his role simply to dispense a folklore-flavored sedative, to be added to the long list of narcotics the Egyptian people bunkered behind as their encounter with the new millennium approached? An addition to the list of tranquilizers we pump into our veins, swallow, sniff, watch, read, think, and recite, day after day?

But when does one's despair reach such a point?

It was the very question he repeated the day following his meeting with the owner of the country's leading employment agency, when he found himself among the pushers and shovers in front of the US consulate.

Actually, the thought only came to his mind after long hours in the burning sun, wrestling with his compatriots for a visa. A visa to heaven, the same heaven he had voluntarily abandoned. Now he was crawling on all fours to be allowed back in.

When neither his American degrees nor scientific accomplishments distinguished him from the billions of crushed souls collectively known as the third world, the dilemma seemed particularly poignant. And just a little later, as the US consul tore down the barrier Abd al-Malak had erected around himself like the enormous billboards the municipality puts up in front of the shantytowns to erase their existence from the consciousness of motorists on our highways, Abd al-Malak's question about despair loomed heavily over him. He was struck by the revelation that America had rejected him just as he had rejected her.

Barely a week had passed when the same question resurfaced as he checked his watch for the tenth time. He awaited his destiny on the pavement facing the Nile Hotel, and it was over half an hour late. In his right hand he held a tape recorder, in the other a black imitation Samsonite briefcase that contained a Koran, two sticks of incense, one magnetic and one drawing compass, and some blank paper. He wore jeans and canvas shoes and perspired August sweat, which refused to evaporate.

He was aware that by waiting on this pavement today, he was taking his first step on an obscure and uncertain path. The way to safety, the path of regret, or the road of no return? A step that was further-reaching than that of the seekers when they entrusted the clairvoyant with their souls. But at that moment he—like them—was driven. It was as though his past empathy toward these people had been, at heart, the manifestation of a secret decision he was hiding from himself, a decision to unconditionally surrender, to acknowledge total and complete defeat, after which there would be no option but to hand over the steering wheel to despair and to entrust his fate to Satan.

As Satan's specter cast its shadow upon his mind, the white Cadillac came to a standstill. It was impossible to see the passengers behind the tinted windows. An extended moment passed. He could feel the perspiration ooze from all his pores. The roar of the car's engine challenged the August heat and doubled his sense of asphyxiation. An elegant chauffeur appeared and confidently opened the broad rear door for him. Abd al-Malak hesitated. The man's hand holding the door was clad in a white glove. He noticed the void of a missing finger.

This chauffeur character made him uneasy. He was built like a professional wrestler and wore a scowl under his cap. Abd al-Malak gathered his courage and leaned forward to shake hands with the car's two passengers, though he had no inkling who they were. Then he stepped inside and, upon the signal of a man in a red Lacoste polo shirt, took the seat facing him with his back to the driver. The other passenger, a child, maybe a teenager, in a beige linen safari suit, showed no reaction. The car dived into the Cairo traffic and set the course for Abd al-Malak's destiny.

When he turned down many an American company's offer, little did he realize that coming home to Egypt would thrust him down this path. All he had hoped for was a job that would afford him a decent living to make up for all his suffering and allow him to take part in his country's development. He had imagined this to be an easy goal, as his country badly needed scientists specialized in the agricultural applications of genetic engineering. Maybe his long stay in America had made him forget how things were over here.

The apprehensive Abd al-Malak waited for the man to take the initiative, but to his surprise he said not a word. Despite Abd al-Malak's malaise, his first physical sensation was comfort. This he soon attributed to the air-conditioned climate. Both the engine's buzz and the hubbub from the street were inaudible inside the car. He sank into the leather seat that hugged his body like a mother's bosom, and dived into his stream of thought. The hum of cool air rushing out of the ducts was pleasant. The coarse, delicious aroma of the man's Havana cigar clung to every surface inside the Cadillac. Its smoke hovered like a cloud in a surrealist dream. Abd al-Malak wondered if the scent would stick to him after he came out into the Egyptian street, if he would spend the rest of the day feeling like an English lord or a fat Egyptian cat.

He was used to the sight of stretch limousines on the streets of Boston, but this was his first time inside one. He looked around in wonderment. The car's interior was more spacious than he'd expected. The compartment was separated from the driver by a thick glass screen. The television set and the bar next to him made him feel he had parachuted into an episode of *Dallas*, the soap opera that had inflamed the imagination of his early youth—in those days he'd considered just watching it an act of extravagance.

"Welcome, Dr. Abd al-Malak. I'm engineer Abd al-Tawab Mabrouk and this is my dear friend, one of Egypt's genius scientists, Dr.—" The man's words took Abd al-Malak by surprise. His voice had a distinctive ring that reminded him of Julio Iglesias. The younger man immediately released a string of fake coughs to stop the other from announcing his name. Engineer Abd al-Tawab hesitated then gave a nervous laugh. "In our university days we used to call him the Cerebellum."

Abd al-Malak scrutinized the face of the child who the man had referred to as 'doctor' and found no signs of manliness or anything to indicate he was over twenty. His immature body confirmed that he was still growing. However, when the young man turned to Abd al-Malak, he could not help noticing that, behind the glasses that covered half his face, his eyes were troubled. The world had indeed dug its fangs into his soul, even if its marks were not readily visible.

"Let's get down to business. I contacted you because of your website. Your credentials are impressive. A PhD in paranormal phenomena from MIT is exactly what I need."

"A doctorate in parapsychology?" said the little genius with interest.

"It's now quite common to deal with such phenomena scientifically." Abd al-Malak's words did not sound convincing to his own ears. His canvas shoes dug into the car's thick cream-colored carpet. Yet Engineer Abd al-Tawab seemed to be taking him seriously.

"Exactly. And we're the kind of people who believe in science and have no time for superstitions or quackery." The man's eyes were hidden behind Ray-Bans. His dark features were stern, tightly strung. Probably in his mid-forties, he too was not really as young as Abd al-Malak had initially thought.

The child genius leaned forward and turned his focus from Abd al-Malak to his friend. His jaw drooped, showing two oversized rabbit teeth. Evidently, he had no prior knowledge of the subject under discussion.

"I've reached a preliminary prognosis, based on our telephone conversation and what was reported in the newspapers. Our case seems to be a phenomenon they call poltergeist in America."

Abd al-Malak looked behind him and noticed, for the first time, a man—even bigger than the chauffeur—in the front seat next to the driver. Silent and alert, he scanned the road and the adjacent cars.

"Poltergeist," the Cerebellum repeated in a hypnotized tone.

"What's important is to bring this whole polter . . . thing to an end." There was a certain impatience in Engineer Abd al-Tawab's voice. Maybe he was irritated by his inability to pronounce the word in English.

"A poltergeist is to parapsychology what a headache is to medicine. It's easy to diagnose, but to treat it you must first determine the cause."

Abd al-Malak could hardly believe the bullshit coming out of his own mouth. A volcano of laughter brewed in his belly. He controlled himself with some difficulty, except for a fleeting smile that he managed to disguise as a twitch. Just then, he noticed a mud stain on the carpet next to his right shoe. He looked up quickly, hoping the two men wouldn't notice. Stealthily, he repositioned his shoe then stole a quick glance downward. A second stain glared up at him. He rotated his ankle until he identified the culprit: a patch of mud that had stuck to his heel. Engineer Abd al-Tawab's voice amplified his anxiety.

"The cause—that's exactly what we're after. I mean if there are spirits who are suffering, we have to relieve their pain and allow them to rest as soon as possible." Clouds of exhaustion started to converge around Engineer Abd al-Tawab's features.

"So that we too can rest," he added.

"Of course. But I'm sure you'll agree that this requires a great deal of effort." Abd al-Malak's words were tentative as he rubbed his shoe against the carpet, hoping the traces of mud would somehow disappear.

He glanced down and his eyes could not break away from the multiple smears that now covered the carpet.

"Results . . . I want results." He heard a note of rebuke in Engineer Abd al-Tawab's voice.

"Of course. I was just pointing out that results require an allocation of time and resources." Abd al-Malak's pennilessness emboldened him, yet the man's tense laughter at his words made his heart drop.

"Money's not a problem. But I have to see results first." Engineer Abd al-Tawab produced his wallet and handed Abd al-Malak a hundred-pound note, adding under his breath, "This is the last time we talk about money . . . until I can sleep."

Abd al-Malak took the money without comment. He wondered what kind of results the man wanted to see. The Cadillac had traversed the heavy traffic of the old-city stretch of the Nile Corniche and was now cruising toward Maadi. After a moment's hesitation he asked, "But what has your sleep got to do with this problem?"

"My sleep *is* the problem."

"I see . . . so you're still living in the apartment?'

"No, I haven't set foot in it for years."

"Aren't you the tower's owner?"

"The tower is owned by Sheikh Wahdan. He very rarely comes to Egypt and never for more than one or two weeks a year. I only own the apartment in question."

"Then who's living in the apartment?" Abd al-Malak tried to cover the stained area with both shoes. A sinking feeling started to spread in the pit of his stomach.

"No one at the moment. There were tenants there until the end of May. But my friend, Dr. . . . the Cerebellum . . . is going to the apartment with you now. He'll be staying there for a while."

"Why did the tenants leave the apartment in May, if this phenomenon only occurred the day before yesterday?" Abd al-Malak's bewilderment was growing.

"No one wanted to rent it after the incident with the actress in May. All the visits by the police and the public prosecutor to the tower didn't help." The millionaire seemed fed up. His sharp tone left no doubt that this conversation was over. Abd al-Malak wondered if the man had been irritated by his interrogatory manner. On his left, the first of the extended chain of towers that have sprouted along the Nile bank in Maadi appeared. Abd al-Malak wondered which one was the tower with which his fate had become intertwined. The Cadillac sped past the side road that led to the Seahorse. On the overpass to Maadi, a flood of memories overcame Abd al-Malak. The Seahorse was his favorite restaurant in the whole world. Oddly enough, his favorite place was where he had received the deepest cuts. Happiness is, after all, love's mortal foe; it smothers love while it is still in the cradle. With all its tenderness and sensuality, love can only feed on tears and heartbreak. A world in which only unfulfilled love may be eternal is surely a merciless place. If grief were truly the best measure of love, then his was the greatest love of all.

After a short silence, Abd al-Malak decided to change the subject.

"You probably spend a lot of time on the internet, Engineer Abd al-Tawab, if you found my website so quickly."

"I'll have nothing to do with the internet and all these new fads. When we joined the faculty of engineering, they hadn't even invented calculators. We used slide rules in those days—the Aristo brand, remember, Cerebellum?" The man went silent, reminiscing or maybe searching for the right words to express an unconventional idea.

"It's hard to explain . . . I just found myself asking my secretary to look up a psychic on the internet." Rubbing his Akhenaton nose with his thumb, he added, "Of course, you were the only one listed in the whole of Egypt."

Abd al-Malak wished the man would take off his Ray-Bans so he could make out whether he was serious or just making fun of him, as things are never what they seem. From the corner of his eye, he caught the amazement drawn all over the Cerebellum's face, in an expression that mimicked the great comedian Ismail Yassine.

Like a ghost from the past, the fleeting image of Maadi Hospital, the unattainable dream during the years of his mother's illness, crossed by the left side window. Had she lasted a few months longer until he graduated, maybe he would have accepted the first job offer he received in America. Who knows, maybe he would have been able to afford her treatment at Maadi Hospital or at an even better facility. The car slowed down, made a U-turn, and proceeded on the other side of the road.

"No need to worry, doctor. Sometimes a person possesses powers even he is not aware of, or he may be destined to fulfill a mission without knowing what that mission is or why he was chosen for it in the first place." Engineer Abd al-Tawab's musings were getting weirder by the word. Abd al-Malak wondered if his anxiety was so evident that the man felt a need to calm him down. But how could such talk calm anyone down?

"If you don't believe me, ask yourself what made you put that advertisement on the internet in the first place."

Abd al-Malak kept quiet. What could he say? How could he reply that it had all started as a joke? A desperate joke by a desperate man. An impulse to make fun of the world and of himself. But the rich man did not wait for him to respond.

"Whatever happens, don't ever forget that we're living pieces on a chessboard. We may believe we make the world go around, but it's the higher powers who direct us according to their whims," the man added with finality, rubbing his nose with his thumb again.

"You've turned into a philosopher, Tutu," said the Cerebellum, still in a state of stupor. He quickly added in confusion, "I mean Engineer Abd al-Tawab."

At that point, the Cadillac came to a standstill in front of a tower whose sheer splendor rivaled Manhattan's best.

✖

Mr. Tutu waited for the chauffeur to open the car door. He hesitated for a moment, took a quick glance at the stained carpet around Abd al-Malak's shoes, gave him one mysterious look, then got out of the car, muttering, "Heaven protect us."

The Cerebellum followed. The bodyguard was already on the pavement eyeing with suspicion the whole of creation. He had a beautiful rosy face, like a movie star, except for a still-raw scar that slashed his cheek from right beneath the eye to his square jaw. Abd al-Malak descended from the other door with his tape recorder and fake Samsonite briefcase. The chauffeur went to the trunk and followed with a small suitcase.

The bodyguard waited at the top of the stairs as the four climbed the seven granite steps one at a time, in a deliberate, ceremonial manner, like heads of state inspecting the honor guard or high officials at a royal funeral. Abd al-Malak glanced sideways at his companions. The Cerebellum, with his jaundiced face, was looking in all directions. Engineer Tutu perspired profusely and proceeded with the stubbornness of one battling powerful winds.

Abd al-Malak, who did not grasp what could possibly make the two men so nervous, could hardly resist looking back at his own footsteps. The mud-stains that marked his progress over the shining steps only added to his confusion.

It occurred to him that the man had not answered one crucial question. He approached Tutu at the top of the stairs and before the man could cross the tower's threshold, whispered in his ear, "But you never told me,

41

Engineer Abd al-Tawab, what does your sleep problem have to do with the subject of my work?"

Tutu turned to him as though he found it difficult to grasp the gist of the question. Before he could say a word, a little boy with a policeman's beret and a whistle that produced a torrent of screeches shot like a guided missile out of the doorway. The child's head slammed into Tutu's stomach. The bodyguard, who had taken up a position at the center of the foyer, dashed to his boss's assistance, but before he could get to him, the child—a reckless train that imposed its racket on the world—was already in the street, rushing ahead without a word of apology. Tutu froze for a few seconds while the others gaped in astonishment. What madness had fate sowed in this strange tower?

"One day, the human race will be gone. We'll be replaced by a much wiser species, who'll want to erect a memorial . . . a tombstone for the entire human race. But what will they inscribe on it?" The millionaire's response, in the wake of the disturbance caused by the speeding child, took Abd al-Malak by surprise.

"I don't understand." Abd al-Malak was totally confused. Was the man testing his spiritual prowess?

"The tombstone of the human race. What would you inscribe on it?" The man's features were completely serious. "I can't make it out. . . . The tombstone is right in front of me . . . but I can't see the writing . . . I no longer get a wink of sleep. But I still can't read the engraved words," he further challenged Abd al-Malak's uncomfortable silence.

Abd al-Malak was only saved by the security clerk, who barked at Tutu, "Welcome, Pasha."

The pasha, whose face was now covered in a viscous layer of sweat and who looked positively sick, did not reply. His eyes drifted in the direction of the three elevator doors and he rubbed his nose with his thumb. One of the elevator doors slid open, but there was nobody inside. Tutu spontaneously moved both hands to his neck as though strangled by an invisible presence. Then he turned to Abd al-Malak

42

and muttered semi-audibly, "I'm sorry I won't be able to take you up. I need to get away from here—I mean, I have an important appointment. An urgent matter." The chauffeur, responding to a quick nod from Tutu, abandoned the suitcase in front of the elevators and hurried back to the Cadillac.

"He'll take you to the apartment. Kasseb knows everything." The Pasha pointed over his shoulder at the security clerk as he headed for the car.

But Abd al-Malak followed and caught up with him just outside the entrance. "What's all this about your sleep, Engineer Abd al-Tawab?" he whispered insistently.

"She appears to me. Whenever I close my eyes, I find her there. She's not letting me get a wink of sleep," the man whispered in Abd al-Malak's ear, then rubbed his nose and hurried toward the Cadillac's open door and the alert chauffeur holding it.

The bodyguard was one step behind him, like a shadow in a nightmare.

"Who?" Abd al-Malak shouted, but the chauffeur had already shut the door.

The three men—Abd al-Malak, the Cerebellum, and the security clerk—watched the Cadillac's rear end as it was swallowed up by the road's rapid current. The security clerk then turned to the two men, sized each of them up from head to heel, and addressed Abd al-Malak. "The Pasha's apartment is 1301 on the thirteenth floor. Mr. Kasseb is across the landing in 1302," he said brusquely and returned to his desk, washing his hands of the two men.

The Cerebellum picked up his suitcase and the two stood next to a pretty woman waiting for the elevator. Abd al-Malak noticed the delicate toes with pomegranate-colored nails visible from her open shoes. He resisted the temptation to look her in the face until they were both in the elevator and exchanged an extended gaze that was only interrupted by the Cerebellum's childish voice, "Which floor, Miss?"

"Tenth please." The beautiful woman made an effort to break free of Abd al-Malak's gravitational field.

"Farah . . .," Abd al-Malak whispered, overcoming the clot clutching his vocal chords.

"No way! Abd al-Malak?! When did you come back?"

That cracked voice . . . how it had inflamed his senses in their youth. He compared it to the howl of a she-wolf calling out to the strongest, fiercest male. But he was never the strongest. Otherwise, he would not have abandoned their love and traveled so far away. Had he been stronger, he would've fought back for her. He would never have given in to her aunt's greed and her uncle's nastiness.

"I've been back for almost three months. But how are you doing?"

"I'm good. I'm great. Thanks be to God." Her shifting eyes exposed her lie, and her voice was saturated with anger, brimming with blame.

"So . . . what are you doing here?" Abd al-Malak tried to think of a way to ask the question.

"It's a long story. . . . What are *you* doing here?"

Farah had small gaps between her front teeth. As always, they added to her animal attraction.

"That's an even longer story," Abd al-Malak said quietly.

"You haven't changed one bit . . . you're the same matchstick, thin and tall with a black head." She laughed in her sensuous, saucy voice, then added quickly, "Are you . . .?" She was first to ask the question that, to him, had suddenly become a matter of life and death.

"No, not at all . . . and you?"

"Me neither." A dense, delicious mist composed of a thousand moments encircled her smile. Living moments preserved in one of the secret mazes of the universe. But what was happening? Was hope creeping back into his heart? Would he allow its ruthless devil to again take control of him?

Farah's charcoal hair had turned blond. Her scrawny figure had gained a feminine roundness. A tasteful pistachio-on-white dress had replaced the jeans and T-shirts of her youth.

The elevator stopped. With feminine deliberateness, Farah turned to face the door.

"You've become so beautiful . . . like a movie star."

Abd al-Malak spoke spontaneously. He had intended no cynicism, but could he forget how critical she was of the girls who put on makeup just to catch a man's eye? 'Candy Dolls,' she used to call them. Now, her beauty was greatly accentuated by makeup. She had turned into one of those very same candy dolls.

"This is my floor . . . I have to go."

"But how will I see you?" Abd al-Malak had not fully grasped that the elevator had stopped, and panicked when she stepped outside.

"I live here." She said after a moment's hesitation, pointing to her right. Then she allowed her magical smile to appear tentatively as the elevator door erased her image and sent him tumbling down the dark well where he had languished all those past years.

"I'm sorry, doctor. Had it been physically possible, I would have vanished and left you two alone." The Cerebellum's voice brought Abd al-Malak back to his bleak existence, after he had touched both heaven and hell with his fingertips.

✼

The elevator door slid open and the Cerebellum stepped onto the thirteenth floor, closely followed by Abd al-Malak. Each carried his stuff. Abd al-Malak was taken aback by the sight of two police recruits on the landing in front of Tutu's apartment. They were involved in an animated discussion and paid no attention to him and the Cerebellum. The blood froze in his veins. Nobody had said anything about the police. The phantom of prison and humiliation had suddenly been added to the army of ghosts that surrounded him.

The Cerebellum headed toward the two recruits, but Abd al-Malak firmly held him by the arm and whispered, "We should see Mr. Kasseb first . . . to avoid any misunderstanding with the police."

In response to Abd al-Malak's ring, Mr. Kasseb appeared smiling. He welcomed the two men and said they were late, as though they'd had an appointment with him. Abd al-Malak assumed that the man's complaint was addressed to the Cerebellum and said nothing. The man showed them into a large living room with loud pink carpeting and invited them to relax on modern grass-green sofas and armchairs. Chrome and glass side and coffee tables carried crystal ashtrays, wooden boxes whose open lids revealed rows of cigars, and small silver-plated trays filled to the brim with assorted nuts.

The exhausted Abd al-Malak sank into a comfortable armchair. Through the French window he could see the Nile. On the other bank, the fields extended all the way to the plateau crowned by the pyramids. The events of the day were beyond his comprehension. Things are never what they seem. He felt an irresistible urge to escape, to get away from this place. This was how he always dealt with trouble: by running away.

But Farah's apparition, a sensual angel in the elevator, her evocative smile that revived past aches, had forever chained him to this building. Abd al-Malak thought he could hear the distant echoes of the police recruits' conversation. Indistinct syllables really. Maybe it was just his imagination, a mere reflection of his own fears.

Yet the handcuffs dangling from the policemen's belts were anything but imaginary. He kept reminding himself that the young recruits were hapless boys who survived their military service as best they could, then went back to their families having gained nothing from the experience. Even the puniest thief felt little fear of these poor lads. Besides, what Abd al-Malak was planning to do was not really a crime, merely an illegal act in a society that no longer respected laws, a drop in the ocean, really.

The apartment's blazing colors made Abd al-Malak nauseous. Despite the air conditioning, he felt as though he were suffering from sunstroke. Dislike for this Mr. Kasseb, with his obscene clothes, bulky gold chains, and the thick black hair that, like a gorilla's, covered his body, increased Abd al-Malak's irritability. He was possessed by an urge to leave this place before he made a fool of himself. Before he exposed his own misdeeds, before he puked on the pink carpet.

"Do you think you can maybe take a quick look around here first? Just to be on the safe side. Prevention is the best cure, right, doctor?"

Abd al-Malak regained his focus as Mr. Kasseb addressed his request to the Cerebellum, whom he had obviously assumed to be the psychic. Maybe he had taken Abd al-Malak for his assistant. But what astonished Abd al-Malak most of all was the Cerebellum's unhesitating "With pleasure."

The small man stood up enthusiastically and pointed to a wide folding door that separated the room they were in from the next one. "What's in there?" he said in his childish voice.

Mr. Kasseb pulled both sides of the door open, revealing the next room to be an extension of the one they were in.

"Touch wood . . . you went straight to the lion's den," the fat man said.

Abd al-Malak caught himself wondering if the Cerebellum was not in fact the real psychic, if his own role was not merely to add a scientific aura to the operation. That would be the worst possible abuse of the MIT brand. Or maybe the whole thing was about the rich contractor's insomnia. Maybe the man thought Abd al-Malak had the cure. This tower was a hornet's nest he had walked into on his own two feet; who could predict how he would leave it? Who could predict what fate had in store for him in this ominous place? Truly, things are never what they seem.

No sooner had the Cerebellum stepped into the lion's den than he came to a standstill before a square platform covered in crimson velvet that occupied a large area of the room. "What's this?"

"Oh, just a bed . . . in case somebody needs a rest."

"This is not a bed, this is a football field. There's room here for you, your family, your family's family, your friends, your friends' friends, everybody's neighbors and there'll even be room left for the people walking down the street."

Then, pointing to the bar in the room's far corner the Cerebellum added, "That bar looks like it belongs in a five-star hotel. So that's why you put the bed here, for people who pass out when they've had one too many."

Mr. Kasseb's enormous belly vibrated under his colorful silk shirt. His laughter sounded like a turkey's cackle. But Abd al-Malak did not find the whole situation funny. Instead, he scrutinized his own footprints on the pink floor, searching for traces of mud. There was not a speck to blemish the carpet.

"What's in here?" The Cerebellum pointed to the near corner, which Abd al-Malak could not see from where he was sitting. But when the still-cackling Mr. Kasseb opened the cabinet in the corner, a classically carved wooden door became visible. Spellbound, Abd al-Malak observed the two men as they peered into the cabinet.

"Oh my God. Oh my God. What's this?"

It occurred to Abd al-Malak that astonishment was one of the Cerebellum's perennial expressions.

"It's called a vibrator." Mr. Kasseb's laughter was beyond control.

"Oh my God . . . and this?"

"They call it a dildo." The man tried to sound serious.

"Oh my God. Oh my God . . . and who's this?" The Cerebellum picked up a videotape and scrutinized its cover.

"*That* is Ginger Lynn . . . the queen of positions." Mr. Kasseb exploded in renewed laughter to the point where his belly was about to declare independence from the rest of his body.

Abd al-Malak followed the whole situation with only a small part of his consciousness, as though he was living a nightmare about to take a dangerous turn. He struggled to grasp what was happening, but it all went too fast. In his imagination, a line of prisoners chained to each other passed in front of him. They were being led to the station by two policemen. The chains molded them together, men and women alike, into one sexless, raceless body, a neglected, subdued beast. The dangerous ones wore extra cuffs around their ankles and walked the streets like penguins or dancers from the Bolshoi.

Abd al-Malak reminded himself that so long as he kept clear of politics, nobody would even notice him. He was trying hard to shrug off the feeling of falling into a bottomless well, when he realized that what was happening to him was anything but arbitrary. On the contrary: the consequences of his decision to operate outside the law gradually sank in. When he did the unthinkable and decided to go against his conscience, to day and night lead a life of sin, to at last seek the open spaces where dimensions and possibilities abound—in that moment he had put himself within range of the sun's arrows and the wind's lances, after a lifetime of crawling in the shadows.

What a terrifying truth. A moment of certainty that, strangely enough, he seemed to have stumbled upon by chance.

Breaking the law for the first time.

The Cerebellum allowed the videotape to fall from his hand. Something else in the cabinet had attracted his attention. "And this plastic doll, what's it for . . .?" Then he cried out, answering himself, "Oh my God. Oh my God!"

Mr. Kasseb's squeals did not cease, even when the Cerebellum shuffled away from the damned corner and said with uncharacteristic firmness, "If you'll excuse me, gentlemen."

"Yes. Time to go." Abd al-Malak seized the opportunity.

"But what were the results of your inspection?" Mr. Kasseb managed to control his laughter, but the mirth spilled over from his eyes.

"After everything I've seen . . . how can you possibly expect an inspection, man?" The Cerebellum's astonishment seemed to have turned to fear.

"But I need to know . . . is the apartment clean . . . or are there spirits around?" Mr. Kasseb succeeded at last in regaining his seriousness.

"Spirits? What are you talking about? I have nothing to do with spirits."

"Then who are you?"

"I'm the one looking for a bed to sleep in." Immediately, the Cerebellum seemed to regret what he had said and pointed to the red platform. "I mean a normal bed."

49

"Oh, you must be Engineer Abd al-Tawab's friend. Then who's the . . . ?" Mr. Kasseb realized his mistake and turned to Abd al-Malak, "And you just sat there and said nothing?"

"It's the apartment across the landing, right?" The Cerebellum interrupted the fat man and picked up the suitcase he had left next to the door.

"Yeah, but you'll need to get permission from the police first. Anyway, you'll find the officer inside the apartment."

"The police!" Abd al-Malak looked around him and picked up his stuff.

"But it's haunted. How are you going to spend the night there?" Mr. Kasseb asked as he caught up with the two men.

"My experience with people makes me look forward to the company of ghosts!" The Cerebellum shouted as he opened the door.

He dragged his suitcase and hurried across the landing. Abd al-Malak followed as far as the elevators and pressed the down button.

"And where are you going, doctor?" Mr. Kasseb called.

"This place produces strong vibrations. . . . I must withdraw immediately in order to prepare myself."

"But there's important work to be done here."

"Tomorrow. Everything will be taken care of tomorrow." Abd al-Malak had lost control. He didn't care about the mission he'd come for. He didn't care about the weird Cerebellum and the fate that awaited him in the haunted apartment. There was nothing left for him but to escape. Just then, the angel of mercy arrived in the form of the elevator.

A traffic sergeant in a worn-out white uniform was inside. His bare head exposed salt and pepper hair. Mr. Kasseb greeted him, saying, "Good man! We were just talking about you." Abd al-Malak assumed that the man had mentioned the sergeant to the Cerebellum, so he could not believe his ears when the fat man addressed him. "This is Sergeant Ashmouni in the flesh, the only person who witnessed the whole thing from beginning to end. You'll need a session or two with him."

Abd al-Malak did not wish to call the man a liar in the sergeant's presence. He hurried into the elevator.

"Nice to meet you," he muttered to the sergeant.

The fat man held the elevator door, toyed with his hair, perspired profusely, and hindered Abd al-Malak's escape with empty chitchat. The blood started to boil in his veins. When Abd al-Malak was about to explode, the man said goodbye and released the elevator door, which shut with metallic energy.

"And you're the maintenance engineer?" As the elevator started its descent, the sergeant sized him up.

The man was about the same age as his father in his last days. His dark face was furrowed, not with the wrinkles of old age but with the landmarks of poverty and hard work. His black shoes told the tale of a life of toil. Like the shoes of his father—God rest his soul—the shoes of a village postman. Abd al-Malak did not wish to start a conversation with the sergeant, but determined not to hurt his feelings, he allowed himself to be drawn into a casual exchange.

Farah's perfume still lingered, he was almost certain. The elevator stopped with a slight vibration. He rushed out, but, confronted with a police officer in the foyer, he slowed down. The officer was talking to a woman who took notes in a small notebook. The two recruits stood a few meters away, alert as guard dogs.

Instinctively, he followed the sergeant's example and veered to one side, waiting for the officer to leave. The journalist would publish the names of all the police bigwigs who supervised the investigation and the officers who rushed to the scene of the crime. But what crime? Would she find an objective description for this incident?

Was an objective description even required?

The journalist was in her early thirties, about his age. Her eyes were black and delineated in kohl, like a woman on the wall of an ancient Egyptian temple. She had a fleeting smile that exposed two delicate hollows in her cheeks. She unconsciously bit the end of her pencil.

Abd al-Malak found her full lips particularly enticing, like the cherries he had tasted in America.

Her questions encircled the officer who seemed anxious to get away. She did not even hesitate to use her slender body to block the man's retreat. An aloofness in her eyes doubled the distance that separated her from erybody else. They were veiled in a light mist, adding an angelic touch to her dignified beauty. A truly cherubic face, except that her short hair, masculine clothes, and energetic movements gave her the air of a mischievous boy. Suddenly, she looked in Abd al-Malak's direction. Something had caught her eye. Her clear olive complexion turned red.

With a swift maneuver, the officer succeeded in getting past her to the door. One of the two recruits raced to the car and the second followed a few steps behind, carrying the officer's briefcase as if it were the valise of the British Chancellor of the Exchequer. The journalist was quick to follow him out the door, but lost interest and stopped after a few steps. The first recruit opened the blue Peugeot's rear door, but the officer froze for a moment before getting in. Something behind the car had caught his attention. Then the Peugeot sped away as the journalist stood laughing at the top of the flight of stairs that led to the tower's entrance.

Abd al-Malak waited for the car to leave, then rushed out of the tower. As he skipped down the steps he caught, out of the corner of his eye, a glimpse of the child who had bumped into Tutu. The boy was in the middle of the road, whistling intermittently and waving his skimpy arms theatrically to the cars. A television cameraman was shooting the sergeant as he rushed to the child, shouting unintelligible words.

But Abd al-Malak didn't really care about any of this and headed for the nearest bus stop.

The Third Page

This space we move in,
a magic lantern to look at
Its light source is the sun, the lantern is our world
Inside we seem uncertain, as images

Omar Khayyam

Islah Mohandes

Poetry was among the things closest to her heart. So was the chirping of sparrows in springtime, Abdelhalim songs on a dreamy summer night, childhood's 'Rocket' chocolate bars as they melted elastically in her mouth, her mother's specialty pigeon stuffed with roasted green wheat, the scent of jasmine at dusk, and the feel of her skin after removing the hair with sticky sugar paste. On the other hand, she hated the sight of cockroaches in the kitchen as she did liars, fleas, the stench of boiled tripe, a man who raises a hand against his wife, the warmth of a toilet seat that has just been used by someone else, the black lipstick and nail polish favored by young girls these days, and a telephone ringing at dawn.

The last is by far the worst, because in a single moment it opens the door to catastrophes of all shapes and sizes, those she dreaded and the ones she had never even imagined, a split second that allows the world's nightmares free rein. The gateway to hell is thrown wide open by a telephone ringing at dawn.

The editor enquired if he had caused any inconvenience by calling at this early hour, but in fact he seemed to relish it. Not waiting for a response, he quickly added that, naturally, he would never discriminate between men and women. As if further demonstration of his obnoxiousness was necessary.

Like a double dose of poisoned honey, he repeated: he would never discriminate between men and women. Her ever-present memory of his cynical smile slapped her across the receiver. They would never discriminate between men and women when it involved throwing an unsavory task at her, but if a woman were to demand her constitutional right to become a judge, she would face ridicule. Something would be muttered about the emotional nature of women and someone would bring up sharia law. And when excuses ran out, they'd simply say this was such a demanding task that—out of consideration for their sensitive dispositions—it was necessary to shield women from its heavy responsibilities.

But where was all this consideration when women were required to prune prickly okra, clean toilet bowls, scrub floors, dust carpets over the balcony railing, or boil their men's dirty underwear in potash? When it came to going out at dawn to chase criminals and report on murders, no one seemed to mind sending a woman, but everyone's great sense of consideration suddenly popped up when it was necessary to protect women from the discomfort of sitting on the bench and adjudicating among people, or—in her case—from the responsibility of being a page editor at a national newspaper with a wide circulation.

Islah put down the receiver and calmed down her mother who stood in her nightgown under her wedding photo. Her father, pictured as a young man in his twenties, was dark and handsome in his military uniform. As a child, she had so wished to wake up one day and discover that the story of her life was really a nightmare and that her father was alive and kicking. A living father gaining wrinkles by the year was so much better than a permanently youthful hero mummified in a picture on the wall.

Exhaustion had grown to be one of the permanent features of Mama's face. Her breasts were two elongated balloons drooping almost to her waist under the nightgown. Time had eaten and drunk on them, as the saying goes. Who would believe that this was the very same blossom smiling shyly at the photographer? What mind can fathom what the clock's arms will bring? Mama was a living hero, but a forgotten one. Maybe it was a manifestation of destiny's justice that living heroes are invariably forgotten, or rather a sign of her sarcasm.

Islah turned to Hamada who stood barefoot in his pajama pants and sleeveless undershirt, rubbing his eyes. Engineer Hamada would always remain her spoiled brat of a little brother, never mind that his muscles were pumped up or that a jungle of hair covered his chest. She told him to go back to bed, and prepared herself for a long day.

The Fiat 128 was waiting for her in front of the house. The editor had sent a car to ensure the job was done promptly. The deadline for the last edition was barely an hour away. After greeting her in a sleepy voice, the driver raced to the scene of the crime. A high-class crime, the editor had said. The victim was a celebrity and everyone would want to know what had happened. And to add urgency, 'the competition' had caught wind of it and would no doubt highlight the story on their front pages. Had a thousand nameless bastards lost their lives, the editor would not have lost any sleep and telephones would not have rung at dawn. But the victim was a young actress, a star in the movies and in society, for men a forbidden dream, and for women an object of jealousy and mindless imitation. The world would come to a standstill.

The journey from Agouza to Maadi took barely ten minutes in that early hour of the fifth of May. The Fiat parked behind a row of police vans in front of the broad granite staircase that led to the tower's entrance. A small crowd had collected in front of the entrance, which was cordoned off by a chain of policemen. As she opened the car door, Islah felt intensely apprehensive, unusual for a crime reporter to whom corpses, criminals, and police stations were routine. Was her anxiety due to the certainty that this case would make the front page, or because she had no way of anticipating what awaited her inside? Or was it simply out of fear of dealing with the stars after all that is said about their deliciously debauched lifestyles?

How uncomplicated are crimes that nobody cares about. Crimes committed in the dark, whose perpetrators are also arrested in the dark, both criminal and victim, faceless, nameless extras in the public prosecutor's daily soap opera. The very same soap opera that, like a speeding train, slices the darkness of the night, or like the automated printing press, waits for no one. How uncomplicated are those crimes that reporters deal with mechanically, without the need for reflection or confrontation with others and their own selves.

The driver rushed ahead of her to clear a path through the crowd of garage attendants and passersby, bellowing in an official tone, "Make way please . . . make way for the lady."

Islah pushed forward, surrounded by a thousand greasy male looks that blended curiosity with sexual harassment. When she reached the policemen, who stared stupidly at her, she waved her press card and pushed past. The police recruits gave way and she found herself inside the foyer.

Contrary to what she'd expected, the scene was calm, with only a handful of people in the foyer. The granite floor was shining, the indirect lighting, soft. In the corners there were trees planted in immense pots, and the high walls displayed colorful murals. There was nothing out of the ordinary except for a police officer and two assistants who were talking to the security clerk, and a fire extinguisher that had been positioned to keep the door of one of the elevators open.

The officer gave her one look, then went on talking to the security guard. Islah moved instinctively toward the open elevator door. Two men wearing medical gloves emerged from the elevator and started to examine the external frame. One of them applied a transparent material with a small brush. Islah's heart beat faster with every step. First she noticed the newspapers spread across the elevator floor, then the truth struck her even before she could fully observe the crime scene. Like an ice sculpture, she froze in front of the open elevator.

Newspapers had been laid casually over the corpse, covering most of it. Patches of skin were visible between sheets and most of the head was uncovered. Not a trace of blood. A clean crime. The color of blood and its viscous crimson luster made her nauseous. But it was the smell that in her subconscious was inextricably linked to violent death. The memory of that very smell had attacked her senses when the car stopped in front of the tower.

Under the newspapers, Ahlam's corpse was rolled on one side. She was petite but her feminine curves could not be camouflaged. Her skin was like fresh cream; her ink-black hair fanned over her bare back and onto the elevator floor and concealed her face from Islah's thirsty eyes.

How complete you are in death, Ahlam.

Innocent and dreamy, just like your immortal image on the screen. Islah felt embarrassed just to be there, to witness the young star in this state, to invade her privacy, the privacy of death, the ultimate privacy. She realized that the photographer the editor promised had not arrived. What a relief. Photographing a scene like this was unconscionable. To disfigure Ahlam's image in people's memories would be unforgivable, an act for the paparazzi, for those who clawed people's flesh in life and in death.

A rod of ice pierced her heart. Nausea took her by surprise. Clutching her chest and stomach, she tried to control it. Like a woman determined not to wake a sleeping child, Islah took small steps backward. The printing press screeched in her ears. With unsteady steps, she moved closer to the police officer and his assistants. As the conversation with the security clerk heated up, the officer started raising his voice. She stopped and leaned on the closed elevator door closest to them. The insolence of the officer's tone doubled her malaise but she resisted the temptation to run away. Thirst for information had become second nature to her. Breathing heavily, she looked up at the floor numbers, pretending to wait for the elevator.

"There's just one thing I want to know: are you a security man or do you sell pickles on the street?!" The officer's voice was deep. She could see his stocky figure from the corner of her eye. The security clerk raised his arms in the face of the three policemen as if staving off a pack of hungry wolves.

Islah took deep breaths. With furious tremors, her heart broke free of the steel fist that held it. The officer's voice had chased away the image of the murdered woman and made the blood run in her veins.

"But Pasha, I told you everything I know. At four a.m., the elevator door opened and nobody came out, so I went to look and found what you just saw. I called the police that second."

Islah turned to face the men with sudden courage. The security clerk's face was the color of a lemon. It occurred to her that the incident had taken place not more than two hours ago and that she was the only reporter here. She had pinned down an exclusive.

"But where did the body come from, you idiot? That's the question I want an answer to."

"How would I know, Pasha? The victim didn't live in the building and I never saw her before . . . except on TV, of course."

Islah took out her mobile phone, an effective electronic weapon against the merciless pressure of the printing press. Impressed by her own self-confidence, she dictated her story to the newsroom. She even tried to follow the men's conversation as she whispered into the phone.

"Then you must've seen her coming in and you should know who she came to visit." The officer banged his fist against the desk. "Or did she parachute in?"

A mouse eyeing a cobra, the security clerk shrank in silence. His eyes followed the officer's every move.

The officer's yelling, which rang throughout the foyer, ended abruptly. He had realized something. He turned and focused the hellish floodlights of his eyes on Islah, still waiting for her imaginary elevator. He took a few steps toward her and hurled his question in thinly disguised courtesy. "Are you a tenant, Miss?"

Islah calmly concluded that it was time to leave.

✖

The moment she sank into the seat of the Fiat 128, Islah was overcome by fatigue, so she decided to go home. Eager as a lover, she threw herself into her bed's warm bosom.

She was awakened from deep slumber by the ring of her mobile phone. She usually turned it off when she went to bed, but in her exhaustion she'd forgotten. The editor's voice was eternal, beyond tedium or fatigue.

"By the way, today's coverage was fantastic. Did you know we were the only paper to carry the news? What's important now is to follow up with one of your great in-depths for tomorrow. Let me guess, you're in the tower right now digging for gold . . . which explains why you didn't come to the office. Actually, I was just calling to thank you for the good work."

Islah rubbed her eyes. The man's insolence was nothing new. The driver had no doubt let him know she'd gone back home.

"An in-depth will require a paid visit to one of the more expensive hairdressers." She tried to camouflage the drowsiness in her voice.

"A hairdresser . . . why does it always have to be a hairdresser?" He went silent for a second, then added with venom, "Well, okay, if that's what it takes."

Not an hour had passed before Islah was pushing open the glass door of Sambo's 'Hairdresser to the Stars' on the ground floor of the Tower of Happiness. She stepped into the air-conditioned atmosphere and was met by a cocktail of cosmetic fragrances and multilingual chitchat punctuated with ringing laughter. In the background, the soft music was almost imperceptible, like the whisper of a neglected conscience.

One of Sambo's assistants greeted her with the compliment, "Your à la garçon suits you beautifully."

"It could do with a trim but don't touch the fringe. I'm really here for a good blow-dry . . . party tonight," she answered quickly.

The cut took only a few minutes. She was then placed under a hairdryer next to an elderly lady who immediately introduced herself as Madame Gawdat. She was not a movie star, the woman explained seriously, but frequented this establishment out of convenience because she lived in the tower.

"It's a pleasure, Madame Gawdat. I envy you, such a distinguished building and sophisticated neighbors, nobody ever hears about improprieties here."

"Don't believe everything you hear . . . standards aren't what they used to be." Then she added in a whisper, "Didn't you hear about last night?"

Madame Gawdat was wearing a navy-blue dress with long sleeves and an impeccable white collar and cuffs, a chic classical frock that ended just below the knees. Despite the heat wave that had prevailed since the beginning of May, she insisted on skin-colored nylon stockings. Her shoes and purse were spotless white. The way she held her purse on her lap reminded Islah of her mother, who had recently started to carry her purse from room to room, as though she had the secret to immortality tucked inside it.

"What happened?" inquired Islah with crocodilian innocence.

"The young actress Ahlam Shawarby . . . the one who looks like a kitten. You've heard of her?"

"Of course. She's a very pretty girl."

"Well they found her strangled in the elevator . . . and what's worse, she was in the state her mother delivered her into this world."

Madame Gawdat was indeed a gold mine, to borrow the editor's expression. A delighted warmth spread from Islah's ears to her cheeks, the tingle of success, victory's fever. She would prove to the son of a dog that the visit to the hairdresser was indeed the act of a professional, and certainly not a female whim.

The woman next to Madame Gawdat, with whom the elderly lady had been chatting when Islah arrived, followed their conversation with interest. Islah might have taken her for the woman's daughter if not for the way she dressed, which belied a modest social background. Who knew, she too might possess interesting information. Islah raised her voice to draw the young woman into the conversation.

"How terrible. Your news shocks me, Madame Gawdat. But I wasn't aware that the young star lived in this building."

"You're right, she didn't. Maybe she was invited to one of those parties that give us headaches every night." A gray pearl necklace was Madame Gawdat's only jewelry. With perfectly rounded pearls the size of chickpeas, it must have been quite expensive.

"So who's the neighbor with an insatiable taste for parties?" Islah started feeling the heat from the hairdryer.

"The woman on the twelfth. Who else?"

The young woman next to Madame Gawdat could no longer contain herself. With a cracked voice she interrupted:

'No, Madame Gawdat, Ahlam never visited the twelfth floor." Then she addressed Islah, "The famous belly dancer, Lula Hamdi, has the whole twelfth floor."

She waved her hands in the air as she spoke. Her fingers were a roving ring museum, displaying anything from solitaire and diamond chips to a rainbow of jewels to a gold scarab and a platinum snake, all of which came to life with her every word.

"She visited Señora Esmeralda a lot," she added.

"Señora Esmeralda . . .? Farah, isn't she the flashy Spanish woman?" said Madame Gawdat.

One of Sambo's assistants came to raise Farah's hairdryer then started to remove the rollers from her dyed blond hair.

"Señora Esmeralda is from Chile in Latin America and a socialite here in Egypt." Farah addressed Islah in her know-it-all tone.

"Farah . . . what a lovely name." Islah became even more interested in getting better acquainted with her.

The hairdryer started burning her scalp. Her short hair did not provide enough cover. Still, she had no choice but to endure.

"Thank you. Actually, Father—God rest his soul—was a great admirer of the Shahbanu. Thank God he left out the 'Diba' part, though. It would've sounded very strange!" Farah released a volley of coarse rubbery laughter, pleased with her play on the Arabic meaning of the second half of the name of Iran's deposed empress: 'she-wolf.'

Still laughing, she followed the assistant to the next room for her hair to be sculpted. Farah walked with a rhythmic gait that made her full buttocks dance beneath her pistachio-green stretch-pants.

After a few moments' silence, in which Islah suffered further torture from the hairdryer, Madame Gawdat whispered, "Did you know, Islah, that Farah Diba was even more beautiful in person than she appeared in pictures? She was a truly distinguished lady, a real empress. I met her when Hamdy — God rest his soul — was still in the cabinet. A party Sadat threw in Aswan. Ah, those were the days."

"Has Farah been living here long?"

The lady raised the hairdryer from her head in irritation. For a moment, the wrinkles multiplied on her forehead. She was clearly exerting a mental effort to regain her concentration. Then she answered Islah somewhat absentmindedly.

"A few months. Just across the hall . . . in Mr. Shaker's apartment. Surely you've heard of Shaker Shaker, the businessman. It seems they're related. In any case, she's a good girl . . . she drops in to see me every few days."

Islah followed Madame Gawdat's example and freed herself of the hairdryer. At last, Sambo appeared. He was dark with kinky hair dyed white-blond. He wore tight jeans and a white silk shirt unbuttoned all the way to his belly. Not one hair cast its shadow on the shining ebony of his chest or arms.

Islah wondered how this man came to own such a profitable business.

"Come on Sambo, I'm in a hurry. The girls are all alone." Madame Gawdat said to him then turned to Islah, "If you come to visit I'll show you my picture with Gihan Sadat and Farah Diba."

Before surrendering her head to Sambo and his gang, Islah remembered a crucial question and hurried — with a disheveled fringe — to Farah who was chatting about fashion with the young man doing her hair.

"When Ahlam visited Señora Esmeralda, was she alone or did she usually go with someone else?" Islah interrupted them without the slightest hesitation.

64

Farah's olive face darkened. She knitted her eyebrows, which were thick in keeping with the current style favored by movie stars. She hesitated for a moment.

"Of course she was alone. Who would she be with anyway?" she said at last.

From the coldness in her eyes, Islah realized how wrong her initial impression about this woman had been. She was anything but naive and there was no way they would ever be friends.

✖

Islah rang the doorbell, slightly out of breath from the three-story climb on the dusty stairs. It was one of those decrepit 1960s buildings that had missed the dignified architecture of the 1930s and 1940s, but had not managed to catch up with the extravagance of the open door policy of the 1970s. The similarities between this building and her own apartment block in Agouza were hard to ignore.

Before she could catch her breath, a strikingly beautiful girl of seventeen or eighteen opened the door. Here was a beauty independent of the color of hair or eyes, of how straight the nose or cute the lips may be, the kind of beauty inherent in the glimmer of eyes, in the purity of skin, in a potential smile at the corner of the mouth, in a bold straightforward look. A unique internal beauty that was in no way undermined by the black mourning attire or the two dark weeping crescents beneath the girl's black eyes. Islah hesitated as to how to introduce herself.

"You must be one of Ahlam's friends. I mean, the late . . . ," the girl said and invited her to come in.

"My heartfelt condolences."

What could she say to the girl: that she had come to spy on her and her family's sorrow? To denude them of whatever shreds of privacy they'd manage to retain, to expose them before the voracious eyes of a world whose sadistic pleasures had become routine?

Islah had still not decided how she would introduce herself. Maybe that's why she'd been so hesitant to pay this visit. She'd managed to dodge her editor for a whole week despite his persistence, that is, until he finally threatened to send another reporter. Islah's thumping heart-beat on the way to the living room told her, however, that her trepidation went beyond simple embarrassment. In fact, she was no longer capable of dealing with this situation in a mechanical unemotional way. She had compromised her professionalism.

The girl led her to a woman with a despondent look. She was sitting on a Louis XV sofa and shook softly under the weight of her grief. The mother was younger than Islah had expected, in her early fifties at most. She was thin with solid features. Her beautiful eyes hurled blame at the world around her. This time-hardened woman was the source of the girl's magnetism and that of the deceased Ahlam. Islah bent to kiss the mother and muttered all the words of condolence she could think of, then she took her place on an Aubusson armchair. She found herself facing the only other person in the room, a young man with a rather familiar face. Through the open door she could see other women mourners in the outer hall. She got distracted for a moment by their low-intensity chitchat.

"A friend of the late Ahlam," the girl whispered audibly in her mother's ear. Then she sat next to her on the sofa.

"I'm sorry I didn't catch your name," she turned to Islah with the same whisper.

"Islah Mohandes."

"And you're also in the movies?"

"No. I'm a journalist."

The girl's question worried her. Wasn't she, at heart, a liar, an impostor, a usurper of the friendship of the dead? In a matter of minutes they'd expose her.

For a moment, Ahlam's mother seemed to focus on what Islah was saying, then she went back to silently blaming empty space. Straight above her head, inside a large gilt frame, hung her wedding photograph. In white dress and flowing veil she sat, gorgeous and bubbling with life. Her husband, an attractive officer, stood behind her in military uniform, alert as a hawk. Tall and slim, every inch of him exuded confidence. If Islah were to die, her mother would no doubt sit beneath her own wedding photograph and, with the silence of a defeated general, count her losses.

Islah wondered how the handsome officer had received the news of his daughter's death. Her eyes wandered around the room searching for answers. The furniture was old-fashioned Damietta style whose gilt had been dulled by the years. The floor, by contrast, was a brilliant ceramic tiling—straight out of the TV commercial starring Omar Sharif and Yousra—and was covered in a navy blue Chinese rug with vivid embroidered flowers. The windows behind Islah were dressed in velvet curtains of the same dark blue. The walls had a fresh coat of white paint, untouched by the dust. A surrealist painting hung on the wall facing Ahlam's mother. In stark contrast with the traditional wedding photograph, the painting featured decapitated horse heads, rounded female forms in peasant dress, and Egyptian villages floating among the clouds like imaginary beehives. Above the open doorway, two stuffed gazelle heads scrutinized everyone who entered or left the room with dusty, ancient weariness.

Islah imagined the gazelles spitting at the man who sat across from her with lowered eyes and tightly closed legs.

As often happens when men find themselves in female surroundings, he had retreated inside his shell. This was a woman's home, covered in the invisible spider web that links the female sex across generations. The apartment was a mixture of old and new, a middle ground between Ahlam and her mother, a halfway point or maybe an armistice line. There was no trace of the young officer outside the brown shades of the wedding photograph.

The man gave Islah a quick look, so in turn she stared at him with the brazenness of a woman in a feminine environment. He was short and skinny with a head too big for his body. His clothes were trendy and his shoes well polished. You can distinguish men by their shoes, her mother used to say when—years ago—she was preparing her to choose a prospective husband. In those days, her mother would say she had but two wishes in life: to see Hamada a distinguished engineer and Islah in marital bliss.

On the wall above the young man's head was a stunning poster of Ahlam Shawarby in a strapless party gown smiling down at Islah. A diamond necklace emphasized the beauty of her neck, and above it, her face was a Nile rose glistening in the dew of dawn. The picture had probably been taken three or four years ago when the young actress was still a starlet. Her smile, full of hope, shouted, "The world cannot contain my beauty, the future is nothing but a slave to my ambition." A fabulous photograph that fate had made a mockery of.

Ahlam lay nude on the Chinese carpet, her body basking in all its glory. Her buttocks had sunk into the rug's thick fleece. Her black hair framed her head like a Coptic icon's halo. The silky tresses spread over one of the man's shoes. He froze in the posture of a pharaoh with eyes gazing toward the distant future.

Islah felt a strong urge to go down on the floor, to sit on the rug and take a closer look at the young actress, to touch her hair and skin, to cover her in a white sheet and take her in her arms. She made an effort to control herself and examined the others' faces for a reaction to what her eyes saw but her mind rejected.

With a flick of his foot the man pushed aside Ahlam's hair and stood up. With funerary steps he walked to Ahlam's mother, who showed no reaction. He produced an envelope from the inner pocket of his jacket and placed it gently on the table in front of her. The wrinkled envelope seemed to take its natural place on the table's marble surface, alongside a rosary of amber beads, a full coffee cup whose contents had grown tepid from neglect, an ashtray of bohemian crystal with three butts swimming in the ashes, and a blue cloisonné vase with gold engravings that was somewhat dusty and denuded of flowers, an item that was probably at the height of style in the sixties.

Ahlam's mother continued to ignore the man. After some hesitation, he muttered, "If you'll excuse me, I'll go now. As I said, I am completely at your disposal."

His voice was pure with a musical ring to it. Maybe he was a singer friend of the late Ahlam. Islah wished the conversation would go on a little longer to see if she could recognize his voice. But the woman did not react, as though his existence belonged to another universe outside the range of her senses. With a gloomy face and confused steps, the man left. The girl accompanied him to the outer door.

As soon as he had left, Ahlam's mother turned to Islah. "Doesn't this just make your blood boil?"

Her focus and clarity of tone took Islah by surprise. She couldn't understand what the woman meant. Islah's eyes instinctively turned to the naked girl on the rug but found no trace of her. She became more confused.

"Please excuse me, my daughter . . . I'm talking to you like I would talk to Ahlam," the woman said. Then with fiery eyes she turned to the beautiful girl who had just come back and ordered her to shut the door behind her. "Give that back to him, Didi . . . catch up with him on the stairs. Tell him we don't need anybody's charity," she said, pointing to the envelope the man had left.

"But these are Ahlam's earnings . . . her entitlement, not charity."

Didi, like Islah, did not grasp the mother's concern, but at least Islah concluded from Didi's reply that the man was Ahlam's producer. Immediately, she gathered who he was. So this young man with the sweet voice was Shoukry Shaker, the son of the millionaire Shaker Shaker.

"If your father was alive, he would've put an end to this nonsense."

So he, too, was dead. A martyr probably, just another name on the martyrs list. Islah started to see things clearly now. So Ahlam, you were obliged to care for your family from an early age. With such a heavy responsibility on your shoulders, there could be no room for flirtations or romantic adventures. You matured and your body rounded and your exterior became soft and feminine, but the thorns grew sharp and dangerous in your soul. A common story that Islah, too, carried like a weight of lead between her intestines.

"It's just a check for Ahlam's earnings. What's wrong with that?"

"You know very well what I'm talking about . . . I don't want to ever see that man in my house again." The woman banged the marble with a shaky hand. Waves of coffee oozed down the side of the cup.

"You should've thanked him for being honest. He could've just kept the money."

"Well thank you very much . . . but this is as far as it goes . . . do you understand?" the woman yelled and slapped her palms against her thighs then rubbed them together again and again.

"All this just because he said I was photogenic?"

Didi's words shed light on what was on her mother's mind. Islah immediately sympathized with the woman. Shoukry Shaker's reputation was the talk of the town and his scandals were constant features in the gossip columns.

"Photogenic . . . it always starts with photogenic." The woman cleared her throat. "As for how it ends, well you've seen that for yourself."

"What happened to Ahlam was a crime that had nothing to do with her work in the cinema . . . and I'm not a child anymore. I know what's right for me."

The woman turned to Islah. "Talk to her, my daughter . . . you're like an older sister to her."

The woman's concern was contagious, but Islah tried to calm things down.

"You still have plenty of time to think about these things, Didi . . . I mean until you graduate from university," she said.

"I'm not arguing with that. My high school certificate exams start in a couple of weeks and—God willing—I'll get good grades. I don't understand why you're all making such a big deal about this!"

Didi's words seemed perfectly reasonable. Islah thought the mother might have been a little hasty in her concerns. In any case, she had her reasons. It was impossible to underestimate the shock she was in. Islah started to feel embarrassed and said something about taking her leave. The woman pressed her hand, whispering, "I really appreciate your visit, my daughter . . . do you know you're the only one of her friends who came? Those 'friends' who were with her day and night—where did they all go? This incident has made people think Ahlam was a bad girl but you, my daughter, you know as well as I do she's innocent. Please keep in touch."

Shaking and perspiring, Islah descended to the street.

✖

Didi Shawarby to succeed the late Ahlam?
Younger sister to take place of murdered star onscreen?
Young producer's offer: Didi, please replace Ahlam
Talent: It runs in the family

Islah sucked the end of her ballpoint pen, then started to gnaw it. Her eyes were fixed on the computer screen in an attempt to uncover the hidden meanings behind the possible headlines for her article. She told herself that the whole thing wasn't worth all this soul-searching. She was merely a journalist doing what journalists do, practicing her profession, sweet and simple. She had gone into Ahlam's home looking for an exciting story and that's just what she'd found. Here it was, fallen into her lap. Besides, Didi and her mother would never guess that it was she who had let the cat out of the bag. They would lay the blame on Shoukry Shaker.

Holding the pen with two fingers, she took it out of her mouth and exhaled as though smoking a cigarette. Success never comes to those who allow their principles to get in the way. Hadn't she learned her lesson when they passed her up for the position of page editor in favor of Hani Mostafa, that degenerate who'd sell his own mother? Hadn't she been stung by her brother's plight, still jobless six months after obtaining his master's degree, wasting unshaven days in his pajama bottoms and undershirt, solving crossword puzzles? Wasn't it time for her to think of her own interest? Would she never learn?

Without realizing what she was doing, Islah deleted everything she'd typed. She stared at the blank screen for a moment then picked up the receiver and asked one of her colleagues for Shoukry Shaker's number. In a matter of minutes and after some give and take with an inquisitive secretary who wanted the story of her life, the musical voice came to her from the other end.

"I'll only take two minutes of your time, Shoukry Bey. It's just that I've received information I need to confirm with you before publishing. Is it true that you made frequent visits to the Tower of Happiness in the company of the late Ahlam Shawarby? Can I take this to be correct?"

The pounding of her heart filled her ears. It was a gamble to adopt such aggressive tactics with influential people like Shoukry and his father. But all other roads seemed blocked and taking a risk with this worthless man was a thousand times easier than betraying Ahlam and her family.

The producer did not flare up in anger as she had expected. Instead, a moment of silence passed, burdened by her heartbeat and the ruffle of his breath, a moment that allowed Islah to calm down but also become more keenly aware of the chances she was taking by fabricating her so-called information.

"May I enquire about the source of this information?"

"As you know sir, my journalist's code of conduct prevents me from disclosing my sources. The important thing is to determine whether this information is correct."

"I had a normal working relationship with the deceased, which means we went to meetings and public gatherings together. Naturally we had mutual friends and it's possible that we may have found ourselves at the same place on some occasions." Despite the man's civil reply, Islah knew he was grinding his teeth.

"Mutual friends . . . such as Señora Esmeralda?"

"My friends and my comings and goings are none of your business!" At last the man's anger was unleashed in a sudden explosion, but even in his outburst, his voice did not lose its musical ring.

Rather than calm things down, she found herself taking a bigger risk. "In fact, I have information that you, sir, visited Señora Esmeralda with Ahlam Shawarby the night she was killed."

"And your name is Islah Mohandes, correct?" His question slapped her in the face. She tried to retract what she had said but he interrupted her, yelling, "You have to understand that in this country there are laws to protect people's rights and their privacy!" The telephone receiver amplified the man's anger.

Before she could compose herself enough to reply, the dial tone announced that the conversation had ended.

Islah turned to her white screen. He hadn't denied that he had been in the tower with Ahlam. What's more, the mere mention of Señora Esmeralda had thrown him into a rage. Islah's suspicions grew, yet the riddle became more complicated with each new discovery. With the confidence of a professional pianist, her fingers raced across the keyboard. The words burst onto the screen. Then she sat back and picked up her pen and started to nibble its end while contemplating her observations on the screen.

The Crime of Maadi

The mystery of the young actress's murder still unresolved after nine days.

Public prosecutor insists: investigation ongoing.

The security clerk to the officer: the victim not a tenant and I never saw her come in through the main entrance.

The coroner: death resulted from nervous shock.

Could death be accidental?

Could killer be someone she knew and trusted?

A professional assassin?

Shoukry did not deny he accompanied the deceased to visit the Chilean Señora Esmeralda.

The Señora left the country mysteriously right after the crime.

A mystery: where did Ahlam's clothes go?

A bigger mystery: when did she enter the tower and with who?

The biggest mystery: how could a famous star enter the tower without being seen by the security clerk, the garage attendants, or any of the tenants?

She withdrew the pen from her mouth, put it on the table, and typed another sentence, then started to suck the pen as her eyes went over her last question again and again.

Is there something fishy about the police investigation?

Islah dared not disclose all that passed through her mind even to her trusted screen. From the start there had been this nagging feeling that something wasn't quite right. The police had not put their fingers on the beginning of the thread, although it was clear as day. When did Ahlam enter and with whom and to visit which of the tenants? Was it so hard for the police to get the truth out of security clerks and garage attendants, when they managed to obtain written confessions from almost everyone accused of any crime? If even the innocent confess in police stations, then what about the guilty?

As her puzzlement peaked, the phone started to ring. She ignored it. Which direction should she take? Whose doors should she knock on? When the phone persisted she picked up the receiver, hoping in her heart the caller would resolve her dilemma and put her on the right track. Her wish was granted, but in a manner she had neither anticipated nor thought possible, when the editor said in his most provocative tone, "We've done well with the story of the murdered actress. Let's follow up when the investigation results are announced."

"What exactly do you mean, sir?" Islah could hardly believe her ears.

"I mean that any further coverage of the story would turn us into a tabloid, and as you know, we are a reputable newspaper with traditions and credibility."

"But sir, I have new information . . . and there's a surge of public interest in this story. . . ." Her words were confused, deconstructed by her shock.

"Not a word is to be published until the official report is out. I think I've made myself perfectly clear, distinguished reporter."

Islah put down the receiver and started to cry as though she had been abandoned by a lover or lost a loved one. Tears gushed and she gulped for air like a drowning person, yet there was no rational justification for her behavior.

Maybe she was crying for the loss of her adopted friend, Ahlam Shawarby, whose friendship fate had put off until after the star's death. With one hot tear balanced on her cheek, Islah smoked her imaginary cigarette and blew invisible smoke into a menacing universe.

※

Three months after the crime—to her, they seemed more like centuries— Islah found herself in a taxi crawling to Maadi and, at last, came face to face with her dilemma. Out of all the misfortunes that plagued the human race, why was Ahlam's tragedy the one that shook Islah to the core? What made the poor girl stand apart from the victims of bus accidents, sunken ferryboats, and overturned trains? What put her above families devastated by drug addiction and children buried alive under collapsed buildings or lost to salmonella-ridden food products, bad inoculations, or incurable disease?

A daily witness of heartbreak, people's lives and deaths were to her, really, no more than front-page stories and attention-grabbing news. Just like the names and photographs in the obituaries that she skimmed through without a second thought. Merely names and numbers, like the latest statistics of people starving to death in southern Sudan or martyred in Palestine or the victims of AIDS in Africa. What then prompted Islah to sympathize with Ahlam and not all the others?

Dehydrated and disoriented by the car's weaving amid the traffic jam, it seemed to her that the answer to her question was straightforward enough: the victim was a woman, a beautiful young one whose life had been plucked like a sad flower at the height of its bloom. Moreover, the murderer was not satisfied with his terrible crime but intentionally left the body naked, even going so far as to discard the corpse—in that state—in a public area that happened to be an elevator, a moving space that spread the scandal from one floor to the next so that the world's eyes would devour her in death as they had during her lifetime.

It was a slap the murderer had delivered on every woman's face, an insult to every human being, an insolent challenge to society as a whole. And what made things worse was the fact that the authorities had failed to shed light on the murderer's identity. So how could she, as a woman, as a human being, be nonchalant about it?

Yet Islah was only too aware that these descriptions fit every crime. A crime represents by definition a violation of a human being's dignity, an affront to someone's humanity. Why then did she place the misfortunes of celebrities above the tragedies of ordinary people?

Ahlam Shawarby's beauty floated like a sad angel around her, the eternal features of an existence that would last forever, even if it were merely the product of the human lens, a mirage like everything else that passes across the golden screen.

She was particularly puzzled by a story she had just read in one of the interior pages of her own newspaper. A story so strange that she was forced to admit that despite her favored status as a priestess at the media's altar, she too was a hypnotized prisoner in its clutches, no different from the millions steered like sheep, forbidden from ever getting to the facts. But even when the truth is obscured by a cloud, a woman's heart never lies.

In her consecutive visits to the home of the late Ahlam, Islah never felt she was in a stranger's house. Indeed, Ahlam's home was closer to her heart than could rationally be explained. Because of the editor's embargo on news of the murder, Islah had nothing more to gain from these visits. But she was not motivated by personal interest. It was as though she actually believed Ahlam's mother when she insisted that Islah had become another daughter to her.

Today, Islah felt partly satisfied, partly apprehensive as she went back to Maadi, as though she were on her way to a date at the Seahorse or the Good Shot. Despite its absurdity and inconsistency, it was the story she had read in the paper that allowed her to reopen the subject after three months, to come in through the window after the editor had closed and locked the door.

She left the cab and, before entering the tower, stood on the sidewalk searching for signs of what had supposedly taken place the day before. She found a pile of broken furniture on the other side of the road. There was some truth at least to what she had read. Immediately, she headed for the tenth floor to belatedly accept Madame Gawdat's invitation, wondering if the lady would remember her from their brief encounter at Sambo's and if she'd insist on showing off her photographs with Farah Diba.

She heard footsteps coming to the door, but it took Madame Gawdat a few more seconds to open it. Islah guessed the lady had been inspecting her through the peephole. Although she could not have expected the visit, Madame Gawdat's face was fully made up beneath her blue-white hair. She wore a dress of green silk and a gold necklace studded with emeralds. Three small dogs greeted Islah with shrill barks, then stopped and sought protection behind their mistress's ankles—white fluffy dogs the likes of which Islah had only seen in magazines. A pink ribbon adorned each of the dog's heads. The lady probably expected visitors, Islah concluded.

"I'm so sorry to barge in like this without calling first, but I was in the neighborhood and simply had to drop in and see how you were doing."

"You're welcome, my dear. Come in."

Islah relaxed in an armchair and was about to remark that her own suit was the same color as the elderly lady's dress, but Madame Gawdat was preoccupied with her dogs, who watched Islah nervously from the middle of the room.

"Come girls!" The three jumped onto the sofa and snuggled up to her. "See how naughty the girls can be! I'm glad to see you, my dear, I missed you."

"Actually, I noticed the heap of furniture in the street and got worried. I was afraid there'd been a fire or something in the tower and I wanted to make sure you were okay." Islah did not wish to waste any time.

"I appreciate your concern, my dear . . . it wasn't a fire or anything like that. . . ." The lady stopped abruptly.

"Maybe a water pipe burst?"

"No, just furniture . . . somebody threw it out of the thirteenth floor." The woman stood up with unusual agility for her age. "Would you like some Earl Grey?"

"I really don't want to inconvenience you. Also, I'm in a bit of a hurry . . . I'll take a rain check. It must've been the tenants then who threw out the furniture."

"At least let me get you a cold drink." The woman headed for the kitchen. "The apartment is usually rented out, but Farah says it's been empty for the past two months," she said over her shoulder.

"Who's the owner?"

But Madame Gawdat was already in the kitchen and could not hear her, so she repeated the question when her hostess came back carrying a tray with a slice of cake and a crystal goblet of soda.

"A rich contractor, Abd al-Tawab Mabrouk, surely you've heard of him? Tell me what you think of the chocolate cake, I baked it myself."

"Aren't you having any?" Islah asked with her mouth full, devouring her cake as quickly as she could. She had gotten the information she needed.

“I wish I could, my dear, but my diabetes is giving me a hard time.”

In a matter of minutes Islah was taking her leave, citing prior engagements.

“But you haven’t seen Farah Diba’s pictures yet,” the lady protested just before the elevator door shut her out.

⁙

Another Neil Armstrong taking humanity’s first step on the moon, Islah entered apartment 1301. She froze. It was as though the apartment had been subject to an organized demolition or shaken by a violent earthquake that left nothing standing but bruised dignity and a profound sorrow throbbing from its dispersed entrails.

A destruction that was not entirely devoid of beauty, a terrible, chilling beauty.

With cautious steps, she navigated the waves of devastation. Then she noticed the corner next to the terrace. There was something unusual about it, something striking. She took another look and could barely take a breath. There was a small table in the corner, its surface polished without a speck of dust. It had a white tableloth and a delicately painted porcelain vase with one rose, a healthy white rose with the beauty of a thousand gardens. Next to the vase, she noticed a thin copybook with a floral cover. Underneath the table the marble floor was a clean, brilliant pistachio-green, a suggestion of the splendor and taste that one day had belonged to this apartment.

It must have taken a miracle for this corner to be spared the destruction that had devoured every inch of the spacious hall. She just knew that the answer to the puzzle that obsessed her was to be found here in this apartment, a rational explanation for the murder of poor Ahlam.

One of the two police recruits, alert on the other side of the room, summoned her. She pretended not to hear. Her eyes were glued to the white rose. She got closer. She felt a certain affinity for it, a desire to touch its petals, to smell its nectar, to listen to the murmur of its music, that familiar song that called out to her. Sensing the recruit approaching her, she instinctively blocked the table from his line of vision, picked up the copybook, and placed it in her purse. Then, innocently, she turned to the recruit, who tapped her on the shoulder after she had repeatedly ignored his calls.

Islah asked to see the officer in charge but the recruit did not dare interrupt the investigation going on in the next room. They were still arguing when a traffic sergeant came out. Gray-haired and in advanced middle age, he seemed quite distraught. Islah wondered if his gloom was due to life's normal worries or a result of the police investigation.

She quickly put the sergeant out of her mind and asked the recruit if the officer was available to see her now. The recruit gave it some thought, then asked her to wait and stepped into the other room. The second recruit came closer and watched her like a guard dog. After a few moments, Islah forgot all about him and started to re-examine the destruction, again unable to believe her eyes.

After a long wait, the officer himself appeared through the doorway. The second recruit quickly moved forward to relieve him of his briefcase, while the first rushed out to call the elevator. Islah showered the officer with questions but he kept walking.

"I have to run . . . maybe another time," he muttered.

Islah forced her way into the elevator with the officer and the two recruits. She produced a small notepad and a pencil which she pointed at the officer like a weapon.

"First of all, can you tell me exactly what happened?"

"The investigation is ongoing." It was the same stout officer who had investigated Ahlam's murder.

"Could there be a connection between yesterday's incident and the murder of May 5th?"

The man just stood there admiring his polished shoes until he was saved by the elevator's jerk upon reaching the ground floor. He rushed out but Islah followed on his heels and managed to block his path before he reached the outer doorway. The two recruits waited a few meters away.

"I know the apartment belongs to Abd al-Tawab Mabrouk, the contractor, and that it has been without tenants for the last two months," she said with confidence.

"Then why are you wasting my time?" The man suddenly sounded exhausted.

Islah wondered why he was grinding his teeth. Could her questions have annoyed him to this extent? But the expression on the officer's rounded face was closer to pain; maybe he had a stomachache.

"All I want to know is who the last tenant was."

After a moment's silence, the officer looked as if his intestines were about to explode.

"Obviously the garage attendants told you everything already, and since you know who owned the apartment then you must also have learned that the last tenant was a young movie producer, the son of a millionaire." He weighed his words deliberately. "But I want you to know that I will never disclose information related to the investigation, so kindly stop wasting my time."

The officer's words rang like giant bells in her head. He had handed her the keys to the investigation that had been locked in her face for the past three months. But could he have done that inadvertently?

By the time Islah regained her concentration, the officer had hurried out of the doorway with the two recruits close behind him. She wanted to stop him for more questions, but she froze a few steps down the main stairs. Before getting into the car, the officer, too, stopped for a moment. He looked toward the middle of the road then stepped into the car and the Peugeot took off.

A little boy stood in the median wearing a police beret that was too big for him, blowing his whistle in short bursts and waving his skinny arms at the cars. There was a television crew filming the incident, a Japanese crew by the looks of the correspondent and photographer. But where had they come from and why?

The sergeant she had seen leaving the investigation room fifteen minutes ago rushed passed her toward the child, shouting incomprehensibly. Her laughter rolled out, washing away her anger and perplexity.

The Fourth Page

In days past was I
Oh pride! A solid warrior, a steadfast knight,
before the feet stamped on my heart,
before the sun and frost whipped me
and bruised my graceful dignity

Salah Abdel-Sabour

Sergeant Ashmouni

"Come on, you stuck-up lord . . . in your shiny black Ford."

Ashmouni contemplates the skyline. The towers extend as far as the eye can see along the Nile's bank. What an impressive sight they present in all their splendor. Then his eyes focus on the shortest of the towers, the one from which the hammering is coming.

"Damn your racket, Charlie . . . on your sleek Harley," he says aloud to himself.

Since early morning the hammering has not stopped. Despite his distance from its source on the eighteenth floor, he's finding it increasingly irritating. The monotonous rhythm makes his head vibrate as if the banging came from within.

"Get going, fatso . . . in your expensive Volvo." Ashmouni enjoys his poetic endeavors.

The workers are demolishing the top two floors. Now they're working on the eighteenth, then they'll get down to the seventeenth. Poor building, it will seem even smaller next to the Tower of Happiness, with its twenty floors, and certainly a dwarf next to the other thirty- and forty-story towers. Even with towers, the small ones are always disadvantaged.

The owner of the short tower, it is rumored, has recently passed away and his relatives quarreled over the estate. There was nobody in charge to keep the city council inspectors happy, so the government decided to apply the legal height restrictions. Serves you right. If you can't agree on splitting an inheritance like that you deserve to lose everything. Greed is its own worst enemy.

But the government has no shame. There's no doubt about that.

"Go on Satan . . . in your brand new Nissan."

He takes a few steps toward the dubious shade of the tiny tree the city has planted on the median, a joke of a tree really, hardly able to block the raging sun. He raises the clay water-jug he keeps there to his lips, takes long gulps, then shakes his sinewy copper-colored hand and allows the water to trickle down his face and neck.

No sooner has he quenched his thirst than a sound booms louder than both the roar of traffic and the workmen's hammering. It is the chirping of the sparrows in his stomach, the daily growl of his hunger that never seems to be satisfied, a call that has now become impossible to ignore. A rather embarrassing question that nevertheless requires an answer: how will he get hold of today's lunch?

A steady hand taps him on the shoulder. He recoils like a spring. All the talk about ghosts these days has left his joints shaky. The reflex has caused him to jump back a few steps, but certainly not into the road. The experience of the day before yesterday still weighs heavily on his mind. He turns to the boy from the kebab restaurant, who sits chuckling on his scooter, an impertinent lad, plump from devouring kebabs.

"Why didn't you call out, boy?"

"Sorry, sergeant, I did but you were daydreaming."

"What do you want?"

If the boy is asking for directions he won't help him. In fact he'll make sure he goes around in circles.

"Just to pass on a message . . . the people on the thirteenth floor of the Tower of Happiness are inviting you to lunch."

The sergeant has misjudged the boy. Maybe he's a good kid after all, just a little slow in the head. Ashmouni shades his eyes from the sun with his hand and looks upward. The spiritual medium, still in jeans, is waving to him with both arms from the balcony. It is the same balcony from which the piano emerged the day before yesterday. The sergeant is about to say it would be inappropriate to leave the intersection, but his legs surprise him by crossing the road toward the tower, so he mutters under his breath, "Come on bloodsucker . . . in your fancy sports car."

⁙

The door is ajar, but Ashmouni still knocks out of courtesy. The policemen have not returned today. The psychic welcomes him with a broad smile and shakes his hand. His eyes are laden with generosity. The sergeant finds no hint of yesterday's strain on his face. He leads him to the dining room. The rubble in the hall has not changed, except that in the officer's absence it's not fundamentally different from the rubble that fills the streets.

"Do you have children, Hajj?" the man asks directly.

Embarrassed, Ashmouni mumbles that God has not willed it. Then he notices a scrawny adolescent sitting at the table behind the unopened kebab package. This is the same unscathed room that was used for the officer's interrogation but the kebab aroma has transformed it, brought it back to life. The boy opens the paper bags and the small plastic containers that hold the tahini and pickles. The psychic gently steers him to a seat across from the boy.

"We're the doctor's guests today. He's the one who insisted our lunch would be more enjoyable if you joined us," he says.

"Thank you for your generosity."

The sergeant scrutinizes the face of the boy whom the psychic referred to as 'doctor.' Clouds of foreboding float in his eyes under his large eyeglasses. Ashmouni realizes he's older than he seems. This is a man with a story. Maybe he's the real psychic and employs the kind young man as a front. Who knows, he may even have manipulated the jinn to enslave and control him. "Heaven protect us," thinks the sergeant.

"With appetite and health, sergeant." The doctor's voice is smooth like a child's. He places a paper plate with a pyramid of kebab and kofta in front of Ashmouni.

"One day at a time," Ashmouni mutters as he rolls up his sleeves.

He refrains from touching the food first so they won't think he's gluttonous, silently enduring his stomach's howls and bites. Only when the two men have started eating their shares does he attack his, satisfied that he has demonstrated he's not desperate for food.

As they wait for the child-doctor to prepare tea, Ashmouni quietly smokes a Marlboro offered by the psychic.

"Tell me, sergeant. What exactly did you see the other day?" the young man asks.

"I swear I saw nothing, sir," he responds without thinking.

The doctor comes in carrying a tray with a teapot and three empty glasses.

"Are you sure you didn't see anything at all?"

"Only the furniture as it hit the asphalt . . . and the pi—"

"And the what?" the two men ask in one voice.

"The pi . . . that thing they play music on."

"The piano!" the psychic exclaims, as though he's stumbled on a thousand pounds.

"Yeah."

"The tea is the color of ink and the sugar intense. This is the kind of tea you can get a doctorate for." The doctor pours the steaming liquid into a small glass, which he places before the sergeant.

Ashmouni takes a sip and enjoys its anesthetic sting. Before he can rest the scorching glass on the table, he's struck by the vision of a cat floating in the air just outside the window. A kitten really, white with apricot patches, swinging like a pendulum with all four limbs paddling the air, as though swimming. The two men watch him with incredulous expressions. He points to the window yet they continue to stare at him comically. The sergeant spills his tea in his lap. He jumps up with a cry, brushing away the scalding liquid from his trousers.

"The tea is good enough for a doctorate, but still not worth burning yourself," the little doctor says, and the two men start laughing.

"There's a cat outside. Look behind you!" he says, trying to hold his trousers away from his skin.

By the time the men turn to look, there's nothing unusual to be seen out of the window.

"Where's the bathroom? I need to put out this fire!"

The sergeant rushes in the direction indicated by the psychic. After a few minutes, he comes back with reduced pain and redoubled embarrassment. He only wants to get as far away as he can from the two laughing men. With a profusion of thanks, Ashmouni excuses himself, explaining he needs to get back to the intersection. As soon as he turns to go, he confronts the same kitten running up to him. The kitten is dragging behind it a long leash tied around its body. It takes refuge beneath the dining table, while the leash, extended on the carpet, points to where it is hiding.

"Did you see that, or do you still think I'm seeing things?" the sergeant challenges the two men, who are still rolling with laughter.

"Meshmesh, Meshmesh, where are you?"

Antar's childish voice is followed by his tiny form speeding into the apartment. Then his bright eyes and ready smile impose his presence. The two young men stop laughing but tears glimmer on their cheeks. They follow Antar's every move as though he were an alien from Mars. But the boy doesn't pay them much attention. He goes down on his knees next to the table and clicks his fingers.

"Come here, Meshmesh . . . . You've been molded in devil's water," the boy whispers.

"You are all guilty and the worst of you knows who he is," a low feminine voice says. Its crystal clarity makes up for its weakness.

The sergeant at first takes this for another of the child's pranks and pays no attention to the words. But he starts to be concerned when Antar remains frozen in his cross-legged position on the carpet. Then the pronouncement comes again.

"You are all guilty and the worst of you knows who he is." The same weak electrical voice emanates from the child's mouth.

The same resolve and confidence.

Could this really be one of the child's practical jokes, or is the psychic trying out the recording equipment he obviously relies on for his work? The sergeant's eyes move from the psychic to the doctor and, finding nothing but astonishment written all over the two men's faces, he bends down and stares at the child, who calmly stares back. The two men come over next to the sergeant and all three scrutinize Antar in his sudden solemnity. His eyes have turned a brilliant green, and again, the words simply flow out of his mouth. "You are all guilty and the worst of you knows who he is."

The three men take slow steps backward until they're in the outer hall. Their eyes remain fixed on the child, whom they can see through the open doorway. Ashmouni turns to the naked woman's statue with the picture hanging around its neck. Antar has not moved. He remains like a block of wood on the floor. The sergeant hears the psychic shout at the child, "You didn't have to dangle the kitten out of the window! Don't you know that cats are jinn in disguise?"

"This isn't about the cat," says the doctor in his soft voice.

The child ignores them, or maybe he's unaware of the conversation going on around him.

"Time to go." Ashmouni rushes out of the apartment door before the others can reply. Not waiting for the elevator, he shuffles down the twenty-six flights of the marble staircase, muttering as he gasps for breath. "Damn kebab . . . and damn the man who wants to eat kebab."

✖

A breeze from paradise has blown after the evening prayers to extinguish the August blaze that has roasted Cairo and skinned its inhabitants alive, sparing nothing and no one. People's features brighten in a ubiquitous Egyptian smile.

"Isn't the night shift wonderful?" Ashmouni ponders during a pause in his conversation with the jasmine vendor. The boy has rushed to peddle his merchandise to the cars in the intersection that await the sergeant's signal to make a U-turn or to proceed to the heart of Maadi. With wit and humor, he makes a living.

The sergeant has drunk a whole jug of water, yet he is thirsty again. Perhaps he added too much chili sauce to the koshary he had for lunch. The Owl's koshary—like all her cooking—is unsurpassed. On her days, he prefers the night shift because it gives him an excuse to avoid her bed, as opposed to the days allotted to the sexy Zuzu, when he is only too keen to get home and dive into that volcano between her arms.

A shiny Mercedes comes to a standstill at the intersection, signaling a left turn. The sergeant sets his thirst aside and blows his whistle then raises both hands in the face of the stream of oncoming cars. When they insolently refuse to heed his command, he steps into the road, waving his ticket book and using his body to block the cars' passage. The Mercedes starts to move.

"Season's greetings," the driver says and hands him a one-pound note through the open window.

"May God protect you, Pasha," Ashmouni replies as the smell of exhaust attacks his nostrils.

A woman on the other side of the road is stuck, unable to cross. She takes advantage of the interrupted flow and hurries toward the sergeant. Although she is dressed like a boy, he feasts his eyes on her confident feminine form. Yet his attention is quickly diverted to a Fiat 132, illegally parked on the opposite side of the road next to the riverbank.

The sergeant initially gave the car a few minutes to move on, but it is still there. The jasmine vendor has managed to sell all his remaining wreaths to the car's occupants and waves to the sergeant, smiling. His night's work is done and he can go wherever he pleases. Here's a story of love and revenge, Ashmouni concludes; love for the car's occupants and fate's revenge that will come at his hands.

He ignores the approaching female and plunges into the flow, expertly avoiding the cars as they roar on to Maadi.

"Get going, you bozo . . . in your beat-up old Renault."

He peers through the driver's open window and catches them red-handed. The young man is kissing his head-scarved passenger and has slipped his hand beneath her slightly raised skirt. Ashmouni allows himself to enjoy the spectacle for a moment then decides to step in before matters get out of hand. First, he takes a grip of his own senses, then he coughs artificially.

The young man looks up in surprise. His eyes squint and beg for leniency but he says nothing.

"Is this kind of behavior acceptable?" The sergeant's question is simple and straightforward.

Swept over by a mixture of animal lust and satisfaction at his own eloquence, he leans with both hands against the car door.

The young man fumbles in his pockets and produces his wallet. "This is just a misunderstanding." He places a one-pound note in the sergeant's hand.

Ashmouni turns the note over in disgust. Does this imbecile know how much a kilo of basboussa costs these days? "What's this . . . one pound? You should be ashamed of yourself," the sergeant says without emotion.

A kilo of basboussa has become Ashmouni's favorite currency. It has, after all, become indispensable if he's going to enjoy the world in the same way as this lad.

The young man hands him a fiver with shaking fingers. Ashmouni pockets the money and pushes his beret back. He turns to go, then stops for a moment. "Take it easy with your fingers or the young lady might have to wash before prayer time."

The sergeant leaves the car behind and strolls down the Nile bank. He heads toward Abbas, the one-eyed lupine bean vendor. Abbas pushes his handcart with its pyramid of lupine beans every day from an alley next to Ashmouni's house in Daresalam. He'll take a long drink from his clay jug and help himself to some lupine beans. How he enjoys a nice walk in the cool night breeze. And isn't it wonderful when cash materializes out of thin air?

A loud explosion of honks attracts Ashmouni's attention to the woman crossing the street. It is the same girl he left a few minutes ago. She has at last managed to get to the Nile's bank after compelling the cars to evade her. Now she obliges him to stop.

"Why didn't you help me cross, sergeant? Where's your chivalry?" She's out of breath. Her hair is short like a boy's and her figure is rather slight, but she walks like a woman.

"I'm sorry, good lady. I had to go see about that guy blocking the road over there, before the officer drives by."

"In that case, I forgive you." The woman stares at the car still parked behind the sergeant. It shows no indication it is about to leave. "Since all is forgiven, can we chat?" she adds in a flirtatious tone.

"Sure. Let's chat. But about what?"

"Well, for example, you can tell me about the strange stuff that's been happening lately."

The sergeant remembers who she is. This is the journalist who was talking to the officer ten days ago. It is definitely her, with her short, straight hair and masculine suit. Women these days think they can turn into men.

"I didn't see anything."

"A friend of mine gave me this pack but I don't smoke. Do you like Marlboros, sergeant?"

A believer never rejects God's bounty. He unwraps the cellophane and lets it fly with the breeze, then opens the box and rolls the silvery paper into a ball and throws it on the pavement.

"I hear you actually saw the piano as it fell."

"True," he responds from the corner of his mouth as he tries to light a cigarette, shielding the flame with both hands.

"I looked for the car they say the piano fell on but couldn't find it. It must've been smashed to pieces."

He draws from the Marlboro and says, "They had it towed away immediately. They're pretty superstitious, you know."

"I guess that shouldn't be a problem for Shoukry, the millionaire's son. If he wanted to, he could replace it with ten cars," the woman said, squinting.

"My dear lady, the car that was destroyed was a Mercedes, the model they nickname 'stealth,' and Shoukry Pasha only drives sports cars."

Ashmouni notices Sambo's BMW come to a standstill in front of the tower. The hairdresser gets out of the car followed by two young men in tight trousers. Their hair is shiny and sticky with gel in the style of Anwar Wagdi, the movie star. Rather than go into Sambo's shop, they head for the tower's entrance.

"Then who owned the Mercedes, sergeant?"

Ashmouni's eyes follow Sambo and his two friends as they disappear inside the tower. He pushes his beret back and scratches the front of his head. He knows his hair is getting whiter by the day. Its spongy, familiar touch helps him to concentrate. Something must be cooking.

"Why are you so distracted, sergeant?"

"Oh, it's nothing, dear lady. . . . The car belonged to his father, Shaker Pasha."

The journalist carries her purse like a bus conductor; she wears the strap on the left side of her neck while the purse dangles at her right hip. Her black eyes are outlined with kohl like a peasant girl's. She seems surprised.

"Mr. Shaker must've been visiting Farah that day, then."

"Mr. Shaker? Did I say Mr. Shaker? My tongue slipped." The sergeant is starting to get worried.

"Then whose car was it?"

"I've been telling you all along, I don't know anything." He finds himself sweating despite the pleasant weather. He takes off his beret and probes his damp hair.

"Then tell me, Sergeant. Who was Ahlam Shawarby visiting the day she was murdered?"

"I really have to get back to the intersection before the officer passes through."

"Stop. Don't you move one inch! I'm just asking you to confirm one tiny little thing, which I already know anyway: was Shoukry Shaker staying at the haunted apartment, yes or no?" she shouts with flaring eyes. This is what we get from women these days.

"I swear I know nothing. I have nothing to do with buildings and towers. I have nothing to do with anything in the world except this intersection."

She produces a copybook from her purse and reads in a low voice,

In days past was I

Oh pride! A solid warrior, a steadfast knight,

before the feet stamped on my heart. . . .

A procession of cars passes by, invading the universe with honks, drumbeats, and trumpets. The weddings of rich folk are noisier than the mock monkey weddings that street performers put up. It is genuine poetry the journalist is reading. She came all the way here just to read him verses from a poem. She pauses until the procession has passed, then continues:

Before the sun and frost whipped me

and bruised my graceful dignity. . . .

"This is a poem by Salah Abdel-Sabour, sergeant. Have you heard of him?"

"Of course. Who hasn't heard of the great poet?" the sergeant replies with enthusiasm.

In fact, Abdel-Sabour's name is quite familiar. The poet is often mentioned on the radio and TV. These high brows think ordinary folks are ignorant and understand nothing. True, he's never heard any of his poetry, but at least he knows the name. Besides, the verses the journalist just read ring so true to his ears, as though they were written with him in mind.

"I fought in '67 and '73."

"This poem is taken from the late Ahlam's notebook." The journalist's face comes closer to his. He needs to be on the lookout for this woman's tricks.

The sergeant steps back. He wants to break free of her, but like a female spider she has him surrounded with invisible threads. He looks upward to the thirteenth-floor balcony and shudders. After the floating piano and the child who spoke in a woman's voice, who knows what could happen. The psychic and his friend are also playing their tricks. Every day of the past week they invited him to lunch but he declined. He'd rather have his onions and turnips than their kebabs. He hasn't even set foot inside the ill-fated Tower of Happiness since that incident with Antar.

"God rest her soul." The sergeant has been genuinely troubled by the loss of the actress.

A procession of stretch limousines stops in front of the tower's entrance. In a sudden whirlwind, drivers, servants, garage attendants, and even the haughty security clerk all burst into motion. There's a lot of confusion. Sheikh Wahdan has arrived on one of his short visits. The sergeant slaps his forehead. He should have learned about this from the garage attendants. He should have read the signs. The mystery that had befuddled him a few minutes ago has been resolved, only too late. Mr. Kasseb's toupee floats smoothly among the Arab headbands. He gesticulates instructions in every direction. In a fleeting moment, the human mass disappears inside the tower's belly. He has missed a golden opportunity. The sheikh's generosity is legendary toward those who welcome him upon his arrival. Never mind, he'll get another chance. But not tonight. The sheikh will be busy tonight at the party prepared for him by Mr. Kasseb and the promiscuous Sambo. "One day at a time."

"What's happening over there?" The commotion has attracted the journalist's attention.

"Would you repeat the part where feet are stepping on his heart?"

"Before the feet stamped on my heart," she repeats with a sad smile, as though she can sense his inner turmoil.

"But what did the late actress know about war, misery, and people walking all over your heart? She was a princess with not a worry in the world." To his surprise, his voice has gained a calm lyrical tone.

"She was murdered, sergeant. You don't get any more miserable than that." Again her face approaches closer to his, staring into his eyes, searching his depths. "Also, her father—God rest his soul—was an officer in the army . . . a martyr. If God had prolonged his life, maybe she wouldn't have ended up this way." *"I was a warrior and a steadfast knight* . . . can you read the poem again?"

"Ahlam was a victim of injustice in life and in death. Do you understand what it means to be the victim of injustice in life and in death? You have to help me, sergeant, to avenge her death."

"God alone can help us all."

The sergeant turns away. It is time to go back to his place in the heart of the racket, at the center of the world's exhaust. He needs to get away from this woman who talks about injustice as though it were the latest fashion imported from Paris. He expects her to block his way as she did with the officer, but she doesn't move. He turns to her before crossing:

"Yes, Mr. Shoukry did rent the haunted apartment but he left just after the murder . . . that's almost three months before this strange stuff started to happen."

She grabs his arm while he's in the middle of crossing. Around them, the cars shoot forward like guided missiles.

"You're a good man," she shouts in his ear so he can hear. "But there's one thing I still need to know. Does Shaker visit Farah regularly?"

"She's a relative, my dear lady. He comes to see her every few days."

"If Shaker is Farah's relative, then Shoukry must be related to her as well. He also visits her, right?"

A steelworks bus misses them by a few inches. The heat from its engine blasts the sergeant's face.

"Wrong. He's never visited her and that's all I know . . . and if we're not careful we'll both get run over!"

The world smiles in his face. He has spoken at least part of the truth. For the first time in his life he has shown courage. Actually, for the second time. The first was in the October War. He gropes for the pack of Marlboros in his pocket and regains his natural smile. Then he whispers to himself as they cross the remaining lane, "Get on, minibus . . . and don't make a fuss."

✼

With a heavy gait, the sergeant climbs the steps leading to the Tower of Happiness. He feels more stiffness than usual in his joints despite the thick red carpet they have laid out for the sheikh. He's going nowhere near the thirteenth floor today, he consoles himself. He'll accomplish his mission: make a few quick bucks, then quickly get back to the intersection. He hadn't wished to impose on the sheikh on a Friday and decided to make his call at noon on Saturday so the man would be awake after the night's partying. This is a duty he approaches with great reluctance. Still, good manners require him to welcome the important guest to Cairo.

Today, an unusually large number of people are waiting for the elevator. Could they all have come to say hello to the sheikh? Then he remembers that two of the three elevators are reserved for the sheikh and his party for the duration of their stay. Only one is left for the tenants' use. He squeezes into the crowd, hoping to find a place on the first one up. A familiar female voice rings in his ear. He turns to find the journalist talking to one of the tenants.

"And exactly how many apartments does the sheikh occupy?" she asks.

"Well, that's a long story. To start with, he occupies the top four floors, three of them for his accommodation while the top one has a gymnasium and swimming pool. Then the next three floors—a total of six apartments—are reserved for his entourage and members of his family."

The man talks to the journalist in a rich, confident voice. He is clean-shaven and his silvery hair is carefully brushed backward. Despite the heat, he wears a red tie and a tight-fitting suit that shows off his slim, well-proportioned body.

The journalist's eyes are captivated by the man. She allows the crowd to push her body against his, then her dreamy face suddenly smiles. "You are Mr. Karim Nafea, right?"

Ashmouni cannot help noticing a red silk handkerchief protruding from the man's coat pocket, swollen like a bouquet of flowers on his chest. He likens the man to a peacock. He's about his age, but the two men couldn't possibly be more different. If he had to choose an animal to represent him, which one would it be?

"Actually, we've met once before, briefly. I've heard so much about you. I'm fascinated with the student movement of '68, and you, of course, are one of its standard-bearers."

"Oh, that's ancient history . . . days of idealism and dreams . . . youth! I have grown children now. This is Aiman. . . ." He points to a young man with a ponytail and earring. If not for the boy's stubble Ashmouni would have taken him for a girl. The boy winks at Islah.

"And that's Tamer . . . the mullah," the man adds, pointing with the other hand to a bearded fellow in a white gelabia and skullcap. The young man looks away the instant the journalist's eyes focus on him. "But why this interest in the demonstrations of 1968? You weren't even born then."

The musical ring heralds the elevator door's opening. People rush in.

Ashmouni manages to squeeze in and leaves behind the journalist and the rebel student of yesteryear who now looks like an aging movie star.

Before the door shuts him in, he hears her say, "That was the golden age. Young people managed to get their voices heard. Actually, I was born in '68."

Like a public bus, the elevator loses passengers with every stop. At last, the sergeant finds himself alone in the final ascent to Sheikh Wahdan. If Ashmouni had to choose an animal to represent him, which one would it be? With typical Egyptian masochism, he repeats the question to himself. He manages an awkward answer before the elevator reaches its destination: he's a warrior like the one the poet talked about in the journalist's poem. He wishes he had learned that poem by heart so he could repeat it when struck by self-doubt. But it wasn't really the journalist's poem. It was Ahlam Shawarby's. These were verses the murdered beauty had chosen to describe her life, or to predict her end.

The elevator door slides open but there's an inner door upholstered in red velvet. He turns the golden knob and it opens. Numb with embarrassment, Ashmouni steps into a wide hall with a white marble floor and walls upholstered in the same red velvet. In the middle of the hall, an unusual table upholstered in green velvet rests on top of a large Persian rug. A young man in a white gelabiya leans on the table, holding a long stick in his hand. He shoots small colored balls with his stick. The collision spreads them across the table. Mr. Kasseb suddenly appears in front of him. The fat man gives him an ugly look.

"I just wanted to welcome the pasha sheikh." Why must a man spend most of his life justifying his actions to others?

"Is that all? You mean there are no new catastrophes?"

Ashmouni isn't sure what the man is trying to say, so he keeps quiet. Mr. Kasseb seems exhausted. After a moment's reflection his face relaxes.

"Well, thank you for the thought . . . I'll inform His Highness the sheikh." Then he produces a five-pound note and puts it in the sergeant's hand. "To celebrate the arrival of His Highness," he adds, grating his teeth.

The young man in the gelabia goes on playing his strange game. Ashmouni makes no attempt to hide his disappointment with the five-pound note. Mr. Kasseb smiles and hands him another fiver. "Here you go, my man. You're worth it. I'll go down with you. I'm in a hurry."

"A thousand thanks, Pasha," Ashmouni barks. He adds in a lower voice as he gets the door, "Do you have a couple of those blue pills on you?"

The elevator rings with Mr. Kasseb's laughter, which he cannot control until the elevator comes to a standstill on the thirteenth floor.

"I would never keep the Viagra from you, sergeant. . . . Come, maybe you'll get lucky."

The sergeant finds himself following Mr. Kasseb onto the damned thirteenth floor. When the man heads for the haunted apartment instead of his own, he can no longer keep quiet. "Aren't we going to your own apartment, Pasha?"

"Of course. But I have urgent business to take care of here then straight we go to get your Viagra. Or are you scared of ghosts, sergeant?"

✣

Ashmouni freezes at the center of the hall that, only two weeks ago, was a playground for ghosts. His legs refuse to carry him inside the dining room, which, with the curtains drawn and lights turned off, is dim in the middle of the day. The room's only source of illumination is a bluish vibrating glow, a nervous rotating beam that plays games with his eyes and exhausted mind. Laughter rings out from the room, mocking his fears. These people have been blinded by their luxury. They show no respect to the powers that lurk around them, invisible, poised to pounce. Then, like background music in a horror movie, the tune explodes. The doctor, with his serious childish features, appears in the open doorway.

"You have a heart of gold . . . we were just talking about you." He looks around the hall as he approaches. Under his eyeglasses, his eyes are two small brown circles, like fish eyes. His confused state further aggravates the sergeant.

"Tell me, sergeant. Have you noticed a strange car driving around the block?" To be heard above the din, he whispers in his ear in a cartoon character's voice.

101

What a strange question. Ashmouni struggles to reconcile it with the surrounding otherworldly atmosphere. Before he can focus, the psychic's voice approaches him.

"Hi, sergeant. Why are you standing outside? Come in."

"Thank you sir, maybe another time. I'm just waiting for Mr. Kasseb and then we'll be going." The sergeant watches Mr. Kasseb who walks into the room and, without hesitation, takes a seat at the table.

"I insist. You'll probably want to tell these good people what you've seen with your own two eyes."

"I swear I didn't see a thing, sir."

As the sergeant repeats his statement for the thousandth time in the past two weeks, the psychic pulls him by the arm and leads him to the same seat where he devoured the kebab meal. The doctor follows like a stray child and sits next to the sergeant.

Chief Bassily, the man with the loudest voice, is the source of the jokes and laughter that shake the place. Ashmouni knows him well. He often passes him by as he sits in front of his roastery, smoking shisha and joking with the passersby. He sometimes gives Ashmouni a quarter kilo of sunflower seeds or roasted peanuts, gifts Ashmouni especially values for their effectiveness in softening Zuzu's heart.

Ashmouni is too distracted to follow the man's joke. His only wish is to get out of here. The others seem to be having a good time. Abdallah Bassily is a human barrel. He laughs at his own joke and his belly vibrates beneath the red checked shirt and suspenders he wears like a character in a Western. The man once told Ashmouni that he had never worn trousers in his life, that is until he bought his apartment in the Tower of Happiness, and that were it not for his children's nagging—being the stuck-up American University students that they are—he would never have given up his soft comfortable gelabiyas. He doesn't seem to mind it when the others laugh half-heartedly at his jokes. His belly keeps on throbbing as he listens to a story Karim Nafea starts to tell.

Karim Nafea's voice possesses a natural warmth. His handsome face is flushed. He beams with pride at his own sense of humor. As he laughs, his shoulders shake from side to side and the red handkerchief in his coat pocket dances to their rhythm. The rotating light shows him in slow motion. He sits directly across from the sergeant. The man's gaze forces Ashmouni to pretend to laugh harder, as opposed to Bassily, who sits at the head of the table opposite the psychic and with whom Ashmouni rarely establishes eye contact.

Between laughs, Bassily addresses the psychic, "Well, Mr. Spiritual Medium, you've played us your disco and still there's no sign of ghosts . . . I hope the masters haven't taken the day off!"

A month ago, the man gave Ashmouni a bag full of sweet Aswan seeds, but when he took it back to Zuzu, she grated her teeth. "This is a crow's present!" she shouted, and hurled the bag on the floor. "Give it to the Owl! Only apples and baklava for me!"

"What's the matter, Dr. Abd al-Malak? I came here to ask you to organize a special séance for Sheikh Wahdan. I hope you're not going to make me look bad?"

Mr. Kasseb's comment seems to unsettle Abd al-Malak, who turns to the sergeant. His eyes plead him to tell what he's witnessed. Ashmouni decides to escape even at the cost of sacrificing the Viagra pills he so desperately needs. Before he can slip away, Antar barges into the room holding his helpless kitten by the scruff of the neck. He heads directly to the childlike doctor, ignoring all the others.

"Uncle Cerebellum, is this apartment really haunted like Soad says?" he goes directly to the point.

"Why don't you ask Uncle Abd al-Malak? He's the one who should explain." The Cerebellum replies impatiently, then turns to Ashmouni and whispers, "You never answered me, sergeant. Have you spotted any strange characters in the neighborhood lately?"

"Has anyone heard the story of the American, the Frenchman, and the guy from Upper Egypt who entered the competition for the biggest. . . ."

Chief Bassily tails off. He glares at the boy who has materialized out of nowhere to restrict his freedom.

Antar repeats his question to Abd al-Malak, who takes Meshmesh from the boy and gently puts the cat down on the table. Then he strokes the boy on the head and starts to chant, "Deoxyribonucleic acid . . . chromosome, chromosome, chromosome . . . speak up. With the help of Adenine and her sister Guanine and her sister Thymine and her sister Cytosine, speak up! Chromosome, chromosome, chromosome. . . ."

This spell is new to Ashmouni, who knows by heart scores of fellah, Bedouin and gypsy spells, plus of course his mother's special charms. She was a blessed woman—God rest her soul.

"I can't believe my ears . . . are you using chemical equations to summon the spirits? That's what we get from an American education. Next you'll make the ghosts appear and disappear by remote control."

For once, the sergeant sympathizes with Karim Nafea when he mocks the psychic. When these educated people encroach on the territory of clairvoyants and soothsayers, what does that leave for poor folk?

"You are all guilty and the worst of you knows who he is."

Taken by surprise, the psychic recoils with his chair a few steps backward. Antar is only a few centimeters away from the sergeant. Under the vibrating blue light, the boy is cut in stone. The sergeant wants to run away from this damned place, but he's paralyzed by fear.

"How interesting . . . the child speaks." Karim Nafea shrugs. He hasn't grasped what's going on.

"You have betrayed those who trusted you." There is purity in the musical feminine voice.

Ashmouni now realizes he should take Antar away from this place, but he doesn't have the guts to make the slightest move. Karim Nafea studies Ashmouni and the laughter freezes in his throat.

"And you, Karim Nafea, have betrayed those who trusted you."

"What's this bullshit, woman . . . I was the leader of the patriotic students." Reflexively, Karim treats the speaker as female. He must've been taken by surprise, hardly expected to become the accused.

"You secretly joined the government's ranks after the students carried you on their shoulders."

"What are you saying, woman? History is witness to my patriotism."

"Today you make huge profits from normalization projects. . . . What happened to the national struggle?"

"Somebody turn off this damned machine!" Karim jumps up and pulls the plug of the machine that emits the blue light, then he repeats the same thing with the tape recorder. The lights and background music stop. He turns on the main lights and remains standing next to the china cabinet, staring at the child. Antar's eyes emit a green phosphorescent glow.

"You are all guilty and the worst of you knows who he is." Emotionless, the voice of a beautiful woman flows through the boy's mouth.

"Why, sergeant . . . I hope you haven't noticed anyone acting suspiciously." The Cerebellum's small fist is like a hawk's talon on the sergeant's arm. His pale face is perspiring. Ashmouni doesn't know what to say to this lunatic.

"Do not worry, Cerebellum, your secret is still intact." Antar iscompletely immobile, with only his mouth moving. His words only redouble the Cerebellum's fretfulness.

"Isn't science wonderful, boys? Bravo!" Chief Bassily still doesn't believe what's happening before his eyes. Perhaps he thinks it is just a new electronic gadget the psychic brought back from America.

"Abdallah Bassily . . . How did you make your millions?"

"I sweated for every piaster I own, Mr. Spiritual Medium . . . And excuse me, but I'm a guy from the streets and you can't play your hocus-pocus on me," Chief Bassily says to the psychic, then produces from his pocket a stick of molasses candy, tears off the cellophane, and starts nibbling.

"Did the money come from your sweat or the sweat of the poor workers you swindled and left stranded in the Western Desert?"

105

For a moment, time freezes in the dining room. Chief Bassily has turned into stone with the molasses stick in his mouth. The Cerebellum, with his two protruding front teeth, is a cross between a boy and a rabbit, totally immobile with the exception of the beads of sweat flowing down his forehead and cheeks. The psychic is still in his chair, which he has pushed further and further back, until he can almost touch the window behind him. As for Antar, poor boy, he's a statue.

Karim Nafea has scratched his hair into a comic shape. But there's no trace of Mr. Kasseb. The discovery shocks the sergeant. The son of a bitch has sneaked off. Ashmouni was duped. What an idiot not to have noticed that, uncharacteristically, the man's voice has not been heard for the past few minutes. Ashmouni realizes that it is his turn now. The ghost will now expose what he has done. He pulls himself together and, without a word, heads for the door.

The voice catches up with him in the middle of the outer hall, "You are all guilty and the worst of you knows who he is . . . . Where will you hide from your conscience, Ashmouni?"

✹

September is here. But the heat and her twin sister, humidity, are inexhaustible. For the past two weeks the sergeant has been avoiding the Tower of Happiness, but he knows from the garage attendants that séances have now become a daily routine. Abd al-Malak, the psychic, has become the most talked-about man in town.

As for Sheikh Wahdan, he left the day following Ashmouni's last séance, after spending only three days in Cairo. The sergeant did not manage to skim one more piaster off him. Ashmouni's disappointment has poisoned the blood in his veins and he finds it hard to bear himself these days. People are making money by the shovelful while he toils and sweats for nothing. Yet there's a diabolical idea he's turning around in his mind, a mind made molten by the sun and eroded by need.

It's a bold idea, and the only obstacle to its attainment is his undeniable cowardice. But the opportunity is now at hand. He must seize the moment before it's too late. When the sergeant is at the height of his indecision, Shaker Shaker appears unexpectedly in his new Mercedes Viagra, as though his form has condensed out of Ashmouni's thoughts. His presence forces the sergeant to make up his mind.

The millionaire leaves his Mercedes at the tower's entrance for one of the garage attendants to park. The sergeant has already crossed the street and now follows him into the tower. He catches up with him as he steps into the elevator and the door locks them in together. The sergeant presses the tenth floor, then raises his hand to his temple in a quasi-military salute and thanks God for the Pasha's good health.

"Thank you, Ashmouni . . . but why the rush, what's going on?" His body is frail and his back bent, as though he's made his millions lifting heavy weights. He studies the sergeant with narrow eyes that emit a penetrating cold. His sickly smile does not abandon his face.

Unconsciously, Ashmouni follows the floor lights, which set him a strict time limit to accomplish his mission. "Times are rough, Pasha . . . but I have hope in God and in your kindness," he answers quickly.

"Please don't tell me you've gone out of your mind and are going to ask for more money." The man exposes yellow fangs and a golden tooth in the front of his mouth. He stuffs an enormous cigar between his thin lips. The elevator stops on the sixth floor. The two men stop talking. The opening door reveals Hani, the tower plumber, carrying his toolbox in his wet hand. He's about to step in, but Dr. Mahgoub stops him. The doctor is in his pajama bottoms, sleeveless undershirt, and plastic slippers. He holds the plumber by the arm and whispers to him in a voice audible to the entire neighborhood of Maadi. "Are you sure that the dripping will stop, Engineer Hani?"

"Don't worry, doctor. Give it a couple of days for the filler to swell and everything will be okay." With a quick movement, Hani escapes the man's grip, steps inside, and presses the ninth floor.

"But this is the sixth time the faucet has been leaking." The elevator door terminates Dr. Mahgoub's existence, but the echoes of his last sentence impose themselves on its occupants.

With a broad, artificial smile, the plumber greets the millionaire. Shaker nods and blows cigar smoke. After Hani has gotten off on the ninth, the millionaire suddenly hits the red button and the elevator stops between floors. "What do you want? Speak up." His eyes are bloodshot beneath his twitching eyelids.

"Only a thousand or two . . . out of the kindness of your heart." The sergeant feels his body shaking. He barely believes he possesses this much courage.

"So you're not satisfied with the five thousand you sucked . . . leech." The millionaire's complexion is nearly gray beneath his artificially straightened and brilliant black hair.

"The situation is getting more complicated, Pasha. The police and the public prosecutor are back—"

"Don't worry. I'll take care of the police, and the public prosecutor too."

"There's also that journalist sticking her nose into everything."

"Leave the journalist to me. I'll take care of her." The man's dull voice is getting impatient.

"What about the masters? Can you save me from them?" The sergeant points to the elevator ceiling, indicating the spirits.

He can feel tears brewing inside his eyes. He's ashamed at his weakness. Had he spoken to the police, the matter would have gone all the way to the public prosecutor and the courts, and who knows? Maybe the hangman's noose would have cast a shadow on a few millionaires. His silence has a price. Still, he's forced to beg for what is rightfully his. But this is an evil, unpredictable man. He wonders if the tears are visible in the corners of his eyes.

"The masters . . . ?" The elevator echoes with the millionaire's laughter. "We are the masters, you fool."

A tear has escaped his eye. The sergeant feels it making its way down his cheek. He looks away from the millionaire, contemplates his dusty shoes. To his surprise the man produces a stack of hundred-pound notes from the pocket of his white coat. He wets his thumb in his mouth and, with quick bank-clerk fingers, counts five notes. Then he returns the rest of the stack to his pocket.

"I want you to think of this as an act of charity."

"May God reward you for your kindness, Pasha."

"Not a word to anyone . . . and don't even dream you'll get one more red millieme out of me. Do you know, Ashmouni, what happens to those who play with fire?"

Before he gets off the elevator on the tenth floor, Shaker presses thirteen and turns to the sergeant.

"Find yourself some business with Kasseb before going down."

※

Ashmouni stands on the landing of the thirteenth floor and wipes the tears from his eyes. Tears of shame and happiness, of fear for fate's retribution. He pockets the money and tries to think of an excuse to ring Mr. Kasseb's bell, then he's overcome by a cascade of dreamy musical notes. It's the tune from 'I Adore You,' Abdelhalim's immortal song, and it's coming from the haunted apartment. Suspicious, he peeks through the door, which stands ajar, then turns to press Mr. Kasseb's bell. No one comes to the door. Attracted by the music, he finds himself tiptoeing toward the other apartment. He says to himself that he'll say hello to the psychic then leave straight away; this way he'll have an excuse for his presence in the tower without exposing his link to Shaker Shaker. Above all, he'll enjoy the magical music.

The music stops the moment he pops his head in. He eyes Abd al-Malak and the Cerebellum, standing in amazed silence. Following their gaze to the corner of the hall closest to the main entrance, his jaw drops.

He shares their surprise. In this corner the green marble is clean and shiny, in stark contrast with the rest of the hall. The walls display paintings in elegant frames. A few steps away from the sergeant there's a stool with a red velvet seat. In front of it, brilliant and pristine, without a scratch or a stain or a speck of dust on it, the black piano sparkles in a pure confident light, as if nothing at all had happened.

The Fifth Page

The last time I saw you
before I went blind,
you were bathing in the nude
in Lake Wan.
Your lips were honey drops
and your right hand searched inside my gown
for the ploughshare of the stars.

Abdelwahab Elbayaty

Abd al-Malak

Abd al-Malak has just left the kitchen with a bottle of cold water and is crossing the battered hall when he notices the piano. He freezes not far from the kitchen door then calls out to the Cerebellum. More than anything, he's struck by the transformation that has taken place in the corner where the piano has suddenly appeared: the floor is again a brilliant pistachio-green, the walls are spotless white with two oil paintings of flowers and fruits in identical frames of black lacquer. The Cerebellum hurries in from his bedroom. His usual expression of surprise attains comic heights.

At that moment the sergeant's head appears through the doorway, which is permanently left ajar. Slightly out of breath, his bronze face darkens. He stares at the piano and, with eyes full of blame, turns to Abd al-Malak and the Cerebellum, as if holding them responsible for all the bizarre things that have been happening lately. Abd al-Malak wonders why the sergeant has chosen to appear at this exact moment after an absence of more than two weeks.

"Who was playing the pi . . . that thing?" the sergeant asks after a heavy silence.

"Nobody was playing. Did you hear something?" The Cerebellum says to Ashmouni then, visibly puzzled, he turns to Abd al-Malak. After a moment he produces a handkerchief from his pajama pocket and starts to wipe his eyeglasses.

"No one was playing the piano," Abd al-Malak confirms. "What makes you ask such a question?"

"Don't tell me nobody heard 'I Adore You,' the Abdelhalim song." The blood drains out of the sergeant's face.

"Maybe the neighbors had their radio on . . ." Abd al-Malak looks for a rational explanation.

In a flutter, two white doves burst into the hall through the glass-less window frames. Abd al-Malak and the Cerebellum pay them little attention. They've gotten used to them coming and going. It occurs to Abd al-Malak that the two doves never leave droppings.

"I'm telling you the music was coming from here—and from that damned thing!" The sergeant points to the piano without looking at it. His eyes follow the two doves until they plunge back into the sky outside. Then he seems to collect his thoughts and voices the question that has been hovering in the air above the three men's heads, like the two doves: imposing but impossible to catch.

"Who brought it here . . . and why is this corner untouched?"

A prolonged silence. The sergeant turns to go. "Ashtatan ashtout," he chants repeatedly as he hurries away.

"Wait, sergeant. I need an urgent word with you." The Cerebellum follows him to the main door but the sergeant has disappeared.

The phone rings. As he hurries to the dining room to get it, Abd al-Malak wonders about the Cerebellum's sudden interest in the sergeant.

"This is Mrs. Hafez, a tenant. I know how busy you must be but I need a consultation on a technical matter." Her voice is dry, lacking a youthful ring.

"I am at your disposal, Madame." Abd al-Malak is getting used to receiving calls from total strangers. After all, he's become a service provider like estate agents or grocers or kebab restaurants.

While talking to the woman, Abd al-Malak turns around to see what the Cerebellum is up to in the hall. The man is passing his fingers over the piano's brilliant surface. Then, with arms raised in the air, he slowly

114

makes his way through the piles of broken furniture onto the balcony, as though reenacting the route previously traveled by the piano to the balcony's edge.

With the wireless handset next to his ear, Abd al-Malak takes a few steps inside the hall to keep track of what the Cerebellum is doing.

"Last night, close to dawn, I heard Mr. Hafez, my husband, growl in his sleep. . . ."

"Growl?" He follows the woman's conversation with barely a quarter of his mind, while the rest of his brainpower tries to figure out the Cerebellum's strange behavior. After freezing for a moment at the edge of the balcony, the little man quickly steps back into the hall, then rushes to the dining room, brushing against Abd al-Malak's shoulder as he passes through the doorway.

"Yes . . . like he was having an argument with someone in his sleep but instead of using words he was growling."

"Growling?"

The Cerebellum stands by the side of the window and inspects the street below. Suddenly, he recoils and remains motionless with his back to the wall.

"Exactly. Like he was talking but in a different language, a language unknown to mortals. . . ."

Abd al-Malak is about to suggest that maybe the man was just having a nightmare, but quickly changes his mind. All his life, he reminds himself, he's been swimming against the current, struggling with the waves, each one more vicious than the one before. He was never really ambitious, with hardly a well-defined objective. All he ever wanted was to survive, just to put off drowning for another day. And now, his survival depends on making money. This woman is a bank vault talking to him over the phone. If he does not grab her money and that of others, the waves will pull him down without a doubt. The merciless black water at the bottom of the waterwheel's well lurks in the depths of his consciousness.

"If that is the case, then we must prepare a séance to get to the bottom of this." He practices the art of his newly acquired profession.

"At your place . . . I mean the haunted apartment?"

"There's nothing to worry about, madame. They are all pure spirits." He's amazed at how serious he manages to sound.

"Yes. We must organize a séance right away," the Cerebellum nervously cuts in.

"But is it necessary for Hafez to attend the séance in person?"

"Only as a precaution, madame. Just in case we need to resort to an exorcism or something similar."

"Tonight. Tell her tonight," the Cerebellum insists.

"Exor . . . what . . .? Heaven protect us! Well, let me try to convince him. I'll call you back. Thanks a lot, doctor."

After putting down the receiver, Abd al-Malak turns to the Cerebellum, "Since you've become such an expert on this whole ghost business, why don't you take the equipment and start drumming up the spirits yourself."

"I hope you don't really think your disco equipment is responsible for conjuring the spirits." The Cerebellum gives a short, uneasy laugh.

"This is the most up-to-date equipment in America." Abd al-Malak tries to maintain a straight face.

"Can't you see, man . . . this whole thing has something to do with *you*. Otherwise why would Tutu have asked for you in person? Millionaires don't just throw away their money."

"He chose me for my academic credentials. . . ." In fact, Abd al-Malak has been troubled by this question all along.

"What credentials, man? You think you're fooling the world, but you're the only one who doesn't understand." The Cerebellum's tone is unusually stern.

"My credentials, my experience, the ghosts just love my looks . . . it's all the same to me. But why are *you* suddenly so interested in this whole ghost business?" Abd al-Malak has no desire to prolong a discussion of his credentials.

"I want to understand. I need to understand. My brain's about to explode and I still don't understand." The Cerebellum's voice is heavy.

Now it is Abd al-Malak who doesn't understand. The small man is a walking mystery. Evidently, he's highly educated, but he avoids talking about himself. He's not rich yet doesn't seem to be interested in money. Abd al-Malak rejects out of hand the possibility that he may be a criminal or a terrorist, but why then is he hiding in a haunted apartment?

And what is this intractable question that haunts him?

"The puzzle is my life . . . how I got here. I never expected my life to take this course. I only wanted one thing, no more . . . to understand the world. The problem is, the more I live and see, the more I learn that I understand nothing. I can't even explain the events of my own life." The Cerebellum's voice is low and tense.

But since when did people try to fathom the course of their lives? With every word, Abd al-Malak's suspicions multiply. This whole business doesn't make any sense. Abd al-Malak moves to the window and inspects the street below. Maybe he'll find an explanation there for the man's strange behavior. What's scaring him so much? What has turned him into a fugitive? The Cerebellum turns to go back to his bedroom, but Abd al-Malak stops him.

"Would you talk to Mr. Tutu for me? I appreciate your generosity with the expenses here in the apartment and everything . . . but, I mean, another advance to speed up the process of summoning the spirits. . . . Would you talk to him?"

✖

Things are never what they seem. Fate always has a surprise up her sleeve: a crucial piece of information will come to light only when it's too late, or an influential person he doesn't even know will constantly be thwarting his efforts. If Abd al-Malak has learnt one thing from life, it is that. Now, after the experiences of the past few months, he has even come to doubt the constancy of things, of people, of facts. The universe suddenly looks like a soup where facts float like green peas and vermicelli, a liquid that is constantly boiling over, whose events interlock then disperse. And people . . . well, like everything else, they drift. They form relationships and break up, walk in and out of his life, they settle at the bottom or evaporate into the air. Like the black piano that was smashed to smithereens only to become whole again. It was equally composed whether floating in the air or settled down in its corner while invisible hands played Abdelhalim tunes only audible to the chosen few.

It has been an entire week since the piano appeared. Since then, the tenants have come in waves, tiptoeing into the hall. They come in twos and threes, make their way amid the scraps of wood and shreds of cloth, freeze in the middle of the hall facing the shining black piano in its clean well-kept corner, then tiptoe back out. They never ring the bell or knock on the door, which is permanently ajar because no one has ever dared to close it. After all, the apartment has been taken over by owners from beyond our world, so who would the tenants ask for permission to come and go?

Abd al-Malak steals down the stairs with the tape recorder hanging from his shoulder and his arm extended with the microphone, a magic wand he waves in the air hoping for miracles to happen. He follows his predetermined course to the tenth floor, an absurdity that has become a daily routine. Here he is, trying to fool the world with an old tape recorder, while ignoring the incredible chain of events. People's triviality constantly challenges the perils of the unknown.

How trivial we are and how blind, he admits to himself.

Abd al-Malak continues to rationalize his dubious afternoon ritual as good publicity, insisting it will attract even more customers. But who's he kidding? He's certainly not fooling his own heart that calls out her name with its every beat, that flutters like a fish just tossed on a trawler's deck. His pulse races with each step closer to her vital space. When he reaches the landing on which she comes and goes, the blood freezes in his veins.

Like a bewildered teenager, he stops before her door, elated and scared, but for the thousandth time does not muster the courage to knock.

He is surrounded by the same perfume that colonized the elevator where he met her after their long separation. He has no way of knowing whether her perfume is actually lingering in the air or if it has only enveloped his mind. He points the microphone at her door. Maybe it'll slide open like Ali Baba's cave. But the cruel, impassive door continues to block his dreams.

"What do you think you're doing over there?" A voice slaps him on the nape of the neck.

Like a scared porcupine, he turns to the elderly lady standing in the opposite doorway. The sensation of being caught in the act ties his tongue.

"I know you're the spiritual medium. Otherwise I would have called the security clerk a long time ago." The lady is wearing a navy-blue dress. Three white poodles scurry around her shoes. Her tired voice rings with the echoes of bygone conversations in circles of culture and power.

"I'm Dr. Abd al-Malak . . . ," he says with difficulty.

"Pleased to meet you, doctor. But you still haven't told me what you come here for every day." Then she turns to her dogs, "Come on, girls."

The lady turns a key in her lock five times, then faces him again. The poodles are interweaving whirlwinds of panting fur and white motion. Her eyes light up with childish mischief. Abd al-Malak feels more secure with her than he has felt in a long time. A connection has been established.

"Well, my instruments indicate that there may be unnatural vibrations coming from this apartment. By the way, who lives here?" He feels rather ashamed of himself.

Ignoring his question, she walks across to Farah's door and rings the bell. "In that case, we have to warn them."

A moment passes and nobody comes to the door. He sighs in relief. The scent of camphor overshadows Farah's perfume for a split second. . . . It had been a long summer morning and he'd loitered on the dirt road, kicking pebbles, broken bricks, and tin cans with his worn-down shoe. He'd waited for a girl to pester or a boy to pick a fight with, but no one crossed his path, and now he'd reached the locked steel gate. Ahmadein the school gatekeeper said the exam results were not out yet. He felt that mixture of relief and disappointment, the same delayed anxiety. Was it cowardice or a masochistic pleasure in extending his torture? Abd al-Malak wonders in front of his darling's door. The only certainty is that nothing ever changes, he answers himself.

Nothing ever changes?

Then where did that bright-eyed, dusty-haired boy in the striped cotton gelabia go? And where is that pretty student with the fluffy black hair? The one who used to make fun of her colleagues and call them candy dolls? What happened to Farah's instant smile and her sneer that froze the heart of any conductor fool enough to try to corner her so she'd pay the bus fare? And Zeina, her aunt who used to sell lettuce and parsley on a palm-frond box in Shoubra Circle? And her uncle who spent his days and nights in the doorman's bar—Kamboura, as the child Farah had labeled him, thus erasing any previous name he may have had? Her family, her life's hidden shame, that terrible secret she exposed to Abd al-Malak only when they were on the threshold of marriage . . . where did they all go?

And if nothing can ever change, if all that is left behind must silently lurk in the depths, then what's the use of their existence here among the high classes? What good will all his efforts do, if concealing flaws is ultimately futile?

Yet despite his terror, he secretly prays to see Farah today. Let this test's result be announced and his incertitude be brought to an end. A thick mist clouds his eyes. Then comes the click of the lock and the world opens up again with Farah's slightly out-of-breath face. She presses her lips to spread the fresh lipstick she has just applied, the stick still in her hand.

"Hello, Madame Gawdat." Her voice is hoarse, like one who hasn't spoken a word all day. She shivers slightly upon seeing Abd al-Malak. "Abd al-Malak . . . what a nice surprise."

Abd al-Malak is sweating all over. He tries to hide the tape recorder behind his back. Madame Gawdat studies Farah's face, then Abd al-Malak's. "I'll leave the doctor to tell you all about the vibrations, dear." She smiles, then turns to her dogs. "Come on girls. Diabetes calls for a lot of walking."

⁂

The two men observe the ship as it glides over the Nile toward Maadi. Its lights, droplets of emerald, ruby, and diamond, shimmer in the embrace of a platinum necklace, which in turn dances on a plane of black satin. The river's pulsating bosom attracts then repels them. Our wise, sarcastic river. The party's merrymaking reaches their ears in intermittent bullets. Each swims with the currents of his thoughts. Abd al-Malak suddenly shatters the barrier of silence.

"There they go, dancing and partying . . . and no one gives a damn about what the country's going through."

"In hard times some people weep, others go dancing," the Cerebellum replies through his enormous eyeglasses, the barricades he hides behind. They remind Abd al-Malak of the bumpers of American cars in the fifties.

"It's all selfishness. If only people listened to their conscience, the country wouldn't be in this mess." Abd al-Malak slams the railing to make his point.

The Cerebellum turns to him with a curious look, stares from behind his bumpers, and says nothing.

The September breeze permeates Abd al-Malak's shirt, tickling his skin. The view from the thirteenth floor is a visual delight. The crowds and the filth in the streets have vanished. The details fade away with elevation and only generalities remain, now just the breeze and the lights.

It has been one and a half months since he came to this place. The first few days, he'd returned to his apartment in Sayeda to spend the night. Today, his clothes hang here in the fancy closet. He's even gotten used to the expensive mattress that reminds him of good American hotels. At first, he was surprised that the destruction had been limited to the main hall while the rest of the apartment remained in mint condition. It seemed like an open invitation to come and enjoy the comfort, a plot to lure him to live here. He resisted in the beginning but now he's thankful for this opportunity. Who knows, this may be the once-in-a-lifetime chance he's been waiting for. He must not allow it to slip between his fingers.

"If only the government were to apply sharia law, we'd regain our past glory," he says.

The Cerebellum just smiles, exposing his rabbit teeth. It dawns upon Abd al-Malak that the man hasn't ventured out of this apartment since he first came here at the beginning of August. Here is a man with a story. But what's essential is his friendship with the millionaire who invited him to live here and who doesn't mind it when he calls him by the childish nickname, Tutu.

"For example your friend Mr. Abd al-Tawab, he seems like a pious man."

"If that's true, then why hasn't he been getting any sleep for the past three months?" The Cerebellum hesitates as though he spoke in haste. "The problem with the religious state you're advocating is that our society's understanding of religion hasn't evolved in stride with civilization . . . Excuse me if I belong to the last generation of believers in the 23rd of July revolution."

"The revolution lifted us up and left us suspended between heaven and earth. It taught us but gave us no labs, made our eyes hazy with hope yet did not pave the way for achievements. It sold us words, fed us illusions, and filled our empty bellies with dreams," Abd al-Malak responds without hesitation.

These are arguments he made over and over again during his university days. Farah was a Nasserist and he always enjoyed a good debate with her. He's on the verge of telling the Cerebellum he's not the last

Nasserist, but he hesitates. After all, she may have turned liberal after moving into this sumptuous tower.

"The revolution committed history's ultimate sin: it lost. And it's the winners who write history." The Cerebellum speaks in a low voice. He stares straight ahead into the darkness.

"Is Mr. Abd al-Tawab a Nasserist too?"

Abd al-Malak's question causes the Cerebellum's body to tense up. The arteries in his neck become more pronounced, as though he had slapped him on the nape of the neck or insulted his mother. "What exactly are we talking about?" he says in a dangerously low voice.

Abd al-Malak takes a moment to collect his thoughts then responds, ignoring the question, "I often say the revolution did this and the revolution did that, then I go back and say, what revolution are you talking about, man? Was there a revolution to begin with? It was just another link in the chain that confines us. We chose a fashionable name with a modern ring . . . but the only true reality is Islam. Yes, we need to evolve our concepts to be more in tune with the times. No one ever said Islam encourages ignorance and extremism."

"Modern Islam is a romantic dream we've talked about for the past two hundred years. You felt proud when the sheikhs called you infidels and the kids stabbed you and the courts divorced you against your will. But where did all your rhetoric take us? We have not moved one inch for two hundred years. Isn't it time to find yourselves a new dream?" The Cerebellum's tension has eased somewhat.

"Islam is neither modern nor classical. It is our past, present, and future—not just a romantic dream!" Abd al-Malak proclaims loudly.

He studies the Cerebellum from head to toe. Finally, he grasps what is so distinctive about the small man's appearance, the explanation he has been subconsciously looking for. His shirt is a least two sizes too big, his trousers would have slipped and bundled around his ankles if not for the tightened belt, his tiny feet are much too small for his slippers. The Cerebellum has grown up accustomed to wearing his older brother's clothes.

"A romantic dream it most certainly is, because it assumes the possibility of revolting against convention using its very tenets. When the Shia tradition first appeared, it was based on personal and tribal partiality, on allegiance, to quote Ibn Khaldoun. When it became established, it based itself on Persian nationalism. In the west, the Protestant Reformation erupted as a revolution against the church's worldly dominion—in other words it was also a political movement. My dear fellow, in order to establish a new Islamic ideology you must first reject the existing Islamic ideology. You've frozen midway up a flight of stairs. You have neither proclaimed obedience nor declared rebellion. Modern Islam is the Perestroika that was communism's downfall." The Cerebellum's voice rings in Abd al-Malak's ears, as though he has awoken from a long sleep or been revived after death. Evidently, he enjoys a philosophical debate.

"Two hundred years? And you secularists dare to talk about two hundred years? Who gave us two hundred years of mirages? You saw the west, got entranced by its lights, and tried to imitate it. You built palaces, theaters, and opera houses, wore suits, ties, and bikinis, devoured McDonald's, gulped Coca-Cola, and chewed Chiclets, then you burped socialism and democracy and babbled in English, French, Russian, and Chinese, twisted your mouths and gelled your hair, but tell me, did you manage to scratch the surface? Have you reached the people? Has anyone, other than snobs, listened to what you're saying? Tell me, what do you do when things go wrong? Do you turn to René Descartes for inspiration, or do you waft incense and recite the Koran, like you saw your mother and her mother's mother do?"

Abd al-Malak's enthusiasm is boiling over. He loves a good debate just as much as the small man who is at least ten years his senior, especially when it comes to religion and its role in society building. He's proud that his years abroad have not weakened his beliefs, but crystallized them. Rather than undermine faith, science reinforces it. Had it not been for the memory of the praying area by the canal and sunset prayers beneath the camphor trees, he would never have survived in a society that claims to be civilized but only respects the logic of power. Friday prayers in the dusty village mosque echoed in his ears. The sheikh's voice, soothing despite Abd al-Malak's childhood inability to comprehend the textual meaning, remained a faithful companion. His father's image fingering his rosary beads on the prayer rug inhabited his days, filled up his small room in the seemingly endless American nights.

"And what does your scam have to do with religion?" The Cerebellum says in his childish, emotionally charged voice.

Abd al-Malak makes an effort to control himself. He'd be the first to acknowledge that he's had to make ethical compromises. But religion remains the compass that will lead him back after his temporary wandering. Yes, he has no alternative but to make as much money as he can. He must finish what he started, build the life he and Farah have always dreamed of. In these critical moments he must not deviate. He ignores the man's provocation and directs the conversation toward his goal.

"Is Mr. Tutu a Nasserist too?"

"Tutu, my good man, is a millionaire who can't sleep, which means that he worships no God but money, and to spare you the trouble of beating around the bush, will not pay one millieme until his problem is resolved. And you have to understand that religion is not empty talk, it's all about deeds."

Abd al-Malak explodes. "And who do you think you are to judge me? I'm a man who follows his conscience, not one who's committed God knows what, who's in hiding and hopes the police won't catch him!"

The small man freezes.

But no sooner has Abd al-Malak said the words than he regrets them. Was his anger sparked by the Cerebellum's implicit accusations or because he made it clear he wouldn't be getting any more money from the millionaire?

"I'm sorry. I got carried away," he adds quickly.

"I'm the one who should apologize . . . I didn't mean to accuse you. But I want you to know that I've never broken the law in my life . . . I have no problem whatsoever with the police."

Despite the Cerebellum's apparent calm, his hands clasp the railing like the talons of a bird of prey. As though if it were not for the railing, he'd drown or, like the piano, float in the air before crashing down to earth. But what is the terrible secret the Cerebellum carries on his shoulders? And why doesn't he ever contact his family or friends; why does he never even mention any of them?

"Well, why don't you tell me your story?" Abd al-Malak's curiosity gets the best of him.

The Cerebellum turns to him. His pale face, like a cartoon character's, is covered in question marks. Then, after a long silence, his childish voice comes from far away. "I agree . . . but on one condition. You too must tell me yours."

⁂

Abd al-Malak rings once. Farah comes to the door right away. This time she was expecting him. She ushers him in and quickly shuts the door. Evidently she doesn't want the neighbors to see him come in. Maybe she lives alone and is wary of people's gossip. On their first meeting in the elevator, she mentioned she wasn't married. But money doesn't grow on trees. She cannot possibly afford this lifestyle out of the fishmonger's alimony. They stand still for a moment next to the door. His entrance has been accomplished with military precision. They catch their breath.

He wonders if he should shake her hand or just say hello. His impulse is to take her in his arms without a word, as he's rehearsed over and over again in his mind, like lovers in a movie. He tightens his grip on the tape recorder with both hands and says nothing. "I missed you," she whispers simply.

Farah looks him in the eyes and causes his heart to melt. She turns and, with a feminine sway, heads to the living room. He follows. It occurs to him he's spent a lifetime out of breath from chasing after her.

"So, you got your PhD?"

"In genetic engineering," he responds like a hypnotized man and takes the armchair she points to. She sits at the far end of the sofa.

"Then what are you doing in the ghost business?" Her eyes turn instinctively to the tape recorder that he has put down next to the foot of his armchair. It was she who insisted that he bring it along today, just as she had fixed the date: one week after the encounter at her doorstep that Madame Gawdat had unwittingly set up. A whole week, during which his heart has been roasting on hot coals. She could've set the date for the same day or the following one, but she allowed a whole week to pass . . . women!

"It's only temporary, until I pull myself together financially, then I'll set up a business and things will get better." Shame eats up his face but he cannot lie to her, he never could.

"I was afraid one of those American girls from the soap operas would steal your heart, and that you'd never come back to me again." Her voice is a basin beneath an open tap of emotions. Tenderness overflows.

"You're talking like it was me who abandoned—" Sound freezes in Abd al-Malak's throat.

"Nobody abandoned . . . it was fate that separated us. Anyway, I paid the price. My marriage lasted less than six months; days too horrible to describe. You can't imagine how I felt waking up every morning with my hair stinking of dried fish. I couldn't stand it anymore. I ran away. Eventually, he agreed to divorce me, on the condition that I drop all financial claims." She holds her head in her hands as if her mind is about to explode or as if the smell of dried fish still clings to her hair.

His Adam's apple has turned into stone. He swallows with difficulty. "But where did all your revolutionary zeal go? And your love, the one thing you said time would never touch. You should've never accepted, Farah . . . to be sold and bought like cattle." He pushes the words out like a difficult childbirth.

"And you, what did you do to protect me? What did you do to defend our love?" Her voice is shrill. She rocks from side to side with her head still in her hands.

"I begged you to resist . . ." His voice recaptures a years-old pleading pitch. Nothing ever changes. Emotions don't die; like tormented ghosts, they linger.

"So it was up to me to resist. You men are all talk!" She jumps to her feet and shouts, pointing her finger at him, "You expected me to wait *five years* for you to come back from America? What was I supposed to do for five miserable years? And what if you never came back . . . what would've happened to me? Should I have waited until they carried me away in a straitjacket?"

"You sold yourself and sold me with you." The tears swell in his eyes.

"You're so clever when it comes to judging others . . ." She sinks back into the sofa and rests her forehead on her palm. "Just shut up . . . you don't understand one damn thing."

The lump in Farah's throat accentuates her natural huskiness, that magical voice that echoed in his ears throughout the years of his estrangement. Her nose is flushed. Her golden cheeks, sparkling with tears like crystal dewdrops, are fresh Kafr Shoukr peaches. Abd al-Malak repositions himself on the sofa next to her. With shaking fingertips, he wipes her tears away and feels his life melt in the depths of her caramel eyes, red from crying. Their bodies are drawn together like magnets. She presses herself against him. Her lips are hot and moist. Their tears mix. Her fingers massage the back of his neck. Her rings' metallic texture numbs his senses. Her teeth dig into his lips. Her breasts are two pomegranates from heaven in his craving palms.

The regular rhythm of her panting fills the universe.

Then, her body hardens like wood. Her words, emanating from tightened lips, ring inside his head, unheard, like a deaf person's sensation of sound. Decisively, she pushes him away. "Stop. Please stop, Abd al-Malak. You've always been a gentleman." Out of breath, she looks up at him.

He raises his body away from hers. They sit side by side on the sofa without touching. She pulls down the edge of her pink skirt to cover her thighs, and starts to do up the top two buttons of her floral blouse. She leans forward and takes a cigarette from a marble box on the table, then ignites it with a lighter embedded in a crystal bowl. He takes another. They blow smoke in silence. He clears his throat.

"A long time ago, I used to watch the ducks swimming in the canal," he says without looking at her.

Farah passes her hands over her clothes, trying to smooth them.

"One day, two of the ducks were trailing each other across the water, separated by a constant gap. When the first one would turn the other followed, like they were attached . . . but the fascinating part was that at the very instant the second duck turned, the first one would too, although it couldn't see its partner."

She turns to him, suddenly attentive.

"Such a special relationship . . . so hard to define. When two people share the same path without the need to explain or argue."

She holds his hand and whispers, "I'm yours . . . I'll never belong to anyone else. But we have to follow tradition."

He presses her hand then pulls away and stands up. "I'll make up for all the time we lost, I promise." He looks at her from above.

"After all, we're back to being two ducks in the canal. . . ." She laughs in that sensuous voice of hers. "I'll see you next week. Same time?"

He stops abruptly in the middle of the hallway. She's a few steps behind. Her last sentence rings in his head. He's astonished at the date she has set. Her choice awakens the question that has remained dormant, buzzing in his subconscious ever since they first met in the elevator, two months ago. He turns to her. "How can you afford this apartment?"

He notices her discomfort, then she breaks out laughing, "I don't own this apartment, silly. It belongs to the company I work for . . . they reserve it for the use of foreign experts who only come for a few days every month. Just between us, nobody in the company knows I live here . . . actually, I'm staying here illegally. Don't mention this to anyone," she adds in a whisper.

"And when the foreign experts are here, where do you stay?" Abd al-Malak studies her face as though he was reading her answer in the flicker of her eyelids, the quiver of her lips, or the tightening of her forehead.

129

"I stay with one of my female workmates, of course. What were you thinking?"

Her sharp retort embarrasses Abd al-Malak. Still, he feels a weight has been lifted off his chest. Her presence in this apartment has at last been explained. And in his heart, he had suspected the worst of her. He has wronged her. Things are never what they seem.

Before his hand touches the doorknob, she says, "I'll miss you till next week." Her voice has regained its romantic tone.

"We can always make it tomorrow?" What a childish request.

"People talk, my love . . . also we need to be careful or the company might find out and it'll be a big scandal." Before shutting the door after him, she adds mischievously, "By the way, Madame Gawdat wants to know if your ghosts can cure diabetes."

⁙

Bassily sits with his short legs wide apart. Beneath his shapeless white suit and red-and-green necktie, his body is composed of two spheres. The biggest is the barrel of his torso. But it is the smaller one between the man's legs that leaves Abd al-Malak dumbfounded. He tries to avoid visualizing which of the man's organs it may be.

Tremors shake the jelly-barrel of a man a split second before the volcano of his laughter erupts. His joke succeeds, where the Johnny Walker Black Label has failed, in melting the ice between guests divided by the oceans of age, wealth, education, and class, with only one thing in common: an invitation from the colorful artiste Lula Hamdi.

Lula circulates among the small, isolated groups that have sprung up spontaneously in every corner of her spacious living room. Abd al-Malak notes that her apartment occupies an entire floor. Mirrors coat most of the walls, enhancing the sense of vastness. The armchairs and sofas are spaced in isolated clusters around the hall's periphery while the inner area is devoid of any furniture or carpets. The famous belly dancer, in a low-cut golden evening dress, glides over the sparkling marble floor toward Abd al-Malak. She is followed by two girls in their early twenties who walk with an exaggerated sway and awaken instincts the ex-genetic scientist thought had dried up years ago.

"Your sense of humor is so sweet, chief . . . it's because of all the molasses you eat," their hostess says.

Abdallah Bassily's belly is still vibrating.

Lula Hamdi turns to Abd al-Malak and leans forward, supporting her hands on the back of a vacant armchair and revealing even more of her explosive breasts. "I have a feeling that tonight you'll treat us to one of those séances the whole country is talking about."

So that's why he was invited. He's the entertainment. As they say in America, there's no such thing as a free lunch. The Cerebellum swore he wouldn't come to this party. Abd al-Malak wanted to network with the greenback millionaires. But would a performance work tonight?

Before he can reply to her request, Lula Hamdi turns to the skinny journalist with the boyish hairdo. She arrived a few minutes ago and was led to a seat facing him.

"Delighted you could come, darling. My artistic program for the next few months is out of this world. I have to tell you all about it. . . . What? Are you drinking *juice*?! That's so bad for your health . . . and our friend Johnny will be offended." She points to the bottle on the table then gives free reign to a burst of laughter that makes her soft parts vibrate.

The journalist signals with her hands that she's fine with the juice and replies with a question, "Tell me, Madame Lula . . . are you acquainted with Señora Esmeralda?"

"So they call that old hag Esmeralda a señora and me a belly dancer . . . ? Believe me honey, it's our inferiority complex with foreigners . . . and I thought the press promoted our national product. Even when it comes to belly dancing they're coming here to compete with us! But I swear on my mother's honor: if that shriveled old hag dares to come back to Egypt again, I'll be the first one to report her to the vice squad. Excuse me for a second, I have to greet a guest." Lula Hamdi walks away before the journalist can follow up.

Abd al-Malak checks out her bouncing behind, but he is quickly sidetracked by the journalist's serious tone, "Sorry, I haven't introduced myself, Dr. Abd al-Malak. Islah Mohandes, journalist."

"Nice to meet you."

Abd al-Malak's coldness doesn't seem to put her off.

"Do you think there's a link between the ghosts that have been appearing lately and the murder of Ahlam Shawarby?" she zeroes in.

"Ahlam Shawarby?"

"Don't tell me you're not aware that the body of the late Ahlam was found in this tower's elevator."

"Have you found any evidence for such a link?" Abd al-Malak crosses his legs. He must avoid probing the issue with her; in fact he'd better not try to come to terms with it himself.

"Did you know that the apartment in which the bizarre phenomena have been happening was rented out, at the time of the crime, to none other than Shoukry Shaker, the producer of Ahlam's last movie?"

"That doesn't prove anything," he replies, his discomfort growing.

The journalist is forcing him to confront his own suspicions. With her bold questions, she's opened up a cave seething with possibilities, like bats shooting out in every direction. Things are never what they seem.

"Did you know that Señora Esmeralda, whose parties Shoukry often took Ahlam to, left Egypt abruptly the day after the actress's murder?"

He shrugs, pretending not to care. What does all this to do have with him anyway, the charlatan whose only concern is to collect other people's money, whose destiny it is to consort with ghosts day and night? At the end of the day, he's no more than an employee of the billionaire Abd al-Tawab. He has nothing to do with crimes and criminals. He'd like to shout in her face, 'I don't care about mortals. I deal only with ghosts.'

"Okay, now did you know that the security clerk who was on duty the night of the crime has also disappeared, and has never been heard from since?" Islah speaks slowly with her right eyebrow raised to signal the importance of what she's saying. Then suddenly something catches her attention. Abd al-Malak follows her black eyes that, like a falcon's, dissect the space behind him. He only turns to look when her focus relaxes and her smile exposes two delicate hollows in her cheeks. Karim Nafea approaches them with a cinematic expression of surprise.

Gently, he shakes the journalist's hand then extends his hand to Abd al-Malak and Bassily and takes the armchair next to hers. A conversation starts off at once between the two as though picking up from where they had stopped earlier. The journalist's unexpected chatter has unsettled Abd al-Malak. Why can't she understand that these matters don't concern him? A tap on his shoulder takes him away him from the conversation he's trying to follow between Islah and Karim Nafea. It is one of the belly dancer's assistants who usually follow her around like her shadow. Abd al-Malak is surprised she's come back on her own.

"You'll take care of me doctor, won't you . . .? I'm scared of ghosts . . . really scared," the girl whispers in his ear while toying with his shirt collar. Her fingertips feel like ice at the back of his neck, the exact opposite of Farah's burning touch. He can hardly believe a whole week has passed since they met and that their date tomorrow is almost here. His ears catch the journalist's whisper:

"I'm here of course as a journalist . . . to gather information for my work."

"Of course, of course. Me, I'm only here in the spirit of good neighborliness . . . only because Madame Lula insisted. Otherwise, I would never have accepted this invitation." Karim Nafea sounds uncharacteristically flustered.

Bassily leans over to Abd al-Malak and whispers, "Listen to the son of a . . . like he's not here every night till dawn."

Then the music blasts across built-in loudspeakers in a pulsating oriental rhythm. The girl sitting on the arm of Abd al-Malak's chair jumps up, strips the scarf from her neck and ties it around her hips, then starts to dance in the middle of the hall. She's wearing a gelabia of golden satin embroidered with colored beads with slits up to her thighs on both sides. It dawns upon Abd al-Malak that Lula Hamdi's living room is designed as a nightclub. Compared to a club, it is only distinguishable by the bright lights whose rays are reflected by all the surfaces, possibly with the exception of the sofas and armchairs whose sensuous gaudy-colored velvets rather than reflect light, emit heat. As for the central part of the hall empty of all furniture, its purpose is now clear.

"The air conditioning bothers me . . . I'm going to step out onto the terrace for a breath of fresh air." Karim Nafea stands up.

"You're right. Fresh air is healthier." Islah follows.

The dancing girl approaches Abd al-Malak. "Come, witchdoctor, let's dance."

He declines. He may be a poor man and a fraud, even a coward, but he won't stoop as low as to shake his belly. A man emerges from a thick cloud of smoke and approaches the girl with his arms high in the air. He jingles a pair of finger cymbals with experienced rhythm and sways unhurriedly on his heels.

"Get over here, man of the people!" the sexually charged dancing girl greets him in a cracked voice.

"Mr. Sherbiny is a member of parliament . . . he represents one of the expensive constituencies." Bassily has apparently taken it upon himself to open Abd al-Malak's eyes to the tower's secrets.

"One of the expensive constituencies?"

"He threw away over ten million to get into the assembly."

"He must be very keen on politics, then." Abd al-Malak feigns interest in the human barrel's conversation.

An unusual commotion draws his attention to the other end of the hall.

"He couldn't tell the difference between a bill of law and the bill in a restaurant, believe you me. He's never even been inside Parliament House. He's basically an immunity member."

"Immunity?"

Lula Hamdi approaches, holding a young man by one arm and a young girl by the other. The threesome captures every eye in the hall in a kind of collective hypnotism.

Bassily finally realizes he no longer commands Abd al-Malak's ear. "How fabulous . . . Shoukry Shaker in the flesh. Can you believe it, when that little slip of a boy goes to the toilet—excuse the expression—he shits dollars."

The famous belly dancer brings the millionaire over and invites him and the girl to take the two seats that had been occupied a moment ago by Karim Nafea and Islah. The young man nods to Abd al-Malak and Bassily.

"This here is the spiritual medium everyone's talking about . . . his voice is heard up there . . . his channels of communication are wide open. Heaven protect us." Lula Hamdi talks to the millionaire as if Abd al-Malak were an inanimate object. Then she calls out to her curvy apprentice, who, sensing she's being watched, wriggles with renewed enthusiasm. "Enough music!" Lula calls out. Then she leans over to Abd al-Malak and whispers in his ear, "The young prince has a headache."

Abd al-Malak stares at the young man across the low coffee table, but he is quickly attracted to the girl next to him and cannot take his eyes off her. The scent of childhood still lingers in her blossoming femininity, her beauty a silent scream. He realizes she's boldly staring back.

Shoukry Shaker repositions his armchair to face the window, walks up to the thick velvet curtain and draws it open. Then he slides open the aluminum window and allows a summer blast mingled with exhaust and car honks to return the party, for a second, to the reality beyond the walls. He pulls his armchair closer to Abd al-Malak's to make space for the girl's chair next to him. Finally, he sinks into his armchair, facing away from everyone.

If Abd al-Malak were to extend his arm he could pull the guy's ear.

The young man turns to him with a head much too big for his body, giving Abd al-Malak the impression he must have difficulty moving it. "Sorry to give you my back, but I have a bit of a headache." He has a clear, serene voice.

135

"Isn't it amazing, sir . . . all the money in the world can't cure a minor headache." Abd al-Malak can hardly believe his audacity.

"All my life I've wondered about magicians and psychics . . . I mean if they really have special powers, why don't they use them to become the richest people in the world?"

"Because money brings headaches," Bassily, a laughing hippopotamus, bellows in Abd al-Malak's ear. The psychic wonders whether the roastery owner is mocking him for being the only poor man present, or if he's making fun of himself and his fellow millionaires.

"If money is that much trouble, then why do people sell their dignity, their honor, and even their organs for a few bucks?" The clear eyes of the young man whose intestines are full of money give no indication he's suffering from any headache at all.

"Well, just because God bestowed good fortune on some people, they shouldn't think they can buy the whole country." Abd al-Malak's anger is rising yet he can hardly believe he's saying this. Why this flash of hatred toward the young billionaire?

"You call us feudal landlords, but at least we've earned or inherited our wealth. Why don't you call ministers and government officials feudal landlords too? Don't they treat their ministries as private property to buy and sell as they please while no one is looking over their shoulders? Except that they haven't inherited or worked hard for anything."

"Sure. Go ahead and divide the country among you . . . ." Abd al-Malak starts to say. He knows he's already gone too far, but was it the young man's arrogant manner or the journalist's earlier talk that provoked him to this degree? Abd al-Malak controls himself with difficulty.

The roastery owner takes advantage of his hesitation to interrupt. "Speaking of money . . . has anyone heard the story of the man who married four women and decided to apply free market rules to his marital relations?"

No one replies. Bassily is about to proceed with his joke then remembers the young girl sitting quietly and gazing out of the window. He hesitates. Just then, the journalist appears and approaches the girl.

136

"Didi. What a surprise . . . what are you doing here?"

Bassily takes advantage of the two women's conversation to go on with his joke, but Abd al-Malak doesn't pay any attention to the man's story.

"I can go wherever I want." Didi's reply stops Islah, who was about to hug the girl. After regaining her composure, the journalist replies:

"But Didi, you're still young . . . there are things you don't understand . . . I'm just saying this for your own good." The journalist holds the girl by the arms like an adult about to shake a child or lift her off her feet.

After his initial belly-shaking, Bassily bursts out laughing. "In true capitalist spirit . . ." he adds, still laughing.

Heeding the stares of Abd al-Malak and Karim Nafea, neither of whom has heard the joke, he stops abruptly.

"I'm not a child . . . and who are you to give me advice?" Didi stands up and shrugs off the journalist's hands. She puts her hands to her waist like a schoolgirl in an argument.

Islah turns to stone, her face distorted in concentration, as if she's about to make a life or death decision. "Didi, I feel I'm almost as close to you as I was to Ahlam." The journalist's voice is clear, untainted by defiance or anger.

"Come on, there's something I want you to see," Bassily says. "It's getting a bit serious in here."

Abd al-Malak follows the fat man without hesitation. They step onto a wide terrace enclosed in glass and crammed full of plants in pots of different shapes and sizes. After the hall's air-conditioned comfort, the atmosphere feels heavy. The heat is aggravated by the numerous lamps that emit a penetrating yellow light. The fat man pauses in front of a plant strategically located in the middle of the terrace. It must be a rare specimen because it has its own separate pot and a low lamp dedicated to it.

The plant has small white flowers and thick boat-shaped leaves as big as Bassily's hands. The leaves are split into two halves poised perpendicular to each other. Their inner surface is covered in thorns and hairs, a pair of jaws menacing the world. Most of the leaves are a pale green,

137

only a few are bright red. These Abd al-Malak mistook for flowers at first glance. He has come across this rare plant in textbooks but has never before seen it in the flesh. He can't remember what is so special about it.

"Shh . . ." The roastery owner puts his finger to his lips.

The two men bend over the plant. Bassily produces two sticks of molasses candy from his pocket and offers Abd al-Malak one. He accepts it with a nod and starts to remove the cellophane wrap while his eyes remain fixed on the plant. He wonders what the fat man finds so interesting about it.

A fly lands on one of the green leaves. Its legs sink in the velvety surface. Entranced, it heads toward the heart, craving the magic nectar. The leaf's curved surface is an open invitation to fantasy and pleasure. Then, with the crack of a released spring, the leaf closes in on itself. Reflexively, Abd al-Malak jumps backward. He turns to Bassily, who bites into his molasses stick, his face red as a tomato. His belly shakes but is not followed by laughter. He returns Abd al-Malak's bewildered look.

"It's a trap, a carnivorous plant that feeds on insects. It reminds me of dangerous women."

The image of one particular woman comes to Abd al-Malak's mind. But he quickly purges its poison. Fatigue is casting its fog on him, playing games with his heart. Here he is, setting himself up. In a voluntary yet involuntary act, he goes back to watching the beautiful predatory plant.

The Sixth Page

That night . . .
we stayed up late singing your heroism
and raising a toast to your health . . .
wineglass after wineglass
to the health of the most beautiful and gallant people,
bottle after bottle
we saluted the girls . . . and patience
we saluted the young men and the grave
Palestine is green inside the wine
a song
a ululation
ever-present
on the map it is not black
not at all under occupation

Abdelrahman Elabnoudy

Islah Mohandes

"I love plants. I talk to them, whisper, sing to them. In my heart I know they listen, that they can recognize my voice and when I'm away, they miss me and they're happy when I come back . . .

"I'm a peasant girl. Fate uprooted me but my heart is green inside, like an alfalfa field glistening in the morning dew. When the world cut me off from my village and my people, plants became my family. Look. I have roses in six different colors . . . and grape vines and jasmine . . . and a swing I can rock on while I sip my tea like the ladies in the movies. But my special one is this naughty girl here . . . a wild plant from the forests of Carolina. She thinks she's the fairest of them all . . . ."

Lula Hamdi's rolling laughter rings true. The belly dancer underwent a metamorphosis the instant she stepped into her greenhouse on the terrace. Her words flow like a cascade in the Carolina woods, a name she can't even pronounce correctly, whose location on the world's map she knows nothing of, not even that the name is shared by a northern and a southern state.

Her breasts are perfect cantaloupes that she flaunts aggressively at the world. Islah finds herself making comparisons. She looks at her own bony knees and says to herself: if women are fruits then I must be a grain. As a young girl she once read that there are two types of women: the apples and the pears. The pears have small breasts and large hips and vice versa for the apples. In the insecurity of her teenage years, she waited for nature to determine which fruit she'd turn into, but she ended up a member of the bamboo family, or a sugar cane or something. Her breasts and behind are more akin to a lemon than a Timor mango or a pomegranate or a watermelon. As for this woman, whose instinctive passion, whose femininity overpowers everyone around her, she is a paradise of fruit.

Before inviting her into her green terrace, the belly dancer took Islah on a quick tour of her vast apartment, to carefully selected corners that, apparently, she likes to show off to visitors. The ritual started with the arabesque fountain near the entrance then progressed to a marble-encased room featuring a red jacuzzi shaped like a giant clam and surrounded by faux roman statues, and ended with a collection of Chinese vases and statuettes carefully arranged on glass shelves.

Islah had followed in silence, Ahlam's slim copybook weighing heavily in her purse. The copybook has been quite a burden, lately. She has only had the time to skim through it, in buses, in crowded elevators, in taxis stuck in traffic jams. Ahlam's features are slowly coalescing. The pages are half filled with a childish handwriting in sharpened pencil. Cuttings of articles and headlines from books, newspapers, and magazines have been carefully glued in. Girlish drawings adorn the margins, and spontaneously scribbled words have taken refuge in pages' corners and the spaces between paragraphs. The copybook reverberates with a pure confident hope that challenges injustice and greed. This is how love chirps away as it eyes death. Ahlam Shawarby's voice echoes in her ears, its silence drowning out the loud belly dancer's witticisms.

In the formal part of her tour, the star dancer recited a list of her upcoming projects: the funny movie she'll star in opposite Mohamed Heneidi, the musical she intends to produce on stage in which she plays the role of a nightclub owner, the new music video she'll shoot in Beirut. Then abruptly, seemingly satisfied she'd accomplished her promotional objective, she stopped talking. After some hesitation, the dancer invited Islah into her sanctum. In the vegetal presence that covered every inch of the greenhouse, she shed her skin like a sweaty belly dancer's costume. Or rather, she took off all her dancing costumes and, without inhibition, bared all.

"The special one is the lady of all flowers because she's a real woman. Her femininity is her weapon. God gave her beauty to allow her to survive, that's why she shows no mercy to her victims . . . I never get tired of watching her."

In Islah's eyes, the plant hardly deserves all this praise. The dancer's admiration is, no doubt, focused on the vivid red flowers not the white, more delicate ones. In our world, bland, delicate creatures are often ignored.

Islah doesn't understand why Lula Hamdi is exposing herself this way. Why not concentrate her efforts on promoting her image?

"Life's a nightclub . . . they sit two gorgeous girls at the bar to draw in the customers, except it's the ugly older women who end up doing all the work."

But what has all this to do with plants? The world the dancer is describing represents a threat to Islah's very existence. Had it not been for her resolve to avenge poor Ahlam, she would've never been here. She takes advantage of the dancer's distraction to lob a question.

"Tell me Madame Lula . . . did Mr. Shoukry bring along the late Ahlam Shawarby when he visited?"

A mystery called Ahlam Shawarby. Islah hounds people with her questions but the time has come for her to get to know the copybook's owner better. To explore her words, to study her thoughts line by line and word by word, to read between the lines, to search for meaning. She needs to reach the depths of the dead actress, and thus genuinely earn her friendship.

"God forgive her . . . that stuck-up brat. She only visited the Señora. Believe me darling, it's our inferiority complex with foreigners. She thought Esmeralda was a high-class girl. What does that make the likes of me. . . diseased dogs?"

The anger in the dancer's voice suddenly evaporates and her eyes brighten. She points to her favorite plant. A fly has landed on one of the plant's green flowers. Islah doesn't quite get the dancer's point until the flower suddenly closes in on itself with a snap like a crocodile's jaws.

Islah gasps.

"That's why they call her Venus's trap," Lula Hamdi whispers.

Was Ahlam then an Egyptian Venus or merely a victim of the goddess's trap? Islah has the urge to bring out the dead woman's copybook, as if reading it in the presence of this exotic plant could decipher its code and expose the truth about the actress and her fate.

Less than an hour ago, Islah took advantage of her time with Karim Nafea on the other terrace to read him a poem by Elabnoudi from Ahlam's copybook. But then, the copybook had refused to disclose its secrets. She read in a fiery voice full of yearning for days past, for a spirit that time had crushed and whose remains it had scattered over the four corners of the earth. As Karim listened with that smile in which she lost herself, Islah read the verses over and over again in the feeble light that seeped in from the hall, and only stopped when embarrassment peered at her from the handsome man's eyes.

His discomfiture had muffled her on the spot, but her conscious mind only produces an explanation now as she contemplates the predatory plant. Only now, with the copybook safely tucked away in her purse, and Karim back in his wife's arms, does his embarrassment expose its nature . . . that man whose every utterance makes her heart shiver in delight. Only now, as the plant whispers, "Beware . . . when the world opens her arms to you, her dagger is secretly poised to stab."

A crimson flow inundates the flower's folded heart, as if atoning for its crimes by shedding blood instead of tears. Its human secret slips through the fingers of its mindless vegetal fist. Colorless only moments ago, the flower now turns an attractive scarlet. Its beauty resides in its thirst for blood.

In her confusion at the plant's beauty and brutality, the significance of what she said to Didi earlier dawns upon her. She said she was almost as close to her as to the late Ahlam. As the words crossed her lips, her own surprise surpassed the girl's. What, is she starting to believe she really was Ahlam's friend? Like a bird released from its cage, her lie circles the sky but refuses to disappear into the horizon

Even Didi had not argued. Not for a second did the girl doubt Islah's relationship with the dead actress, that goddess Islah has only encountered on the screen of illusions. Despite her youthful rebelliousness, the girl opted to leave rather than bruise the friendship of the living with the dead. And Islah was left with the dancers and millionaires, lonely but comforted by the actress's ghost, and of course her knight in shining armor, that handsome man old enough to be her father. Karim: a hero of the national movement, a relic from the days when there was a movement and the word national still occupied a line in the dictionary.

Didi had not asked what she too was doing here at the belly dancer's party. Had she asked, Islah would have stuttered an excuse that would have confirmed her guilt. Despite her anger and rebelliousness, the girl had spared Islah that embarrassment. Islah too had not mentioned the visit she paid Didi's mother barely two days ago and did not repeat what the woman had said in confidence. Surrounded by the pictures of the husband and daughter she'd forever lost, the still-mourning mother had simply declared that she was cursed and that everyone she loved was destined to perish. Today, Islah chose not to remind Didi she was all her mother had left in the world and did not make her miserable by warning her not to repeat Ahlam's tragedy.

After her initial impetuousness, Didi abruptly went quiet. Instinctively, Islah took her in her arms. Then, with tears on her cheeks, the girl left with the millionaire. Islah stayed, her mission like a midnight mosquito nagging at her. Now, she collects her thoughts, turns away from the predatory flower, and asks the dancer:

"There's talk of a big commercial deal . . . a new canal in the desert. The price of land will skyrocket. Nothing has been announced yet, but you've probably heard something?"

"Why don't you stick to the ghosts, darling, and stay away from the living . . . or instead of reporting the news you'll become a news item yourself." The dancer's voice is an ocean catching its breath between hurricanes. Her eyes, bottomless wells, watch Islah. Then the music bursts from the loudspeakers dispersed all around the apartment. The sirens of Lula Hamdi's world clamor for her attention, a call she can't refuse. Without a word she returns to her guests and their rowdiness.

Islah relaxes on the swing like Faten Hamama or Magda in a fifties movie and draws the copybook from her purse. She opens it on a newspaper clipping too big for the page it is pasted to. The clipping's carefully folded half is starting to turn yellow. Gingerly, she spreads it out. The headline takes her breath away. It's cut from one of the new tabloids. This is what you get from the freedom of the press. She looks behind her; she doesn't want anyone to see her reading this stuff. Then she remembers to check her watch and gasps as she just did in front of Venus's trap.

It's almost three a.m. and she hasn't warned her mother she'd be late. Mama never complains but always waits up in chronic anxiety. Hamada likes to play man of the house and sometimes complains, but when she makes fun of him, he shuts up. Except that he's rather edgy these days; a man's joblessness cuts deep into his pride. Islah folds the page, returns the copybook to her purse, and hurries away. She'll read the article another time; besides, she's skinny and so it doesn't apply directly to her. She repeats the title many times without actually grasping its meaning: "Obscene Exercises for Fat Women."

✖

She rings the bell without an appointment. The security clerk has gotten used to her; he now simply returns her greetings without asking where she's going. It is already five; the sun is about to set. October is half gone and the days are getting shorter. This time of year always takes Islah by

146

surprise; the heat imparts the confidence of a midsummer day then, suddenly, darkness sets in.

A buxom stylish maid, reminiscent of maids in the movies, comes to the door. She invites Islah into the living room and walks away at a leisurely gait.

Islah is in a good mood. An immense burden has been lifted: Hamada's problem has suddenly resolved itself for no apparent reason other than a mother's prayers. He was offered a job with one of the big construction companies, including an air-conditioned car and a salary beyond the young man's expectations, and what's more, it was they who actually sought him. They said they'd been looking for months for the right person, then well-wishers had recommended him. She's never seen her mother so happy. The idle son has found a job. Only the spinster daughter has yet to land a husband. Hamada can now at last ease some of Islah's burden, carry the responsibility on his broad shoulders. No longer responsible for anyone but her own self, Islah feels like a butterfly, a wonderful feeling she's yearned for, maybe subconsciously. Her one task now is to seek justice for Ahlam Shawarby.

After a few minutes, Dr. Mahgoub appears, preceded by the cracking of his slippers. His pajama top is unbuttoned, exposing a white T-shirt and a mat of protruding chest hair. The hair lost its way, Islah thinks, contemplating his bald head. The little boy Islah remembers well follows, mimicking his father's every move. The man seems unaware of the kid's presence.

"Welcome. What a pleasant surprise, Miss Islah."

He crosses his legs, his toes a cluster of fat dates wriggling inside his open slippers. Islah had intended to begin by introducing herself, but now that the man seems to know who she is, she doesn't know where to start. Besides, it is hard enough to contain her laughter, as the child, hiding behind his father's armchair, raises his head from time to time and makes faces at her.

"I have to admit I'm impressed with the press. There's no hiding anything from you guys. You must have very good sources, Miss Islah."

147

The man's talk adds to her confusion. If only he knew that she doesn't have a single bona fide source. All she can hope for is to find one tenant in this tower willing to tell the truth, a last-ditch attempt to confirm her suspicions. Now at last it looks like she's found a man who has something to say. Who knows, maybe today her happiness will be complete?

"I'm sure, Dr. Mahgoub, that you have useful information on the story I'm working on." The trail is getting warmer; her enthusiasm grows.

"I was sure the media would be interested in my story. As you well know, traffic problems affect each and every one of us." The man pushes his enormous head and trunk back. Inside the slippers, his toes wriggle with extra vigor. Confused by what the man is saying, Islah tries to overcome her anxiety that the man will tip over with his armchair and hurt the child.

"Soad. Soad! Would you be so kind as to prepare a glass of your very special lemonade for our guest?" he bellows.

"Naturally, the situation created a traffic jam . . . but we shouldn't allow that to distract us from the terrible murder."

"Exactly. That's what I always say . . . incompetence in organizing traffic is just as bad as murder," the man interrupts Islah, this time leaning forward.

Soad's prompt appearance with a glass of lemonade on a tray suggests she was waiting for his signal. She sets the tray on a small side table next to Islah. The man—transformed into an angry gorilla—lunges unexpectedly toward the maid. He passes his finger over the table's surface next to the tray then raises his blackened fingertip in her face and nods at the dark line his swipe has left on the dusty table.

"Cleanliness is next to Godliness, Soad. . . ."

The maid walks away without a word as if all this is no concern of hers.

"Cleanliness is next to Godliness . . . and filthiness, next to women." The man intensifies his accusation at the space she had occupied. Then he goes back to his armchair. "Excuse me, Miss Islah. Of course I didn't mean educated women like yourself," he adds casually.

Islah tries to ignore the whole episode. "Do you have any recollection of the night the actress Ahlam Shawarby was murdered?"

"Of course I remember. But what does that have to do with the matter at hand?"

"Fantastic . . . do you know then who Ahlam was with that night?" Her mounting anger at the man allows her to continue to ignore his questions. Islah takes a sip of her lemonade and discovers she's consumed her entire drink; only the ice cubes that fill the glass are left.

"She came with Shoukry Shaker like she always did. I ran into them in the elevator that night. Now where was I?"

Islah can hardly believe her ears. Without giving it a second thought, the doctor has just dropped a bombshell. Impossible to ignore, the boy's head keeps popping up like a buoy in the Alexandrian sea. She cannot control her laughter much longer, but who cares? She's already obtained the information she needed. As a matter of fact, her article is written and carefully folded in her purse next to Ahlam's copybook. When the editor refused to publish it, she used a pen name and now that her suspicions have been confirmed, she'll send it to one of the opposition papers.

The man's voice is a vibrating device like the one workers use to compact concrete. He drowns the world in his buzz but she can no longer identify individual words. Traffic on Egyptian streets . . . in different circumstances she would have been interested, but today all she wants is to solve the murder and get justice for Ahlam. All is clear now; her objective has become a sacred duty. Then laughter overcomes her. Once again, the young devil has won.

The doctor's eyes silently reprimand her, then he realizes what's going on and turns around and pulls the child out by the ear. "What are you doing here, you little devil?"

With a well-rehearsed twist of the head, the child escapes his father's grip then stops a few meters away, contemplating the man as if seeing him for the first time. He answers the question like a student in an end-of-year exam. "Other people's kids are good and smart but our kids are the worst in the world."

Islah impulsively applauds. The child has put down the model answer and the examiner can only give him full marks. Under the weight of the doctor's look of surprised injury, she quickly returns her hands to her sides. Abruptly, she stands up to take her leave. She hurries to the landing, ignoring the doctor's entreaties:

"But I haven't told you everything yet . . . the juicy parts are coming up."

"I'll come again in a day or two . . . next time I'll bring along a photographer."

The elevator door shuts out Dr. Mahgoub from her world. She's escaped, freed herself from the clutches of his donkey voice, bald head, and fat toes. The elevator's tranquility makes her realize how much the man had succeeded in colonizing her world with his noise. But the hush also permits a distant drone to surface into her consciousness; her decision has metamorphosed from a mildly annoying fly into a raging beast she must either kill, or perish. It occurs to her that publishing her article is the first real decision she's ever faced. Before this, she merely went with the flow, a serious student who did what she was told without arguing with the teacher or revolting against the curriculum.

Today, she's going to challenge the newspaper. The editor will undoubtedly learn what she's done. She'll set loose a chain reaction whose outcome is unpredictable. A strange heat permeates her body. She finds herself repeating in an almost audible chant: "Cleanliness is next to Godliness . . . and filthiness, next to women."

✖

Like a child playing a prank on the neighbors, Islah presses the bell intermittently. She gives up and is about to head for the elevators when high-heeled steps approach unhurriedly. She presses the bell with a vengeance until Farah's face appears in the half-open doorway. She's wearing black stretch pants and a pomegranate-red sweater of soft wool. Her makeup is a rainbow of sensuality. Islah is not sure which is more annoying; the coldness of the woman's eyes or her aggressive beauty.

"Hi, Farah. I hope I'm not disturbing you."

"Hello . . . Ihsan . . . isn't it?"

"Islah."

"Of course, Islah. We met at Sambo's a while back . . . must be over three months now." Farah's hourglass figure blocks the half-open doorway, but still she holds the door as if anticipating that Islah may try to force her way in.

"I think we met more recently at Madame Gawdat's." Islah produces a pencil from her coat pocket and unconsciously positions it between her lips, like a cigarette.

"Possibly."

"I wanted to check on Madame Gawdat . . ." Islah realizes she's talking with the pencil in her mouth and quickly returns it to her pocket. "Looks like she's taken the girls out for a walk."

She laughs nervously at her failed attempt to lighten up the atmosphere. Farah's features are frozen in ennui. Islah decides upon a less tactful approach.

"You don't mind, do you, if I stay a few minutes till she gets back?"

A charged moment, then Farah pushes the door open.

"Sure, come in," she gestures, making no attempt to hide her annoyance.

Islah relaxes on a pistachio-green sofa whose fabric reflects rich waves of brilliance. Her heels sink into the fleece of a thick Chinese rug of the same color. Its sponginess feels suspicious following the hardness of the shiny parquet.

"Wow, you have a beautiful place here, Farah. How cute, a whole zoo on your coffee table." Islah points to the crystal figurines spread in two parallel lines atop the thick glass surface of the metallic coffee table.

151

"Thank you. I love collecting beautiful things."

"I see you have very sophisticated taste. . . ." Islah adopts her mother's tone when provoked by some arrogant friend. A tone that brings back childhood embarrassments, the sensation of her body stiffening in the presence of children with fathers who brought them apples, Cadbury chocolates, and sweaters purchased from overseas. "Actually, I've been looking for Mr. Shaker for the past few days . . . I thought maybe I'd find him here." She enjoys watching Farah's face turn red.

"He's not here," the woman snaps back, evidently struggling to remain composed.

"You own this beautiful apartment, don't you, Farah?"

"Not exactly . . . anyway it's none of your business," she says through gritted teeth.

"It's just that when the piano fell from the thirteenth floor, it wrecked Mr. Shaker's car. I assume he must've been here . . . visiting, of course."

"This apartment is owned by the company I work for . . . nobody's using it right now, so Mr. Shaker—the company's owner—was kind enough to let me stay here for a while . . . I don't see anything wrong with that." Farah's voice is cracked, threatening, imploring.

But Islah is on a mission and there's no going back. "I'm interested in a homicide . . . not a vice case." Islah can't believe she actually said that.

"Who do you think you are?" She jumps up, her eyes on fire.

Islah recognizes Farah is about to pounce on her yet, with a degree of composure she wasn't aware she possessed, she contemplates the other woman's beauty as it evaporates beneath her makeup, like gasoline on a hot day. A woman's beauty is ephemeral—she remembers the observation that stood out as she skimmed through Ahlam's copybook—her animal attraction fades away by the time she's twenty-five. From then on, she can only count on her intelligence. Islah now sees how true that is and how momentous: the misery women everywhere must endure, the injustice. Ahlam's observation leaves no doubt that the train of feminine desirability has already left Islah's station, and

152

that hereafter she must content herself with a cart pulled by the donkey of intelligence.

"I'll say what I want . . . at least I haven't sold myself or let dogs tear at my flesh." The words shock Islah, as though there's someone else using her voice. She never imagined she could be this cruel, this vulgar.

"That does it, bitch . . . now you've gone too far." Farah rolls up the sleeves of her blood-red sweater.

"You don't scare me . . . if you want to humiliate yourself in front of the whole building, go ahead." But what if she doesn't mind a scandal? Islah wonders behind her bravado. Alert, she examines the features of her wounded victim. A tense moment. Hurricanes brew in Farah's eyes. Any moment the woman will attack, but she's never learned how to physically defend herself. Maybe she should run away or apologize for her insolence.

"I'm going to tell Mr. Shaker that . . . that you're trying to implicate him in a murder. He'll know how to handle you," Farah sputters.

Islah realizes Farah is controlling herself with difficulty. So she dreads a scandal, after all. Islah starts to regain confidence. "You need to understand that in this country we have free media. No one can scare us into silence."

No sooner has Islah made this declaration than she remembers the editor banging on his desk and disallowing any story on the murder of Ahlam Shawarby. The reality that has eluded her for months now dawns upon her. She wonders what Shaker Shaker will do to her now that she's found a way around his embargo, after her articles have appeared in a number of independent papers under a thinly disguised pseudonym.

"I've never done anything wrong . . . except when I had no choice," Farah mumbles in her hoarse voice, as though to herself.

"What do you mean when you had no choice? What kind of an excuse is that? There's no difference between stealing one pound and a thousand, honey."

It occurs to Islah that she's not talking about ethics or virtue or right and wrong, but about sex. Here she is preaching about that magical forbidden relationship between a man and a woman, something she knows next to nothing about. Her childhood curiosity ever growing, never satisfied; the mysteries of Mama locking her bedroom door when father was still alive, of her belly filling up with Hamada, or of Mama forbidding her father to touch her when she was fasting . . . Islah now recalls her bewilderment at this magnetic yet unclean effect of a male touch. When her father was gone and the family had adapted to the new situation, her mother often revealed she had sacrificed her life for Islah and her brother—she meant by refusing to remarry. But what exactly did she sacrifice? What is the secret a man hides in his pants? Why did her brother Hamada suddenly become the uncrowned king of the house? How can she explain her own and her mother's decision to dedicate themselves to serving him, a decision neither of them ever spelled out, yet to which they adhered as if it were a fundamental law of nature?

"You don't understand anything because you've never experienced need . . . a person who steals out of hunger can't be called a thief." Farah's eyes are bloodshot and her voice is broken.

"You think I was born with a silver spoon in my mouth? My life story can be summed up in one word: struggle." Every word she says is true, if only this promiscuous woman knew.

"Your struggle, darling, is a luxury. You were breast-fed principles and bathed in morality then you were allowed to pursue your precious struggle . . . as for me . . . I suckled from the garbage of the streets." She shivers. Her body is contracted like a compressed spring. "That's it . . . I've had enough." She points to the apartment's door.

Islah doesn't move. She wonders what's gotten into her to spurt this poison. Is it self-righteousness or revenge or jealousy?

"I'm sorry . . . maybe I went too far," she says.

Farah's volcano subsides instantly. The pain spreads gray shades beneath the foundation on her face, a physical pain that disfigures her features as though her entrails were being torn apart. She leans on the back of the armchair.

"An innocent girl was murdered. I'm sure Shaker Shaker and his son Shoukry had something to do with it . . . and why did all this have to happen in this particular building? There's something off about this tower. For example, why would Shaker and his son take private apartments in the same building . . . isn't there anywhere else for a millionaire to go?" Islah sets aside her growing compassion. The other woman is in a position of weakness now; she'll ultimately reveal everything.

"I have no answers. You're wasting your time. You'll end up involving me in a scandal and still not get what you want . . . plus, Shoukry rarely used the apartment he rented and then only for business meetings," Farah squeaks. Then she whispers, as if to herself, "Scandals . . . I never cared about them . . . but right now . . . I can't believe he's back . . . I'm tired. Please leave me alone. I need to rest." Farah lies down flat on the sofa.

Islah leaves and shuts the door behind her. She wonders if she has so rudely invaded Farah's privacy to collect information related to Ahlam's murder or if from the beginning she's been possessed by a deep desire to insult the woman, to take revenge for sins that have hurt no one but herself. Then the elevator door slides open and she faces Madame Gawdat and her panting girls.

⁙

The waiter approaches with a bottle of Stella for him and her glass of lemonade whose surface is quivering. He spills a few drops as he sets it on the table. Islah follows the droplets as they meander down the glass's surface to be absorbed by the white tablecloth, already stain-specked.

She asks herself what she's doing here with him. What if someone were to see them together in this romantic café, this lovers' hideout? Would anyone believe it is no more than an innocent encounter? She pushes her bewilderment to the back of her mind, smiles and, once the waiter has gone, continues her conversation.

"They say political detention is the one real school of politics in Egypt . . . true?"

Karim passes his trembling fingers through his silver mane. The gold ring reappears as he flattens the locks tousled by the Nile breeze. He opens his mouth as if to say something then changes his mind.

Islah continues, "All my life I wished they'd send me to jail for defending my principles . . ." She laughs nervously. "But Mama would have a heart attack."

He joins her, his laughter even more on edge. Then his face turns serious. "The people who speak so fondly of prison are those who've never even driven past a prison wall, let alone served time in one."

"I didn't mean to trivialize the suffering of our heroes . . . but the important thing is for a person to know he had the courage to stand up against oppression . . . that he didn't give up . . . never said it's none of my business . . ." She can feel the heat of her words in her cheeks and skull.

"Prison is an intensely personal experience . . . so hard to explain. There are no words to describe the smell of a prison cell." His voice is low. He swallows the bitterness of his words with a long gulp of beer.

Her eyes are captivated by the slight tremors at the corners of his mouth. Her mind is enthralled by his deliberate manner of speaking, the way he pronounces every syllable. This is a man who knows what he's saying, who has lived every word. He has never been content to read about life in books and magazines.

A sad tenderness peers at her from his eyes, melts her heart.

With shaky deliberateness he touches her hand, then cradles it in both of his as if to protect it from the world's cruelty. She rotates her fist to feel the contours of his palms. A fleeting electric delight. She presses his fingers. The heat of contact is only restricted by the solid touch of cold metal. She's not sure whether it is the fancy ring on his right hand or the wedding band on his left. Alarmed, she withdraws her hand.

She sips her lemonade. The ice cube feels like fire on the tip of her tongue. The flow of the over-sweetened liquid clears the lump in her throat. She regains concentration.

"Your generation's worst fears have materialized in the New World Order . . . and even worse." Her voice is soft but her words lethal.

"When we were young . . . enthusiasm sometimes blurred our vision. We were afraid of colonialism, exploitation, and foreign domination. It turns out marginalization is a thousand times worse." He passes his fingers through his hair again, then rests his chin on his hand and caresses his lower lip with his finger.

"I admire your humility. Someone else would have gone on about his past glory."

"I resolved a long time ago not to live in the past . . . life is the present and the future. Life is reality."

"And what battle is consuming your present, then?"

"To expand the role of civil society, of course. We need to liberate ourselves from the control of corrupt and lazy bureaucrats. If each of us were to pick up one scrap of paper from the sidewalk, Egypt would become the cleanest country in the world . . . and if each of us would plant one flower, our country would become a piece of paradise." His orderly voice jumps a pitch with every word. In a few seconds he has adopted a well-rehearsed oratorical tone.

"Wonderful, Mr. Karim . . . I'm sure if we had a few others like you in the country things would be much better. To be honest, when I found out you were living in this expensive tower, I said to myself he's into business and money now and has forgotten all about the country's woes . . . but I can see you're still a revolutionary . . . just that you managed to adapt."

"Do you realize that you sometimes come across like a little boy who takes the world too seriously?" he laughs.

"I've gotten used to that, Mr. Karim. Even when I was young, I felt responsible for Mama and Hamada. I never had the time to be a girl. I'm still scared to feel . . . feminine. I don't know how to explain . . . ." She removes her hands from her lap and rests her elbows on the table.

She looks him in the eyes. He looks away. His hands tremble on the table's edge. His veins are blue bulges. He's old enough to be her father, but so what? This is perfectly innocent admiration, she tells herself.

"I thought we'd agreed to drop the Mr."

"Okay, Karim . . . it would make me happy if you talked a bit about yourself," she says softly.

"There's not much to tell. I have two sons; one wears a devout beard, the other a ponytail. The intellectuals will have nothing to do with me because I drive an air-conditioned car and use a mobile phone—they still think that behaving like a vagabond is the mark of culture—and when I say we must be pragmatic, my old comrades go wild and accuse me of high treason. On the other hand, the business community considers me a communist and believes I bring bad luck . . . Yes, and Zeinab—my wife—well, she's gotten into the habit of visiting this new psychic who's moved into our tower."

Her hair stands up on end at the mention of his wife. "And which one is the real you?" she responds quickly.

"The real me is a prisoner. When I was in detention, at least I could see the bars that constrained me and I knew who the jailors were. But today the bars are success . . . and the jailors are the people closest to me. In my prison days there was always hope for release . . . either I'd escape, or the ruler would decide to set me free, or he could die and his successor would need to free up prison space for his own enemies. But now, my sentence is for life . . . and as long as I'm around the jailor is alive and kicking." He stares at her, eyes ablaze with desire.

Islah doesn't know what to say. She feels a tingling up her spine. She never thought this great man could open up to her this way. What an honor. There's no denying that a connection has developed between them. Her eyes wander across the Nile's dancing waves. The old river, cynical and omnipotent, bubbles on. Silence is a barrier she needs to overcome, but before the right words come to mind, he adds:

"Every living creature carries the seed of its destruction in its heart. Everything in the world has a cycle and turns into its own opposite. In his intestines, man carries the very maggots that will ultimately devour him. As the world rotates, the revolutionary activist becomes part of the system. Your enemy turns into a friend and your brother's stab tears through your heart. Greatness generates hubris, which brings on its heels weakness and humiliation. Love quickly turns to possessiveness then jealousy, conflict, and hate. Satisfaction becomes boredom. The moment you attain happiness, you discover it's a prison cell from which there is no escape."

She cannot fathom what he's saying. But this is not the time for understanding. Contemplation has become impossible with the erupting volcano in her soul. For the first time in her life, she'll follow her heart blindfolded, anything to break that murderous silence that has engulfed her past years.

"Daddy used to take me on his lap and allow me to hold the steering wheel as he drove . . . it was a Fiat R, sky-blue. God rest his soul, he was martyred in '73 . . . at the battle for Canada Camp, one of the fiercest of the war. He sacrificed his life for the nation, for our sake . . . for Mama, Hamada, and me."

"A martyr's daughter . . . I should've guessed. People like you are a rare breed these days. I mean people who have kept their hope alive."

"I'm doing a story on the murder of Ahlam Shawarby," her voice rings aloud for the first time this evening.

"God rest her soul, she was beautiful, like an angel," the man's face lightens up. Islah realizes he's one of the few people who hate to talk about themselves.

"I'll never let her killers get away."

"This one may be bigger than the two of us, Islah."

He touches her hand again. She withdraws it and looks him in the eye. "Didn't you just say that power carries the seeds of its defeat? Following the same logic, then weakness must contain the ingredients of its victory . . . right, Karim?"

His smile is a fountain of nostalgia, an evocation of revolution and innocence, a torrent of wisdom, adventure, sorrow, and pleasure. He sends out vibrations that enrich the whole of existence. This is just an innocent friendship, she repeats to herself.

⁙

The truth . . . but where lies the truth, where does it reside? Where does it spend the night in the cold of winter and where does it nap on a sleepy summer afternoon? Happiness is a prison cell, strength is weakness, and love . . . an early morning mist that hugs the desert road, certain to quickly expire.

What about death, is it really a barrier that separates different worlds? A gateway permitting passage in one direction? A unique experience known only to those who have tasted it, but once initiated they're pledged to eternal silence? Or is death a bridge people come and go across, one of the levels of illusion, another self-deception we simply cannot sweep away because we avoid awareness?

The CNN screen shows no black boxes. Hamada has gone out with his friends to celebrate the new job. Mama sits next to her on the sofa, slapping her thighs lightly. She rubs them a little then slaps again, leans forward and backward.

"No news of the black box?"

Islah does not answer her mother's question. She lets it circle in space, hover in a dimension of the cosmos beyond our perception. She allows her mother's question to merge with the uncertainty of two hundred and seventeen souls at the moment they face the truth, as their world drowns in the rattle of metal, the shrieks of children, and the hiss of flying objects, the collective horror of flight 990.

A veiled woman sobs onscreen. The pallor of her face is contagious and in a second, Islah feels miserable. A new widow is born. One widow embodies all the widows of the world. What's the use of reasons and explanations? The only reality is this televised widow, a woman condemned to go on living after being buried alive. Islah takes a sip of her coffee. She's added sugar yet it's bland on her tongue. Her eyes are glued to the screen, captured by the giant who stares back at her from the magic box.

Life is a widow.

A bald American explains for the thousandth time the flight's graph: its sudden drop from thirty-one thousand to nineteen thousand feet, its futile ascent to twenty-four thousand, then its disappearance altogether from the radar. A dot of light in a video game, followed by a screenful of debris; images she's scrutinized ad nauseam. Fragments of torn metal salvaged from the deep, a broken seat, the remains of a suitcase, shreds of cloth, part of the aircraft's tailpiece, other blurred objects that make her heart fall. She's terrified that human remains will suddenly come into focus, someone's hand or foot caught in the wreckage.

"Isn't that the area they call the Bermuda Triangle?" Mama will not rest until she has a convincing explanation.

An elderly man stumbles onscreen. An airline employee steps forward. The man leans on him. How many young girls have been orphaned in this crash? The living take precedence over the dead, right? Except that the dead take with them a piece of those left behind, and the living, for their part, cannot help but cling to ghosts.

What if Islah herself had been on the passenger list? What if her life had been switched off like a sitcom in a power cut? A few months ago that thought would not have worried her in the least. Now she can't even bear the idea. Between lost lives and onscreen sorrows, Islah can sense life pulsating in her veins. For the first time, life kicks like an embryo in her belly.

After thirty-three years of running away from life, it has at last caught up with her. The lifetime she considered interminable suddenly seems so short. Now's the time to make her claim. Karim Nafea's delicious and somewhat exhausted features smile at her from her inner screen. She needs to remain alive for a few more days at least, just to look at his handsome face, to listen to his voice that is desire incarnate.

"When will they find the black box?"

Islah finds nothing to say to her mother.

⁙

It was a sunny winter's day. Their mother had decided to take them to the zoo. Ahlam was a primary schoolgirl and Didi, a wide-eyed baby who stared at the world from the security of her stroller. Their father was still alive, away at an army camp in the distant desert. The grim events that were to claim his life years later were still beyond the horizon; Desert Storm, stealth aircraft, cruise missiles, Hafr Elbaten, Norman Schwarzkopf: all words still concealed inside fate's pouch.

There was nothing to disrupt the serenity of mother and daughters or undermine the ecstatic Ahlam's encounter with the elephant, pony, giraffe, and monkeys, the seals and the hippo.

Today, the sun is blocked by a black blanket of pollution that has descended upon Cairo's inhabitants like fate's retribution. Islah dashes across the studio courtyard. Ahlam's copybook pulsates inside her purse, which she carries like a soldier with his weapon. Each day her relationship with her friend Ahlam is further consolidated by the dead actress's scribbled words, her favorite poems, and the articles and cartoons she found relevant enough to cut and paste in the copybook.

These past few weeks, Islah's interaction with the copybook has become more ceremonial; her affection and respect for the copybook's deceased owner are now enshrined in ritual. Islah always keeps the copybook close at hand. When she's out of the house, she carries it in her purse under her left arm, a few centimeters away from her heart. At night, the purse rests on her nightstand, as though the copybook, deprived of its owner, can no longer bear to be alone.

She only approaches the copybook when her mind is completely at ease and her emotions drummed up for an exceptional encounter. Then, with an almost religious reverence, she turns the pages one at a time and never a page turned before it is fully absorbed; the poems learned by heart, the notes carefully dissected. Islah has even learned to read between the lines, inferring intimate details from generalities and from her growing understanding of her friend's world.

Through the copybook, she explores the strengths and weaknesses of the deceased, tries to develop their relationship in the way living people do: step by step, day by day, never pretending affection or anticipating events. Despite her professional curiosity, she's not yet halfway through the copybook. She's even resisted her temptation to jump directly to the article on obscene exercises for fat women, turning her inquisitiveness into an incentive to continue to devour the pages.

The copybook's second half may well contain a clue to unravel her friend's murder, but ritual has attained a sanctity she doesn't dare to challenge. Most of all, Islah dreads the day she'll turn the last page and stand face to face with her friend in the blackness of the night. The construct of their friendship accomplished, there will be nothing left to say but their long-delayed goodbyes.

Islah struggles through the heavy November air. Her purse, with the copybook inside, swings to and fro. She can visualize the child Ahlam in front of the tiger's cage, clinging to her mother's strong, youthful hand. This is childhood's garden, lush-green, awash in sunny days, and gone never to return. "They've even poisoned the air . . . damn their military exercises," Islah mutters between coughs.

"Wait, Didi!' she calls out in a breathless voice, as though trying to catch up with a phantom before it disappears into thin air.

Didi and Shoukry stop, only steps away from his red sports car. They turn. Their mirth freezes on their faces. Didi clears her throat with low-pitched coughs.

"I've been looking all over for you, Didi."

"I've been busy." Her eyes are lowered despite the coldness of her tone.

"Can I talk to you for a minute . . . alone?" Islah stares at Shoukry, making no attempt to hide her scorn.

"I'll turn on the AC, I can't breathe!" the man says to Didi then disappears inside the car. He's put up the leather top today, probably to allow for air-conditioning. Maybe he's worried the pollution might damage his vocal chords, Islah thinks mockingly to herself. She holds Didi by the arms, half in familiarity, half threateningly.

"Your mom is really worried. She can't take this much longer, you come back late every night and you don't even listen to her anymore. If you don't care about what's best for you, at least have pity on her."

"What do you all want from me? Why don't you just let me live my life and have a real shot at a future?" She avoids Islah's fiery stare.

"You can make a future by concentrating on your studies. After you graduate, go act or do whatever you want." Islah gulps for air but there is little oxygen in the atmosphere.

"Shoukry will make me a star in less than a year. If I throw away this opportunity now it won't come again. I have to go."

Suddenly, Islah's senses are assaulted by the combined buzz of the car's engine and air conditioner. "Shoukry is a snake. The moment he gets what he wants he'll throw you to the dogs!"

The two women turn their eyes to him, sitting calmly behind the steering wheel, sheltered from the smell of exhaust that saturates the air around them. Islah controls the urge to smash the low-suspension car, to scratch his eyes out with her bare hands.

"Why don't any of you accept that I'm talented too?! You keep saying that no one can replace Ahlam . . . well I accept that, but at least let me follow my own destiny." Flares shoot out of the brilliant blackness of Didi's eyes.

"Do anything you want but stay away from Shoukry . . . he's the one responsible for Ahlam's death," Islah shouts. Her emotions conspire with the polluted air to bring tears to her eyes.

"You're lying. You'll say anything just to stop me from taking this opportunity," Didi challenges. Her hair flutters in the dusty breeze, its luster enhanced by some unknown chemical reaction.

At the zoo, the child Ahlam observes the tiger lazing behind the bars. As they approach, the beast springs up, and she can't contain her excitement. His bulging eyes are glued to Didi. Big cats too like to cuddle babies, she thinks. Suddenly, the tiger attacks but is repelled by the bars. He tries again and again. It dawns upon the little girl that the brute wants to harm her baby sister, suddenly a helpless delicious meal to be devoured with predatory relish. The vision of the pouncing tiger kept recurring until Ahlam's last days, provoking renewed puzzlement and endless questions.

The copybook groans in Islah's purse, piercing her heart. She knows Ahlam is calling out to her now, asking for help. "If you have no pity for your mother after all she's been through, at least show respect for the memory of your late father . . . the martyr, the hero, the man who gave up his life for the country . . . for you and me."

The girl's focused gaze dissolves in the thick black cloud. Her focus fans out, beyond Islah's face, beyond the motion picture studios, beyond Cairo and our limited world. Islah is not quite sure whether the girl has understood her.

"My father was a martyr too . . . he died in '73. That's why I feel I'm Ahlam's twin, despite our age difference," she adds, not sure whether she's talking to herself or to the girl.

"You didn't need to say it. You have 'martyr's daughter' written all over you." Didi laughs suddenly then stops just as suddenly. Her features are stern once again. She adds quickly, "Ahlam was a martyr's daughter too. As for me . . . when I was a kid I kept on repeating: Dad's a hero, Dad's a hero. Until one day I asked myself: what exactly did he die defending . . . oil? George Bush and the New World Order? I'm not a hero's daughter after all, I'm the daughter of a fool."

"How can you say that, Didi?" Islah can hardly believe her ears. "Did you expect Egypt to stand by and watch as Saddam Hussein occupied Kuwait? Doesn't Kuwait deserve to be free like all the countries in the world?"

"I'm not defending Saddam . . . but there's a huge difference between the war of '73 and the war of '91. Your father crossed the canal to defend everything he valued in life, but mine treated the war in Kuwait as a contract job. I realize that the world has changed and that we have to change as well . . . that's the difference between us."

The wind has caused Didi's dark sweater to stick to her, emphasizing the perfect curves of her breasts. Where did the baby that Ahlam describes in her copybook go? When was she transformed into a woman of overwhelming beauty and femininity? Islah realizes that the real difference between them is beauty. Had she been as beautiful, had she been offered Didi's opportunity . . . who knows what she would've done? Let her act or do whatever she pleases so long as she has nothing to do with this son of a bitch waiting in the Ferrari's shelter.

"Wake up, Didi. Wake up." She shakes her as if actually trying to wake her from a profound slumber.

"Leave me alone. Why don't you all just leave me alone?" The girl breaks free; Islah's grip was weakening anyway. As Didi turns to go, in despair, Islah grabs her again by the wrist. Her attention is drawn to the girl's gold bracelet, studded with diamonds and other precious stones. She stares at the girl then the bracelet in disbelief; it's a work of art, no doubt worth thousands. The tiger's roar merges with the buzz of the car's engine and the hum of its air conditioner. Tears are starting to swell in the girl's eyes. Islah relaxes her grip.

"It's an innocent gift . . . don't get any ideas," Didi responds to an accusation Islah has not pronounced.

Islah's eyes wander back to the girl's wrist. The bracelet is in the form of a tree branch with a ruby, a sapphire, or an emerald embedded in each leaf, all surrounded by a scatter of diamond shards. Then Didi's warm skin slips away from her exhausted fingers and the escaping Ferrari disappears. She finds herself all alone in a nightmare of pollution. She curses military maneuvers, Israeli explosions, and irresponsible factories, but her swelling eyes are prisoners of the bracelet's lingering glimmer, whose beauty was amplified by Didi's silken skin.

The Seventh Page

An Evening at Señora Esmeralda's

*Amid drunken cheers and adolescent remarks, the Señora
screened a documentary about sex in the animal kingdom. One
scene showed a long queue of female baboons facing a big male.
The male started to mount them, one by one in quick succession.
In a matter of seconds he'd satisfy his desire for one female, push
her away and beckon the next in line. If she waited, hoping for
more, he'd bite her, and shove her away.*
*The men cheered the baboon like he was a mythical hero. Their
common dream was materializing on the screen.*
*Before that day, men were a mystery to me. Suddenly, everything
became clear. I understood.*
Beneath your suits and ties, you're all monkeys.

Ahlam Shawarby

Sergeant Ashmouni

For a split second, her bracelet captures the rays of the setting sun. Its jewels pulsate color. Her hair is like a movie star's in the breeze. Her beauty is so familiar . . . it is her. Impossible. Your mind's playing games on you again, Ashmouni.

He gives me an impatient honk, tries to capture my attention. As if I wasn't familiar with his car: its red paint without so much as a scratch, its luster unblemished by a speck of dust, and an engine that purrs like the desert wind.

I used to jump to attention upon seeing this car like a dog picking up his master's scent. Now, I want to puke. As usual, he hit the brakes at the intersection. His left signal indicates his intention. Haven't we had enough trouble from you? He drives with the roof down despite the November chill. If I spit, I could splatter him, or maybe the beauty next to him. Her bracelet shines as she lifts a lock of hair away from her eyes, the same black velvet. Her beauty is a slap on the back of my neck: the same eyes and eyebrows, the same bold look. She is the spitting image of the deceased, only younger. Could time be flowing backward? Can this be a new test for you, Ashmouni, a make-up after failing the original exam?

"Hello, Ashmouni." The son of a gun has a sweet voice.

I don't reply.

"Take this . . . for your tea." Ten pounds. I refuse to take it but he stuffs the note in my fist. It feels like fire between my fingers. And I had

169

taken my skin—time-weathered, desensitized to heat or cold—for dead. How often do I repeat to myself, 'You're calloused from head to toe, you have no shame anymore?' I withdraw my hand . . . the same hand that has been soiled by everybody's money.

"No Pasha. I can't accept this."

He turns to the girl. He's not interested in what I have to say. He thinks I'm repeating my usual proclamations of virtue: there's no need, Pasha . . . by God no need at all . . . you've already been too kind. I can't find the right words. I don't know how to say no. All my experience in life hasn't taught me how to say no. The girl is her identical twin. God bless her soul wherever she is. Her spirit is watching me from the third heaven . . . or the thirteenth floor.

Another honk. He looks at me in surprise. A whole minute has passed and I haven't cleared the way for him yet. He's getting impatient, well, why shouldn't he? He's bought the road and everyone on it, now it's his mother's private property. I give him back his money, throw it in his face. He watches the note fall into his lap. The demons go wild in his eyes. I know the question that's spinning in his head. His bewilderment merges with anger. What have you done, you lunatic? Save yourself, Ashmouni. I raise the whistle to my lips. Before he speeds away, my eye catches hers. An inexplicable familiarity has developed between us. His wide tires leave a mark on the asphalt. But I've angered the pasha and lost ten bucks. What have you done, Ashmouni? How stupid can your stupidity get? Has the last remaining screw in your head gone loose?

Whatever . . . One day at a time.

He ditches the car at the tower's entrance and leads the girl up the steps. The cars pile up in front of me. I won't set them loose. It's not the end of the world. Let them think some big shot's motorcade is about to pass. I cross to the other side. The honks follow me. I hurry to catch up with the pasha and the girl. Something tells me, 'Don't repeat your terrible mistake. Apologize to the pasha.' The moment I give them my back, the cars at the intersection rush forward in a dense turbulent stream. They can all go to hell.

The girl turns around and hurries down the steps, like she read my mind. Shaker follows. He calls out to her but she ignores him. She stops right in front of me on the sidewalk. She looks me in the eyes as if she knew me well. Ashtatan Ashtout, may heaven protect me. Poor girl, are you turning to me for protection? You're leaning on a crumbling wall.

"Can you stop a cab for me, sergeant?" An angel's voice.

"What's the matter, Didi?" He seems so innocent and sincere.

"I can't . . . my head's going to explode." She cups her head in her hands. "The cab, sergeant, please."

"But you were okay a few seconds ago." She's got a headache, you idiot, what's wrong with that? Instead of interrogating her you should rush her to a doctor or at least give her a ride home.

"Never mind, sergeant . . . you go back to your intersection before the officer passes through." He orders me around as if I was his servant's servant. He only wants to have his way with the girl. You eat their flesh and throw their bones away. But all this is no business of yours, Ashmouni. This is your chance to regain the pasha's favor. After all, she got into his car of her own free will. Nobody forced her. Who knows, she may even be the dead girl's ghost come back from the grave to take revenge.

"Taxi . . . here you go, Miss. May heaven protect you."

I open the door for her. But what's gotten into you, Ashmouni? Now you're really in trouble. She fumbles in her purse, finds a one-pound note.

"Keep your money, Miss." The way you look at me is worth Qarun's treasures. You used to look right through me without ever seeing me. Today, after you're dead and buried, you finally realize I'm human, made of flesh and blood. I close the taxi door behind her.

"Forget the taxi, I'll drive you home." Too late, moron.

"I wouldn't want you to miss your séance," she rolls down the window and replies. The driver takes off in relief. Shoukry and I, we watch as the taxi melts away in the sea of cars.

"What's wrong with you today, sergeant? If this goes on, I'd start getting worried about you."

171

"You see, Pasha . . . old cheese breeds worms." Your open threats no longer scare me, Shoukry.

For the first time in my life, fear has abandoned me. Just like that. Could this be a case of temporary madness, a momentary lapse of reason provoked by the girl, or merely a delusion of courage that will bring my entire house tumbling over my head?

"Well, smart-ass . . . we'll see what good your peasant proverbs will do you." Sparks shoot out of his eyes.

✖

"Turn off the lights, woman . . .

We're the burglar policemen."

Antar carries a football. It looks enormous under his threadlike arm. His knees are lemons covered in scars and fresh wounds. Here is a true devil, but what a sense of humor. If only he'd learn to respect his elders. Kids these days respect no one.

"No little guy, that makes no sense. Policemen can't be burglars. The song goes: we're the vigilant policemen." His genuine leather football is my childhood dream that never came true. My only wish in life was to own a ball like this one and paste it with tomato sauce so it would last forever. Unfulfilled dreams . . . the story of my life.

"Yeah they're burglars . . . that's why they want people to turn off the lights."

"Listen to what you're told, little guy." If only God had given me a son to fill up my world, a little sergeant as Zuzu's father sometimes jokes. A little devil whose one laugh is worth more than the Tower of Happiness and all its inhabitants, more valuable than the fortunes of all these pashas, sheikhs, belly dancers, and pimps. But we don't always grasp God's wisdom. Who knows maybe if I'd had a child he would've turned out like the kids in our neighborhood: popping pills, sniffing gasoline and glue or, in line with the latest trend, collecting cockroaches in

172

jars then setting them ablaze to sniff the fumes. Poor devils, cockroaches fill their lives even when they're trying to have fun.

One day at a time.

"Let's throw the ball around!" With your clubs and playgrounds, you still want to play football on the sidewalk, what have you left to street kids?

"It's dangerous to play football on the sidewalk, little guy."

"I mean pass the ball, not kick it."

"That's not allowed, little fellow."

"Everyone does what they want except me . . . everything is not allowed. Not allowed."

You're right, my son. How can we ask you to respect anything when we've turned principles into shiny slogans to cover up our rot? But Antar, you're something else. You must never become like us. They stepped with their boots all over our dignity. But you . . . life's bubbling in your veins. You must turn out better than we did. What other hope do we have?

What a great blessing to have a little boy. I used Suma's infertility as an excuse to take another wife but then forbade Zuzu from getting pregnant. I married her on an impulse, for pleasure. Okay, I bought her . . . so what? Just like the government bought me. Just like those big guys buy and sell me every day.

"Alright, little guy, but pass the ball very slowly so it won't roll into the street."

Gently does it. You pass it to me and I'll pass it back. Slowly, I'm an old man. Watch out, Antar . . . .

"No, Antar. Stop...stay where you are . . . never mind the ball. I'll get it for you. No . . . no!"

God help me. The cars are guided missiles . . . rabid dogs. The whistle . . . yes, the whistle . . . the honks . . . brake! Brake! The boy will be turned into mincemeat. Damn kids! Damn you, Ashmouni! How will you face his father?

The bus comes to a standstill perpendicular to the road. I can't hear the driver's voice, but I can see he's cursing. I cling to Antar, and Antar clings to the ball. Everyone is safe and sound. Saved by God's mercy, nothing else. I carry him to the sidewalk as he holds tightly to his ball. We can all die but you must survive, Antar. We're already dead, turned into mummies like our forefathers . . . but you . . . they haven't managed to suck the life out of you yet.

"You're a scaredy-cat, sergeant." He pushes my hand away. "Let's play some more?"

I would've cursed his father except the sound is blocked in my throat. If my joints weren't too loose, I would have kicked his behind.

"Okay forget it. . . you're not such a good player." He bounces the ball as he hops up the steps to the tower's entrance. He stops midway and turns to me. "I used to be scared of the dark but now I say Uncle Sergeant is there. You can't be a scaredy-cat. Or how are you going to scare away the bad guys?"

He continues up the steps. Your words break my heart, Antar. He turns around again, laughing.

"Turn off the lights, woman . . . .

We're the burglar policemen."

✖

The white Lada has been out there for over an hour, lying in ambush in the shade of one of the boulevard's few remaining trees. Its two passengers are silent, the kind of men who put on a scowl along with their clothes before going to work. Frankly, I'm starting to get worried. They're watching me like I'm a terrorist emir or a member of a communist cell. I could be wrong, of course; they may just be waiting for an unpunctual friend, or they could be staking out somebody else and have no bones at all to pick with my poor self. But their glares chew up the back of my neck. Could someone have reported me for leaving the intersection unattended?

The car starts to move. I pretend to be absorbed in the traffic. Maybe they'll go away and I'll never see them again, but Satan will be admitted

174

into heaven before that happens. He calls out to me. The car has stopped in the middle of the road. How are you going to handle these ruthless guys, Ashmouni?

"Get in, sergeant." The driver's voice is coarse. His hand is a sledge-hammer he waves in the air.

Who the hell does he think he is? How am I going to deal with this?

"Stop wasting my time, Ashmouni. Get in."

The second man gets out of the car. He pushes me into the front seat where he'd been sitting. Why are you pushing me like that? Leave me alone, you brute.

"What's going on?" The car starts to move. I get no answer from either of them. I'm a dog: let him bark.

Silence. The Lada is as quiet as a grave. The driver has taken a short-cut through Maadi's side streets, then crossed the railway line and taken a left behind the satellite relay station. Now, houses are getting scarce. Where is he taking me? What have I done?

"Excuse me, Pasha, but there seems to be some misunderstanding."

"Why are you talking? Did anyone tell you to talk?" The driver is worked up for no reason at all, like he actually believes it's a crime to talk. He struggles with the steering wheel. He could easily bend it with his bare hands.

"All I'm saying is the intersection's on its own . . . it's a big responsi-bility, Pasha."

"Responsibility? Who are you to talk about responsibility?" The man in the back speaks for the first time. His head is completely shaved, like a fresh army recruit or Ahmed Zaki in his recent movies. These men talk like guard dogs bark.

"How come, Pasha . . . I'm glued to the intersection."

"What intersection, you retard? We're talking about Shoukry Pasha . . . when he gets upset, heaven help you."

Did you really have to stop that cab, Ashmouni? Why interfere with these powerful people? So what if he does get his way with the girl, so

175

what if he corrupts the whole world as much as he likes—is she a member of your family? But no, I did nothing wrong. There must be an end to injustice. An end to fear. Like Antar says, how will the bad guys fear you if you go on like this?

"Old cheese breeds worms, Pasha." Did you have to say that?

"Keep that old-cheese talk for your mother. Don't open your mouth except to say yessir. If someone says good morning . . . you say: yessir. When they tell you to get in the car you say: yessir. When I say you've heard nothing and seen nothing, what do you say . . .?" The man in the back has an enormous nose, like an eagle's beak.

What do you want from me, you dogs? I, who carried my shroud over my shoulder in two wars for this country. In days past I was a solid warrior and a steadfast knight . . . before their boots stepped all over me, before the sun and frost whipped me. Where's that journalist right now to record what's happening to me? God forgive you, Miss. This is what we get from you people, poetry and high-sounding words, but when the going gets tough where can we find you . . .? Like a pinch of salt, you disappear in the soup.

"What do you say, Ashmouni?" The eagle beak slaps me. His palm feels like a sledgehammer on my shoulder.

"Yessir." My voice is hoarse. You've swallowed a frog, Ashmouni. It's better to play it safe. Let it pass. This has been one rotten day from the start. But what are you doing, you son of a bitch? His grip is made of steel, I can't get him to let go of my ear.

"Have pity, Pasha . . . I'm old enough to be your father." The tears are warm on my cheeks. Take my life, dear God. Spare me this humiliation.

"Remember, this time we're gently pulling your ear . . . next time we'll rip it off." The driver talks to his steering wheel, doesn't even make the effort to look at me. But what's he doing? He leans over me. Why is he opening my door?

Damn you to hell, you lunatic!

The slap of the asphalt scorches my back. The lights are off. Picture

176

and sound have merged, a rare harmony. The taste of sand mixes with tears in my mouth. The sting of the Sinai sand in '67. Mirage fighters pounce upon us like heaven's fury. Don't worry, Ashmouni, they target the officers. We've lived to see officers pretend to be soldiers. They contest us even for our misery. The dust blurs my eyes, but my mind's light is clear. The world smiles calmly as I roll over like a ball kicked by Maradona into the goal.

A crowd has gathered. You're crouching on the sand. It looks like you've landed safely this time. Only the good die young. Maybe you did die but they wanted to have nothing to do with your ugly face in paradise. Living or dead, does it matter? But why are you cackling like a madman?

I laugh.

In all your faces, I laugh. I wipe the blood from my eyebrow and laugh. I shake the sand from my hair and laugh. Of course . . . what's the alternative?

�֍

"What's going on, sergeant . . . you're always daydreaming."

"What do you want?" He never fails to take me by surprise, the dim-witted boy from the kebab restaurant, fat from stuffing himself all day with meat and grease. The idiot's broken my chain of thought. Good, they were poisoned thoughts anyway. It is Satan, no doubt, who brings up these painful memories from time to time. In waking hours and in slumber, he whispers in my ear. A big blue fly buzzes in a dream. It says, 'Women spawn children by the thousands and you've been denied even one. When you die you'll leave no trace you ever existed, like a castrated sheep. What's your crime, Ashmouni, that you may deserve this fate?' I wake up in the middle of the night and pray to God to dispel the devil.

"I've been trying to get your attention for an hour."

"Who can hear anything in this madhouse?"

177

"The gentleman on the thirteenth floor sends his greetings and says your mother-in-law loves you."

My mother-in-law? If she got the chance she'd slit my throat, cut me to pieces, and feed me to her ducks. Still, she makes the best layered ghee pastry in the world—my new mother-in-law of course; the old one said her goodbyes in the days of the stone pound. She too, was a great cook—God rest her soul. My neck still aches. Since the affair with the Lada, it feels like a rock. Looking up makes my head spin. The ghost doctor waves from the balcony. Why can't he leave me alone?

"Did you get grilled testicles this time?"

"Yeah. He ordered bull testicles especially for you . . . have to run, these are busy times."

Everybody's ordering kebab while us poor folk can't even get plain bread. I swore not to set foot in that jinxed apartment again but the birds in my stomach demand to be fed.

I swore not to bathe, sir . . . until you get me a glittery dress . . .

The washbasin said . . . The washbasin said . . .

The washbasin said that hunger breeds despair. Also, tonight is Zuzu's night; at your age a good lunch is essential, Ashmouni. Who knows, maybe I'll manage to hustle them for the price of a tray of 'aysh saraya with nuts and cream, to make tonight the creamiest of nights.

One day at a time, Ashmouni. One day at a time.

The elevator is saturated with cigar smoke. The gentlemen walk in and out with lampposts in their mouths. They should've called it the Tower of Cigars instead of the Tower of Happiness. I thought this cigar thing would do wonders for one's mood, until one day Hani, the plumber, gave me a cheap one. When I tried it, I said these rich guys have surely never experienced honey-mixed tobacco, otherwise each of them would stock a shisha in his Mercedes. But after what Clinton did to Monica, it turns out cigars are pretty essential and have more uses than one would have imagined. God help you, Ashmouni, you're always drawn to politics. Wouldn't it be out of this world if I could sneak Zuzu into this elevator, then make an emergency stop between floors? And what if I had one of those cigars on me; I'd say, 'Shut up woman, this is how the high-class do it.'

The thirteenth has always been an unlucky floor. I'm pretty sure all the catastrophes that happen in towers are on the thirteenth. If I was the minister of housing, I'd pass a law banning any building to go over twelve floors. The apartment door is still ajar. The debris remain untouched. The piano is black and shiny in its tidy corner. Ashtatan Ashtout. Everything in the apartment is the same except it is dimmer. They've stuck cardboard sheets on the windows where the glass was broken. Makes sense; winter is at hand. The aroma of kebab calls out to me from the dining room. The two doctors are just where I left them over two months ago. The kebab packages are on the table in front of them, untouched. They're decent guys after all.

"Where've you been hiding, sergeant? You haven't come by in ages." I have no idea why the psychic doctor treats me with such affection.

"With appetite and health, sergeant. Dig in before it gets cold." The smaller doctor constantly switches from a child's character to that of a middle-aged man and then back again. You're right, let's get some food down before the catastrophes start happening.

"You probably don't know this, sergeant . . . but you remind me of my father—God rest his soul. You're a good man." The psychic seems sincere. He doesn't touch his food. The other man unwraps his and gobbles up a piece of kofta as he scrutinizes me.

A question has been buzzing in my head for some time. I don't want the psychic to think I'm an unbeliever, but he's a learned man, besides, I remind him of his father. Maybe he can lead me down the righteous path. Maybe he can help banish Satan from my sleep.

"Tell me, doctor, does God punish sinners in advance?"

"In advance, sergeant?"

"I mean: would He punish you for a sin before you even commit it? After all, isn't God's knowledge extended in time?"

179

It's the only plausible explanation; God has punished me twenty years before my crime. All the time, the sin was eating up my liver like a bilharzia larva, and I was unaware of its existence. In that case punishment was warranted.

The small man nods and dips half a pita in the container of tahini. The psychic just stares ahead as though allowing his thoughts to take shape or receiving inspiration. Suddenly, he starts talking, slowly and in monotone. "There's a message I'm required to relay to you: the world has its ups and downs, Ashmouni . . . the weak man will one day wake up strong and the powerful go to bed in decline . . . weakness is the weak man's strength . . . and the strong man's strength, his weakness." The psychic has still not touched his kebab. His talk is disturbing. God help me.

"Wouldn't it be best to leave this discussion until after lunch, Abd al-Malak?"

Right you are, weird guy. Anyway, the psychic should have at least answered my question out of politeness, and then what good can come of this kind of talk that makes my joints feel loose when I've had nothing to eat all day?

"Who's this message from, doctor?" My question hits the two of them like fate's revenge. The psychic's face turns red, the other stops chewing. I knew from the beginning I should've kept away from this apartment, from its weird comings and goings.

"Hello. Am I barging in at a bad time?" This is just what we needed. The journalist is in the doorway. She has sneaked in without announcing herself. This place is turning into a public meeting point.

"I'm really sorry. I didn't mean to disturb you while you're having lunch."

"Not at all, Miss. Please join us." The psychic grates his teeth. His weird friend almost chokes on his food.

"Thanks, I'll take a rain check. I just wanted a word with the sergeant . . . it's kind of urgent." This is just like you educated people, you always appear when you're not wanted, but when you're needed, you're nowhere to be found. From the start, I knew this day would turn out bad. In any case, I've lost my appetite.

I guess you have no choice, Ashmouni. The psychic catches up with me and hands me my kebab package. He's a good man.

"There's really no need, doctor . . . if you didn't insist I . . . well, thanks a million. But you haven't answered my question."

"Later, sergeant, we wouldn't want to waste the lady's time."

Maybe it's for the best. I didn't really want to know, anyway. I follow her to the elevator like a prisoner being led to his cell.

✖

"I insist, Miss. One pure morsel can satisfy a hundred people's hunger."

"Merci, sergeant. You go ahead . . . with appetite and health." In her checkered trousers and heel-less shoes, the journalist sits cross-legged on the worn-out grass. What could she possibly want? Probably more questions, but I'm used to that.

"I swear on everything that's holy that you have to join me!" We're poor folk but we know our manners. "I haven't forgotten that your father—God rest his soul—was martyred in the October War."

Would she be too stuck up to join me in a meal?

"I'll have a quick bite so I don't offend you." She spills some tahini into half a pita and stuffs it with a kofta finger and a pickled eggplant. I do the same. Although the kebab is starting to get cold, its taste produces a delicious electric shock in my mouth.

"Like I said, sergeant, this isn't just about getting justice for the late Ahlam." She talks with her mouth full, like a man. How does she expect justice for the dead woman when nobody else gets any justice?

" . . . What's important now is to save the innocent Didi." She wipes a drop of tahini from the corner of her mouth.

"You should talk to her, Miss . . . tell her the truth, open her eyes." The girl is truly innocent. Apparently, she's started to smell the stench behind Shoukry's cologne. But why is the journalist so keen on talking to me about this? What can I possibly do?

"I tried many times, but it's useless. Her head is hard as a rock."

"I'm sure you have your ways, Miss . . . a couple of articles in your newspaper, then everything will be out in the open."

Damn the Lada that has just appeared out of the blue. Heaven help me. I caught a glimpse of the car a few minutes ago, but my tired old mind only recognizes it now. Silent under the tree, ready to pounce. Who knows how long they've been spying on me. What do I do now, where can I escape?

"I've written one but it's not enough. I can't link Shoukry to the crime. I do have some evidence but it's just not enough. Also, the editor is taking his side. If someone could give me a tip on the where-abouts of the security clerk who was on duty the night of the crime . . . with some prompting, he might be willing to tell the truth." She stuffs the remaining part of her sandwich into her mouth. Me, I've lost my appetite.

What does she expect of a mere sergeant who was thrown out of a moving car and did not even have the courage to weep, when the edi-tor, in all his glory, is scared? Anyway, who knows where Abdelaty may be now; is he still alive or have the bastards done him in? She devours my face with her eyes. You on the one hand and the brutes in the Lada on the other: I'm in a worse fix than the kofta I find so hard to swallow. An educated journalist like you should know how things go. What can I possibly do?

"To save the innocent Didi, it takes a solid warrior, a steadfast knight. Right, sergeant?"

That's what we get from you; verses of poetry, truthful but not worth the paper they're written on. War isn't a word you chew like Chiclets. Your father—God rest his soul—should have taught you that. War is a story that will one day be told. In '67, I was freshly drafted when the Jews attacked. The other soldiers took flight so I too, fled. When we stopped to rest in the desert darkness, I started to reproach Sheikh Abdelmohsen. God rest his soul, he was like a father to me. "Would it not have been more honorable to die in our places," I shouted. After all, I was in the prime of youth.

"But what are we defending?" the sheikh said. "Did you believe that this is really our country?"

When the war ended and the ugly face of defeat could no longer be ignored, when people piled abuse on us in the streets and on public transport, I had a chance encounter with Sheikh Abdelmohsen in a café. I repeated the same reproach and the same question. I said, "Maybe if we'd fought we could now raise our heads."

He said, "You're stupid and don't understand a thing . . . Don't you see what those in power are doing to us? How they mistreat us even in their defeat? Did you want them to win the war and be able to get even more abusive?"

"Father—God rest his soul—was martyred at Canada Camp . . . have you heard of it, sergeant?" the journalist asks.

Have I heard of it? I heard, saw, tasted, smelled, bled, puked, lived and died it. Should I tell her about the shell that landed between my feet? Fate willed it not to explode and it has now become my most prized possession. A couple of months ago I met a young man who wanted to immigrate to a country called Canada. I said, you're walking on your own two feet to scorching hell.

"I've heard of it."

If she mentions her father's name maybe I'll remember him, maybe I'll visualize his shredded body.

"Sadat was wrong." Now she's approaching deep waters. Your tongue is your protector, Ashmouni, keep quiet. "He sacrificed men's lives to achieve his political agenda. Since he envisaged negotiations all along, he should have opted for them from the start . . . and let my father live." I wonder if the sons of devils in the Lada are monitoring our conversation with their equipment.

"No Miss, you're the one who's wrong. You have to understand, we really fought in '73 . . . it was serious, nothing to joke about." This is my testimony and it's my duty to tell it.

"What really drives me crazy about the '73 War is that the soldiers never realized the futility of their fight, not because the enemy was invincible, but since their own leadership had decided it only wanted a superficial victory, a partial victory."

"But we really fought in '73 . . . and we won." They convinced us it was all for our country, so we fought. We didn't do it for them but for our own selves, so we could raise our children in peace . . . had we been blessed with children, that is.

Abbas, the one-eyed vendor who sells lupine beans in summer and sweet potatoes in winter, approaches. His handcart puffs smoke like a small locomotive. The smell of kebab has probably attracted him. I should invite him to share my meal, but what if he heard the journalist's crazy talk?

"Listen lady, I don't understand most of what you're saying but I know it's wrong. We fought like men in '73. There was no difference between officers and soldiers, rich and poor, Muslims and Copts . . . if it wasn't for Sadat's decision to go to war, all this wouldn't have happened. The problem is that this spirit did not last after the war."

"The spirit still lives, sergeant. If only each of us would speak up when someone is wronged. If only we'd shout out at the top of our voices . . . that's why I have so much hope in you."

The Lada starts to move slowly. It's the same two men. They stare at me from the other side of the road then the car gets smaller. It reaches the intersection and makes a U-turn toward me. God help me. It comes to a standstill next to the sidewalk. Now the two men are only meters away. What do they want? Damn kebab . . . and damn the man who wants to eat kebab. When people like us start eating kebab all hell breaks loose. We're destined to eat worm-infested beans and felafel fried in motor oil.

"I saw nothing and know nothing . . . you're wasting your time." I raise my voice so they can hear. May God will this ominous day to end in peace. One day at a time.

"Sergeant." His vocal chords are made of steel. I go to him like a lame dog.

"Did you notice anything unusual this past week?" His nose is a perfect replica of Aboulahab's, Abousoffian's, and the noses of all the historic infidels in the sitcoms.

"No, Pasha. Everything is under control." What's the pig talking about?

"Keep your eyes wide open . . . a group of hooligans are going around damaging people's property." He has a convict's haircut.

"Yessir." Thank God it's over. The man's yellow-toothed smile floats in the air after the car has disappeared. He left it behind to terrorize me until his next visit. Old cheese breeds worms. A hair in my ear irritates me. I need to scratch. Control yourself, Ashmouni, no need to look bad in front of the journalist.

"A group of youngsters are going around Maadi with sticks. If a driver runs a traffic light, they break his headlights. If someone litters they beat him up and force him to put his trash in the bin. The latest incident was at a construction site for a building with no provision for a garage. They beat up the watchman and set the cement bags on fire," the one-eyed vendor volunteers to the journalist. Who asked for your opinion, you fool? Take the remaining kebab and get out of my face.

"Interesting . . . tell me more." The journalist stands up and heads toward Abbas.

"I swear I don't know anything." The son of a cowardly woman picks up the kebab package and pushes his handcart away.

"If you remember anything, call me." Having lost hope in the one-eyed man, she turns to me and hands me her card. It feels like fire in my fingers. It could be held against me. I won't even put it in my pocket. I'll throw it away as soon as she goes. The hair in my ear is so damn

185

irritating. Before she crosses the street she turns again. She shakes her head and starts to laugh when she catches me scratching my ear with her card.

※

The aroma of cooking greets me at the door. My mouth waters every other day. The Owl's day is for the stomach, the Coquette's for the heart. I live one day at a time. She's sitting on the straw mat with her legs crossed and a white goose trapped beneath one thigh. She squeezes a bean into the bird's beak then shuts it tight and massages its neck until the bean passes through. Then she fills her mouth with water and spits it into the submissive bird's throat, almost kissing the bird in the process. The Owl is kissing the goose; birds having fun together.

Uncharacteristically, she's wearing a clean cotton gelabia. She's spread a newspaper on her lap to protect her gown from her prisoner's droppings. Behind her, the kerosene burner is on. While still holding the goose, she turns, raises the aluminum pot's cover, and returns it.

"Give me five minutes . . . go wash and dinner will be ready."

She talks without looking at me. Her bare head is like a shriveled olive. Her white hair is braided into two short pigtails on each side of her neck. She'll demand her lawful rights tonight and I'll have no excuse after eating the napalm she's cooking.

The Coquette's door has been left ajar. She's lying on the bed pretending not to care, naked under her pink nightdress. What a wild girl, impervious to the cold. It's almost December, woman. The covers are bundled beneath her bent leg. The contours of her body are waves rolling on the ocean of her desire.

"Hurry up . . . it's spiced oxtail with onions and potatoes cooked in mutton fat and nutmeg. You'll be licking your fingers and your hands too," the Owl calls after me.

The goose tries unsuccessfully to shake free.

"Is that you, Mouny?" Zuzu's voice is sleepy, croaky like a child's. As she says Mouny my heart melts like asphalt on a hot day.

"Yes, I'm home, Mouny's darling." A slip of the tongue, heaven help me.

"Shut up, slut, or you'll regret it . . . and you, Mouny pig, do you want this pot and everything in it on your head?"

The toilet door feels soft from the humidity and rot. The place stinks worse than a sewer; the latrine is overflowing. Still, we should be thankful. Others live fifteen to a room and must share the toilet with the neighbors. The urine fans out then consolidates itself in two divergent streams. What am I going to do about this prostate thing? The doctor's examination; what a terrible experience that was. My manhood, my only wealth, was trampled in the dirt. "Sergeant, your prostate is as big as a sweet potato," the doctor at the municipal clinic joked. In my stupidity I felt proud. I told him my generation grew up eating natural farm butter. He laughed at my ignorance. Abdul the assistant tells me surgery is inevitable, but I turn a deaf ear. I say one day at a time.

The barrel of clean water is filled to the rim. The Owl works like a mule, unlike Zuzu who spends the day lazing in front of the mirror. When will the government have pity on us, provide us with running water, spare our agony rather than spend a fortune on palaces on the North Coast? They call our communities irregular settlements and refuse to spend one red millieme on us. All the city council does is erect giant billboards to hide us from motorists on the highway. I walk out of the toilet in my underwear and head for my gelabia.

"Mouny, can I talk to you please?"

The meal is spread out on the low table. The bread is perfectly risen; Souma must have bought it from the bakery just before I arrived. The arugula and pickled lemon are to die for. Why won't the girl keep quiet and let the night pass in peace? I throw my work clothes on the bed. My thick cotton gelabia is perfect for this cold weather.

"God grant me patience . . . shut up, girl. This is not your day." The Owl's patience is running out. The oxtail, spicy and delicious, melts in my mouth.

"What's the matter . . . all I want is a word with my husband . . . after that, you can enjoy him all night."

"After dinner, Zuzu," I intervene—otherwise the Third World War will break out. I try to secure my peace of mind. The Coquette doesn't reply. Her sobs come in installments. She pretends to be hurt.

"Delicious, Souma . . . you're a gifted cook."

"With appetite and health, sergeant . . . may the meal give you strength," she attempts to flirt. She exposes a leg like a goat's. The Owl has put on the perfume they give away in mosques. It reminds me of Sheikh Abdelmohsen. This is no scent for bed, woman. With this perfume you'd be better off giving the Friday sermon.

"Try this delicious morsel." Before I can catch my breath, she stuffs a piece of oxtail in my mouth.

The Coquette's sobbing breaks my heart. I can't bear the thought that she's upset with me.

"Listen Souma, you're the wise one . . . there might be something urgent she needs to tell me," I mutter as I stand up.

I close the door behind me.

"You old man . . . with a nose like a mug," The Coquette whispers as though talking to herself.

"Forgive me, princess of goodness and beauty . . . I'll even kiss you on the forehead."

"And all I asked for was a word with my heart's sergeant." She exaggerates her sobbing. Damn television that teaches girls these tricks.

"Have a word, a sentence, a whole dictionary, Ashmouni's heart." I lower my voice so the monkey in the hall won't hear.

The sun suddenly shines through her eyes. She exposes her thigh as though unintentionally; it looks like marble and feels like farm cream.

"Where are you taking me on New Year's Eve, Mouny?" Her huskiness ignites my fire. She caresses my chest.

"Stop fooling around, girl . . . the food is getting cold," the Owl shouts. Zuzu must be joking. She called me here just to provoke the Owl.

"Don't I have the right to celebrate like other human beings?" She pushes my hand away from her thigh. Good. I should get back before my dinner gets cold.

"Be reasonable, girl . . . do you want me to wail like a woman?"

"Are you saying I'm not as good as the women who go out to celebrate New Year's Eve?" Damn television.

"Did your mother—God bless her—ever hit the town? Had she even heard of New Year's Eve?" Unintentionally, I raised my voice. Keep it low Ashmouni, or the Owl will hear and make our lives miserable.

"This time it's different. It's the celebration of a thousand years, not just one. When I celebrate, I'll be celebrating for all the women who've never had a moment of fun in the last thousand years. I'll be celebrating for my mother and her mother and her mother's mother." Damn you. Who taught you to talk this way?

"This has gone too far. The silly girl has finished the whole dictionary. Come back to the table, you ungrateful man, before the demons take control of me."

Despite her ear-piercing voice and the poison that pours out of her mouth, the Owl is less threatening than you, depraved girl.

"I never want to hear this kind of talk again, Zuzu. Understood?" I leave her with an enormous scowl on her face.

The Owl's face is contorted. I direct my frustration at the food. The molten mutton fat and the pickles are delicious and the arugula, well women grow it under their beds . . .

Mint tea and a cigarette . . . you know exactly how to satisfy me, Souma. By the prophet, I've wronged you. I blamed you for not bearing a child and took a second wife, a girl young enough to be your daughter, and you endured it. My immoral intention was exposed when I forbade

Zuzu to become pregnant and still you didn't protest. Tenderness is slow burning. How I treasure you, Souma; you've served me all your life and never complained or asked for anything beyond my means. Time and again, I mistreated you and then God always punished me. Yet I never came crawling to ask for your forgiveness. Your breasts used to be like navel oranges, healthy and firm in my palms. Your skin was clear and sweet like honey. You were a woman when I was a real man. But now . . . well, the world has its ups and downs.

The oxtail's fire runs in my veins. The Owl's recipe never fails, more potent that the Viagra the pashas pay an arm and a leg for. Now the Owl is calling to me from her room. She turns on the bed, exposes a lumpy bluish leg. At times just looking at you repels me. I wonder who I'm more disgusted with; you or myself. And the Coquette is like a cup of cream within my reach. God, this is unbearable. Everyone but me eats their meals salted. If I find the food it'll be without salt and if I get the salt I have to lick it off my palm with no food in sight. This isn't just punishment . . . it's the worst form of torture.

And you, Zuzu, lying effervescent in the other room, your thighs so soft and dewy. I close my eyes and I can almost touch you. Yet the pleasure you give me is sinful. Your dowry was the bribe I forked over. Just as they bought me, I bought you. Our marriage cannot possibly be blessed; it is fornication with an official certificate. If you beget a child it'll be a bastard. Yet sin is deliciously irresistible, and pleasure, the seed of guilt. It is written that I must live with one foot in heaven and the other in hell, condemned to be more than one person at the same time.

"Come on man, come to bed. It's almost dawn."

"One last cigarette, then I'll be right there." What a liar. Your packet is empty; not a cigarette left.

I stand up. I tiptoe like a burglar in my own house. The Coquette senses my body heat. She had started to fall asleep. I undress her completely. My hands tremble. Her hand finds its way beneath my gelabia. Her eyes grow wide at my hardness, then she smiles. I can see my life in her eyes. I read in them an understanding of everything. My fornication with you comes at the price of perjury, of keeping quiet about injustice. But I cannot resist my desire. All this you understand and you raise your legs. Me, I'm a wild bull, But, ah . . . the pinch of pain on my naked behind, a normal extension of the stream of pleasure. It is the Owl's cry that draws me out of my trance.

"Men like you only behave when you beat them with a wooden slipper."

At first, I didn't realize what was happening. As though the devil inside me was willing to endure anything just to extend his pleasure.

"You have no respect for God's rules . . . you traitor . . . you infidel."

Zuzu tries to push me away, but in vain. Then surprise returns to her eyes. She regains that instinctive understanding. The Owl is still beating me with her wooden slipper and my body shakes, incapable of reaching climax.

"I've been working my hands to a pulp all day, to prepare you a dinner that would wake up the dead . . . and this is my reward." She leaves sobbing and slapping her chest. I raise my body with difficulty. Shame makes me heavy. The sourness of frustration lingers in my throat. I've lived unfulfilled and that's how I'll die.

Living in holes makes us act like insects.

"Mouny." She stops me before I leave.

"What do you want now?"

"Don't forget about New Year's Eve."

⁙

The Suzuki driver boogies in his seat. With each turn he spills some of his Kamanana rhythm. Kamanana is a destructive weapon he invades the world with. I left Mansour, the electrician, hanging the lights that will embellish the entire façade of the Tower of Happiness. His apprentice too was playing Kamanana. This is turning into a Kamanana day. I asked

Mansour if the lights are put up to celebrate someone's return from the pilgrimage to Mecca. He laughed. He said, "You're ancient, Ashmouni." It turns out the lights are in preparation for Christmas and the New Year. I said to Mansour, "In that case, they're celebrating Ramadan a little early." He said, "Do you think these people even care about Ramadan?"

The Suzuki driver weaves among the traffic. He must have started off as a horse-and-carriage driver. God's will has promoted him to automobiles. Even the mini-truck seems to be in the mood for Kamanana. Reflexively he turns the volume down, then presses the brakes and comes to a standstill in front of the police station.

"A pleasure, sergeant." He darts away.

The police recruit on guard is a small fellow. His shoulder slants under the weight of the automatic rifle. The station's steel gate is unhinged and leans over the fence. Garbage is everywhere.

Reconsider, Ashmouni. This is getting serious and will no doubt turn out badly.

The recruit lets me wait outside the officer's door. I've put my trust in God. I'll wait until he feels like seeing me. Let him take his time. I said to Mansour, "This year's celebrations will probably go on for forty nights since we're turning one thousand years old, like a car's mileage counter when it reaches a hundred thousand then restarts at zero." He said, "Didn't you know that people are arguing over whether the new century starts in 2000 or 2001?" I said, "These guys really have nothing better to worry about."

The officer's door leads to my grave. Reconsider, Ashmouni; you're committing suicide. There's still a chance to turn back. You haven't even said goodbye to your women. What will they do when you don't come back home in the evening? Will they rush out in their nightgowns looking for you on the streets? And what will happen to them when they discover you're not coming back? No need to worry about the Coquette; she's still in her prime. She'll sell herself to others like she sold herself to you. But Souma . . . she'll roam the streets and squares cursing the day she set eyes on your face. She'll shout, "He ate my flesh and threw away my bones." She'll say, "After I gave him my best years, the madwoman's son chooses to go to prison." She'll say, "I wish a train had run him over. At least it would've been fate's will."

My joints ache. The recruit has shut the door. I'm alone with the officer. I support myself on the back of a chair. He's talking over the phone and doesn't notice me. He softens his voice like a teenage girl. He must be talking to someone important; his mouth delivers words of honey. In a matter of seconds it'll turn back into the sewer he opens when addressing common folk.

He puts down the receiver and looks through his papers. Maybe he hasn't noticed me. Maybe he wouldn't notice if I quietly slipped away. And even if he did, I could make up an excuse. The important thing is to leave this place in one piece.

"Yes?" he mutters while reading. Damn your voice, it gives me diarrhea. Did he really speak or was I imagining it? Even if he did speak, it's not certain he was speaking to me. Maybe he talks to himself, like I do all the time. I'm not even sure he's aware of my presence.

"Speak up, man." He doesn't raise his eyes off his papers. I'm a son of a bitch not worthy of one second of his time. This is your last chance, Ashmouni. Say, "Happy New Year, Pasha," and limp away like a pathetic dog. What's wrong with being a dog if it means surviving?

"I have come to confess, Pasha." No, I'm not a dog. I'm a solid warrior, a steadfast knight. I'm the one who crossed the canal in '73, when this officer was only a child soiling his pants. After all, weakness is the weak man's strength . . . and the strong man's strength, his weakness. Have you forgotten?

I wonder how this officer will celebrate the new century. Will he dance the night away or prostrate himself before God or spend the evening with his children watching TV? I can't imagine him doing any of that. Maybe he's one of us common folk, with never a thought about celebration. For us, the century has neither beginning nor end. A lifetime is just one year;

it begins when you're born and ends on your deathbed. When they start to celebrate a new year, we're being carried into the grave.

He raises his head for the first time. There's laziness in his eyes.

"I saw the late Ahlam Shawarby enter the tower on the night she died."

He says nothing but grates his teeth. His round face is wrinkled in disgust. These are ruthless people. Why did you get yourself into this mess, Ashmouni? You can't face up to these people. Do you want to spend the rest of your days behind bars for the sake of justice?

What justice, you loser?

And if you did manage to get away from the government, where would you hide from Shaker Pasha and the men in the Lada?

"She came in with Mr. Shoukry. They went up to visit the foreign Señora."

He taps his fingers on the desk. Disgust is written all over his face. He doesn't look me in the eye. Now, he'll remind me of the question he asked me again and again during the inquiry. He'll condemn me for denying I knew anything about anything. He'll accuse me of perjury.

"I've received many reports about you, Ashmouni . . ."

"They bribed me to keep quiet. I accepted five thousand pounds, and another five hundred two months ago."

Your reports are true, Pasha. I've witnessed wrongdoing with my own two eyes and helped to cover it up, and not only in this case but in everything else. I see a thousand injustices every day of my life, and I help to cover it all up. Turn off the lights, woman . . . we're the burglar policemen.

So you confessed. Happy now?

"I have specific information that you're imagining things . . . to cut a long story short, you're starting to lose your mind." The officer seems distracted, as though he's been daydreaming and hasn't quite understood what I'm saying.

"Mr. Shaker is the one who paid me."

Mr. Shaker and friends. You've accepted everyone's money. You even used bribe money to get married; a fornicating marriage really, a

194

Kamanana marriage. And now she wants to celebrate New Year's Eve. Who knows, maybe the guards will call you Mouny in the penitentiary.

"Get back to your intersection . . . you've caused enough trouble." The phone rings. He picks up the receiver. Surely he didn't get what I said.

"But Pasha, I . . . ." I interrupt his telephone conversation. He goes wild, throws the receiver on the desk.

"I said get out . . . I don't want to see your face here again. Understand?"

What does he expect me to do? Walk the streets shouting, 'I'm guilty,' or to start making preparations for a New Year's party? But even if I had all the money in the world, would I know how to celebrate? I, who never understood what they were celebrating to start with?

"You're a good man, but you need a rest," the officer says softly, then picks up the receiver.

The Eighth Page

Would that you could live on the fragrance of the earth, and like
an air plant be sustained by the light.
But since you must kill to eat, and rob the young of its mother's
milk to quench your thirst, let it then be an act of worship,
When you kill a beast say to him in your heart,
"By the same power that slays you, I too am slain.
Your blood and my blood is naught but the sap that feeds the tree
of heaven."

Gibran Khalil Gibran

Abd al-Malak

The telephone is a silent devil that I circle around but dare not touch. Her number is a hymn to love I repeat in my secret of secrets. I extend my hand then withdraw it, fire-struck. Farah, my heart's Farah, my soul's Farah. She said: "Don't call me, I beg you. Sometimes there are co-workers around and I fear a scandal." She said she'd call as soon as she could. I promised to be patient. I've suffered in silence but she hasn't kept her side of the bargain.

The ring tone cuts through the silence. She hasn't forgotten me after all, and I unjustly accused her. She'll say she's sorry she took so long to call. She'll make excuses and I'll forgive her. I'll melt in her voice.

I pick up the receiver. Slowly, the way I used to unwrap a chocolate's silver wrapping in the old days, so as not to tear the fortune strip. My fascination with reading my fortune was even greater than my love for the chocolate. The nuts had often gone stale, yet how delicious that chocolate tasted. I wonder what the telephone lines hold in store for me today, this communications network that controls every aspect of people's lives. We're all captives in a spider web of technology. With small, nervous movements we delude ourselves into thinking we're free. We kill time and wait for the false promise of happiness to materialize. Happiness and technology, the technology of happiness. Happiness: that great lie of the twentieth century.

It is Mr. Abd al-Tawab on the other end. I speak in an exaggerated military tone, like the minor functionary who stands up in respect when he receives a call from the department head. I used to make fun of those who kiss ass but I'm no better. We make fun of ourselves so we can bear the humiliation.

"Sleep, doctor, has become more valuable to me than all the world's money." His voice is worn out, beyond the cracked exhaustion of the day we met inside the Cadillac. Now he's fed up, as though he's suffered to the point of giving up on life. "You've spent the last four months summoning ghosts and I still can't get a wink of sleep." He doesn't give me a chance to reply.

But it's all of your own making. Why don't you ask yourself how you made your millions, how much bread you snatched from people's mouths to double your fortune? Haven't you understood that sooner or later God's justice must prevail?

"It'll be any time now, Mr. Abd al-Tawab. Put your mind at ease, I've already established the cause." Congratulations, Abd al-Malak. Now you talk like a professional psychic.

"You say 'any time now,' but I'm starting to lose my mind."

"The masters have revealed to me that the cause of all your problems is a big business deal that will only bring you bad luck." What a great idea, Abd al-Malak. This man's whole life is made up of one big business deal after another. He must have a bad feeling about one of them. His silence exposes the telephone line's hum. He's turning my words over in his head.

"But why would this particular deal bring bad luck?"

A barefoot Cerebellum comes out of the kitchen. A book protrudes from his pajama pocket. He holds a glass of tea in each hand. His spectacles are loosely hinged on his big ears. He has aged dramatically these past few days. His imprisonment in this place is arsenic eating away at his body. He's prepared tea for me too, thoughtful.

"Listen, doctor, I hired you to solve my problem, not to accuse me or give me sermons." The millionaire replies to his own question without giving me the chance to say a word. Who said I accused you of

200

anything? The man is getting extremely irritated; the result of insomnia or people's hatred?

"Excuse me, sir . . . ."

"Well, many people have been done in by foul play . . . still, their spirits must rest in peace. Understood? The spirits must rest in peace." His words are a scimitar raised against my neck, as though every word I said carries some terrible accusation against him. "I want a quick and effective solution or else I may lose patience, and no good can come of that . . . and keep in mind that this country offers opportunities a million times better than those in America."

But what could he possibly mean? Is he promising me a great reward if I achieve what he wants? But foul play . . . people have been done in by foul play? The spirits must rest in peace? He's no doubt aware I'm starting to make money off this scam. Could he be threatening to fire me, or even worse: foul play?

"Who was that?" The Cerebellum asks drowsily. Maybe he heard the dial tone come back while I was still holding the receiver. He speaks without interest, probably just to break the silence.

"Mr. Abd al-Tawab."

"What did Tutu want?" He opens his book and passes his thumb down one page, then another, then turns the page. At first, I could hardly believe the speed with which he reads. In this way, he finishes at least one book every day.

"Tell me, Cerebellum, why did Mr. Abd al-Tawab choose me?"

"Don't waste your time, you'll never understand Tutu's motives. He's always had a dark side to him, special powers I mean . . . he's established a special connection with the other side, as you would say. But since he asked for you in particular, then he must see something in you . . . something even you may be unaware of." He shoos a fly away from his tea. "But you didn't say what Tutu wanted."

"To tell me that the opportunities in this country are a million times better than those in America."

I don't know which of the two of you is crazier.

He bursts out laughing, slightly hysterical. He bangs the dining room table. Had it not been for his small size, I would have worried his violent rocking could break the chair.

"That explains why two geniuses like you and I are buried in this hellhole," I say.

Well, at least I have my excuse; I'm here to make a living. But you . . . your story is hard to believe. I turn it around in my head for the thousandth time and I'm still not convinced. The truth lies hidden in the Cerebellum's belly. I bared my soul but he only offered a few sentences, incoherent and largely unintelligible. He goes back to his book. The title, *Black Magic in the Era of Globalization,* is printed in blood-dripping letters on the white cover.

"What's this you're reading . . . are you planning to compete with me?" I laugh . . . out of confusion, really.

He smiles and looks at me like a sickly child. The words form on his lips but no sound materializes. We sit solemnly on our opposite sides of the dining table, like we were on the board of the International Monetary Fund—the International Misery Fund as people call it. He looks behind him then whispers, "I get more and more puzzled every time I try to make sense of the course of my life. I've reached the point where I'm starting to doubt that people have any free will at all. As though there's a blueprint, carefully laid out for each of us, which we cannot deviate from . . . except we're not allowed to see it until it has come to pass." He seems agitated.

You're right, Cerebellum.

"Who would've thought I'd end up being a psychic?"

"Or that I'd end up a fugitive from Mossad and the CIA?" he mutters from beneath his gigantic glasses. "You were keen to hear my story . . . now you know it." He takes his first sip of tea. He prefers it lukewarm. I've almost finished mine. He goes back to his book as though we were in the middle of a perfectly mundane conversation.

There is loud knocking at the apartment door, always left ajar. All this time, neither of us has gathered the courage to close it. The

Cerebellum shrinks in his seat. His face is sickly pale. It is the voice of the newspaper vendor. He breathes in relief, then heads for the door. They have an agreement: the newspaper boy brings him a big stack of books and magazines every day. I have no idea how he can afford all this. He claims to have worked for the Iraqi nuclear program and that he escaped when it was dismantled. He says he's terrified of the revenge of Mossad and the CIA. Maybe he's joking, or the superstitious nonsense he's reading has affected his judgment. But he could be right; these days reality has become stranger than fiction. Who knows the truth about anything?

Things are never what they seem.

His legs are unsteady under the weight of the pile of books he's carrying. Strange, since the newspaper boy regularly carries twice as much with no problem. He releases the books on the dining room table. That's odd; he usually takes very good care of his books. He leans on the table for support.

"What's the matter?" I catch him just before he collapses, and help him into a chair. I pass his tea glass. He takes a sip, allows the liquid to remain inside his mouth for a second before swallowing.

"The newspaper boy . . ." He takes a deep breath. His face is pale. "I had asked him to tell me if he noticed anything unusual."

I stand next to him. I don't trust his ability to remain upright on the chair.

"He says two men in a Lada have been observing the tower for the past two weeks."

"Get a grip, Cerebellum . . . snap out of it! Do you really believe the CIA and Mossad have nothing better to do than look for you?"

His eyes flare up. He pushes my hand away. "Why can't you understand . . .? Since they dismantled the Iraqi program, they haven't figured out what to do about the scientists . . . they must eliminate them, otherwise someone else can use them to restart their nuclear program."

"You'll have a nervous breakdown locking yourself up in a haunted apartment. You're getting paranoid, Cerebellum. You need to get out of this place . . . walk around the streets, breathe fresh air, meet people."

"They're tracking down the scientists. One by one, they're dying in unexplained accidents. As you know, anything that threatens Israel is taken very seriously."

"Screw Mossad and the CIA. It's up to you to decide what you're going to do with your life. What's the use of being alive if you're going to be locked up in this rat hole like a convict serving a life sentence?" I talk to him, but in reality I'm speaking to myself.

How long can I go on lying and cheating? What's your excuse, Abd al-Malak . . . survival? To make enough money to get established and marry the woman you love? But what's the use of survival if it comes at the cost of giving in to corruption? What's the value of love when a man must lose his self-respect?

What seekest thou, my son? A question asked by an old man in a school textbook, ingrained in my mind since childhood. The old man repeats the question. The son gives a string of wrong answers. First he says wealth, and the father explains that money cannot cure disease. Then he says social status, and the father explains that success is short-lived. Finally, the old man reveals the correct answer. He defines the objective the young man must aspire to for the rest of his life. Funny, but the answer has evaporated from my mind and only the question remains, nagging day after day. What seekest thou, my son?

"One day, during my college days in the seventies . . . I was running late for a lecture when I heard a call for help. I turned around and saw a plainclothes policeman grab a student and try to pull him outside the university gate, no more than twenty meters away," the Cerebellum says as, again, he pushes my hand away. He stands up, takes a few wobbly steps, and points to the corner of the hall where the piano is located, as though he can see there something I cannot see.

"The student resisted . . . I knew him to be a leftist radical. The cop was on his own, surrounded by all the students. He hesitated for a moment. I could see fear in his eyes; if the students got involved, the police car waiting outside the gate would not be able to save him. Only three or four students gathered but even they stayed a few paces away . . ." He hugs himself, fidgets, tries to stay upright. Then he waves his arms in the air, struggling with an invisible opponent.

"Most of the students went on with their business as if nothing was happening. The cop recovered his courage and with redoubled violence managed to drag the student back to the police car . . . I'll never forget the look in the young man's eyes when he discovered that the time for slogans had passed and the moment of truth was upon him. In a moment of truth, everyone saves their own skin."

I'm sick and tired of your childish old man's voice, Cerebellum. Why tell this story now? What use are memories and acquired wisdom? You faced a cop and lost your nerve, so what? Who hasn't bowed to authority? Who do you think you are to talk like that?

I can no longer bear the Cerebellum, his wasted genius and sick fears, his secular talk, his smell that in the past few days has turned foul as a grave. I can no longer bear this apartment where devils and enraged spirits have played their ugly game, the child who speaks in voices from the underworld, or the traffic sergeant who carries a terrible secret. I can no longer bear to pretend I'm just another professional living in just another apartment. I can no longer . . . my relationship with Farah, my desire's obstructed flow, this deprivation that's driving me crazy. I can no longer bear to wait for a phone call that never comes. I'm sick and tired of all this.

My clothes are in the bedroom. I leave the Cerebellum trying to stand upright, wrestling with the spirits, and make my way through the wreckage for the last time. The two white doves flutter inside the hall; they've come in through the window we left open for them. I tell the customers these are pure spirits who bring benediction in the flapping of their wings. They believe me and dig into their deep pockets. Even the Cerebellum has come to believe. Will this assumption on my part turn out to be truthful or just another superstition? Who knows?

"You're leaving me . . . where are you going?" His steps are heavy behind me. His weak body is burdened with anxiety. He realizes I'm making a vital move. He stops in the middle of the hall. I turn around to make sure he won't drop in a heap. Good, he's holding up. He stares out of the gap through which the doves have just left, at the clear sky. Then he focuses on the two birds circling in space.

"What about me, why should I accept this?" he mutters to himself.

"Put on some clothes and come with me right now." I shouldn't leave him alone in this place.

"The piano has returned whole again, without a scratch." He always says irrational things, but today he's going too far. "The white doves are calling out to me."

"Stop, you madman . . . what are you doing?" He opens the balcony door and rushes to the railing.

"Calm down, Cerebellum . . . are you going to commit the eternal sin?" I catch him in the nick of time and drag him inside. At first he resists, then completely surrenders, distracted. The wailing of women suddenly attacks my ears. The sound has been there in the background, but I only recognize it now. He must have heard it first. I release him. He looks around in bewilderment, then clings to my arm. Insanity has made his face serene.

At last, he speaks in his normal voice, the one I haven't heard for days. "What's this . . . are the women wailing over me already . . . am I still alive or have I embarked on the ultimate journey?"

⁙

"God forgive you, Abd al-Malak. The day you finally convince me to leave the apartment, you bring me to a funeral," he chuckles.

I've never seen the Cerebellum in such a state of jubilation. He entered the funerary tent like he was approaching a wedding. My heart fell as he pressed Mr. Hafez's hand, then proceeded to mutter his condolences to the rest of the bereaved family. I could see the waves of laughter gather at the corners of his mouth and feared he'd succumb to the euphoria that erupted when his confinement came to an end.

The Cerebellum's transformation is unexpected; his decision to confront death seems to have been profoundly liberating. Maybe he'd never tasted freedom before and started to value life only when he thought death had, at last, caught up with him. Then he decided to come to the funeral. The death of others seems to have reminded him how delicious it feels to be alive.

We both face the mokrea, the chanter of the Koran, who sits in the manner of an ancient Egyptian scribe on an elevated gilt sofa. His voice is pure. Ever since I moved to the Tower of Happiness, I haven't listened to Koranic recitation. I refuse to use the Koran in my con act; it's essential to keep at least a part of my soul truthful and pure. Ah . . . how beautiful are God's words! I didn't realize how much I missed this tranquility, this serene light that makes no distinction between rich and poor, cherishes genius and dimwit alike.

The Cerebellum has succeeded in liberating himself, but I wasn't strong enough. I had intended to leave the haunted apartment for good yet I couldn't muster the courage. It's because I only need a few more months. One way or another, I must endure. Then I'll have enough money from my business to marry. Please forgive me, God. A few more months then I'll make the pilgrimage and turn a new page.

The Cerebellum won't leave me alone. I'll keep on ignoring you no matter how hard you dig your elbow into my side. If you have little or no respect for death, at least listen to God's words. The genius has been transformed into a teenager and is acting like one.

God rest your soul, Mrs. Hafez, you were my favorite customer, a first-class dupe. You were so scared for your husband's health that you'd panic and rush to doctors and astrologers whenever he had a nightmare. Mr. Hafez made fun of you but put up with your silliness, and now he's receiving condolences for your loss.

A mobile phone rings. Half the people present dig into their pockets. The ringing goes on. The mokrea looks tense. He has every right; people should show some respect. Is it so hard to turn off their phones before entering a funerary tent? The mobile phone is an electronic fly that won't stop buzzing.

Everyone stares at the worn-out carpet. A funerary tent is an exhibition of shoes; expensive and cheap, shiny and muddy—like the Cerebellum's, which have never tasted shoe polish. Mine are well polished. Shiny shoes are the sign of social standing. Dr. Victor was the only man in our village whose shoes were always shiny. I spent my childhood dreaming that one day I'd wear such shoes. During university I used to wear sneakers, even in America sneakers ruled. I only started to look classy when I became a con man. Glitter covers the rot.

The telephone is still ringing. The caller must be a real pain in the neck. I'd love to find out who this phone belongs to. I make circles with my shoe on the carpet, a shiny shoe on a worn-out carpet, navy blue, concentric circles . . . .

Circles with my muddied shoe with the big hole in its sole. The shock of the cold tiles tickles my cracked child's foot. The classroom floor is dusty. The Arabic teacher is a sheikh with a lightning-fast bamboo stick. Now, what was his name, Abd al-Malak? It was first grade and he was a vicious, impatient man. "Shut up. I don't want to hear your voice." When I could no longer hold it, I moved my shoe in circles over the wet tiles. The warm urine gushes inside my shoe. Circles and circles. Maybe the puddle will disappear, maybe the tiles will absorb it. The students' laughter whistles in my ears. An insistent, untiring whistle. Time will never absorb the nag of embarrassment. Its relentless ring shows no mercy.

"The pond is in a state of eternal silence," the Cerebellum whispers in my ear. But how did he find out? He smiles, a smile that comes from far away. Might I have spoken out loud without noticing it, or in any other way exposed my thoughts?

"Suddenly, a frog jumps in . . . plop." He makes a plopping sound with his mouth. He moves his hands in the air depicting the pond's widening circles. You've totally lost your mind, Cerebellum. But at least his rambling has nothing to do with my childhood.

"What do you mean?" Anything to distract me, to liberate me from the ringing.

"It means he who has tasted knows." I've never seen his face this brilliant. Despite his short stature, he peers at me from above as though rather than being seated he's floating in the air, like an Indian fakir or a Native American shaman.

The mokrea stutters and stops midway through a verse. He swallows, clears his throat, then starts from the beginning. His hand creeps into the folds of his kaftan and produces the culprit. Son of a gun, it's been your phone all along. He presses a button and the ringing stops.

"Hello . . . hello." The caller's voice is a mosquito in my ear. Or am I just imagining it? *Hello . . . hello . . . we're all here,* Laila Mourad's old song. He rests the phone on the sofa next to him. Rather abruptly, he ends the Koranic chant and raises the phone.

"Asalamu alaikum," he says.

The mourners start to queue.

"Shouldn't we get going?" the Cerebellum says.

"Let's wait for another round of Koran . . . this is a blessed place."

Mr. Hafez is an important man, he'll appreciate our staying longer and in any case, it costs us nothing. I hope I manage to attract him. It's imperative that he takes his late wife's place in my séances. Will I muster the courage to raise the matter tonight?

"At least we can speak freely now that the Koran has stopped."

We've been speaking freely all day. What do you have to say that's so pressing, Cerebellum?

"There's been talk about the currency crisis . . ." I say to distract him from his hallucinations. Well done, Abd al-Malak. Nowadays you have bank accounts and can worry about the currency crisis.

"Ugliness, no matter how extreme, holds beauty in its soul . . . and danger comes hand in hand with security."

He's not interested in talking about currency, but what is the madman talking about? The mokrea resumes his Koranic recitation and saves me from the Cerebellum's nonsense. I wave away a waiter with a tray of bitter coffee and glasses of water. Mr. Hafez ushers a man in a navy-blue suit to the VIP seats, then returns to the entrance. It must be the government's representative. The Cerebellum pokes me in the rib. I ignore him. Here's an important man whose sole function in life is to offer condolences to people he doesn't know. Imagine that. Perhaps he does weddings too, or if they have it all organized at the protocol department, some people specialize in weddings, others in funerals. The important man is surrounded by empty armchairs. Curious stares bounce off him from every direction.

The mokrea concludes his second quarter with no interruptions from his cell-phone. The Cerebellum stands up without waiting for my signal. We queue to pay our condolences. No one ever notices the tent material's genuine artistry and beautiful balance of colors because they're always covered in the dust of death. The government representative is the first to leave; he has other funerals to tend to. I wonder if I might raise the subject with Mr. Hafez. I press his hand. His eyes are unfocused. I lean closer. He becomes alert. I've caught him by surprise.

"The Missus. would like you to know she's in a place flooded in light and happiness."

There, I've done it!

The Cerebellum pushes me onward. The December wind splashes against my red-hot face. The street's freedom is a delight after the funeral's claustrophobia. The InterContinental Hotel is flooded with light, bubbling with merrymaking. The Nile Corniche is something else in winter. How beautiful Cairo can be after the daytime hubbub has dissipated. The Cerebellum goes on talking nonsense.

I don't understand a word he's saying. What use is talk anyway?

✖

"Is this the piano?" She points at it like a Japanese tourist or an inquisitive child. Mrs. Shaker's fleshy arm is covered up to the elbow in gold bracelets. She wears them over a tight-fitting black sweater whose soft cashmere exposes her gelatinous parts.

"It is the very one, Madame . . . as for the rose, it's out there on the balcony." What's this Abd al-Malak, have you converted from a psychic to a tour guide?

"We have plenty of roses in the garden. I'm interested in the piano everyone is talking about." Maybe we should've posted a sign saying, 'House of Ghosts,' and collected an entry fee.

"Do you expect me to believe this is the same piano that fell from the thirteenth floor and smashed Shaker's car to pieces?" Even this idiot doesn't believe the story. Maybe the whole thing is a hoax. Who knows?

"I'd like to see the rose, if you permit. Doctor." Shaker Shaker's tone is decisive. The wheeze in his throat betrays a lifelong love affair with hashish. He pulls me by the arm to the balcony, a wicked wizard making his way across a wasteland. His wife wants to come along, but he turns to her. "Better stay where you are, Nafitha. I don't want you to trip over anything." The way he pronounces his wife's name is unusual, yet familiar. Some actor used to pronounce the same name that way in a soap opera, a long time ago.

The rose is vibrant, virgin-white. Just looking at her brings joy to my heart. Although I never water her, every morning I greet her like an old friend. Were I not intimately acquainted with her velvety touch, I would have thought someone brought in a new rose every night. Mr. Shaker doesn't show the slightest interest in the rose. He produces a roll of hundred-dollar notes. With a money-changer's fingers, he counts a sum and quickly withdraws it from the roll. He stuffs the money in my pocket then looks me in the eye. He has two dark valleys beneath his eyes, like an owl weighing heavily on my chest in a nightmare.

"Is this enough?" He blows his cigar smoke in my face.

"Pay whatever you like, Pasha . . . it all goes to charity." A perfect reply, Abd al-Malak.

"So long as you keep away from NGOs . . . even talking about them these days can land you in jail." He laughs like a coffeehouse owner.

211

His face suddenly turns serious. "All I ask of you is a small favor . . . two, actually. First, I want you to convince the Missus never to set foot in this building again. Say some tragedy will befall us. Second, I need to sleep . . . I can't get a wink these days, doctor . . . not a wink." His expression is somber.

What is it with millionaires and insomnia these days? If you listened to your conscience just a little you'd sleep like a baby. In the old days, men went to astrologers for help with sexual performance. Nowadays, all they seem to want is to sleep. Damn Viagra.

"Kiss the money, Hajj . . . so you'll be compensated a hundredfold." I give him back the money. He accepts. He kisses the notes and presses them against his forehead thee times then gives them back to me.

"As for the missus, consider it done. But the sleep issue is a little more complicated."

His fangs are a repulsive yellow-brown, like a rabid dog's. How fate mocks Adam's progeny and their vanity. Abd al-Malak, son of Tafida, has become the healer of sleep disorders. How I wish you were here, Mother, to see with your own eyes how far I've come. You, who used to tie me by the ankle to the goat before I went to bed so I wouldn't get far if I walked in my sleep. You were terrified I'd fall into the waterwheel's well. Your ploy didn't work; one day I woke up in the alfalfa field with the goat munching happily next to me. I have no idea which of us led the other to the field. Even today, I sometimes walk in my sleep. The masters call out to me, as the old folk used to say. Even in your sleep, you search. What seekest thou, my son?

But why is the man so keen on keeping his wife away from the tower? Didn't she say the piano fell on top of his car? What was it doing here to start with? Why, of course . . . it must be Lula Hamdi, the man must be having an affair with the belly dancer; that's why he doesn't want his wife around. Perhaps Farah knows the truth; women sniff these things in the air. I'll ask her tomorrow when she comes back from Alexandria. A business trip, she said. Her boss sent her. She had no choice, really.

That's okay, it's only work. I hope she calls when she has a free moment, just to say hello. In any case, Farah's a strong woman. No need to worry about her. It's only a matter of time, my love. We'll soon set up our business together, then you won't need to work for anyone.

"How much will the sleep problem cost me?" Due to his bent back, he looks up at me with the insolence of a sickly vulture.

"Please don't misunderstand me, Mr. Shaker. All the good work I do is for the love of God . . . I only meant you may have to visit us a few times before—God willing—the symptoms are completely cured. By the way, that's the rose you wanted to see, over there."

"Pretty. Now let's get on with the ghost business." He turns.

The Cerebellum and Mrs. Shaker are already at the table. The little genius is telling her about the piano's ability to maintain a brilliant surface even though no one ever dusts it. She pulls her sweater collar and spits superstitiously into her bosom. Hello millionaires.

"All businessmen in Egypt are facades for foreign interests." Damn you Cerebellum, you haven't even been introduced to the man yet. I wink to the madman to be more diplomatic. I should really start the séance before this idiot poisons the air . . . but Mr. Hafez is late. He'll be upset if we start without him, and he may turn out to be very useful some day.

"Empty slogans . . . look at all the factories and other successful projects coming up everywhere . . . and in any case what difference does it make if the ownership is Egyptian or foreign?" The millionaire calmly relights his cigar. He isn't being defensive about the Cerebellum's comments.

"Capitalism will never resolve Egypt's problems . . . from the moment Mena unified the two States, Egypt's riches have been owned by one-half percent of the population and everybody else is their slave." I start to wave to the Cerebellum to stop. Has he lost his mind?

"I can see you're a pessimist, doctor. Don't forget that for the first time in history, we're starting to settle beyond the Nile Valley; for the first time we are liberating ourselves from geography. Why then not liberate ourselves from history too?" Wow. I never imagined Mr. Shaker could muster such eloquence.

"Actually, what we've seen so far points to the opposite. The new business barons are even worse than the old feudal landlords because they lack all sense of belonging. With all due respect to your good self, of course, this country needs a new revolution . . . to clean up all this mess and liberate the people."

"This kind of talk is inappropriate, Cerebellum . . . and you shouldn't forget we're gathered here for a noble cause . . . we don't want to offend the masters." I'm forced to intervene before the Cerebellum messes everything up.

"Just consider for a moment the possibility that the business barons you referred to may be the very ones who'll lead the new revolution, that they may succeed where others have failed. Who else can challenge the absolute power of the State? Historians have depicted authoritarianism as emanating from the pharaohs, then the revolution occurred and they painted the feudal landlords as the culprits. Both points of view are naive and simplistic.

"Authoritarianism was, and still is, the rule of bureaucrats, soldiers, and the clergy. The authoritarianism of the pharaohs is nothing compared to being controlled by these types . . . and the problem is: no revolution can ever get rid of them. Today, the business barons have actually succeeded in limiting the cancerous growth of government bureaucracy. For the first time in Egypt's history, we have created an alternative to the State. You must understand, doctor, that only free markets can achieve prosperity for Egypt, something that was never accomplished by socialism and its coalition of the working classes."

Wow, Mr. Shaker. It turns out you're a full-fledged philosopher. Who said today's millionaires are ignorant? The Cerebellum is starting a coughing fit. The pasha's cigar smoke has saturated the air. Mr. Hafez's white head appears in the doorway. Thank God he's here. Let's get on with it before the Cerebellum begins his rebuttal.

"Welcome. Good to see you, Mr. Hafez."

The man takes a few hesitant steps. He walks with a slight limp. His eyes are weary, yet they glitter in anticipation. He never realized how much he loved her until she disappeared from his world. Now, he needs to get in contact with her at any price. He knows his need has turned him into easy prey; he's ashamed of his weakness. This business teaches one to peer into people's souls. I never realized it was so easy. Why then doesn't everybody do it? Why doesn't everyone try to understand other people's needs? No, they choose to blind themselves. Each of us wraps himself in his own ego until he can perceive nothing else in the world.

Mr. Shaker's golden tooth glitters as he warmly welcomes Mr. Hafez. I quickly turn off the lights and put on the lighting system before the Cerebellum can resume his nonsense. The tape recorder is next to my foot under the table. All the equipment is ready. Only Soad is missing. Today's séance is important. The usual quackery will not suffice; real ghosts will be indispensable. It's all in Soad's hands now. I only hope the Cerebellum gets back to his senses and doesn't mess everything up.

⁙

The hall resounds with the flapping of wings. The two doves circle over the wreckage, searching. What seekest thou, my son? An explosion of sound and motion, a white pulsating energy, blind resolve. They cross over into the dining room. For the first time, they've penetrated deep into the apartment. They flutter over our heads. Pure spirits, I must announce. I'll pretend they're part of the routine, a new act for my customers' entertainment. But my voice is mute. A sudden nausea. The customers look around in disbelief. Wings beat the air.

Dizziness.

Pure spirits, I have to say. But are they really spirits? Are they truly pure? What does all this have to do with him? A whirlwind of feathers and small red eyes. A whirlwind of destruction. What does all this mean? A whirlwind. How is it that I find myself at its epicenter? Am I destined to get out of here in one piece? Will I survive in any shape?

What seekest thou, my son?

Nausea.

They observe us from above. What do I look like in the eyes of a dove? The ruins are everywhere; in the apartment, in the streets, inside people. Shards of souls torn apart. Words we say, acts we conceal. But the truth shouts at us from every corner. All the lies we fool ourselves with, the idols we create then worship. Cruelty. Cruelty. Cruelty. Injustice and suffering. Oppression. Oppressor and oppressed: you are all guilty and the worst of you knows who he is.

A moment to catch my breath.

The doves have taken off to the hall and from there, to space, to the endless heavens. What is your message to us? I don't understand. What does all this mean? Chatter reclaims the room. The Cerebellum argues. Shaker lectures as though addressing a large audience. Flabby Nafitha tinkles her bracelets. But all they're saying doesn't reach me. The circles surround me. The doves' circles of flight. The circles of neglected truth. Ghost circles. The circles of my shame.

Call it a game, a big lie, a great illusion. Say what you wish, what's essential is never to stop for a moment to think. Don't give yourself one second to wonder. If you object you're finished. If you ask the question you're lost. If you stop to take your breath, you'll be trampled by the herd.

"Pure spirits." They all stare at me.

"Pure spirits," I repeat in the voice of a scared toad.

⁙

"What a corrupt government." Damn. The Cerebellum has completely lost his marbles. He used to be scared of his own shadow, now he's more brazen than the whores of Pyramid Street. He seems to think he's a member of the British House of Commons. He throws his accusations at Mr. Hafez as though the man was the prime minister. He should at least respect that the man is in mourning.

"Did you just say the government is corrupt?" Mr. Hafez stares the Cerebellum in the eye. The shoulders of his navy blue coat are specked with dandruff. "You think the government possesses a magic wand that'll solve all problems?"

Why did you have to answer the Cerebellum, man? Just ignore him.

"It is the government's responsibility to introduce reforms. Leadership is everything." The Cerebellum is a feisty gnome; nothing seems to scare him anymore.

"You know why you refuse to give up on the dream of the enlightened despot? Because you're lazy. Things are bad because the government is corrupt. Okay, so how do we reform the government? When the enlightened despot appears he'll know what to do. Until then you're all sitting on your butts . . . and feel no need to think or do anything." Mr. Hafez's oratorical style is overdone as though he's preparing himself for membership in parliament, or — who knows? — the cabinet.

"If you want to lose all hope, you need look no further than our educational system. Now who's responsible for education, isn't that the government?" The Cerebellum waves his skinny arms in the air.

"If we would only go back to religion we'd find solutions to all these problems. . . ." Everyone turns to me as though I pronounced the worst of heresies.

"Actually, religion could have compensated for the political establishment's neglect of the people, but unfortunately, the religious establishment chose to transform religion into a series of empty rites. You cannot say hello over the telephone, you should never celebrate your children's birthdays . . . because these are foreign customs. So the religious establishment has failed to fulfill its primary function of shaping the Egyptian individual," the Cerebellum answers me in his quiet, provocative tone.

Before I can respond, Soad's well-rounded form appears. My dizziness has left with the doves. Their circling must have caused the feeling. I take a deep breath. I'm a composed human being once more. I spring up and go over to her. Let's get on with it before the Cerebellum drives all the customers away.

"Well done, Soad." I take the kitten and hand her the charm she asked for. Now she'll go back and tell Antar where he can find Meshmesh. "You have to keep it close to you day and night, and—God willing—your wishes will come true." Even the maid wants to land a Sheikh. Whatever happened to girls hoping to meet a nice guy, the gentle, handsome, ambitious man of their dreams? Such romantic notions have obviously gone down the drain. Nowadays, we make good luck charms to land Arab millionaires.

Her behind bounces as she turns to go. A walking volcano of voluptuousness. She's undoubtedly endowed with the right equipment to achieve her goal. Women like her have little need of a good luck charm. Meshmesh tries to break free of my grip. I hold him tighter. Maybe the trick will work and Antar will come looking for him.

Finally, Meshmesh calms down on the table in front of me. I keep an eye on him so he won't escape and hide underneath the table or behind the cabinet. Meshmesh mews. I head to the kitchen, carrying him with me so he won't run away. I come back with a saucer full of milk. Watch it! He's thumped into me. His head in my stomach. A dull pain. But at least the plan has worked. All we need now is for the ghosts to respond.

"Careful, young man . . . no more running please."

"Meshmesh, what are you doing here? You stole him!" Now even the children are hurling accusations at me.

"Not at all, young man. He came to visit on his own. I was just getting him some milk, see?" Everyone can see right through your lies. But a man must have thick skin to make a living.

"Okay, he can drink his milk, then we have to go home straightaway." Antar regains his instinctive smile.

"Patience, my son. Patience is bitter but its fruit is sweet," I say. Classical Arabic is such an effective weapon in the hands of psychics, astrologers, and assorted con men.

"Are you gonna start talking funny like Mr. Mohamed, the Arabic teacher?" He says Mister in English.

Mister Mohamed, the Arabic teacher, deliciously hilarious.

"Everyone insists their children must get a university education although we all know that university graduates are a dime a dozen and cannot find a job. Under such circumstances how do you expect a functioning educational system?" Mr. Hafez says soberly to the Cerebellum.

"This is a people that for five thousand years has been treated worse than slaves. The small ruling elite has shown less regard for the average person than for cattle: humiliating people in government departments, slapping them around in police stations. Do you find it so strange, then, that every laborer or farmer wishes his children would join the educated elite so they can be treated like human beings, even if they'll end up working as cab drivers or waiters . . .? This is a people that has been truly mistreated, now you're saying they're not even worthy of getting an education." The Cerebellum is as animated as a lawyer making his case before the judge.

"Let me give you a concrete example, sir; when the High School Certificate exam or even the Primary School exam is a little difficult, the whole country is up in arms, and the issue becomes politicized. Don't the parents know that when an exam is difficult it applies to all students equally? So we've made the exams like taking a stroll in the park, and the student who gets a ninety percent mark is considered a failure . . . happy now?" Mr. Hafez seems to speak out of conviction.

"That's no excuse." The Cerebellum, having liberated himself of his fear, has adopted the role of a public prosecutor.

But Mr. Hafez interrupts him, his face red as a tomato. The corner of his mouth trembles. His entire body is tense, as though he's waited all his life for this moment. At last he's got the chance to defend himself, perhaps even in the presence of his late wife's spirit."You kept on demanding free education . . . free education! Now degrees from Egyptian universities are not worth the paper they're written on . . . you kept on calling for equal opportunities; today the only respectable university in Egypt is the American University, soon to be followed by the French, German, and British."

"But . . . ." The Cerebellum attempts to respond but Mr. Hafez won't give him the chance.

"What about the parents who bribe officials to get hold of their kids' exam questions in advance, or those in the rural areas who wait outside their children's schools with loudspeakers during exams and call out the correct answers . . . honestly, do you think educating such a people is worth the trouble?"

The Cerebellum bangs the table to make the man listen to him. The son of a dog will almost certainly get us into trouble today. Antar is standing next to me like a little angel, waiting for the cat to lap up its milk. I sure hope all this talk about corruption in our schools will not have a negative influence on the boy.

"Of course it's worth the trouble. Despite its shortcomings, the Egyptian educational system has produced Ahmed Zewail, Farouk Elbaz, and thousands of Egyptian geniuses all around the world. And why go further; you have yours truly here and that guy over there pretending to summon the spirits . . . multinationals would bend over backward to have us work for them. All this talent could have been put to the service of our country, if only you had provided the right environment."

The problem is not that I'm a con man and the Cerebellum a fugitive, but that we could've turned out so much better. Keep quiet, Abd al-Malak, your mouth can be your downfall. There's no need to pour oil on the fire.

Mr. Shaker scratches his chest with nervous fingers. He's lost interest in the ongoing debate.

"Environment . . .? And where do they grow this environment thing? It seems like a good idea, let's import a few million barrels of environment

220

from Taiwan . . . My good doctor, in the poorer districts when a patient dies in hospital, when it's nobody's fault I mean, the doctors and nurses conceal his death from his family until they've quietly slipped out of the hospital, because they know that the moment the family finds out they'll go on a rampage. This is the environment you're talking about, unless you want us to import a whole new people, that is." What is that idiot talking about? Why are they looking far and wide for solutions when we've had them here for over a thousand years, divine solutions that can never go wrong?

Mr. Shaker scratches his body nervously. "I hope my talk hasn't given you a rash, Mr. Shaker." The Cerebellum sets aside his debate with Hafez.

"It's an allergic reaction. Fleas can completely mess up his body. . . . must be from the cat." His fleshy wife pats him on the back.

I steal a glance at Antar. I'd be in a fix if he were to take offense at the woman's reference to his cat and decided to leave. The boy doesn't even seem to be following the conversation. Thank God.

"Can someone tell me what would've happened to Ahmed Zewail had he remained in Egypt?" The Cerebellum's voice comes from afar. Nobody seems to take his question seriously. I must intervene before the Cerebellum messes everything up.

"I have a message from the underworld for Madame Nafitha . . . ." I wave my arms in the air and roll my eyes. Now I remember: it was Fardous Abdelhamid and Elsherbiny in that soap opera. Elsherbiny? Yes of course but what was his first name? Ali Elsherbiny? Mimi Elsherbiny? I observe the millionaire's wife from the corner of my eye.

"God preserve us from the wicked devil . . . let's hear the message, doctor." The fat woman perspires heavily. I seize the moment:

"You've come here of your own volition, nobody forced you. Know this Nafitha: we are not a toy for you and your friends at the club to play with. This time you get off lightly, next time warm blood shall be spilt." I shudder with emotion, more authentic than Youssef Wahby in his most moving role.

221

Shaker nods, he approves. Now all I need to deal with is the hot potato of his sleep that he's thrown in my lap. But it's just as important to make Mr. Hafez happy. Now how can his late wife be summoned? For that I must depend on Antar.

"No need to worry. These are pure souls." A new, more profound level of my voice that I only discovered recently. Meshmesh doesn't touch his milk. He freezes like a statue. Antar, too, has turned into a block of wood. Thank God. It's happening. I slip my hand under the table to turn off the music.

"You are all guilty and the worst of you knows who he is." The same woman's voice, from the child's mouth as usual. Such a beautiful voice, so familiar now. Sad but serene, its anger is justified. A profound hush, a guilty silence. Antar is cast in stone. I conspired with the maid to draw him here. But he's been molded in devil's water. There's no way to control him. Anyway, thank God he never remembers anything in the end.

"You are all guilty and the worst of you knows who he is." A judge from another world, uninterested in your silly debates.

Nafitha remembers what she just said and turns to Meshmesh, her fleshy face a ripe tomato. "Excuse me, I never meant to insult cats or anything . . . Shaker probably ate something and got food poisoning."

"You are all guilty and the worst of you knows who he is."

Shaker scratches his chest like mad, then tears off his tie and undoes the top two buttons of his shirt.

"You are all guilty and the worst of you knows who he is, Shaker." The voice, a surgeon's scalpel, knows no hesitation. The table shakes beneath our hands and starts to rise; an earthquake of anger emanating from another world.

"I'm innocent. By God, I'm innocent" He denies the charge even before he's accused. His gray face turns paper white. The table floats in the air. We freeze.

"You must be the one who murdered the actress." The Cerebellum, attorney general to the ghosts, intervenes. A comedian trying to play a serious role or a man serious to the point of being funny? He reminds me of Shouikar when she sings, "You must be the one who killed my father."

"I didn't murder anyone. By God I have nothing to do with it. Since when has it been a crime to protect one's own son?" The arteries are about to burst in his neck. All eyes are on him, digging into his dilapidated skin. He looks around the room, realizes the danger of what he's saying, and stands up: "Let's go, Nafitha." His voice is almost blocked by the lump in his throat.

The fat woman's mouth is an open trapdoor. She leaves the room with her hand on her chest and her eyes roaming from face to face. The table drops to the ground with a thump, taking the two of them by surprise. They freeze for a second. Damn the spirits and the conjuring of spirits if they will implicate me in a murder investigation.

The fleeing millionaire and his wife disappear. Meshmesh starts to mew and Antar comes to. The cat ignores its milk and flees like the wind. Antar follows, calling, "Meshmesh, wait."

"Soheir . . . where are you . . . can you hear me . . . do you see me?" Mr. Hafez's gaze moves haphazardly from the ceiling to the corners. He's confused. He stands up and, without a word, walks away.

✖

The haunted apartment vibrates to the beat of a Mohamed Heneidi song. The Cerebellum has turned on the recorder at full blast. He dances in the hall while putting on his oversized clothes.

"It turns out, doctor, you're a fan of *Hammam in Amsterdam*," I say dryly.

There's something about his abrupt transformation from angst to joy that infuriates me.

"So what? I'm a fan of New Generation music." He waves his arms in the air like a teenager at a pop concert.

"Or in other words, New Fornication music," I reply with disdain.

"This is what I call the democratization of music . . . I respect the taste of the vast majority of Egyptians. Actually, the cassette revolution is the only successful one in our long history. Ahmed Adawiya was the most popular singer in the country for years, yet the radio and television authority refused to broadcast his songs, can you believe it?" He buttons his shirt as he talks. The Cerebellum's talk gets more provocative by the day.

"What democratization of music . . .? Call it rather the deterioration of public taste."

"Do you know what really pisses you off, you and the rest of the intelligentsia? That the working class and the kids are now setting the standards after thousands of years in which their voices were muted." He allows his pajama bottoms to drop, then steps into his room and reappears with trousers in his hand.

"Why do you insist on confusing the issues? What has democracy to do with music? In music, at least, democracy is far from desirable. It is the intellectual's role to improve public taste. Otherwise garbage collectors will turn into critics and teach us all about art, doctor."

"I beg to differ, sir. Democracy is not just about elections. It is a culture: the way the teacher treats his students, the headmaster the teacher, the boss his employees, and the minister his department secretary. Democracy isn't merely about politics but about everything, about respecting opposing points of view, respecting New Generation songs even if they're trashy and in bad taste." He slips into his trousers as he gives me the benefit of his intellectual gems, then disappears again into his room.

"Where are you off to?" I ask, but he walks into the bathroom and shuts the door.

He comes out exuding strong cologne, a familiar fragrance. The son of a gun has helped himself to my bottle without bothering to ask.

"If you'll excuse me. I have an appointment with the girls."

"The girls . . . aren't we getting overambitious? Wouldn't one be enough for a start?" This story is impossible to believe.

"There's actually three of them: white, small, and cute . . . and they pant all the time."

"They pant all the time? Then Mr. Kasseb must have introduced you to them."

"God forbid! How can you even think that . . . all I said was they pant. I'm talking about Madame Gawdat's girls." His face turns red.

I take a few seconds to grasp what he's talking about. "Ah, the girls . . . you're taking the girls for a walk. Or to be more precise, walking the girls." I can't stop laughing.

"Exactly . . . Madame Gawdat isn't feeling well because of her diabetes." He disappears through the half-open apartment door.

No matter how liberated you become, Cerebellum, there'll always be shackles you can never shake off. True, you no longer tremble at the mention of the CIA or Mossad; the cops and even the entire government can't make you flinch, but hearing Mr. Kasseb's name still loosens your joints and makes your ears redder than a tomato.

✖

"The best thing about the month of Ramadan is that everyone stays up late." Farah smiles.

Is she agreeing with what I just said or mocking me? Or is she merely trying out one of her seductive smiles? She loves to inflame my senses, always has. She knows the secrets of my soul like the palm of her hand; my desire to take her in my arms without a word; to press my body against hers, impervious of the crowd; to bite her lips; to dig my fingers into the Turkish delight of her flesh; to devour her, my love, the candy doll.

God help me conquer these evil thoughts. In Ramadan, the struggle against one's desires takes precedence over fasting. Be patient, Abd al-Malak, soon you'll be a legitimate couple. Yet, I no longer know whether restraint is possible. It's easy to preach, so hard to practice.

Ramadan is upon us . . . we're overjoyed. After this long wait . . . welcome, Ramadan. God rest your soul, Teleb. Your song is eternal, so different from today's lyrics that possess neither taste nor smell nor color, like a textbook definition of water. Layers of noise; the band are trying out the loudspeakers. The waiter brings tea and a couple of shishas. I hadn't envisaged smoking a shisha in a five-star tent like this one, but Farah ordered apple-flavored tobacco with her tea. It seems that my period of absence in America has left me behind the times.

The waiter puts down his tray. The teapot's enamel is peeling off. The cheap glasses remind me of the Yassine brand of olden days. Most glasses used to be tinted in blue or green, size fifty for tea. Today everything is imported from Taiwan. The rectangular table is low, its brass surface covered with sticky rings from previous customers' orders. The waiter sets two white plastic objects on the table. I hold one up with two fingers and study it inside the see-through wrapping.

"That's a mouthpiece for the shisha. Don't you know anything?" Farah starts to laugh. She reclines on the cushions made of tent material. Her thighs, inside black stretch pants, are two of the marvels of the universe, pillars of marble as Father—God rest his soul—would say. A true Scheherezade: beauty, delicious curves, sensuality, cunning, sense of humor and all.

But this is the tip of an enema!

"How about sharing the joke?"

My laughter overflows but I can't tell her the reason. This says it all about Egyptians: when we want to play civilized, we use an enema's tip as a mouthpiece for our shishas.

"I'm laughing because I'm so happy, Farah."

She starts to laugh seductively, an encouraging sign.

"Farah, after all the years we wasted . . . the time has come to mend what was broken . . . I mean, get married." A torrent of words races to my lips. I suppress it all. A sudden lump in my throat, a lonesome tear at the corner of my eye. If you speak you'll expose yourself, Abd al-Malak, you'll drop the mulberry leaf that shields you.

She listens without looking my way and says nothing. She produces a small velvet case from her purse, perhaps a cigarette case or a makeup kit. She opens it and produces a mouthpiece, ivory or maybe white marble. She fits it over the brass mouth and pulls vigorously turning the shisha's water into a bubbling volcano. She seems more experienced than a coffeehouse owner.

The blood boils in my ears. Left and right, all the girls are bubbling away. I'm profoundly embarrassed; coming back from America, I'm still the old farm boy. I pour the tea in the size-fifties made in Taiwan, drop six cubes of sugar and a mint stalk in each glass, and stir.

"What are you doing . . . are you crazy?" Her sudden laughter attracts a few stares.

Music bursts from the giant speakers. People applaud.

"I don't take sugar with my tea anymore, those days are long gone," Farah shouts to be heard above the din.

An effeminate performer appears from behind the curtain onto the low stage. The applause is like fireworks. Farah leans over to me as she claps.

"The whole world has changed, but you're still the same."

How true. I for one still dream about getting married and settling down. I perform my prayers on time. I fill up my tea with too much sugar. I still don't like a lot of noise. I don't know the name of this Lebanese singer who's driving women crazy all around me. I don't even own a marble mouthpiece for the shisha.

"Let's get married by Eid . . . and make a new home . . ." I shout the words of an old Lebanese song in her ear. I adopt the Lebanese dialect; maybe it'll soften her heart.

The entertainer ends his song and the whole tent explodes in applause. For the second time tonight, Farah ignores me. She's caught the fever of adulating the singer— and I thought celebrity worship was a Western disease. It turns out we, too, are idol worshipers.

"By pure chance, the great artiste Lula Hamdi is with us here tonight." The MC is wearing a red jacket. The applause is deafening. My head is about to split. Ramadan is supposed to be a month of calm and contemplation, what's wrong with you people?

"Ladies and gentlemen, a warm round of applause for Miss Lula Hamdi. Perhaps she'll consent to grace us with one short act." In the midst of the applause, a new musical band takes its place. The man in the red jacket leaves the stage. The belly dancer bows then takes the scarf from her neck and ties it around her waist. Bastards, this whole thing is only an act to get around the prohibition on belly dancing in Ramadan.

"By the way, I'm serious. I mean about marriage and everything." I pinch her arm to get her attention. But why the silence when I raise the issue—hasn't this been our shared dream for years?

"You can't imagine how I longed for you to ask, but now that I hear the question, I feel nothing." She still avoids my eyes.

I fit my enema into the shisha and pull hard. The smoke seeps out of my nostrils. I pull again before the coals die out. It is futile to try and understand a woman.

"You'll feel happiness when my words become reality, when we build our lives together, the life we've always dreamed of."

She looks away. Such is the human condition; we chase a dream like mad until we attain it, only to realize it wasn't that important after all. But I'm not talking about a new toy or the latest electronic gadget. I'm talking about the dream of our lives. If we don't take our dream seriously what else do we have left? Why can't you understand, Farah? I don't know what else to say.

"You come back from America after seven years and think time has frozen in Egypt. The world goes around, doctor, life's train waits for no one." She shouts above the surrounding noise. Her courage abruptly fails her. She looks away again.

I can hardly believe this is Farah speaking. Maybe years of disappointment—maybe anger and despair—kept building till they developed a voice of their own. Perhaps the girl I loved no longer exists, except in my memory. Who knows—maybe her laughter, full of hope and defiance, is no more than an echo perpetuated by my mind, a mind drained by deprivation and failure. My voice freezes; my tears are trapped in my heart. But I can't lose hope. Things are never what they seem.

"Let's go. I've had enough noise," she says.

Without counting, I throw some money on the table and follow her. My burning face's encounter with the December air is another shock.

�֍

"The past is more real than the future . . . that's your tragedy and mine." Her sorrow shatters the calm of her apartment. There's a sleepy warmth about her. "The past is dead and buried . . . the future, resurrection and everlasting hope."

Her hand is a block of ice. I try to warm it between mine, maybe to make up for the triviality of my words.

You're my only truth. I was born again when we met by chance in the elevator. Farah, when the waves toyed with me according to their whims; when ferocious storms decimated my sails, when the currents landed me on unfamiliar and terrifying shores, your love was the anchor I clung to. I acted foolishly, I'm the first to admit. Cowardly, I agree. In the restlessness of my youth, I saw your love as shackling, a backbreaking load, a weight pulling me downward, drowning me. All mere excuses to justify my desertion, but no excuse could dampen my longing for you day and night. In my folly, I tried to shed your love, but can a patient spill the drug that is at once his disease and cure?

There's so much to say but it all freezes in my throat. Eloquence has abandoned me. My tongue is unable to produce one syllable. Where have all the poems gone, the verses I composed to the sparkle of her eyes, the love my heart overflowed with, all the words I wished I could one day utter?

Words. What is the use of words?

229

"The past is made of flesh and blood . . . the future, of mirages and illusions." Her hand is an inanimate object she surrenders to my will. I press it and squeeze it then, in tenderness, I caress it. Still no response on her part. I raise her hand, my lips quiver. I stamp a kiss on her marble skin, a kiss to last a lifetime.

The conversation has withered away. Her cold body sitting next to me on the sofa barely touches me. Her lips twitch. Without thinking, I get closer. The fragility of her body in my arms. I press against her. The taste of tears is salty on my tongue. Perhaps my hope will drive away her fears. Perhaps my fire will melt her ice. If only she'd say yes we'd get married this very moment, spend the night embracing love. We'd melt together, fuse into our long-sought perfection.

The doorbell. Its buzz is an act of aggression against our privacy. Her grip stiffens around my arm. Her body is a tightly strung chord. The bell rings again. Her eyes are two circles of surprise.

Who could it be at this late hour?

"I'll get it."

She holds me by the wrist. Jumps up. The coldness of her hand is a rheumatic pain. Her finger on her lips pleads for silence. Her face pale, she pulls me to the kitchen. You're right to fear scandal. I wish I could go up and down the tower shouting: "Hear ye all, Farah is my wife in the eyes of God and before our own consciences. Hear ye all and henceforth it shall be known."

I follow her into the kitchen's darkness. The service door. Firmly, she pushes me, her eyes pleading. The doorbell's assault continues. Her eyes amid the shadows are the mystery of my life. She shuts the door in my face. In the pitch-black I turn around. A metallic clang; I just overturned a garbage can. The angry mewing of cats from upstairs and downstairs. I grope my way to the next floor. Only three floors to go, Abd al-Malak. My heart shudders, not out of fear of the dark. Calamity surrounds me but I fail to identify it. I must hurry. I jump up the steps in the darkness. I lose my balance. A sharp pain in the knee. I go on. A soft body against

230

my leg, a momentary touch in the dark: cat, burglar, or ghost? It hardly matters. Faster, Abd al-Malak, faster. The drums and trumpets from the belly dancer's apartment sound like a zar or a dervish dance. Every season has its rhythm. The noise is fainter as I reach the thirteenth floor. The door is cold and hard under my palm. I bang with my fists and kick it.

"Who's there?" someone calls out from Mr. Kasseb's apartment. The question is then echoed in the Cerebellum's shaky voice.

"Let me in, Cerebellum, it's Abd al-Malak. Open up, there's no time." I can hear him groping around the kitchen. I shout to him. I don't know what more I can say. The blood rushes to my head. The friction of metal on metal. The lock's ring and the flooding lights from the kitchen revive the service staircase. His face is engulfed in darkness, his small body poised to strike. He's holding the large kitchen knife. I push him out of the way and rush out of the half-open main door. I jump down the stairs: no time for the elevator. I come to a stop in front of Farah's door.

Voices ring inside the apartment, blend with my heavy breathing. A man's deep voice. I hold my breath. My heartbeats make my body vibrate like a drum. Her voice is heavy. The world around me is red. My pulse is getting back to normal but I can't stop shivering. The door amplifies the voices inside.

"I beg you . . . don't forget we're in Ramadan." Her voice is suddenly clear. She's approaching the door, walking as she talks.

"I'm all respect for Ramadan, but we can do whatever we want till daybreak." The voice is familiar, rough around the edges, dangerous. The man has followed her into the hallway. He has the voice of a drug dealer or a coffeehouse owner.

"I beg you . . . Sh . . . ." Shaker, who else? The owner of both the company and the apartment. It was clear as daylight but you were blind. Blind, you seer of what no man knows. Even blind people can hear, touch, use their other senses, but you, spiritual medium, soothsayer, your blindness is total. You've intentionally blinded yourself. She must have married him in secret, or . . .

231

"Have fear of God!" A cry for help. Her voice, even in this situation, is not devoid of sensuality. But who do you think will come to your rescue, my love?

What makes you think they're married, you jackass? Shaker's kind have no need for marriage; there's no shortage of whores. But how can they keep this relationship secret? The security clerk, the garage attendants, even the tower's inhabitants must know what's going on behind this polished door. Everyone knows except you, brilliant scientist. Everyone is talking about your woman. The scandal is ever-present. It was out of God's mercy, mother; that He summoned your soul before you could be tainted by this scandal. The funny thing is, we made a point of leaving the tower and coming back separately, so no one would suspect we were lovers. Of course: a girl's most valuable asset is her reputation.

This is how Farah, the revolutionary, has ended up, the outcome of the big talk of her student days. Where did Zeina, the lettuce seller, go? Shouldn't you be here to congratulate yourself on how brilliantly you've brought up your daughter? And Kamboura, you filthy beast, how do you look your scoundrel friends in the eyes at the doorman's bar?

And Abd al-Malak, where were you, when all this was happening? Now that you've found out, what will you do, brave, honorable man? And the greatest love story, where has it gone? We thought ourselves two ducks in the canal; it turns out we're two pigs in the sty. And why hang around now in front of the doors of the high classes, anyway?

In prostitution, we're all together.

And things are never what they seem. Not at all: they're exactly what they seem. Only we choose to bury our heads in the sand. So, what seekest thou, my son?

The three-floor walk is more grueling than Mount Everest. My body suddenly crumbles, as though the whole tower has collapsed on my head. The static sound of a radio out of channel. And the world: how black it has turned. But the stairs are brilliant white, clean, and shiny as if nothing has happened.

The Ninth Page

Those runaway tits
from the gown's bosom,
brimming with passion,
I worry for them;
a little hot sun
and they could burst

Azza Eid Abdelmawla

Islah Mohandes

The staircase is dusty. Blotches readily blend with the mosaic tiles. Layers and layers of stains; consecutive generations of negligent janitors; the enduring chain of disintegration. Atik, the Nubian, washed the staircase every day at dawn. He'd swipe it with a jute rag starting from the top seventh floor all the way down to the basement. A mixture of water and kerosene would cascade down the steps. He was the last of the respectable janitors. The stairs used to be squeaky clean in my childhood, when Atik was still alive, when Hamada was a cherubic baby, before he turned stupid and selfish. Yes, stupid and selfish: manhood's two unmistakable signs.

"You're stupid and selfish!" I shouted at him before I had a chance to think.

My brother's talk confused me so I exploded in his face. Yet I can't deny the significance of his message. All your life, Islah, you've been a ticking time bomb. You never learned to maneuver. You should have absorbed the shock and given yourself time for a studied reaction. You always return fire with fire. You burst out, you shout. You bang the door behind you then freeze on the dusty stairs and ask questions between the floors.

I was totally unprepared for what Hamada said. Not just the substance, even the way he said it. I've gotten used to his anger and shouting—they think a loud voice is the mark of masculinity. Selfish and stupid bastards. But today, he took me by surprise. He was unusually quiet and he pleaded—almost begged. He begged me in Mama's presence. He said, "My future is in your hands." For a second he went back to being a pampered child and Mama's eyes watered. She didn't say a word, only looked at me. But the accusation in her eyes was loud and clear.

Hamada's talk was truly frightening. Frightening and confusing. The air is heavy and the world spins. I lean on the wall for support. Its texture is soft, bursting with humidity. I didn't believe Hamada at first. 'It's a silly prank,' I said to myself. Then my eyes instinctively turned to Mama. I watched her happiness freeze. This couldn't possibly be a joke. And his face was pallid; his voice hoarse, as he said his new job—his lifelong dream and the fruit of his mother's prayers—was in jeopardy. Everything was suddenly under threat.

I lean on the concrete railing. I need to reach the street; the December air will revive me. I need to regain the ability to concentrate, to absorb what's happening. They told him, 'Your sister is a journalist with a bad reputation.' They said, 'This is a respectable firm, there's no place here for scandals and scandalmongers.' 'We don't just pick our employees; we take into account their families and friends. All this we consider before making our decision.'

The janitor is reclining on his bench. He picks his cracked toes and doesn't pay me the slightest attention. When Hamada comes through he sits up straight. These days, with the new job and all, he stands up at attention, 'Good morning, Mr. Engineer.' As for me, he doesn't care. A woman, no matter how successful, merits no more than a wag of his toe then a long look at her behind. They're all selfish and stupid. The winter sun is feeble, the wind slaps my cheek, makes me alert.

They haven't signed Hamada's contract yet. They haven't even told him what he'll be doing. So far it's been just talk. They gave him hope then left him hanging there and he begged me, and Mama thought I was to blame. I carry the whole world on my shoulders and nobody gives a damn about me. I shouted at them both and banged the door as I left. But there's no escape: I'll be back tonight and the problem will still be there. At least I'll have had a chance to reflect, to absorb. What the hell!

"You filthy bastard!" I hear my own voice, my helpless cry.

The motorcycle disappears behind a mini truck. I've got mud all over my trousers and he simply slipped away, the filthy bastard. It's a small puddle he could've easily avoided. The filthy bastard did it on purpose. Whether on purpose or not, what's the difference?

My trousers are muddied all over, a mean, filthy pattern. He did it and disappeared. The janitor smiles, still reclining. They're all selfish dogs. Now I have to go back again to change my clothes. I have no choice. The tears blur my vision. I turn around so the moron reclining on the bench will not see I'm crying. I wipe the tears with my sleeve. I need to control myself. But why did the firm choose Hamada to begin with? There's nothing outstanding about him, no work experience to mention. How did they learn about him and why did they seek him out at a time when people are slitting each other's throats over jobs?

Bastards.

✖

The elevator door shuts us in. I'm alone with him for the first time. This is the seclusion of a man and a woman as defined by sharia. The mirrors magnify his every facet: the tiny white hairs on the back of his neck, his backside straight like a general's, the creases of his jacket beneath the shoulders, his nose perfectly straight in profile, his smile surrounding me from a hundred and fifty different angles, his apparent calm.

You're fully exposed, Islah. Your turbulence is clear as daylight. Your face, the color of tomatoes, peers at him from every direction. The pain in my shoulder has been coming and going since morning. My night was restless, besieged by apprehension. He smiles readily. His smile melts away all problems, clears my mind of worries. The floor numbers turn on and off above his head, announcing we're quickly approaching our destination. His pink scalp occasionally shines beneath the soft silvery mane eroded by time. Pink the color of a baby in an advertisement, the color of the girls in the *Playboy* magazines Hamada hides beneath his mattress, Souso's color.

Souso, my beautiful doll, Father's present on my fifth birthday. I nurtured her like a baby. "So you can pass her on to your own daughter when you grow up," Mama used to say. "I'll never give her up no matter how old I get," I resolved in secret. She was Father's last gift before he went off to war. She bears the scent of the living. I'd comb her hair, dress her up and confide in her. Soon, she became a friend. Yesterday, for the first time in years, I took her out of her box at the bottom of the cupboard. I found myself hugging her, whirling with her in dance. The dizziness of a tango, a waltz, inner music, a sensuous animal blur like an elevator's confusion. Like the confusion caused by the slightest touch of his hand, this man old enough to be my father. I found myself kissing Souso on the lips and saying, "I love you," but in a low voice so Hamada and Mama wouldn't overhear.

Karim has a virgin girl's full lips with vertical lines like a skinned tangerine segment. Their parting holds the secret of prohibited pleasure, a pleasure that can never be mine. After all, he's a respectable family man. Careful, Islah, the devil is sly. Mama's face is full of generosity, of confidence in my good judgment, with a hint of blame just in case. She knows what goes on inside a girl's soul; blame will always be justified. The recorder weighs down my purse. I'm here for an interview with the well-known thinker. It was an excuse to call him really, to hear his voice on the other side of the line, to sink into the net his eyes set up as they devour me in the elevator, to enter his private sanctum on the eighth floor of the Tower of Happiness.

"Bahia is visiting her mother in Alexandria." He breaks the barrier of silence, his tone apologetic.

His embarrassment is a shock to me. The elevator jolts slightly and comes to a standstill. Why does your heart ring like a frantic alarm clock? In your heart you knew you'd be alone together in his apartment, it is one of the unenunciated laws of the universe. Certainly not a plot on his part, but a simple acceptance of the laws of nature. How dangerous wishes can be when they come true. I follow him like a hypnotized woman. He thrusts his key into the hole.

The air is putrid with cigarette smoke. It smells like a bachelor's place. The wooden floors are blanketed in a thin layer of dust pocked with footprints. With a quick gesture, he invites me to relax on the love seat. Its cushions are thick and comfortable and hug me in their warmth. He takes the rocking chair on the other side. A square coffee table separates us. He makes no attempt to get closer. The coffee table is mahogany, its luster still visible beneath the dust. There are three used tea glasses and tens of sticky rings. Bookshelves cover the length of the wall behind me, imposing their presence on the room. I turn around to examine them. They force a solemn hush on me. The books are colorful and dusty, stacked vertically, horizontally, or allowed to slant in rows. The shelves are overflowing and random piles of books are scattered on the floor.

"Tea?" He heads to the kitchen and leaves me in the company of his and his wife's things, the living proof of their common life. He leaves me alone with my disappointment and a faint guilt that I suppress as soon as it creeps in. Karim disappears and, for a moment, leaves me with the unknown.

The woman has been away from home for only a week and order has totally collapsed. The fingers of anarchy have crept in to tear down what she spent a lifetime erecting, to enable mother nature—always on the prowl—to re-impose her supremacy. The universe is destined to drown in anarchy, predicts the second law of thermodynamics. Women, in their desperate courage, are trainers of beasts of prey, involved in an impossible struggle against instinct, the instincts of others and our own. Bahia, Mrs. Bahia, Madame Bahia or comrade Bahia from the revolutionary past, which is the most appropriate?

Photographs are scattered across the bookshelves. How can I resist heading for them? With two fingers, I hold a silver-plated frame enclosing the picture of a small boy in shorts, his knees splattered with scars and fresh wounds. Which of the two sons would it be? Fukuyama's *The End of History and the Last Man*, Heikal's *Autumn of Fury*, Edward Said, Garaudy, Achebe, a chubby baby—the object of his parents' pride—smiles at the camera inside a mother of pearl frame, *Thus Spake Zarathustra*, Noam Chomsky, Gabriel García Márquez. My fingertips are black with dust. Karim's footsteps behind me. A porcelain picture frame, pink on white with small protruding flowers: a middle-aged woman of average beauty, ordinary in every sense. Pleased to meet you. Behind her there's Soyinka, *The History of Egypt* by Vatikiotis, Bahaa Taher's *Love in Exile*, and *Agamiste*, short stories by an author I've never heard of. In the photograph, her smile is faint, tired. She's no communist leader, just another housewife. Madame Bahia, how is your dear mother doing today, a little better I trust?

"Tea from white water!" He uses a coffeehouse waiter's jargon to call me back, to make me stop groping his life with my dusty fingers. How dirty they've gotten. What if he chose to hold my hand right now? I get out a tissue and go back to the love seat. The Love Seat.

"I thought maybe I'd find a picture of you . . . leading a demonstration."

"A photograph like that could have landed me in jail. If you're that interested, you might find one in the archives of the secret police." He abandons himself to laughter, seems to regain a long-lost spontaneity. His shoulders shake uncontrollably. He's a rebel student once again. Bahia's eyes dig into the back of my neck. I turn to face her.

Ahlam Shawarby was something else, different from you and me, Madame Bahia, different from all the other women of the twentieth century. She succeeded where we all failed. Men rolled over in her footsteps but she never surrendered the key to her heart. She never submitted to them. She rejected a life of okra and sweet peas and hairdressers and tearful evenings in front of a soap opera. She never proclaimed: "Whatever you say, greatest of men." But she didn't rebel against her nature either. She didn't wear her hair short and put on men's clothing and speak of herself in masculine terms, and she certainly did not compete with the editor in his juvenile games. She never shouted in the mirror: 'I'll never get

240

married!' or swore she wouldn't become just another dairy cow. Ahlam succeeded in preserving her equilibrium as a woman. Her strength was in her femininity. She forced them to deal with her on her own terms and lived and died a free woman. True, when they failed to break her in, they killed her. But ultimately, she came out victorious.

"In my day, students had given up even demonstrating." I say as soon as he stops laughing.

A sip. The delicious tingle of tea on my tongue.

"Good. Let them concentrate on their studies." He lights a cigarette. His nonchalance is getting on my nerves.

"Well what's the use of studying if they're only going to join the queue of the unemployed when they graduate? And if they do end up with a job, they'll ultimately become corrupt, kiss ass and if they're lucky, become crooks and fraudsters, and if their consciences prick them they'll have no alternative but to turn into extremists. What's the use of study and what good will come from education, sir?" I explode. Didn't you know that women are time bombs?

"In these difficult times, it is wiser to deal with matters 'Calmly,' in the manner of Ibrahim Nafea's weekly column, rather than 'Frankly,' in the manner of Hassanein Heikal's." He hides a smile behind his tea glass. He rocks his chair, taking my words lightly. Suddenly, he whispers, "You can't imagine how much I admire you." His eyes brim with tenderness. "You're beautiful, sensitive, smart, and fearless." He must be sincere. The world opens up to me. I misjudged you, Karim. This is how my emotions vacillate in your presence, like rides in a fun park. I drop from heaven to earth in a second.

"I've come to admire you too . . . ." What are you saying? Have you gone completely mad? I quickly correct myself, "I mean . . . because you've always advocated total war against Israel."

He lights a fresh cigarette before putting out the old one. Don't worry; I'm not going to mention that you've become one of the leading proponents of normalization with Israel. The cigarette shakes between his fingers.

I continue, to fill the gaping silence. "I was only a child in '73, but when I grew up I came to recognize Sadat's terrible mistake. We should have fought to win, not to heat up the situation in preparation for peace talks. The blood of martyrs was spilled in vain."

He blows his smoke toward the ceiling and rocks his chair then pulls again at his Marlboro.

"That was my conviction at the time as well, but . . . there were many things not apparent to us in those days: the Soviet Union turned out to be hollow; the truth about Arab unity was later exposed in the Gulf War; it has also become evident that Israel and America are connected umbilically . . . In Sadat's day, I experienced imprisonment and humiliation, horrors I can never tell anyone about. Nevertheless, I think maybe Sadat did Egypt the greatest favor in its modern history." The smoke escapes through his mouth and nose as he speaks.

Naturally, you're trying to justify yourself, to explain how you traded away your principles. Tell me, revolutionary comrade, how did you come to own this sumptuous apartment? But I don't blame you; you acted like everyone else, you've become a citizen of the New World Order. I produce the recorder and place it on the table. He puts his hands in front of his face defensively.

"Can we avoid this recording business . . . ? After all, I'm neither a politician nor a movie star . . . nobody's really interested in what I have to say. Why don't we just call it a chat between two people who are bound together by many things?"

"We're bound by many things . . . like what?" The words escape me. No doubt, Islah, you're exhibiting your silly, broad smile. At university, I once said penile code when I meant penal code. All the students laughed at me; a trip of the tongue or a Freudian slip? Sooner or later all that you have suppressed will come to the surface.

"We're bound by enthusiasm, patriotism, and naiveté . . . plus something else I can't find the right word for. Something natural and spontaneous . . . a special attraction, magic maybe. One of these days,

242

I must tell you all about your eyes . . . ." The cigarette shakes in his fingers.

I've never tried smoking. All my life I've considered it a luxury I couldn't afford, but so wished for. In my heart, I wanted to be the girl in the ad with the handsome guy; holding a cigarette while her blond hair flutters in the air. One of these days, he'll tell me all about my eyes. Yes, smoking is a luxury, just like love. I wish this very instant he'd blow his smoke inside my mouth. The smoke would open up a new channel of communication between us; we'd merge together without needing to touch. He'll tell me all about . . . is there so much to tell about my eyes? I wish . . . Is this it? Can this be love?

"When I first set eyes on you, I felt that my life, with its sweet and bitter experiences, had suddenly gained meaning. As if everything that ever happened to me was merely a prelude to this moment. . . ." He talks to the cloud of smoke surrounding his face. Our eyes don't meet, as though we're each living in a different world, or as if our souls are hovering in a special ether unique to lovers, separated from the material world. I've never really tasted love before. Definitely, another luxury. No, a sweet pain. My one experience was on the bus . . . .

"Have you ever been in love, Islah?"

You read my mind. You smile. From behind a thick mist, your eyes devour me.

"Once . . . but it doesn't really count."

He waits.

"It was a young man I used to see every day on the bus . . . on my way to university."

The bus line was 888 and the boy was skinny, an engineering student, I could tell from his T-shaped ruler. He got on before my stop. We never spoke and I never heard his voice, but I got to know his eyes intimately. Every day I'd seek out his eyes in the mass of cramped bodies. We met every morning at precisely the same time but I never discovered the timing of his return journey. I knew him without really knowing him at all.

"So you met on the bus and then started to date?" He crosses his legs. His shoes are imported, well-shined. You're perfectly right Mama: you can tell a man by his shoes.

"Actually, we never exchanged words. We never even got to know each other's names." We got pretty close without actually touching. In my dreams he whispered in my ear, but in real life an invisible barrier separated us. I so wished he'd start a conversation. I wrote so many love letters to him, but then tore them all up. "At last, one day, he got up the courage to press my hand as we were getting off the bus . . . but I never saw him again after that."

Why are you telling this man your deepest secrets, exposing to him what you've never spoken out loud before, simply and without the slightest embarrassment? What will he think of you? An experienced man like him will not content himself with only boyish looks.

"I've never really known love . . . I mean until these past few days . . . . And now, I experience love so late in life. I always used to say that the Cause was my first and last love . . . the Cause . . . ." He lights another cigarette. You're a walking chimney, Karim. "The first time I saw you, it felt like an electric shock . . . but when I got home, I quickly said to myself, 'You no longer have the right to fall in love. It's not for people your age. And then you could end up hurting this innocent woman.'"

Who's the innocent woman, me or Bahia?

"When I'd come across respectable men who started acting like teenagers and made fools of themselves, I used to say 'They've gone mad.' I found it hard to believe that people would actually do this to themselves. Then I met you. At that moment, my wisdom, my dignity, the advice I used to dole out right and left, all that evaporated. I said to myself, 'You just need a change. Take a trip. Introduce a variation in your life's routine to make it more bearable. Go get drunk, have yourself a sexual escapade.' But my heart wouldn't go along with that. I could only see your face. Your voice refused to leave my ears. Even in the middle of the night, I think of you." A lump in his throat forces him to stop.

This delicious pain in my chest. I breathe with difficulty. Your words have captured my soul, melted my heart. A moment more intense than anything that has happened to me before. Like you said, all my life has been merely a preparation for this.

"I tried to resist . . . with all my might I tried . . ." A tear trickles down his cheek. I find myself hugging my chest. "Trotsky once said, 'Process is everything. The objective does not concern us,' a statement that always confused me. Until now, I never understood it. As it turns out, this is the golden rule of love: only the current moment counts. Past and future— indeed the whole world does not concern me." He turns to me, tears glittering on his cheek.

I release my arms from around my breasts; I don't want him to get any ideas. God forgive you; you've turned Trotsky into a romantic poet.

He puts out his cigarette and approaches. "What's this, have you hurt yourself?"

Anesthetized, I feel nothing. He passes his finger over my lips. A bright drop of blood; I bit my lip, no big deal. The feel of his palm on my cheek then his finger again on my lips. The tears sparkle on his face, warm and salty. His lips are soft under the pressure of mine. This delicious sensual dizziness. What's happening?

What would happen if a woman unveiled the truth of what goes on inside her soul? The world would split apart and bare its darkest secrets . . . . a question, an answer, a piece of wisdom I must have read. Where? I don't remember. A statement that assumes that this can never happen. Never ever. A wise man's assumption, except humanity is nowhere close to wisdom.

It was my initiative. Yes. It was I who started things. Funny, in the movies, it's always the guy who makes the first move. The first time I ever kiss a man and it's I who initiated it. No one warned me of this possibility, this devious power. I've discovered my softness, the feminine volcano I've been carrying unwittingly. But what could have prepared me for this? What would happen if a woman were to expose . . . ? It can never . . . at least that's what the wise man thought. Never ever.

245

This instant is the moment of a lifetime.

All things past are memories. What is to come, hopes, words, the product of thought, excerpts from rationality's dictionary. Salwa, Seham, Soha: names in a telephone directory. My grandmother, my uncle, my aunt's aunt's ex-husband: names on tombstones. Islah Mohandes also is a name on a tombstone, only with a delay of execution. Pristina, Timor, Grozny, Jerusalem, the Prime Minister, the Minister of Information, the Secretary General of the United Nations, the woman who bore septuplets, a string of news items on TV. All exist as part of reality but outside the realm of truth. The only truth is right now . . . .

Him.

He's my only truth.

The taste of cigarettes in my mouth, his taste. He kisses my eyelids, bites my lips, holds me close, sucks my neck with a full mouth. My fingers dig into his hair, pull it, mess it up. His fingers steal closer. The forbidden pleasure. Without a man, a woman is incomplete. My poor mother. Her and all the world's wasting widows. My moaning fills the universe, my freedom, the freedom I never knew. Aladdin's genie was a woman. When he released her from her urn, she was still unaware of her feminine truth. He pulls me. I follow. One step, two steps. But no. Not the bedroom. Not Bahia's bed. My first love on another woman's bed? Never.

"Here . . . right here on the sofa." You're shameless, Islah.

I pull my hand away from his. The bookshelves. Bahia's agony bites at my entrails. I turn her photograph upside down. My breasts swing right and left in their nudity. My nipples are erect. The touch of velvet is a cold fire, the love seat again. He folds my body like a spring. His hair smells of apples. I bite his neck. A fleeting pain. The moment of discovery. The pleasure of exploration and the exploration of pleasure. The living instant; all that is past, all that will come to be, does not concern me. The earth can no longer hold my emotions. Such is love, all clichés. The blood of my virginity is a stain on your sofa, Bahia. On your love seat.

When it's over, I'll ask him for a cigarette. I'll blow the smoke in the air. Now, I press my lips against his. Hamada in his yellow fiberglass helmet motions to the crane; the job he's always dreamed of. A pain in my neck. I'm pressed against the sofa's arm. My shoulder; the duality of pain and pleasure. The editor and his yellow smile. Mama bites her lips, her heart chewed up by worry. The inquisitiveness of a thousand books peers at me from the shelves. Ahlam Shawarby is naked, her hair spread out on the elevator floor. Karim's sons, in their childhood photographs, listen in on the moans of my eroticism. My internal laughter cracks. He raises his head, eyes bewildered. The genie is out of the urn, haven't you heard? You're such cowards, men. I press his head against my heart and whisper in his ear, "Process is everything."

※

Why does the story of Karim's son come to mind right now? It invades my foggy mind while I wait for the editor-in-chief to end his telephone conversation with the high official. The man rocks in his posh leather seat with a cigar between his fingers. A forest of long white hairs stares at me from his ears and nose, mocking, provoking me.

Last night at the police station, Karim was in a state of confusion. His face was pale, his hair unkempt. Men: how attractive they are when they're most vulnerable. "Men are like fish in the sea . . . . the smart woman is the one who attracts the fat eel to her net," Teta would say. God rest her soul. Naturally, she was talking about marriage. Oblivious to this other world called love, she never imagined there was any alternative.

The officer had seated Karim in front of his desk, out of respect for his age and social standing, or just in case he had connections in high places. Karim was overjoyed to see me. He almost took me in his arms, but at the last moment, controlled himself. Over the phone he'd said his son was in trouble and that he needed my help. But why did he turn to me

247

in his hour of need? Does he have that much confidence in the power of the media, the fourth branch of government, as the joke goes?

The officer said, "It's a State Security crime, sir. You should be thankful your son is still alive." I was certain he was talking about Karim's bearded son; some shady operator must have turned his head in the mosque. These are strange times; people feel their children are safer at nightclubs. As it turned out, the accused son was Aiman, the playboy with the ponytail and earring. "How can he be involved with extremist religious groups?" I asked. It would have made more sense if the officer had said a drug-related offence or a lurid act in public.

My article rests on the desk in front of the editor-in-chief. Sure enough, it deals with the Tower of Happiness, but from a new angle. I will not rest until I uncover the truth. When my editor rejected the article, I took it all the way to the editor in chief. A hot story like this and he rejected it out of hand without giving one reason. "What is this, the rule of Karakosh?"

"Yes. You can call it the rule of Karakosh,' he said with a poison smile, referring to the despotic Fatimid minister from the history books.

We're talking about séances attended by the rich and famous, by people in high places, and the idiot thinks himself Karakosh. My heart beats violently. If the editor-in-chief rejects the story, no one can blame me for what I'll do next; the opposition papers are always willing and pen names are a well-tried method. Unconcerned by all this, he cackles into the receiver.

Karim, my lover who looked the State's wrath in the eye without flinching, yesterday begged for his spoiled son. The officer accused the young man of being the ringleader of the infamous gang that has imposed a modicum of order on the streets of Maadi. He called them a dangerous terrorist group, specialized in smashing cars, breaking the windows of shops that sell defective goods and perished foodstuffs, and setting fire to buildings whose owners had turned the parking areas into boutiques and warehouses. The officer said he hadn't made up his mind if they were terrorists, drug addicts, or even Satanists.

"Damn these kids and the years spent bringing them up," as Teta often said. "They bring you nothing but problems and heartache." The police brought in the boy in a wretched state: tousled hair, dirty face, and a swollen left eye. His yellow sweater was soiled and his trousers torn at the knees. He struggled to keep his composure but upon seeing his father, one big tear broke loose. For once, Karim looked his age. You've fallen in love with an old man, Islah.

"He organized an attack on a patrol car!" the officer shouted at Karim.

"The police car was driving in the wrong direction," the boy was quick to reply. "We threw a brick at the windshield. If the government doesn't punish violators but is itself the biggest violator, it's up to us, young people, to do something about it. Otherwise, we've surrendered and buried our heads in the sand like the rest of you."

In the end we managed to secure the boy's release. It turns out I underestimated the influence of the fourth branch of government. But what has all this to do with the hairs protruding from the editor-in-chief's nose? He puts down the receiver—as though he's read my mind—and turns to me.

"This is an exciting story. It'll catch the public's attention," I say to hide my confusion.

"Thank you. But isn't it a pity that your talents should be wasted on such trivial stories?" The words emanate from the hairs of his nose. It's as though men have been allocated a specified amount of hair and when it starts falling off the head it has no option but to protrude from the nose and ears. An interesting theory.

"I appreciate your confidence, sir. I hope it will be reflected in your approval to publish my story."

"This is much bigger than one story, Miss Islah. I'm sure you agree with me that journalism is, above all, a mission . . ."

Journalism is above all a mission! If journalism had indeed been a mission they wouldn't have chosen someone like you to be editor-in-chief.

Media is a great void, an air bubble. The media bubble. Sure, sure, go on bullshitting me.

"For some time now, I've been looking for the right person to be editor of the women's page. As you know, women make up fifty percent of our society."

So it turns out we're half of society. Just you go on with this crap.

Ahlam's copybook is in my purse. I take it wherever I go. It's become part of my life. Its poems have become a bridge binding the living and the dead, a tangent between different levels of human existence. 'Obscene Exercises for Fat Women.' Such an unforgettable headline, an article that has more than aroused my curiosity. What could these obscene exercises be, anyway? And why did Ahlam include such an article in her copybook? Anyway, I simply cannot read it in the presence of others. Whenever I resolve to lock myself up with it, something has to happen. Something is always diverting my attention.

"What do you say, Miss Islah?"

"What do you mean, sir?" Can anything good come out of this ugly character?

"I would be pleased if you'd accept the position of editor of the women's section. I have the impression this is the promotion you've been dreaming about for quite some time now . . ." But what's he saying? My mind is too exhausted. The hair protruding from his nose is so distracting.

"Naturally, I expect some new ideas . . . and a lot of extra effort. I'm keen for our women's section to play a significant role in the development of our society."

"It . . . it would be a great honor . . . but what about the story?"

"What's the matter, Miss Islah? It's time to leave such trivial work to the regular reporters. I want you to put together a blueprint for a total revamp of the women's page. I expect it on my desk in twenty-four hours."

What's happening? I'm sinking in quicksand. Lately, my world has been turned upside down. Its rhythm has jumped from dead slow to the speed of light. All these crazy events going off around me faster than I can grasp: my relationship with Karim, his son's story, my friendship with Ahlam and Didi, Hamada's job. Could there be an invisible link between all of these? I don't know what to say to the editor in chief. The emotional whirlpool makes me dizzy. I don't even know what I want any more. At this moment I only have one desire: to pluck one or two of the hairs protruding from his flat nose.

⁙

She's beautiful enough to be in a television commercial. Her dress has a slit on the side all the way up to her thigh. Her figure is soft and rounded. The young billionaire's secretary disgusts me. There's something repulsive about her. Perhaps it's plain female jealousy, but no. My disgust is linked to this place. The marble floor, a little too brilliant; the Scandinavian furniture; the secretary's false smile: all cogs in a diabolical machine, a trap set up all around me, leaving no possibility for escape.

She gave me a same-day appointment, while millionaires have to wait for weeks or months. She set the appointment on the spot, without checking with him first. Didn't even ask why I wanted to see Shoukry Shaker. She had expected my call. My spontaneous act had been anticipated, part of a master plan I'm not even aware of. I'm a pawn on a chessboard: deaf, dumb, and manipulated by fingers beyond my perception.

She smiles as she pushes open the broad door. She radiates a false sense of security that can only be explained as absence of awareness. One day they may well find your naked body in this distinguished tower's elevator or in another's. What good will your beauty do you then? Will you keep on smiling when that happens, or rise up in your death and demand justice and revenge? She shuts the door behind me ever so gently, producing the least possible disturbance. She's well trained in the shutting of doors.

Shoukry greets me with a beautiful voice and the lingering smile of a man who knows more than he cares to admit. Through the French window, Cairo is a modern city of light on the banks of the Nile, a metropolis showing off her luster, reveling in her prosperity. This city has nothing to do with the one I live in, stacked with garbage in every corner, reverberating with human voices, corroded by the dust and pollution that mix with every atom of its air. In fact, the city I live in is the exact opposite of the beautiful picture behind the young millionaire, the one they've skillfully erected to erase poverty, depravation, lost dreams, and the wasted years of youth, a perfect picture that shows no trace of the volcano brewing in the depths of each of us.

My greetings are subdued, my voice coarse. I don't know what to say. He saves me the trouble of finding a suitable introduction. "I hear you'll be occupying an important position in your newspaper, Miss. Are congratulations in order, then?"

Occupy? That's exactly what has been offered me . . . to occupy . . . . And naturally Shoukry Shaker knew about it all along.

"Ahlam Shawarby—God rest her soul . . . ." I start to reply but the words get entangled.

He fidgets in his seat but says nothing. The mere mention of the dead actress angers him. He offers me a cold drink or a Nescafe. No thank you. He insists. I say no. I'll never break bread with a scoundrel like you.

"Anyway . . . the living must take precedence over the dead," I say.

He smiles, probably thinks I'm here to declare surrender, unconditional surrender like a nation whose backbone has been broken by a nuclear attack. I quickly manage to collect my thoughts:

"I mean . . . what's important to me now . . . Didi . . . she has to concentrate on her studies and start to build a successful future."

His chin is the shape of an Indian mango. He toys with it with two fingers, deep in thought. I was wrong to take him for a fool.

"You asked to meet me urgently . . . please get to the point."

"This is the point."

"Try to be specific." His voice has a musical ring despite the dryness of his words.

"What I'm trying to say is that Ahlam chose the entertainment industry . . . and we all know where that led her. Now we have to save Didi before it's too late."

God have mercy on you in your eternal rest. Your copybook is in my purse, your words in my heart. I'm sure you support every word I say.

"Poor Ahlam—God rest her soul—was the victim of a terrible crime. But in this day and age, a crime like this can happen to anyone . . . it had nothing to do with her work." Like a pop star he raises his eyebrows and gesticulates as he speaks.

"I can't tell if her end was related to the nature of her work or to the circles she moved in. The evidence has been tampered with . . . many of the facts have not yet been uncovered . . . ."

"That's for the police and the public prosecutor to decide. Can you please tell me what you want from me?" He rocks his lavish chair impatiently.

"That's a big issue I don't want to get into again. What's important for me now is Didi, that young innocent girl . . . ."

"But what do you want from me?" he interrupts.

"Leave Didi alone."

"Has anyone told you I kidnapped her? Didi is free to do what she wants like everyone else."

"She's young. She doesn't know what's good for her."

"Why don't you try talking to her?"

"It's no use . . . she's so stubborn. I've come here to convince you."

"I make it a point not to get involved in the private affairs of actors who work with me."

"Either you leave her alone, or I'll go on publishing my articles until the public prosecutor reopens Ahlam's case."

He laughs suddenly. Son of a . . . even his laughter is rhythmic.

"So, you've come here to threaten me . . . ."

"Not at all, sir. I'm just trying to convince you."

"To convince me? You don't understand one damn thing." He looks at me with genuine pity. "There's nothing you can do that would even annoy me . . . all your horses and all your men couldn't even touch one hair on my head."

You're right. I'm not in a position to threaten a chick, let alone one of the richest men in the country. Then why did I ask for this appointment in such a hurry? I came here looking for something that I hadn't quite defined in my mind. Perhaps I came here hoping for an apology for what happened to my friend Ahlam. I may have even believed I could save poor Didi. Or rather, did I come looking for a way out of my personal dilemma, an honorable way to accept the editor-in-chief's offer and save my brother's job?

"But what do you stand to lose by letting Didi continue her education? After that she can act if she still wants to." What can I do if he refuses? He holds ninety-nine percent of the cards, to borrow Sadat's expression.

"You don't get it when I say you don't understand one damn thing . . . . I'm simply not used to denying myself anything I want," he whispers. There's a delicate sadness in his eyes despite his insolence, as though he really pities me.

How true. Your request is indeed unreasonable, Islah. You want honor, heroism, success, money, and happiness for your family, and you want it all at once. You thought this man would offer you an easy solution to an impossible equation. If that solution was readily available, government offices would not be packed to the gills with bribe-seekers, whores wouldn't crowd the pavements, and every Egyptian would be able to live and die an honest person.

In the heat of my desperation I find myself liberated from all anxiety and confusion. The situation's terrible reality takes form in front of me, but in tranquility. Cairo's image behind the man is suddenly so attractive.

"Egypt looks so beautiful from up here," I hear my voice say as I turn to go.

�֍

She greets me with a hug. I've only seen her in mourning and with a sullen face. Grief has become second nature to her, smiling an alien act. Her skin has turned ashen, aging her by an extra twenty years. This is the first time I see her face in sunlight. The velvet navy-blue curtains are drawn open today. The sky is clear outside the window. Ahlam's mother returns to her usual position beneath her wedding photograph, protected by her long-lost youth, by her martyred hero. Her face is lit up by a composite beam of sunshine. But can the sun's warmth possibly melt her ice? I trace the corrosion on her features as if I'd known her for years. This is how much I feel for her. Her hopes have become mine, her tragedy no less so.

"You haven't called for some time, my daughter . . . but it's good to see you." There's warmth even in her blame.

She reminds me of Mama. Each of their life stories is a Greek tragedy, but they've both accepted their fates with neither remorse nor objection. A submissiveness that I've always found disturbing. Until, that is, I came to recognize my generation's tragedy: the illusion that happiness is a birthright. So we continue to demand, object, rebel, and we never accept — indeed, we're incapable of accepting — reality. We insist we've been denied our rightful happiness. In my childhood, when we'd all get carried away with laughter and our hearts opened up in a rare, transient happiness, Mama would quickly mutter, "God have mercy on us," three times. In my heart, I'd get upset with her; why did she have to feel privileged for a taste of happiness when others had it for breakfast and dinner? But I was fooled by appearances. Little did I realize that happiness is no more than a stolen moment which was never ours to start with, an unintended twist of fate anything but legitimate, a debt that once incurred we must sooner or later repay in blood, sweat, or tears.

"I've been so busy lately . . . but you're always on my mind and in my heart."

For a long time I was convinced I'd been tricked, I was angry at the world, blamed others for my shortcomings — then I met Ahlam Shawarby's mother.

"I know you're a decent girl, Islah." The smile that had started to form abruptly vanishes. "I know you've been worrying about . . . our rising star," she adds.

"Actually, I did watch Didi in a soap, right after breaking my fast . . . I came over to see how she's doing. I mean in her studies."

Bleeding horse heads and farm girls oozing eroticism follow our conversation from the surrealist painting on the wall.

"She hasn't opened a book since the beginning of the year . . . now, she's even stopped going to university altogether."

"Can I talk to her? Perhaps God will grant her wisdom." The two stuffed gazelle heads nod slightly above the doorway. In agreement, I wonder, or are they just making fun of me?

"She's not around . . . traveling, my dear . . . they're shooting in Alexandria. Who will she listen to, now that she's a star?"

Ahlam's gigantic image smiles down at me. This dangerous, dazzling illusion called stardom.

Desert or rural? I stop myself from asking.

I wonder if you ever took Ahlam and Didi to Alexandria when they were children. And if so did you prefer the desert or the rural roads? This was the chronic debate between Father and Mama; desert or rural? They'd always end up taking the rural route, to be on the safe side. Father would make a stop at every café on the highway. He'd raise the hood of the 1100R and we'd have fettir pastry with sugar and honey, and I'd relish the sensation of the bubbles in my Spathis soda as they gushed into my mouth, tickled my nostrils. The trip to Alexandria would take five or six hours. Just getting the car moving required forty-five minutes at least. Father would heat up the engine then start reading verses from the Koran. Mama was always late getting dressed and putting on her makeup. And I'd wait in growing impatience.

"Shall I call her tonight? Will she be back?"

"Not before next week."

"A whole week?"

"If you'll excuse me for a second, my daughter . . . I've got something cooking on the stove."

Ahlam's smile encircles me, the friend I so wished for in my childhood loneliness. Mama never allowed me to go to the beach on the first three or four days, until my skin got used to the sea breeze. So I'd spend three days on the balcony sniffing iodine. And when I'd complain, Teta would explain how lucky I was, recounting the story of how her own parents insisted on tying a rope to her waist before she went into the water. A couple of servants would stay on the beach, holding the other end, just to be on the safe side. Teta smelled of garlic, a clove of which she'd swallow every morning. I felt ashamed of her when my classmates came over. This is how we are in youth, Ahlam, blind. And when we grow older we don't really improve. Humanity: how blind we all are.

She'll spend a whole week with those scoundrels. Didi is not stupid; she can take care of herself. But a whole week . . . in the end, she's just a child inside a woman's body. Isn't that why men find her irresistible? Directors, producers, members of the public: all wolves.

"Can I help you with anything?" I shout. The flood of memories has kept me from showing some basic courtesy. The smell of home-cooked food invariably brings hope. Vine leaves; eggplant; beef tajine; chicken casserole; moussaka; oven-baked macaroni; pickled lemons, olives, and cucumbers; citrus, date, fig, apricot, and rose marmalades—how can things go bad in a home where such food is prepared? I wonder if Ahlam's mother is in the habit of preparing certain dishes on particular days of the week. In Mama's case, it was koshary on Fridays and fried sole on Wednesdays. Ramadan, of course, has its special rituals. But all that was in the past. Today, nothing is predictable anymore; the world has lost its bearings.

"I have everything under control, dear." Her voice floats on the aroma of frying onions.

I close my eyes then reopen them to Ahlam's face. She dominates the room from her poster. How can I save your sister and mine? And my brother and yours? Her magical smile provides no answers. Outside is a crystal ball of infinite clarity. How can wars break out under such a sky? How dare evil expose its bloody fangs? Two white doves circle on the other side of the window. A dove couple, all love and loyalty. They land on the windowsill. Only for a split second; then with an elegant fluttering of their wings they take off and dive into the translucent ocean of lapis lazuli.

A Page Never Read

It is impossible to define precisely what the soul is.
Definition is an intellectual enterprise anyway;
the soul prefers to imagine.

Thomas Moore

Obscene Exercises for Fat Women

Albayan *Newspaper*

Ahlam Shawarby

Two angelic circles in lapis lazuli: the dance of air and feathers. Despite its irregularity, their flight is serenity. The doves land on the balcony railing, then head into the apartment. My two friends flutter over the men's heads. Abd al-Malak and the Cerebellum have gotten used to their presence. They do not touch the men's food and never leave droppings. Their presence is pure and innocent. The men are busy moving chairs from the kitchen and bedrooms, setting them around the dining table. They are preparing for a séance they think will be special: the last séance in the millennium, before the counter turns and restarts at zero.

31 December 1999.

A turning point, according to the game of numbers. And how we humans have become captives of this magical game of numbers, the answer to our eternal dream of containing time, of preserving it in tin cans, to our quest for a device to freeze the ticking of the clock, at least for a while. For this purpose, we invented endings and beginnings, created the illusion of defining time's continuous flow. Definition, after all, is delineation, and delineation, control: a means to control our lives and everything around us. And can any of this be achieved without resorting to the weapon of numbers?

Except that our achievement extends no further than illusion's limited zone. The narrowness of our horizons—such a blessing, it turns out. We define the world we live in by our absence of vision and the darkness

261

in our hearts. We perceive time's flow as linear by means of a human invention called chronology. Sequence; cause and effect; past, present, and future: mere words we set loose, that carry neither substance nor meaning. Past and future merge, interweave, coexist in time's turbulent whirlpool. The present is an oversimplification, no more, a futile attempt to trap an illusory moment that has already elapsed by the time we perceive it. And vision . . . .

It was never about sight.

The heart's eye: can vision occur outside the realm of the heart?

Everything has been given, although, mostly, we are not aware.

⁙

When you find yourself contemplating your own body the way you study someone else's, you realize you have died. Except that your realization—despite its obviousness—stays within the realm of assumption, a mere hypothesis supported by an indicator here, a piece of evidence there; the reality of death remains beyond your awareness. Like life, death is a journey, an adventure imposed upon you with no prior warning, without the option to accept or reject it, with neither questions asked nor explanations given. You embark unprepared. A sudden fall or ascension: which of the two, in your confusion, you cannot tell.

My long hours in front of the mirror, my magnificence enthroned on the golden screen, my starry eyes on magazine covers, my narcissistic pride and deceiving modesty, all never satisfied my yearning to be truly beautiful. I had to await my demise to enjoy my physical allure. For this, I had to watch my corpse being pulled across the shining marble and flung, inert, onto the elevator floor.

Before the moment of my unwitting liberation, I had never seen my body this exquisite. My beauty only emerged after the body had shed its anger; the same anger that accompanied me throughout life's journey, then pursued me in death. Cast out by the body lying in its final rest, it caught up with me and started to besiege me. Here was anger more durable than the body that engendered it. Like a jinn, it materialized before me, ugly in form, terrifying in tenacity, to intensify my grief and panic. It returned my glare with impudence; its fury the fury of the moment—the moment of my violation after I was already a lifeless corpse; a finale for my previous rapes, my recurrent rapes in more forms than one, my ongoing rape over the days and years.

Latin rhythms resound throughout Señora Esmeralda's apartment. The night feels overstretched, flavorless. The beats of salsa, samba, lambada, and merengue combine with overused jokes and stale laughter. This instant, I am overcome with boredom with my whole life—this instant that still lingers in space. Everyone starts cheering, clamoring for me. With little enthusiasm, I climb on the table and the air spins in a whirlwind of drunken wobbly cigar smoke. Little by little, my dance develops a sensuality I had not anticipated. My repressed femininity finds expression, taking me and everyone else by surprise. Shoukry's eyes light up. It'll never happen. Haven't you learned that what you desire is farther away from your reach than the moon and the stars? Haven't you understood that you can only have me the legitimate way? I promised Mother and swore by the dear one. "This is a solemn oath I'll never break no matter what," I repeat to myself but go on dancing. I inflame his desire and mine with no hope of satisfaction.

He ends a quick call on his cell phone and joins me on the table. He sways smoothly with arms extended in the air. He whispers in my ear. I don't believe him at first. The marriage official is on his way, he insists. His apartment is on the thirteenth floor. We'll have a big wedding later but let's get the official part over with tonight. He speaks and to my astonishment, I accept. He hands me a glass of almond syrup; its bittersweet taste is my favorite. I say okay, it's my body talking now. My imprisoned desire has cried out, and with that, released the sequence of events that had already been floating aimlessly over my head.

And my shadow.

I tussled with it all night, inquiring about its significance.

It was a long night, seemingly everlasting, and then, the vision came to me.

⁙

My brother and sister dart out of the balcony. They leave the two men to their preparations. The Cerebellum moves loosely in his striped pajamas, a few sizes too big, stretched on one side by the weight of a book squeezed into a pocket. Abd al-Malak glows in a new black suit he wears with a white shirt and black tie, looking more like a mafioso than a psychic preparing for a séance to predict the events of the upcoming New Year. They leave the two men behind and circle in space then drop as if in response to an unpronounced call. They swoop into the Member of Parliament's open window on the third floor.

A shrill cry escapes Mrs. Sherbiny, the MP's wife. Like an extra in a burlesque show, her artificially straightened hair stands up on end in a halo around her face, which has turned ochre. She turns around in confusion but remains seated behind the desk she has placed on the floor landing just outside her apartment door. Her two bodyguards' hands shoot into their jackets but they decide against producing their weapons.

The two doves calmly glide above the heads of Mrs. Sherbiny, the distributor of alms, and her two bodyguards; above the public-bus driver who instinctively tightens his grip on the ten-pound note just handed to him by the generous hand; over the heads of the bus conductor, who is next in line, the radish vendor, and the garage attendant. They flap their wings down the staircase above the one-eyed lupine bean vendor with the two missing teeth and the queue of heads extending all the way down to the foyer. Finally, they fly over the last of the charity-seekers, patiently lined up on the pavement in front of the Tower of Happiness.

They circle above the petite Japanese correspondent talking to the camera in short unintelligible bursts and her TV crew who, with scholarly earnestness, are filming the queue; above the three public buses parked on the other side of the Nile Corniche; above Sergeant Ashmouni, whose worn-out shoe—this very instant—lands on the top step leading to the tower's entrance, either in an attempt to bypass the queue or on his way to participate in the séance of predictions for the New Year.

The two doves drop almost to road level just as the red car comes to a standstill in front of the tower. The sergeant looks back and freezes, staring at the car and its occupants. Shoukry whispers in Didi's ear. How beautiful she is, my kitten. The two doves flutter their wings right above their heads but neither of them takes notice.

Shoukry leaves her seated in the Ferrari and heads for the steps. As he approaches the sergeant, he waves a hundred-pound note. Ashmouni shakes his head in refusal. The two men wave their arms at each other theatrically. Shoukry stops and faces Ashmouni for a second. Their stares wrestle. Locked in a momentary exclusion zone of anger and confusion, the two men freeze. Finally, Shoukry manages to break loose and moves on. As for the sergeant, he wavers between continuing and turning back. He gives Didi a prolonged gape, then makes up his mind and proceeds toward her. Didi smiles at him.

How innocent is her smile, how honest.

"Take care, my daughter."

She doesn't reply.

"Watch out for the wolves . . . that surround you."

"I can take care of myself." Her stubbornness is doing the talking.

"The late Ahlam came to the tower with him, the night of . . ." He points to the tower's entrance that has already swallowed the young millionaire.

I did not think you possessed that kind of courage, Ashmouni.

"What are you saying?" My little sister is bewildered.

"He's responsible for your sister's death. Now his eye is on you."

What a violent moment it is, when words collide with reality—the moment we hear what we've been pondering for so long, except that now it resonates in the air. The truth: what a terrifying affair.

"Have you gone crazy?" she lashes out like a wounded tiger.

"I assure you, madness is not too far off for someone who's seen as much as I have," he says as he turns around.

Again he wavers between climbing the steps and returning to his intersection. He gives her a final, sidelong glance before making up his mind and heading for the steps. The doves beat the air insistently above Didi's head but she closes her eyes and presses her palms against her ears. It is time for the two doves to rise.

✖

Like a statue, Shoukry remains in the doorway, face to face with the hall's destruction. He examines the aftermath of my rage, in astonishment or in fear, I cannot tell which. Abd al-Malak approaches him, muttering unintelligibly. He pulls the millionaire by the coat sleeve and walks him through the outcome of my fury. The two men stop, overwhelmed, amid the piles of broken furniture. Neither of them utters a word. Shoukry puts an envelope in the false psychic's palm. The two men shake hands; briber and bribed. Abd al-Malak opens the envelope and spreads the banknotes in a fan, which he stares at in astonishment.

Shoukry clears his throat then whispers in his melodious voice, "My girl is waiting in the car downstairs."

The hall suddenly resounds with the fluttering of my brother's and my sister's wings. Shoukry turns around in terror. Abd al-Malak does not raise his eyes away from the deck of dollars in his hand.

"It would be good if . . . you'd talk some sense into her. I mean, assure her that the whole thing will end in marriage . . . the spirits foresee a wedding . . . something like that." Shoukry looks behind him as he speaks. He's finding it hard to control his rising trepidation. Same trick, same place, with the victim's little sister, her twin in beauty and femininity. If damnation is cast upon a person, its burden weighs forever on his heart. A crime is a continuum. He fools himself, he who thinks it is a

266

fleeting moment quick to come to an end. Injustice, like a cancerous cell, will constantly multiply.

Abd al-Malak does not respond. He nods to the money in his fist. He understands what is expected of him. The human race nods in unison. The act of nodding fills up existence, in regular, monotonous repetition.

It is my turn to nod. At Señora Esmeralda's, Shoukry whispers in my ear. He says the wedding sheikh is on his way and with a semi-drugged mind, I accept. I swallow the last drops of almond syrup. I have a liking for both its bitter and sweet tangs. I nod again and follow him to the elevator. With a lamb's submission, I walk. Two floors up then he turns the key in the lock. How many times have I refused to cross this threshold?

Today I cross, so long as the wedding sheikh is on his way. I kind of like the idea of getting married to Shoukry. I don't love him but Mother will be overcome with joy and she'll drown the world in ululations. I don't love him but I don't hate him either and what is marriage, if not legalized prostitution? The apartment is saturated with stale cigar smoke. A sudden nausea. I rest on the sofa as the world spins.

Abd al-Malak does not respond to Shoukry but he understands what's required . . . .

The devil of my anger blows like a storm inside the living room, defying its phony elegance. It completes ninety rotations before the window-panes explode in panic. Objects take flight with every additional round. The shelves release their books and the vases leap off the tables. Colorfully embroidered cushions tumble off the sofas, yet my rage continues to spin like a whirlwind out of hell. I had assumed that my rape lay at its source, but now my rage appears to be a tree with interweaving roots, multiple branches. I cannot distinguish where it starts and ends. I don't even know where it is leading me.

But the act of trashing the apartment rests suspended in time's spiral: recurrent, continuously replayed, stuck in the everlasting present, while I drown in perplexity, waiting for the truth to emerge.

"I'll bring her up now . . . can I depend on you?" Without waiting for an answer, Shoukry turns to go. In the doorway, he narrowly avoids the sergeant.

Ashmouni makes his way to Abd al-Malak across the wasteland left behind by my rage.

"Wouldn't it have been better to hold the séance after we break the fast . . . so you could invite us to kebab as usual?" He laughs cynically.

Abd al-Malak stares at the sergeant, struggling to understand what he is saying. After a moment he responds, dead serious, "The evening— after breaking the fast—is reserved for the New Year's party . . . it seems you're not living in this world." He waves the pile of banknotes in his hand as proof that the sergeant is not living in this world. "This is what they buy us with," Abd al-Malak adds after a moment's silence.

"For them to buy us . . . first, we have to put ourselves up for sale." Ashmouni's smile is pregnant with sadness.

✖

I always thought death snatched people away, disconnected them from the living. The truth is, the dead are concerned with life the most. Yes, death has—in spite of me—pushed me closer to people, to all creatures, to inanimate objects, to all things irrespective of their shape and color. Could the love of creation be the sole path to truth?

"Does anyone know why they call a maiden, a maiden?" Abdallah Bassily asks, laughing.

"Because her beauty drives us mad!" he answers himself, then realizes it's not funny.

"We're mad enough as it is." The Cerebellum speaks for the first time. He has exchanged his pajamas for a suit that also fits too loosely.

And what do any of you know about a woman's beauty?

A woman's beauty is more captivating than a genie's, more dominant than the grandest of empires, more destructive than a multiple-warhead

268

nuclear missile, longer lasting than time itself. A beautiful woman never grows old; the secret of her success is her unwavering belief in her own beauty. And I . . . after beholding my lifeless corpse in its serene splendor, I realized I had been predestined to be a beautiful woman, to bear beauty's burden and pay her price. So I came to accept the inevitability of my time running out while I was still in the prime of youth. And how grateful I felt for that.

"As long as we keep saying things like that, we'll never advance. In today's world there's no difference between a man and a woman." All this talk about beauty provokes my friend Islah. Finally, Abd al-Malak has given her permission to participate in his séances. At last, she has gathered the courage to come.

"Who can blame you, Miss . . .? Ever since you women were granted the right to divorce yourselves, you've gone out of control." The Cerebellum teasing her.

"Why does any of this interest you, doctor? You're not married or a millionaire." Abdallah Bassily produces a molasses stick from his pocket then realizes it is fasting time and returns it untouched.

"What does being a millionaire have to do with a woman's right to divorce herself?" The Cerebellum is curious.

"All the millionaires are scared to death, my friend. To avoid paying taxes, their possessions are officially in their wives' names . . . they all felt pretty secure knowing that the missus wasn't going anywhere. But now that women can simply divorce themselves, they can take off with the lot." Abdallah Bassily is a fat teacher explaining a lesson.

Abd al-Malak studies the faces around the table in silence. He does not try to hide his contempt for their silly laughter. The hundred-dollar notes are spread on the wooden surface in front of him. This time, he has not tried to turn on his lighting and sound effects. He has come to accept their futility. He understands how ridiculous he's been. Today he has not even bothered to shut the curtains. You are right, until when are we going to hide behind lies and illusions? Today the game will be played out in the open.

"The first prediction for the New Year: the black cloud of smog will cover Cairo all year round, then spread out to cover the whole country." The Cerebellum is full of enthusiasm for this prediction game.

Shoukry enters the room. He leads my little sister by the hand. Same man, same place, and the same dirty objective. They were late to come up. Perhaps she resisted. Maybe the sergeant's words raised her suspicions. In both beauty and stubbornness, you resemble me, Didi. You replicate my existence. The same damned recurrence, the present that multiplies and will never go away . . .

. . . Shoukry leads me by the hand, brings me here. Nausea. I rest on the sofa but my dizziness is getting more intense. My mind continues to rotate but slower. My ability to move is gradually eroded. What if? The idea flashes through my mind, then comes back again. Really, what if? Impossible! True, he's the one who handed me the glass of syrup, but impossible. Could he?

Where is the wedding sheikh in any case, why hasn't he appeared . . . ?

Shoukry pulls a chair for Didi then sits next to her. All eyes are on them. Abd al-Malak understands what is required of him. The magic wedding word, the same wedding sheikh who never materializes.

. . . Shoukry helps me sit on the bed then sits next to me. The son of a bitch has done it; he spiked my drink, added a yellow liquid as they say in Arabic movies. He has led me to the bed like a sheep to be slaughtered in the feast. And as my limbs grow paralyzed, my anger grows . . .

It is the same apartment, the same place where I was led into the trap. Now they are conjuring my spirit. The same apartment that has tasted my fury.

. . . It blows right here, in consecutive stormy cycles with neither beginning nor end, suspended in time. Circles of red mold the whole of existence. Cushions explode and feathers float in the air. The pages of books race like the wind. The sofas are lifted into the air until they touch the ceiling then dropped, then again and again until they've released their entrails. Armchairs are crashed into the walls. The legs of smashed chairs are driven into their seats until their springs and straw are dispersed everywhere . . . .

"Hi, Didi." Islah grates her teeth.

Islah faces them from the other side of the table, devours the two of them with her eyes. My one and only friend. I knew nothing like her friendship during my stay on earth. It has come very late, but there's always room for friendship. My copybook of secrets is in her purse. Where she goes, it goes. In return, her secret is now mine.

My sister, taken aback at first, starts to regain control.

"The second prediction: Palestine will remain occupied . . . and the Jews will remain masters of the world," the Cerebellum jokes under his gigantic eyeglasses.

Antar comes in carrying Meshmesh by the scruff of the neck like a mother cat carries her kittens. He stares at all the people sitting around the table. "Why are there lots of people sitting around the dining table with no food in front of them every time I come here?" he asks.

"The third prediction: our parliament will issue a new law legalizing bribery; the ultimate solution to the problem of corruption," the Cerebellum says.

Antar turns to Abd al-Malak. "Where is the chocolate you promised me, uncle? Don't worry, I'll eat it after I break my fast."

"The fourth prediction: Zamalek and Ahly, our two leading soccer clubs, will be shunted to the second division . . . and all the sports associations in Egypt will be dissolved," Abdallah Bassily responds to the Cerebellum.

"They'll legalize narcotics, on condition the trade is run by members of Parliament." The Cerebellum is an aggressive rabbit.

"You're very beautiful, auntie," Antar says to Didi. She smiles in delicious girlish bashfulness.

"They'll appoint a Coptic governor," Bassily whispers, hesitant.

"They'll appoint a woman judge," Islah joins the game.

"They'll appoint a man minister." Bassily's laughter shakes the room. And Shoukry lets loose his yellow smile.

⁘

With claws of steel he grasps my breast. He lifts my dress and digs his greedy fingers where they should never go. Feebly, I push him away. I bite. He slaps me with full force. My groan rises in a powerful wave. My shriek builds up in acuity and resolve, transforms itself into unremitting ringing. Ring ring. Shoukry howls in anger, lifts himself away from me, stands up, adjusts his necktie in the mirror. As he leaves the room, he pulls the door behind him . . .

Today, he smiles to my little sister. Her innocence adds a halo to her beauty, a quality he finds irresistible. This is how opposites attract: her beauty, his malice; her serenity, his guilt; her purity, his filth. Away from her, he can never be complete. Without corrupting her he will know no happiness. And she too, is drawn to him, drawn to her certain doom.

She smiles at him. The body of a woman, face of a child; every man's dream . . . right?

The voice of my rage explodes from Antar's lungs. He's still hugging Meshmesh. "You are all guilty and the worst of you knows who he is."

Islah checks under the table, searching for the source of the voice. She stands up and walks to the child, circles around him. Her face approaches his lips. Suddenly, she jerks a couple of steps backward. She realizes that the sound actually originates from the boy's vocal chords.

"I admit it. I'm guilty . . . but I'm also a victim. He who delivers the first blow is guiltier and I was never one to start . . . correct me if I'm wrong," Ashmouni says in a crystal clear voice.

"Who are you? Who does this voice belong to?" Islah asks, addressing herself to Antar.

"Search in your heart . . . you will find the voice's owner," I answer her calmly.

"All I ever hoped for was to, someday, not be an aggressor or victim," Ashmouni interrupts.

"If it's you . . . if it's really you, give me a sign," Islah addresses all those present. She stares at Abd al-Malak with suspicion. But he doesn't care. He just sits there, lost in his stack of cash.

"The proof lies inside your own purse. Turn the pages and you'll know," I reveal all to her. Today, everything must come out in the open.

Islah moves closer to Didi, holds her hand, and whispers in her ear, "Didi, it's really her . . . believe me."

My sister and my friend look all around the room.

"I no longer fear a living soul . . . or even the jinn," the sergeant shouts at Shoukry.

Didi stands up and throws herself in Islah's arms. Each seeks protection in the other's company. Didi, my darling, how I wish I could hug you, protect you from the beasts, from the tiger at the zoo. How I wish I could kiss our mother, lay my head in her lap, tell her not to worry about me, somehow alleviate her burden, reduce her agony. How I wish I could tell her: "You're the world's greatest mom, you are a mythical hero." But the barriers have been erected and the distances too vast for reunions. Life is a widow. Little by little, I'm drawn westward. Pulled, in spite of me, to another level. Didi allows herself to drift a few steps away from my friend. "Ahlam, can this be true . . . can it really be you?" she asks.

✵

I get up with difficulty. I grasp the bedpost in order to land on my legs. The mattress creaks. The bedpost screeches. An electrical shock passes through my body. My heavy breathing, a pulsating roar, shakes my head. Men's voices approach from a faraway nightmare. I hold onto the doorknob for support. I turn it; he hadn't quite shut the door. The wall's cold sensation on my shoulder. I try to keep steady, face the doorway's narrow

273

gap. The voices outside are my only safe haven. I'm just one step away from them, from being rescued, only one step.

"It's Tuesday, sir . . . not Wednesday." Shoukry's voice is shaken.

"Are you sure our meeting is for Wednesday rather than Tuesday?" The voice has the ring of Julio Iglesias that I love so much. "In any case . . . the situation allows for no delay," the voice answers itself sharply.

"But my father is traveling . . . he'll only be back tomorrow morning." Fear is creeping into Shoukry's voice. His crime is about to be exposed, he'll be disgraced before the world. I must keep steady for a few moments more. Soon it'll all be over. I push the door, heavy as a rock blocking a mythical cave. I pull together all my resolve.

"The route of the new canal will be announced next week. We only have a few days to buy up all the plots of land," spoke another voice, more calmly. There are two men with Shoukry and two others in the background, near the main door. Suddenly all is quiet. All eyes are on me.

"What's she doing here?" Julio Iglesias's voice is projected at me. The voice's owner is thin and dark. His face is stern, tense. He's wearing sunglasses in the middle of the night.

The other man turns away abruptly, to avoid me. I thought his face was familiar. Now I can only see his back. He moves away, sits facing the piano in the far corner.

"It's because . . . the meeting was supposed to be tomorrow," Shoukry stutters. The mean dog.

In the corner closest to the balcony, I can see a delicate white flower. In a vase of painted porcelain on a small table, one white rose, vibrant, full of life. The world can't be all black. There must be some mistake. Perhaps this is not really happening; mere hallucinations. Maybe Shoukry has carried me to the bed and we're waiting for the doctor to arrive. Maybe . . .

"I thought I had warned you that this apartment was to be used only for business purposes. I made it clear you weren't allowed to let anyone in other than your father."

"Forgive me, sir. It's no big deal . . . the girl's high on heroin. She won't remember a thing." What are you accusing me of, you lowlife? Was it heroin, then, that you spiked my drink with?

"Now you're using my apartment as a drug den?" the man with Julio Iglesias's voice shouts.

"No, no. . . she was already high when she came. When I realized, I was just about to throw her out . . . ."

"And how can we be sure she won't remember anything?" The man rubs his nose with his thumb.

The one sitting on the piano stool with his back to me remains silent. His cigar smoke is a ghost floating over his head. He raises the keyboard cover and starts to play.

✖

The notes from the piano bounce off wrecked furniture, books torn apart, tattered paintings, and shards of glass spread across the hall, and smoothly impose themselves on the séance. Didi throws herself again into Islah's arms while Abdallah Bassily starts shaking in his chair, almost turning over. *I adore you . . . but wish I could forget you.'* Shoukry is frozen in his chair, staring straight ahead. He dares not take a breath until the music stops.

"I, too, am no longer scared . . . I took part in building the Iraqi nuclear program before the Americans brought it down . . . I thought I was helping to build up the power base of the Arab nation but found myself a participant in the greatest Arab catastrophe since '67 . . . but that's not important anymore . . . besides, it's not really my fault . . . was I the one who played roulette with the destinies of millions or the one who uses nations as pawns in a chess game? I'm merely a man who was deceived by history, no different from a million other fools." The Cerebellum is a marionette in a puppet show, waving his arms in the air.

You're right, Cerebellum; the world's perfection is deceiving. Except that the fault lies only in people's eyes, in our egoism, in the triviality of our concerns, in our chatter.

Silence is perfection.

The sin of all humans is that they blind themselves to the perfection that pervades them. They intentionally tighten their own blindfolds; blindfold their hearts; intentionally . . .

"Help me!" I whisper with difficulty. I seek assistance from the man in sunglasses who has Julio's sleepy voice. I approach him, leaning on the back of the sofa for support. He does not respond, looks to the man who has turned his back on me, who's playing, 'I Adore You.' How did he guess it's my favorite song? The man with sunglasses takes a few steps and whispers in the other's ear while he plays.

I adore you . . . but wish I could forget you. He sways right and left then stops playing. Why are you stopping? I adore you . . . but wish. What warmth and beauty! Why did you stop playing?

"Take care of it," he replies sharply.

The man with the sunglasses paces back to me but the other does not resume playing. The man with the sunglasses says nothing. Take care of it. He's not going to help me. I feel his burning glare from behind the Ray-Bans. I limp toward the door. My legs are no help. I tumble to the floor. The shock of my collision is silent. All sounds have escaped and there's nothing left but flashes, reflections from the pistachio-green marble in my eyes.

"Ihsan, take care of the young lady," says the man in the Ray-Bans. Julio's voice reaches me from far away, from another world. The marble floor shudders with slowly receding footsteps.

Cigar smoke blends with the pistachio-green luster. The cold penetrates my cells. I shiver. The cigar's aroma is an invisible fist pressing hard against my chest. This is a soundless, motionless ocean. Where have you gone, Ihsan? Take care of the young lady. Could he have left with the others?

An eternity. My eyes are on the white rose. The colors of its cheeks taste like dreams. Its red is pomegranate; its purple leaves a flavor on the tongue; its yellow smells like a lemon tree in blossom. An eternity. An eternity of waiting, then the earth trembles beneath my head. His steps are calm and confident, his shoes black, well polished. He stoops. His face approaches mine, handsome and rosy. He stares me in the eyes, then stands upright. He produces a pair of gloves from his jacket pocket, fills them up with his steel fists, then bends. He lifts me by the elbows. I have lost the will to move. I have turned into an inanimate object that he pulls toward the apartment door.

"Such great beauty . . . what a pity," Ihsan whispers to himself.

✖

"You're the killer!" Islah's finger is a canon pointed at Shoukry Shaker's face. All eyes turn to him and Abd al-Malak waves his bunch of dollars at him. "You murdered Ahlam . . . and now you want to do the same to Didi." Islah holds Didi tightly as if to protect her from a pack of wolves surrounding them from every direction.

They're all wolves . . .

Ihsan, the bodyguard, throws my body on top of the piano. I reach out for support. My hand lands on the keyboard producing an explosion of notes that echoes throughout the hall. His handsome face leans over me.

"Such great beauty . . . what a pity," he sighs.

Suddenly, he grasps my breast then releases it. His athletic body presses me against the piano. He takes his gloves off, produces a pen-knife. The blade briefly glints in my eyes. I wait for the stab but he lifts my dress instead. The hiss of tearing cloth. My clothes. The fabric parts with certainty as the knife slits through it. I look down at my body. He's cutting through my underwear with the same calculated coldness, the same criminal precision. He throws the knife on the surface of the piano and attacks my body with voracious fingers.

277

The blade shines again in my eye. I extend my fingers. I endure. I raise the blade in my weak grip. The blood explodes from his face, a longitudinal cut from right beneath the eye down to his chin. My head shakes under his blow. The knife is flung away. He grasps my neck. The warmth of his grip freezes me; his hands' heat conducts all the world's cold. He stares into my eyes as he squeezes. The color red drowns the piano's cries. His blood drips into my eyes. My own blood roars in my ears. He relaxes his grip. A gulp of air. The hardness of his body preempts all resistance. The white rose smiles to me from her far corner. The light gets dimmer, sound recedes. Abdelhalim's voice comes from within. I adore you but wish. Ihsan repeats, "Such great beauty . . . what a pity." I feel my body slip over the smooth surface as darkness blindfolds the world's eyes . . .

"I'm innocent . . . I swear to God, I'm innocent," Shoukry shouts suddenly.

"You're the guiltiest of us all." The sergeant bangs the table.

"Never . . . I've never in my life even hurt a fly." The millionaire's voice is rhythmic despite his confusion.

Abd al-Malak waves the dollars at him.

"I didn't kill Ahlam . . . I loved her . . . if I knew . . . I would never have agreed."

My rage . . . who dispelled you and where have you gone? Like a sudden gale, you blew for a reason. Your mission accomplished, now you disappear without a trace.

"And Didi . . . do you love her too . . .? You must have a really big heart." Abdallah Bassily's words are pure poison.

"Are you happy with what he's saying, Ahlam? Why don't you answer him?" Islah looks around her in all directions and so does Didi, then both their eyes focus on Antar.

"Let bygones be bygones . . . and don't worry; friendship is forever," I reply to my friend. I can sense a profound transformation; I'm no longer concerned with what happened to Ahlam. My connection to the woman I once was is slowly disintegrating.

"But Ahlam . . ." Didi is asking for my support.

"Let bygones be bygones . . ."

Meshmesh mews and Antar shudders. "Why do you people keep bringing me here . . .?" The child comes to and asks in a low voice.

Silence.

"It will be the last time, I promise," Abd al-Malak says at last.

"Each time we come here, Meshmesh acts mean afterward."

"The chocolates are over there . . . you can have the whole box." Abd al-Malak is still holding onto the bunch of money.

"I don't want your chocolates . . . I want you people to think of me for once. I'm cold . . . so is Meshmesh." He holds Meshmesh close to him then turns to Didi who appears very confused: "Aren't you going too, auntie?"

Didi hugs the child just as he hugs the kitten, then she turns to Ashmouni, "Sergeant, can you stop a cab for me, please?"

"Right away, my daughter."

"It's getting colder," Bassily remarks as he stands up.

The cold . . .

The cold that goes beyond any cold I have experienced, an inner frost against which wool and fire are ineffective. The necessary fall before a possible ascent. It comes to me between alternations of light and darkness, amid sporadic sparks. The weight of a merciless monster. The touch of flesh. Flashes of final moments. My teeth chatter. Ihsan's viscous blood is on my face. I hold onto the piano's leg, dazzling black, like a drowning woman. The white rose is in the background. Its colors explode suddenly. A penetrating white light. Millions of white butterflies transform into white doves. Thousands of wings welcome me. The dissipation of anxiety. The end of fear. There is no context for the struggle anymore. I can see for the first time.

Light.

The light flows inside my veins, penetrates my cells. My worn-out body has been transformed into a ray of light, a new light that revives the world's colors, a light that, in its purity, permeates everything. Under its intensity, my killer appears transparent. A lightness of being beneath the cover of flesh, the encasing of fat, bones, and intestines. A lightness of being beneath his injustice, greed, fear, and pettiness.

I see the world for the first time.

Suddenly, he is scared. He's realized that he's been having intercourse with a corpse. He stands up in panic. He's been touched by death, and he'd thought death was the monopoly of others. His face has been bloodied by my stab.

He rushes to the main door, freezes with his hand on the knob, then bends down, shuddering. He turns around to inspect my corpse. He paces around the hall like a tiger in a cage. He stops, grates his teeth, tears off what's left of my clothes, tries to avoid touching my skin. He wipes his face with my dress then cleans up his own blood from my face. He stuffs my things into a plastic bag, drags my body to the main door, leaves me there, then gets my dress out of the plastic bag again. My things fall out, scatter on the green marble.

He's noticed the bloodstains and sweat marks on the piano and floor. He uses my dress to clean up the mess he made then returns it and the other things to the bag. He opens the door cautiously to make sure there's no one on the landing. He summons the elevator and leans the plastic bag against the wall next to it. He drags my body into the elevator and leaves me there without a piece of cloth to cover my secret. I have only my violated innocence to protect me.

He presses the buttons to all the floors and steps back again onto the landing. The door locks my corpse in. The elevator embarks on its downward journey. My naked body lies in peace.

✖

But why have I remained mystified, suspended in time? Perhaps I felt insulted in my death, felt I needed an apology. Or maybe I felt a need to offer my own apologies. If that is the case, then every Egyptian deserves an apology, and must in return apologize to others. Each of us is both executioner and victim.

And we're all mystified, suspended in time.

The séance is over but Islah, paralyzed by confusion, does not leave. She looks all around her, searches in the midst of the wreckage, excavates for an answer to an unspecified question. Your perplexity, my friend, is mine. I wish I had the capacity to illuminate your way.

I had imagined that with death, questions disappear and answers crystallize, but time has proved me wrong. Could questions, then, be the sole truth? Might answers exist only in people's imaginations?

She approaches my corner, comes to a standstill before the small table. She observes the crochet tablecloth and the brilliant surface unblemished by a speck of dust, contemplates the porcelain vase hugging my vibrant rose that, all this time, has refused to wither. Beneath the table, the pistachio-green floor shines like crystal. My rage has spared the entire corner; even for this, I have no explanation. This whole situation is beyond me, just as it is beyond you, Islah.

She remembers my copybook, which I left here for her. She produces it from her purse. Of course . . . the copybook. It must carry a message for her, a special kind of code, a password. Open sesame. Randomly, she turns the pages. She chooses a page and starts to devour it when my two friends' fluttering catches her attention. She follows them to the balcony. For a second she contemplates their aerial acrobatics then goes back to the page.

"My heart embraces every form; it is a pasture for gazelles, a convent for monks, a temple for idols . . . the pilgrim's Kaaba," she reads out aloud. She stops, allows the words to sink into her soul, then repeats in her loudest voice: "My heart embraces every form; it is a pasture for gazelles, a convent for monks, a temple for idols . . . the pilgrim's Kaaba," she shouts in Cairo's face, in Egypt's face, in the face of the entire globalized world.

Then she listens. What, are you waiting for the world to respond?

She turns the pages then stops. Her eyes trace the letters of a new page's title, again and again. "Obscene exercises for fat women," she whispers. She keeps it down; no shouting this time. Her eyes are again drawn to the words. You're still searching, Islah, prospecting, deceiving yourself that the answer lies in the copybook.

Before she can digest the first line in the article, the copybook slips from between her fingers. She tries to catch it but it flies away. The wind flings it into the empty space beyond her. She stares at it as it drifts then starts to soar, follows it with her eyes, her arm outstretched. Her shock over the copybook's loss grows. Helplessly, she looks around her. It crosses her mind to rush down and catch the copybook as it reaches the ground. But she's frozen in place, watching the copybook rise rather than drop as anticipated. The sense of loss gradually dawns upon her.

A single tear flows down her pale cheek.

Then the copybook explodes, dispersing thousands of miniature papers of all colors in the air. All the colors of the universe sparkle in her eyes, colors that metamorphose into butterflies. Millions of colored butterflies fill Islah's world and return the smile to her heart. She's a child again, fascinated by a magician's sleight of hand. She mutters, "Let bygones be bygones . . . and don't worry; friendship is forever."

Islah waves goodbye to the butterflies as they head toward the horizon.

There is an invisible relationship that binds us all; the living and the dead. That binds me—after the maggots have devoured my flesh—to a child that will be born in a far-off land in the distant future, links the two of us to all living creatures, even to inanimate matter, which pulsates though it is not permitted to make a sound. Alchemy. An umbilical cord that connects the whole of existence. A love affair that links me to meteors and volcanoes. The music of the ocean's waves and the roar of colliding galaxies. The unity of existence is the unity of creation. Nothing happens by chance. Serendipity. Parallelism. The rotation of constellations. Nature is harmony.

Equilibrium.

The colors have adopted an orange hue with the approaching sunset. The shadows have stretched out and forms seem less tense, more at ease. Islah starts laughing on the haunted apartment's balcony. She laughs long and loud. She opens her arms to the world before her, opens her heart to the two doves, my friends who have become hers. At that moment, Mansour, the electrician, lights up the chain of colored bulbs, the pattern he's toiled for weeks to mount over the entire façade. Islah shines. Without knowing it, she's at the heart of a giant white rose, a rose of pure light.

A Page No One Noticed

My heart embraces every form:
it is a pasture for gazelles, a convent for monks,
a temple for idols . . . the pilgrim's Kaaba,
the tables of the Torah . . . the tome of the Koran.
In the religion of love I believe,
its course I have chosen to pursue.
For love is my religion and it is my faith.

Mohyiddin Ibn Arabi

Ahlam Shawarby

"Yesss! Got you, got you, got you."

Your laughter cuts like a knife. You take pleasure in the man's revulsion. To your cheerful applause, the sergeant spits out what seems like vomit onto the pavement. At first, his face lit up, thankful for your generous gesture. He welcomed the sandwich after the meager meal he broke his fast with, prayed for you before biting into the soft bread. But what overjoyed him most was that you had thought of him. The sandwich was proof that a special connection bound the two of you. You, the spoiled middle-class brat bubbling with an inner force, the child whose every move, whose every look, pulsates with the vitality of existence; and he, the aging man whose heart has been stepped upon once too often, who has been whipped by the sun and frost, the traffic sergeant whose existence pedestrians overlook and whose signals cars ignore, who was born and bred in poverty and never blessed with a son to make up for all his suffering.

"But it was a good one, right?"

You wrap your cruelty in your child's lisp. Since morning you've been planning your prank. You immersed the soap in water to soften it, then spread it with a knife, watched the thick, soft layers saturate the bread. You used up a whole bar from your mother's Camay box. Then you eagerly waited for the canon to announce the end of the fast, so you would feel less guilty about committing your sin. And now you're overjoyed for the man's humiliation.

But you're not to blame. No one ever taught you anything but blind obedience: to conform to a social order that subdues your freedom, subjugates your nature; to treat as sacrosanct edicts that are merciful on the surface but rotten to the core. You have assimilated your society's class-consciousness, absorbed it to the marrow. In early childhood you learned to despise poverty, to look down on the social classes beneath you. People's misery now makes you laugh. You do to others what has been done to you. You pass on the torch.

You Antar . . .

You Antar . . . are me.

"Is this kind of behavior right, my son . . . ? I'll be scared to take anything from you after this." You don't respond when the sergeant reproaches you.

But one tear restores your humanity. The lone tear that escapes from the sergeant's eye electrifies your heart, makes you realize what you've done. You instinctively know that you're not incapable of influencing others, that you're not incapable of giving. So you hug the man you've just insulted. You pat his dusty jacket with a small palm and say, "No uncle sergeant. You can't ever be scared."

Only your innocence remains in the almost-vacant vessel of hope. Without your natural luminosity, my voice would have been unable to materialize in your body and shake the foundations of this miserable Tower of Happiness.

But you recognize none of this. You don't have a clue about the reason for the sergeant's sudden laughter. You turn and rush home in a victory dance rather than a child's hop. Little do you realize that despite what you've done, you're the only ray of hope that remains to him and the others. Actually, you do know, but this awareness is relegated to the margins of your soul. You jump in the air and sing loudly,

"Turn off the lights woman . . . .

We're the burglar policemen."

✖

And you, Bassily . . . you revel in the exploits of soccer legends Hamada Imam, Hassan Shehata, and Rouka, describe the Zamalek–Tottenham match as though it was played yesterday. You tell stories about Abdelkarim Sakr's acrobatics on the field and his private exploits in the brothels of Claude Bey, although you've never set eyes on the man. You whisper to yourself, "Ali Kouta welcomes Ahly and Zamalek: Egypt celebrates a feast, today," and smile. Then you say, "You bring us good luck, Latif," to young people who don't have a clue who you're talking about. How you miss chewing sugarcane and devouring tangerines in the third-class stalls. In bygone days, you used to play simultaneously in the positions of goalkeeper and striker, the days of youth, so much closer than anyone can imagine. Tell me, Captain Zewar . . . is the name correctly pronounced Falcao or Falsao?

In the roastery, you start telling one of your jokes. "Pope Shenouda, Sheikh Sharawy and a regular guy like us stand before God on Judgment Day . . ." then you stop. It's a great joke but you're tongue-tied. Today, a cloud covers your clear-skinned round face. You clasp your hands together. You're about to bite into a molasses stick but refrain, put it back in your pocket. You should show courtesy to those who are fasting. "El-Kosh, Part One or Part Two?" you cynically ask, referring to the village where Muslims and Copts clashed. You laugh while the knives carve up your intestines. But you're not alone; the heart of every Egyptian bleeds.

You Bassily . . . .

You Bassily . . . are me.

You are me, and I am you,

There's nothing to separate us but the illusion of individuality.

✹

And you, Cerebellum . . . you've given the chicken-and-egg conundrum a ton of thought. You debate Abd al-Malak in his area of expertise; insist that people make a mistake when they say that a chicken lays an egg to pass on its lifeline to the chick. In your conversations with the sergeant, you stress that it is the egg that hatches so that the chicken can lay another egg. You explain to the newspaper vendor that genes control our lives, employ us to ensure their continued existence. When no one will listen to you, you stand in the balcony of your friend Tutu's apartment and shout that the egg is the origin, not the chicken. You yell that individuality is an illusion, our consciousness merely a secondary element in the window-dressing of existence.

You mutter the names of Nasser and Saddam in your sleep. Your nightmares are inhabited by the CIA, Mossad, and the festival of sexual paraphernalia in Kasseb's cupboard. With your mind's eye you can see colliding galaxies, pulsars, black holes. You try to visualize the curvature of space, the duality of light, absolute zero. You've devoured books in every field and turned your extraordinary mind into an information warehouse. You whisper that had it not been for the revolution, someone like you would never have had the opportunity to get an education, let alone become a scientist. Then you wonder: what good is learning and what's the use of knowledge, anyhow?

You insist that neither government nor civil society has a monopoly on corruption, that what we're faced with is rather a culture of corruption. You declare that until society reaches ideological consensus, a democratic system will never take root, that ideas are at the heart of all reform. And you smile calmly because in the world of ideas, you are king. But the truth kept on eluding you until you received 'The Mother of All Battles Award' in a country whose children are dying by the hundreds of thousands.

You smile. But where were you when your mother lay moaning in the throes of death? Were you blessed with a son to carry your name or a wife to wail at your departure? In fact, you've provided empirical proof that more knowledge equals less understanding. If only you'd accept that egg and chicken are two sides of the multifaceted truth, maybe then you'd enjoy some peace.

You . . . little genius.

You, Cerebellum . . . are me.

You are me, and I am you,

There's nothing to separate us but the illusion of individuality.

Time is one, our places we've exchanged . . . and space is our common heritage.

Lover and loved, oppressor and oppressed, executioner and condemned . . . we're all of them at once.

⁙

And you, Shoukry, heir to billions . . . you've grown fond of giving your father lessons he cannot understand. You tell him about the dream of noblemen across the ages—he who was born on the sidewalk, toiled as a laborer, and never wore a new shirt until he'd made his first million. He smiles. You explain that science will at last allow the aristocracy to become ethnically and physically superior. You proudly insist you'll live to be a hundred and fifty and your son will make it to five hundred. You'll still be young when you turn ninety while the riffraff will find it hard to climb the stairs at forty. Beaming with enthusiasm, you ask him to imagine the amount of knowledge, experience, wisdom, and power that will belong to you and your peers. You'll all finally achieve your blue-blood fantasy.

And when—in a rare moment of contemplation—your father confides in you, says that the tragedy of his generation and yours is that you'll never witness your nation become a developed, sophisticated state, that in fact you'll never meet a person who has either seen or may possibly see such a day, you make fun of him and wonder when he got to be so blind. You tell him that perspectives have changed, that we live in a 'Me' era, an era that knows no national allegiance. This is the age of money that recognizes no boundaries, the age of those who own money, who make up the new-world aristocracy, the masters who will control the course of history for centuries to come. Their allegiance is to one another, not to states and nationalities. These are the Hapsburgs and Tudors of the twenty-first century.

Your musical voice rings out when you repeat to the astonished old man that Egypt today is living its golden era. After decades of turbulence, society is at last taking shape. The new class is coming of age. And the Egyptian people, how lucky they are, at last, to be blessed with the leaders who will put them on the map of the world.

And when he reprimands you for ignoring his warnings and continuing to visit the Tower of Happiness, you think to yourself that the man, despite all the wealth and influence he's amassed, has never managed to liberate himself from fear and submissiveness. You point out politely that a master never fears to go wherever he pleases.

You're taken by surprise when he scolds you, accuses you of stupidity, shouts that your country is one thing, America—from whose universities you graduated—another, that here, in old Egypt, wealth is an illusion because possession is, ultimately, pharaoh's exclusive prerogative, one that he shares with no one, no matter how eminent he may be. You respond calmly that he's a prisoner of the past, while you are the son of the future.

You sit alone with your dreams, your only companion a tumbler of Grand Marnier. Whenever your victim's specter emerges, you proclaim innocence, repeat your list of lame excuses, as though standing before an incorruptible judge. Then you push all your black thoughts aside and go back to humming a sweet tune . . . to which song? You can't remember.

You, Shoukry . . . .

You, my murderer . . . are me.

You are me, and I am you.

There's nothing to separate us but the illusion of individuality.

Time is one, our places we've exchanged . . . and space is our common heritage.

Lover and loved, oppressor and oppressed, executioner and condemned . . . we're all of them at once.

We move in coinciding circles that we thought to be detached.
Their colors: a rainbow of crystal white.

⁙

And you, sergeant . . . you fought in two wars but could never figure out why the defeat of '67 did not dent our resolve, while the victory of '73 . . . You turn from one psychic doctor to the other and say, "Would you, educated people, please explain?"

You've remained silent in war and in peace, mute in sunshine and frost. You never spoke out against injustice and humiliation. Then, suddenly, after your hair has turned white, you rediscover your voice and the words flow. You say, 'We're all thieves and have all been robbed.' You disapprove of Zuzu, the flirt, when she wants to hit the town on New Year's Eve. You say, "They're celebrating one thousand years of plunder, exploitation, and promiscuity. Naturally, they look forward to another thousand." You add, "So what do we celebrate . . . a millennium of oppression, misery and crawling in the mud? What do we have to look forward to . . . another millennium of the same?"

And when, flirtingly, she persists in her request, you find yourself bombarded by the same erotic dream. You can't get your mind off the elevator with the smoky mirrors, soft music, and floor lights that turn on and off. Your desire mushrooms. You say to yourself, "Aren't we human too?" You turn to her, "You can't imagine how special you are to me . . ." Then whisper in her ear that you'll take her, allow her to feast her eyes on the tower, its lights and extravagant parties. You mention you'd do anything to make her happy but sharply add that all she can expect is a quick tour from floor to floor, she can only watch, no more. You won't tolerate any dancing or such nonsense. You quickly whisper that she'd be wise to keep quiet about this, or else the Owl will smell something cooking.

Then you take a nap, prepare yourself for the celebration of a thousand years.

You, Ashmouni . . .

You, sergeant . . . are me.

You are me, and I am you.

There's nothing to separate us but the illusion of individuality.

Time is one, our places we've exchanged . . . and space is our common heritage.

Lover and loved, oppressor and oppressed, executioner and condemned . . . we're all of them at once.

We move in coinciding circles that we thought to be detached.

Their colors: a rainbow of crystal white.

Before our individuality was generated . . . our existence was real, and after the maggots devour our livers . . . where will our egoism reside?

✖

And you, Shaker Pasha . . . you provide banquets for the poor, distribute alms and charity, then go off to seek happiness in the Tower of Happiness. With no prior notice, you impose yourself on Farah and go mad if she declines. You say to her, "I've just gulped a glass of 'sers elzalou,' the aphrodisiac from Lebanon that's known to work miracles, and won't relent until I get what I want." You stand there in surprise when she tells you, "It's Ramadan. Have fear of God!" You argue that the canon has already gone off, signalling the end of the day's fasting. You shout that you won't go home until you've quenched your thirst. And when she persists you accuse her of being cynical. A whore's a whore, Ramadan or not.

And when she still does not comply, you fly into a rage and resolve to take what is rightfully yours by force. Yes: what is rightfully yours, the goods you paid good money for. By the time you feel the numbness creep up your arm, you've already torn the bodice off her nightgown. Then come the chest pain and shortness of breath. Suddenly, you're all alone, as in reality you've always been, in good times and bad. You lie down on the sofa and, in your solitude, face the truth.

You, Shaker . . .

You, kingpin . . . are me.

You are me, and I am you,

There's nothing to separate us but the illusion of individuality.

Time is one, our places we've exchanged . . . and space is our common heritage.

Lover and loved, oppressor and oppressed, executioner and condemned . . . we're all of them at once.

We move in coinciding circles that we thought to be detached.

Their colors: a rainbow of crystal white.

Before our individuality was generated . . . our existence was real, and after the maggots devour our livers . . . where will our egoism reside?

The spirit is everlasting, and the ego, an illusion soon to dissipate.

⁙

And you, distinguished journalist, editor of the women's page, owner of a living conscience, who bears responsibility for your brother's future and your mother's contentment . . . Since childhood you've carried the world's burden on your shoulders, and today, you demand revenge for the injustice suffered by your friend. In your zeal to protect your little sister, Didi, you smile at her and search for the right words. But you cannot find them.

You contemplate Didi, who occupies her mother's place on the sofa beneath her parents' wedding photograph, and repeats that she has the right to find her own way in life without people interfering. She has the right to make choices, good or bad. In the end she's the one who'll have to face the consequences. She says "You and Ahlam are no better than me." And you shake your head, still searching for the right words.

You mutter that you only want to open her eyes to the realities of the world. You address your words to Ahlam's poster, the photograph of me in my phoniest of states. "No, we're no better than you," you admit after a long silence. You talk to the gazelles' stuffed heads. You wonder if she's heard about your affair with Karim, if the truth is out in the open as is the way of all truths. Maybe she's heard that your brother is now working for Shoukry, the murderer, or that you got promoted. Has the world exposed your dilemma? You wonder if all eyes are on you, silently observing, mocking you in filthy, sadistic curiosity.

You, my best friend, my alter-ego in all aspects; in self-respect; in being honest with yourself; in your resolve to say the truth come what may; in dedicating your life to an illusion that will never come true. When you sit alone with yourself you say, "I made mistake after mistake after mistake, but I tried. I did my best."

Questions about your next move surround you but you find no answers. You realize how much you admire this gorgeous girl. For the resolve that shines in her black eyes, for the hope she fills the world with. And you ask yourself, "Who do you think you are to open this girl's eyes to the realities of the world?" And again you search for the right words but cannot find them.

You, Islah and Didi . . .

You, my friend and my little sister . . . are me.

You are me, and I am you.

There's nothing to separate us but the illusion of individuality.

Time is one, our places we've exchanged . . . and space is our common heritage.

Lover and loved, oppressor and oppressed, executioner and condemned . . . we're all of them at once.

We move in coinciding circles that we thought to be detached.

Their colors: a rainbow of crystal white.

Before our individuality was generated . . . our existence was real, and after the maggots devour our livers . . . where will our egoism reside?

The spirit is everlasting, and the ego, an illusion soon to dissipate.

Oh ye white rose . . . guardian of secrets.

✖

Curiosity killed the cat.

And you, Meshmesh, hide beneath the wrecked furniture that once epitomized good taste and fashion and cost a fortune to purchase from Roche-Bobois.

Your eyes glow in concentric circles of color, waves in the mighty ocean of desire. Your innocence exudes tenderness, warm and delicate, idolizes caprice. You know no shame and promise nothing. And when you do, you break your promise without the slightest sense of guilt.

Your eyes shine in the dark, equally unsettling to the sleeping and those who are awake. You see what we cannot. You understand the meaning of our ancestors' saying, "Darkness provides intelligence and nutrition." In fear, you puff yourself up, expose your claws. In play, you toss and turn like a tame tiger. And in the coldness of the night, you rub against us and your mewing spreads an intuitive warmth across the world.

You, Meshmesh . . .

You, Meshmesh . . . are me.

You are me, and I am you.

There's nothing to separate us but the illusion of individuality.

Time is one, our places we've exchanged . . . and space is our common heritage.

Lover and loved, oppressor and oppressed, executioner and victim . . . we're all of them at once.

We move in coinciding circles that we thought to be detached.

Their colors: a rainbow of crystal white.

Before our individuality was generated . . . our existence was real, and after the maggots devour our livers . . . where will our egoism reside?

The spirit is everlasting, and the ego, an illusion soon to dissipate.

Oh ye white rose . . . guardian of secrets.

If neither death provides an ending . . . nor birth a beginning . . . then extension is total, complete.

✖

"Straight ahead," you, Abd al-Tawab Pasha—Tutu—instruct your chauffeur in your deceptive calm.

The exit to your right slips behind, the one that would have taken you, beneath the flyover, to the private hospital where your grandmother lies. The driver pushes on along Nile Corniche toward Maadi. After a few minutes he slows down and, without waiting for instructions, makes a U-turn at the intersection. The Cadillac comes to a standstill in front of the Tower of Happiness.

Without a word, both the driver and bodyguard get out. They wait outside, alert among the shadows. You, in the Cadillac's solitude, rest your head against the upholstered car body and close your eyes, feigning drowsiness. As though you could fool the devils that surround you from every side, the mocking devils who block your sleep, leave you writhing like a child eyeing a piece of candy he'll never have. You press your eyes shut but there's no way to keep the sound out. The echoes of youth, your private devils, advance upon you from afar, across the ether of time and space, through the Cadillac's insulated windows.

The sun is in the middle of the sky and the road is the coastal strip between Sokhna and Zafarana. It is just after the war and the road is narrow and worn-down. The curves are tight and dangerous. The car is moving too fast. To your right, the mountain is a giant whose rocks are scattered like children playing at its feet. To the left are the minefields, narrow and decorated with barbed wire and small signs with black skulls. Beyond them lies the sea, with its seemingly peaceful waves and the veiled rage that lingers with the ever-alert sharks, the coral sharp as knives, and the sea urchins with poisonous spikes.

The road is narrow and the curves are getting tighter. The potholes play with the Cadillac's suspension, as you observe the nurse wipe away a drop of custard from the corner of your grandmother's mouth. The nurse is one of three whom the hospital has dedicated around the clock to care for the elderly woman's every need. The nurse lifts the bed tray and puts it on the table then she neatly straightens the sheet over the lady's chest. It's all paid for.

"Lands and acres . . ." your grandmother mutters unintelligibly. The words' openings start off clear then they are submerged by an inner flow. Her speech is a surrealist flood that leaves a haunted glint in her yellowish eyes. She argues, waves a shaky arm then stops suddenly and her eyes focus on you, her millionaire grandson. They brighten up but are quickly overtaken by the same glint. Her river continues to flow in nonchalance, "The Rolls redder than a rose . . ."

She had only one wish, a prayer she repeated thousands of times in your presence. She'd raise her palms to the sky and say, "Gracious God, please take me before my mind slips . . . before I start talking nonsense . . . and the riffraff start looking upon me with pity."

She never asked for money and power; those she took herself. She never asked for health and happiness; she never cared much about either. Instead she prayed for an early death, assumed it was her legitimate claim.

When humanity's turn has come in the queue of extinction, and a new race, wiser and less evil, has taken over the planet, then a monument will be erected in our memory. A fact you recognize, Tutu, in your delirium. You've known it for some time. The memorial will take the shape of a tombstone. You can visualize it but cannot get yourself to focus on the writing.

"Here lies a race destroyed by its folly," you whisper a guess in the calm of a Cadillac parked next to a ghost tower. Surely this must be the right answer. Still, you're unable to make out the words engraved in the black marble. You have no way of easing your burning bewilderment.

"Won't you say hello to Abd al-Tawab Pasha?" the nurse shouts in your grandmother's face.

Your grandmother regains consciousness for less than a second then wanders back and the Cadillac hugs the curves on the coastal road. Its broad tires shriek like wailing women. The vibrations create a parallel sea whose waves blow from inside the vehicle. Your shouts to the driver produce no sound. The lid of the car trunk flies away, torn by the hinges. You don't know what makes you look back out the rear window. With every curve, banknotes burst out of the trunk. Dollars here, pounds sterling there. The Cadillac leaves behind a cloud of stray paper that slowly sinks into the indifferent Red Sea.

"What's this . . . shouldn't we be more careful?" The nurse treats her like a child. The elderly lady has passed gas with a deep extended sound.

Your grandmother suddenly becomes lucid. She stares at you, her glare punching a hole in your head. "I blew some air . . . so what?" And she turns loose a long, liberated laugh.

A moment of serenity. Then something in the room's corner catches her attention and the glint returns to her eyes. You hear the nurse clicking her tongue as you leave. The same way your mother used to click her tongue when, as a child, you did something wrong. A metallic click screamed by a Cadillac speeding from Sokhna to Zafarana, fleeing the smell of rot, leaving behind the voice of reason amid an endless cloud of dollars.

Inside your big car at the foot of the Tower of Happiness, you shut your eyes. You know that your grandmother's journey is approaching its end. But you don't rush off to see her; you no longer can. You smile to yourself and whisper, "I blew some air . . . so what?"

⁙

"I put my faith in God," you stated, Gamil, at thirty-three thousand feet and became a murderer on CNN; a mass murderer, an indiscriminate killer, a man who's killed total strangers—a phenomenon that has become so common in their society that it has started to make sense. Rationalizing the absurd: humanity's main achievement in the twentieth century. In the past we explained these things away as acts of the devil, wrath of the Gods, or sorcerer's spells. Or people would simply fold these incidents away in a dark corner of their consciousness. Today, the worst of atrocities have become live pictures on our screens. Either disbelieve our own eyes or accept, so we rationalize.

They claimed that, Batouti, you were suffering from depression caused by your daughter's illness and missing the promotion to captain. In their insolence, they even asserted you were in the habit of exposing yourself in public, in New York hotels. This is how the Americans dig up people's secrets. Even in death, they're not spared. This is how CNN rationalizes the absurd. Or is it a CIA conspiracy? A way to protect the Pentagon's diabolical secrets? Or is it all about the price of Boeing's jumbo stocks? A unique logic invented by the multi-headed hydra that is America. This is how truth is blended with fiction; illusion becomes a cheap craft they disseminate right and left in virtual reality.

And you, the people of Egypt, you flood the streets, volatile, bewildered. Injustice on the screens is nothing new to us. They've exchanged the facts and now truth no longer exists. Their truth has silenced us, frozen the words in our mouths. Our vagabond truth sleeps on the sidewalks, beneath bridges. Nobody pays it any attention anymore. What use is the wounded truth anyway, after it has fallen into their trap? And what good is rationality when they've rationalized the absurd?

Two hundred and seventeen cries echo across the North Atlantic, in the airspace of the Island of Nantucket; magical in her transient summer, laden with anger in winter—a long dark anger. The fates perform a symphony of pain for each of you. In life ambition and envy divide us. We're distinguished by passports, places of worship. We identify ourselves by those we love and hate. But death is the one and only unifier.

"I put my faith in God," you, the passengers of flight 990, declared. Then there was silence.

✖

You, Batouti, Antar, Tutu, Islah, Didi, Meshmesh . . . .

You, Ashmouni, Abd al-Malak, Shoukry, Esmeralda, Sambo . . . are me. You are me, and I am you.

There's nothing to separate us but the illusion of individuality.

Time is one, our places we've exchanged . . . and space is our common heritage.

Lover and loved, oppressor and oppressed, executioner and victim . . . we're all of them at once.

We move in coinciding circles that we thought to be detached.

Their colors: a rainbow of crystal white.

Before our individuality was generated . . . our existence was real, and after the maggots devour our livers . . . where will our egoism reside?

The spirit is everlasting, and the ego, an illusion soon to dissipate.

Oh ye white rose . . . guardian of secrets,

If neither death provides an ending . . . nor birth a beginning . . .

then extension is total, complete

and truth is a connection,

existence, unity,

and differences merely

a fabrication

that in our selfishness

we believe.

✖

What seekest thou, my son?

You shuffle across the landing, Abd al-Malak, raise a knife that's not even yours. The knife belongs to Tutu, the millionaire, or to the ghosts, the masters, the dead who live among us. You raise the knife that encapsulates human history and stride down the stairs. You've just finished your evening prayers and the world surrounding you is all red. You've prayed for the millionth time, but you've never touched its essence.

You stop. Rather than ring the bell, you kick the door. You leave an imprint of mud and excrement on its varnished surface. It is the very shoe whose shine you're so proud of. Farah opens at once. Without makeup, her face is pale. You don't find it surprising that she didn't bother to put on makeup on the night of a thousand years, the mother of all nights. You don't find it surprising that her nightgown is torn. You don't find it surprising that she's not surprised to see you. Nothing surprises you anymore. You've passed the station of surprise on your predetermined tracks. The knife now sums up the course of your life. The tracks are straight and parallel and lead all the way to the precipice. Your destiny is an assured fall. The cascade of red has exploded at the center of the universe. Nothing can stop it now. Its pulse has seduced then drowned you.

She makes way, silently invites you in. She pays no attention to the knife, makes no attempt to resist. She no longer cares about life. All she wishes for is to avoid scandal. After all she's done, after all she's lost, she still dreads scandal. You too.

No matter how liberated, rebellious, revolutionary she's become. No matter how intensely people have ostracized her, their talk is still her greatest fear.

And yours too.

You push the door shut behind you, then shout, "You sold yourself, whore."

The door's crash is violent yet hollow. The lock hasn't clicked in. You realize—as she does—that you should turn back and shut the door properly, but the train of events has already left the station.

"I had no choice," she states a fact, neither showing remorse nor seeking forgiveness.

"What about your dreams . . . and your honor? What about my honor that you trampled in the mud?" Your eyes are two pieces of solid glass. "You sold yourself, whore." You rhyme it like a line from your favorite song.

Then you see him lying on the sofa. Your emotions boil over, flow into the knife.

"I was sold anyway . . . my mother sold me to the fishmonger and split the profit with Kamboura . . . when I sell myself, at least I get to keep my own price." She seems oblivious to the man's presence.

Shaker studies you with eyes burdened by a thick mist. His body is inert, incapable of motion. His hand clutches his neck as though trying to liberate his windpipe, or out of fear of the hangman's noose. Could Farah have poisoned him? Or did she wear him out in another way? In your confusion you allow your arm to drop. The knife is heavy and your mind is getting foggy.

"You're no better than me." Her words, a dagger, rip your entrails. Yet it takes ages before the pangs of pain start shaking you. Then the world turns black as it spins around you. The floor shudders like a mechanical room in a funfair in hell. You realize that the knife has risen again, that it has developed a life of its own. The knife is master now, both you and Farah its obedient servants.

"Then I'll kill both you and myself." The knife's voice is crystal clear.

"So what . . .? Aren't we, after all, two ducks in the canal?" Her smile is ochre, poisoned.

"But first, I have to kill this scum."

"He's not worth it . . . he's already leaving this world."

The referee whistles. A goal, a foul, or is it halftime already? It's the doorbell.

"Are you playing movies?" It is Antar, the little devil. He wears a sorcerer's conical hat, silver with stars and crescents, and has a rolled paper whistle in his mouth. When he blows, it produces a foot-long erection. The official whistle at parties and celebrations: such an obvious phallic symbol.

"Antar, what are you doing here now, my boy?" Your voice is dampened by a lump in your throat.

"Yes, sweetie, we're playing. But you have to go back to Mommy now." Farah's eyes suddenly fill up with tenderness.

"Can I play with you, uncle . . .? Look what I can do." He walks toward you with both hands raised, moves sideways, pouts his lips and hoots, pretending to be a ghost. Then he notices the man lying on the

304

sofa. "Is this how you die when you lose? Does he stay like this until the end of the game?"

"There's still hope, Abd al-Malak . . . you still have the chance to set up the business you always dreamed of." For the first time her eyes focus on the knife.

"Antar, go away." Your voice is low. Your larynx has turned to stone.

You suddenly remember the raised knife and allow your arm to rest. You wonder what you're doing here. Nothing in life makes sense anymore. What seekest thou, my son?

"It's still possible to turn the desert green . . . to do something great with your life."

To turn the desert green. Her phrase provokes you, but Antar's presence restrains your angry soul. You rest the knife on the table and raise the child off his feet. You carry him to the door. He resists, blows his whistle in your face. Kicks and hits the air.

"Let me down or I'll pinch your ear, uncle." Tom Thumb threatens you. Despite your anger you find yourself trying to control your laughter.

"There's still hope, Abd al-Malak." Her plea reaches you as you lock the door, leaving the boy outside. You reach for the knife on the table. Antar presses the bell. If only she realized how the word 'hope' provokes you. A lie we keep on repeating. Where there's life there can be no despair. Nonsense. Life is all about despair. Words we toss right and left without a second thought, words like 'love' and 'faithfulness.' Two ducks in the canal. Words are colored lights like the ones they've adorned the tower's façade with. They fool only idiots. The Tower of Happiness. They call it the Tower of Happiness, how ridiculous.

"Don't soil your hands with my blood. I'm not worth it." There's not a hint of fear in her voice, only tenderness in her eyes. She's beyond fear. You too. There's nothing left for the two of you but despair and anger. But where did her eyes get that tenderness?

Could there still be an atom of love left in her heart?

305

"You and I, we deserve each other," you whisper, to mask your constricted voice. Antar rings the bell again. You allow the knife to drop to the floor. Your arm has lost the will. The man's wide-open eyes watch you while his mouth gasps for air. All the world's oxygen is no longer sufficient for him, or you. You have lost all sense of taste and smell. Even anger has abandoned you.

Could there still be an atom of love left in your heart?

You open the door and the boy rushes in. Her voice reaches you as you walk into the elevator. "It's too late for me . . . but there's still hope for you, Abd al-Malak . . . otherwise, there'll be no hope for Egypt, no hope left for the world."

Then the elevator door shuts you in.

"What seekest thou, my son?" you whisper to yourself.

⁙

What seekest thou, my son?
People are prisoners of their happiness
but I worship on freedom's altar.
Cleanliness is next to Godliness
and filthiness, next to women.
There are two types of women, don't forget:
the apples and the pears.
And men are like fish in the sea.
I adore candy dolls.
A white rose of supreme purity is what I pursue;
a lovely flower, with bloody thorns;
Venus's trap.
I liken us to two ducks in the canal . . .
But I'm the tiger in the cage; my mouth waters
at the sight of an innocent child.
Things are never what they seem;

old cheese breeds worms;

weakness is the weak man's strength . . .

the strong man's strength, his weakness.

And nothing ever changes . . .

One day at a time.

Life is a widow

and the masters must rest.

Ha. Ha. We are the masters, stupid.

You are all guilty and the worst of you knows who he is:

Every moment, I commit an act of deception

against others and myself;

I find satisfaction in excessive cruelty;

a desire to dominate God's creatures.

So turn off the lights, woman.

But what seekest thou, my son?

I seek a mythical truth,

I seek my lost dignity,

a shining black piano,

a vagabond violin,

this century's promised happiness,

I seek the runaway tits.

A Page Composed by the Clock's Strikes

Truth has allowed me to witness the scene of veiled light
and the rise of the ascendant star,
And told me: do you know how many layers I have veiled
    you with?
I said, no . . .
With seventy curtains, He said,
if you lift them, you do not see me,
and if you lift them not, you do not see me.
Then He said to me, if you lift them you see me,
and if you lift them not, you see me.
Then He said, beware of burning.
Then He said to me, you are my eyesight so be secure,
and you are my face so veil yourself.

Mohyiddin Ibn Arabi

The First Strike

The rose has turned yellow-brown. Its once-velvety petals now feel like paper. The vase has aged; its surface is covered in fine cracks. But the child—who has sneaked out of his early bed—is oblivious to this. The shadows engulf the corner that shelters the secret—what a secret!—and Antar's eyes cannot make out the transformation. Instead, he relies on memory's eye and her false confidence in the constancy of things.

He hugs Meshmesh, who turns his head, focuses on the vase and rose, then shrinks into the child's embrace. Antar shakes his head, covered in a sorcerer's conical hat made of silvery paper decorated with crescents and stars.

"What do you think, Meshmesh, let's give this beautiful flower to Auntie Farah so she'll stop crying like a baby?"

Without hesitation, he extends his arm to pick up the rose from the vase, but it disintegrates in his fist, turns into a thin powder. A whirl-wind erupts in the hall, disperses the powder across a night sky cloaked in radiant darkness.

The sudden cold rush makes Antar shudder. His eyes vacillate from his fingertips to the vase, searching for an explanation that his little mind can accept. Then he leans closer as he starts to suspect that it has turned duller in color and that its surface is all cracked. Instinctively, he picks up the vase from the bottom, takes a few steps backward until he's within the arc of light flooding in from the dining room and realizes how it has aged.

Suddenly, the vase's upper half collapses while he still holds it. He's sure he hasn't touched it or, in any way, caused it to break. With its jagged edge, the lower half remains a sharp weapon in the child's shivering grip.

"It broke," he says to his cat.

The child discards the vase, and still holding the kitten, runs like the wind, flees this cursed apartment that his father has so often warned him to avoid.

As for the vase's lower half, the child's jerking action propelled it into space out of the thirteenth floor balcony. It embarks on a journey, an extended fall in time and space.

The Second Strike

On its journey, ultimately to the bottom, the vase's lower half passes by the belly dancer's balcony. At this point, it makes three turns in the air along time's mercurial spiral. The laughter emanating from the apartment is beyond promiscuity, the music has reached boiling point. The dance extends a bridge to mankind's primordial past. Cigar smoke has erected dark tents. The champagne overflows and fills the revelers up to the top of their heads. Conversations have become intermittent, ideas scattered, and instincts now have the final word.

Supporting himself on the bare shoulders of two beautiful extras from a movie set, Mr. Kasseb gets to his feet. He pulls the two girls, in their glittering red and green dresses, up by the hands, and shouts to all the women wriggling around the hall and the men parked hypnotized on the sofas, "Everyone get up . . . let's go . . . let's say bye-bye to a thousand years and hello to a new millennium . . ."

Mr. Kasseb and his two dazzling companions form the head of a train that, in a matter of seconds, collects hundreds of twisting men and women. The wobbly dancing snake starts making the rounds while its tail keeps on growing until the wide hall suddenly feels claustrophobic. Mr. Kasseb throws open the apartment door and the noisy snake bursts outside to explore the horizons of the Tower of Happiness, chanting:

"Hello, hello . . . bye-bye, bye-bye . . . .

Hello, hello . . . bye-bye, bye-bye . . . ."

Mr. Kasseb waves his dainty hands in the air, supported by extensive shaking of his flabby arms and shoulders. A thick gold bracelet, more glittery than the belly dancers' costumes, dances on each of his wrists. His thick bluish lips deliver a hoarse, experienced singing voice:

"When the clock strikes . . . 'Welcome' we say.

When the clock strikes . . . let the music play.

Let the clock strike . . . let's rewind the counter.

Let's say hello to Oslo and Madrid . . .

and bye-bye to Jerusalem and Baghdad."

The Third Strike

With heavy steps, Abd al-Malak descends. He's wearing jeans and blue canvas shoes. In one hand he holds the tape recorder, the black Samsonite briefcase in the other. The Italian suits and French neckties he's left behind for the ghosts. He's departing the tower just as he came. He waited a long time but all the elevators were occupied. He doesn't mind taking the stairs, doesn't seem to be in a hurry.

Abd al-Malak is a matchstick both in appearance and substance. The world has lit then extinguished him. But a matchstick can light up only once. Can a man's honor be compared to a matchstick?

Both he and the vase's lower half tumble down to their destiny. At the twelfth floor, they share the same elevation. It's also at this point that the laughter and the raw, sensuous drumbeats catch up with him. He's concerned by none of this. Yet the dancing snake noisily approaches. In a philharmonic composition made up of a hundred male and female voices, it chants:

"Hello, hello . . . bye-bye, bye-bye . . . .

Hello, hello . . . bye-bye, bye-bye . . . ."

Abd al-Malak pays no attention to the flood of dancers that surrounds him. His broad forehead is furrowed; his hazel eyes murky; his dark features near black. Lula Hamdi, the belly dancer, clicks her finger-cymbals and sings in a powerful voice emanating from her flabby gut:

"Dance till you drop . . . let your mood run high.

Let the dollars flow in . . . and the milliemes scram!

Say hi to fun, and to stubborness bye-bye.

Bye-bye to misery . . . and hello to Uncle Sam."

The parade of dancers, propelled by an inner energy and rhythm, a unique collective spirit, waits for no one. Reciprocating Abd al-Malak's attitude, it ignores him. Each goes his own way, and the frenzied snake quickly overtakes Abd al-Malak, leaving him to his painfully slow progress. Mr. Kasseb, Lula Hamdi, her two assistants, Sambo, and Bassily blend with other faces and bodies Abd al-Malak has never seen before—or if he had come across them, they haven't left an imprint on his memory. At the very end of the flow of bodies comes Antar in his sorcerer's hat, holding Meshmesh who looks around him in tense alertness.

Abd al-Malak becomes aware of Antar. He wants to say something but the right words don't come to mind. He stares at the child as he moves away, hopping to the same rhythm as the others. Before he disappears around the stairwell corner, Antar looks back and, for a second, studies his dark, gloomy features, then he starts to chant:

"He'll sigh, he'll die . . . like a scaredy-cat, he'll cry."

Surprisingly, the hundred voices repeat after the child:

"He'll sigh, he'll die . . . like a scaredy-cat, he'll cry."

The Fourth Strike

The falling vase makes one somersault in the air just beyond the tenth floor of the Tower of Happiness. The vase's motion is a spiral in time and space. It belongs to an alternate universe whose laws do not coincide with those that govern the tower and its tenants. Nevertheless, an obscure yet potent interaction links the two worlds.

At that very instant, Madame Gawdat sits motionless on a Louis XV armchair whose seat and back are upholstered in navy-blue Aubusson, the same color as her dress. As usual, her makeup is delicate yet ample. She's wearing black patent-leather shoes. Her necklace's gray pearls, uniformly sized and fully rounded, have regained a unique luster they'd lost years ago. Just like her eyes; today, all exhaustion has dissipated and serenity radiates from them.

She picks up a framed photograph from the side table. She shakes her head slightly to the rhythms of an Om Kolthoum song emanating from an ancient Grundig recorder. With eyes fixed on the photograph, she sings along:

"They mentioned you again ... and reminded me .... They reminded me."

She lifts the telephone receiver and presses the buttons. "Can I speak to the small doctor please? Ah it's you ... hello, doctor ...." Her eyes remain fixed on the photograph. "Of course I'm aware you're not small ... please excuse me, my son, diabetes has been eating away at my

317

memory . . ." Gently, she returns the silver frame to its position on the side table. "Why not? I'd be happy to call you Cerebellum like everybody else . . . surely it's an indication of genius . . . but in your case it's not only genius, but also kindness of heart." She shifts the picture frame to the right and left until she's satisfied it is dead-center on the crochet tablecloth. "I'm sure you're the best person to take care of the girls." She lets go of the picture frame and sits up straight. "Would you be kind enough to put the receiver close to the girls' ears?"

She waits for a moment then says, "Hello my darlings. No matter what happens, you have to remember I love you, and will always love you."

The dogs' wailing across the line sounds like mourning women. She puts down the receiver.

She stands up, tucks her black patent-leather purse under her arm, and heads for the kitchen. She comes back with a yellow cleaning cloth, then rests her purse on the seat of the armchair she'd been sitting on. With the cloth, she wipes a few specks of dust from the marble surface of the low coffee table. She picks up her purse from the armchair and returns to the kitchen to hang the cloth from its plastic hook inside the broom cabinet. Then she opens the pistachio-green Westinghouse refrigerator whose color was all the rage in the seventies.

Madame Gawdat rests her purse on the squeaky-clean Formica counter then takes a cake from the refrigerator, a chocolate cake decorated with whipped cream flowers and preserved cherries. She places it on the kitchen table, contemplates it for a moment then pulls a dessert plate from the drying rack and a fork and knife from a drawer. She cuts a sizeable slice then takes a spatula from the drawer, which she uses to lift the slice onto the plate. Before she digs her fork into the cake, she repeats after Om Kolthoum, "They mentioned you again . . . and reminded me . . . They reminded me."

The sugar's sting on her tongue washes away years of depravation. Gradually she starts to distinguish the chocolate's sour tang from the cream's richness, a symphony of taste she has so missed.

After twenty minutes, she stares at the remaining quarter of the cake and smiles, slightly embarrassed at what she's done. She stands up, shakes a few crumbs from her dress, washes her plate, fork, and knife and gently places them in the drying rack. She dries her hands, lifts her purse, walks back to the hallway and stops before the mirror. She produces a lipstick from her purse and spreads a thin film over her lips, then presses them as she has done every day for the past fifty years. She returns the lipstick to her purse then quickly arranges her hair with her fingertips, careful not to get her hair entangled in her wedding band or the solitaire wedding ring.

Madame Gawdat heads for the living room, where she picks up the silver picture frame from the side table and contemplates the photograph. She's surprised at how young she looks, standing next to her husband, Sadat, and the first lady, with the Giza pyramids in the background. This woman, smiling at her from the picture, could just as well be someone else. The picture depicts a totally different world; a world she can no longer bear to be separated from; a world that, at last, she's returning to for eternity.

Still holding the picture frame, she heads for the bedroom. She starts to make out the drumbeats and trumpet calls from the landing outside her apartment and smiles. She doesn't mind the noise. She rests her purse on her late husband's side of the bed and balances the picture frame on his pillow, facing her. She takes her shoes off then lies on the bed. Suddenly, her body shudders violently. Soon the tremors weaken and nausea sets in. She forces herself to remain focused, gets on her feet, steps into her shoes, pulls the prayer rug from the dresser and returns to bed. She takes her time settling in then covers the exposed parts of her legs with the prayer rug. Then she passes her hands over her dress to straighten the creases and finally allows her head to rest on the pillow.

Madame Gawdat hears the rhymed words. She's not sure if this is the world's farewell, her requiem, or if it's a melody emanating from her luminous, inexhaustible inner space:

"Hello, hello . . . bye-bye, bye-bye . . . ."

319

Before the coma finally overtakes her, she repeats after the tape recorder, "They mentioned you again . . . and reminded me . . . They reminded me."

Then she looks at the picture, poised on her late husband's pillow, and smiles.

The Fifth Strike

As the falling vase makes its second consecutive roll outside the tenth-floor window, Shaker lies on the pistachio-green divan with the floral design. His bloodshot eyes emit a penetrating frost. The pangs of pain have melted away as his body turned into wood. His eyelids flicker continuously; he can move nothing else. His face is gray beneath his dyed, artificially straightened hair, which, in its brilliant blackness, has come to resemble a porcupine's spines.

Unexpectedly, his sense of hearing is doubly acute. In his mind, the thoughts come and go, crystallized, sharply defined. He's only too aware that his ailment is serious, but he has escaped death—for today at least. Except there are fates worse than death.

He's suddenly overwhelmed by drunken singing and dancers' patter. Intently, he listens to the noisy celebration as it stumbles down the staircase. He tries to guess the merrymakers' identities, attempts to cry out for help but fails to move even his lips. He finds himself encircled by that crazy song:

"Hello, hello . . . bye-bye, bye-bye . . . .

Hello, hello . . . bye-bye, bye-bye . . . ."

There's no escaping it, with all the meaning it bears. Yet, as the hubbub outside intensifies, his anxiety starts to subside. He feels thankful for the merrymakers' company; thankful to all the revelers and drunks; to all the philanderers of this universe. Above all, he's thankful for the breakdown of the barrier of silence that is life's mortal foe. Serenity gradually blossoms in his soul. Then there is calm.

Making a gargantuan effort, he succeeds in moving the corner of his mouth and the words tumble out in rhythmic mutterings:

"Bye-bye . . . bye-bye."

The Sixth Strike

Flanked by Shaker's door on one side and Madame Gawdat's on the other, it is Farah's turn to wait for the elevator that, tonight, is uncharacteristically late. From time to time, she glances at a large suitcase next to her. She's wearing an unbuttoned mink coat over a chic pink dress. Her olive face is pale and her thick eyebrows almost touch one another. She finds herself encircled by the ocean of dancers. She turns around, smiles and nods to some familiar faces, but nobody returns her greetings.

With a finger crowded with rings, she presses the elevator button repeatedly then takes out a cigarette and lights up. As she mutters impatiently, the music's rhythm spreads through her curvaceous body, and involuntarily, she starts to sway. Soon, Farah finds herself singing to a universal beat:

"My lover and I . . . we were almost happy.

In love's canal . . . we nearly swam,

pretended to be a couple of ducks,

But the world showed us its fangs,

reminded us that love is not for the likes of us."

And the dancing mass responds:

"Hello, hello . . . bye-bye, bye-bye . . . .

Hello, hello . . . bye-bye, bye-bye . . . ."

She waves to the line of dancers cascading down to the bottom, although most of them have already passed her by.

"Auntie Farah. Auntie Farah ... have you stopped crying now?" Antar's musical voice takes her by surprise.

As she turns around to face the child, she becomes aware of Abd al-Malak's skinny, exhausted form approaching amid the crowd. He nearly bumps into her then freezes. His eyes are bulging and he mutters something unintelligible. She has so much to say but doesn't know where to start. In her confusion, she can only answer the child, who has already disappeared around the bend of the staircase. "Yes love. I've stopped crying."

The Seventh Strike

By the time the vase's broken lower half has reached the eighth floor level, Karim Nafea is pulling Islah by the hand, decisively but in tenderness. She refuses to enter his apartment. With peasant-girl eyes, black outlined in kohl, she stares at him.

"Come in, Islah . . . we don't need a scandal." His voice is less confident than usual.

"My life is a mess . . . everything is wrong . . . I just don't get what's happening around me anymore." She passes her trembling fingers through her hair, which she has allowed to grow longer than usual.

"Alright . . . let's talk about it." He tries to pull her in but her slim body is tense, firm as an anchor.

"I feel that if I come inside your apartment today, I'll be drawn into a whirlpool from which death is the only escape." Islah speaks slowly, raising her right eyebrow. Then with a quick movement she pulls her hand away from his grip.

"Please get in . . . before someone sees us." He has stroked his silvery mane into a comical shape.

"I can't . . . I'm lost in an endless desert. I need to find my way before it's too late." Her wandering eyes amplify the gap that separates them.

Abruptly she regains her concentration and whispers, "Do you hear music?"

"Yes . . . people are coming down the stairs . . . get in here quick!" His handsome face is bright red.

The advancing soundwaves pave the way for the dancing flow. A thousand voices clamor:

"Hello, hello . . . bye-bye, bye-bye . . . .

Hello, hello . . . bye-bye, bye-bye . . . ."

"You go in, Karim . . . and don't forget to lock the door." Her eyes remain glued to his face as it distorts with despair.

"Why did you come here today, then?" Karim's anxiety has taken control of him. His red face and unkempt hair add an aura of insanity.

Islah is struck by an epiphany. For the first time in her life, she realizes that a body may harbor more than one person at the same time; that people are reshaped by time's unrelenting pressure; that in the rare event that dream and reality converge, the experience they give rise to can only be temporary. She calmly replies, "To say to you: bye-bye, bye-bye."

The Eighth Strike

At the sixth-floor level, the half-vase rotates in a horizontal circle. At this very instant, Dr. Mahgoub makes a move on Soad, the maid, who skillfully dodges his extended arm. She recoils then comes to a standstill a few steps away from the apartment door. With both hands on her waist, she calls out in a hushed voice, "Madame!"

He's dressed in a gray woolen robe and plastic slippers out of which his toes protrude like aggressive sticks of dynamite. Here he is: the esteemed professor, who has educated consecutive generations of our oil brothers, then brought home his savings in order to restart his postponed life in Egypt. He sends his murmurs after the maid in a voice incapable of whispering, "Girl, you shake your goods . . . and you drive me nuts."

Youth has passed him by and the years have eroded his capacity for pleasure. Mahgoub had fancied that time would freeze in Egypt pending his homecoming, but he was to learn that the Earth's rotation waits for no one. Upon his return, he discovered that people had changed; their morals had sunk to unprecedented lows, and more critically, that the savings he'd put together from years of hard work were mere pennies. The people who make the millions snatch their wealth out of thin air.

"No, doctor, not all birds are easy prey." As she talks every cell in her soft, feminine body gyrates inside her tight orange dress.

It crosses the doctor's mind that he started off high and mighty, but that a piece of his dignity got chipped away with every new petrodollar added to his bank account. But the knockout blow, he muses, was waiting for him back home. His eyes are on the corridor leading to the bedrooms. When his wife doesn't show up, he approaches the maid, "All right, all right . . . just give me one kiss . . ."

"Everything is possible . . . following God's law." Her seductive moves follow the rhythm of the music that is gradually consolidating its presence outside.

By mentioning God's law, she's stepped on his Achilles heel. He whose flesh has been pecked by the oil sheikhs, followed by the savings and loans sheikhs, then by the stock exchange sheikhs. Everyone has abused him and now she's demanding that he respect God's law. The whole world violates the traffic laws with impunity but he's required to stop at every red light. That may have been possible at the beginning but now he must catch up with life's flowing stream. He must snatch every look, every musical note, every kiss.

Soad turns sideways. In one move, she amplifies her curvaceous breasts and behind, and allows him a generous view of her assets in profile. Then she turns the doorknob and spontaneously throws herself in the middle of the dancing crowd and starts to sing in her brazen female voice:

"In accordance with God's law . . . anything will go."

And the crowd responds:

"Hello, hello . . . bye-bye, bye-bye."

Dr. Mahgoub cuts in, in his loudspeaker of a voice:

"You shake to the right . . . and you shake to the left.

And my heart has fallen victim to theft.

My soul has been burnt by love,

I can no longer resist your stuff."

He starts to dance in his woolen robe, surrounded by all the men in tuxedos. Suddenly, he turns around, "Antar! What are you doing here . . . you little devil?"

The Ninth Strike

Sergeant Ashmouni gasps for air as he reaches the second floor landing. He pulls Zuzu by the hand. She's wearing jeans that hug her curves. Her plastic slippers are purple to match the scarf covering her head.

"Why didn't we just wait for the elevator like everybody else?" The two-story climb doesn't seem to have exhausted her, though.

She studies everything around her: the brilliant marble, the polished apartment doors, and the indoor plants in the corners. She cannot see the broken half of the vase, however, which just then intersects the second-floor level in the air outside the tower.

"Keep quiet, girl . . . did you want us to wait . . . in the lobby . . . for the bad-tempered . . . security clerk . . . to come back . . . and start asking questions?" he gasps.

"And why would he ask questions? Aren't you supposed to be the government?"

"Of course I am, you stupid girl . . . I come and go as it pleases me. But when you're on an official mission, you're not supposed to bring along the Missus, if you know what I mean." He pushes his cap backward, exposing his hair streaked with white.

"Yes, but didn't you say you wanted to take me for a ride in the elevator?"

"Sure."

"Then why are you making me climb the stairs . . . ? Or was I born to be miserable?" She turns around as the music and laughter starts to rise.

"Spit the words out of your mouth, woman. May God never bring us misery . . . we'll take the elevator from here . . . and now, let it take its time." He presses the elevator button.

"Are they having a wedding . . . or is this what they call a New Year's celebration?"

"Now listen here, girl . . . there'll be no dancing or any of that business. I'll just give you a ride in the elevator . . . then straight home we go." He presses the button again, his impatience growing.

With his finger still pressing the button, he feels her hard talons dig into his shoulder. Before he can turn around, her cracked voice slaps him, "What are you doing here, Ashmouni?"

The sergeant's face is the color of pure yellow turmeric. For some reason, the Owl's appearance doesn't surprise him; he's overwhelmed by a sense of déjà vu. Anyhow, why is it so strange that the Owl should show up right now and deprive him of a pleasure that, to start with, he had no claim to? He who's never enjoyed a single uninterrupted pleasure. Did he think that his erotic fantasy with Zuzu in the elevator could possibly come true? He swallows and, with the calm of a man condemned to death, replies, "Damn these women. What are you doing here, old hag?"

"Men with a sense of shame no longer walk the earth! You ungrateful man . . . were you going to let this worthless wench have all the fun and dance all night . . . and keep me in the dark?" Abetted by the drumbeats that are creating tremors up and down the staircase, the Owl wriggles her dried-up body to make her point.

Caught red-handed, he's covered in shame from head to toe. The words simply refuse to come to his rescue. Before he gets the chance to pull himself together and come up with an excuse, the elevator door slides open, releasing a woman's flirtatious giggle. The laughter, mingled with a sensuous perfume, quickly invades the sergeant's world. A girl in a short black glittering dress emerges in rhythmic strides. She is followed by the respectable Mr. Hafez.

The sergeant freezes, unable to utter a word. His envious eyes focus on the lipstick stains on the man's cheeks and collar.

"Let's go, Ashmouni. Aren't we going to ride the elevator?" Zuzu whispers with eyes fixed on the girl and the big-shot pasha. For no apparent reason, the two start to climb the stairs.

"Elevator my foot . . . It's over. The plan has gone bad, bust, kaput, it's been called off, cancelled, terminated . . . We'll take the stairs, wenches. We come down just as we came up." The sergeant watches the elevator door slam shut. Despair is written all over his face.

"But . . ." Before Zuzu can voice her objection, they are swamped by the dancing horde. Without the slightest hesitation, she joins the gyrating dancers and repeats after them:

"Hello, hello . . . bye-bye, bye-bye . . . .

Hello, hello . . . bye-bye, bye-bye . . . ."

Ashmouni stands there, having lost all sense of control. Zuzu easily blends with the flood of dancers but the Owl clings to him like a drowning person. If not for his weakness and bad judgment he wouldn't have found himself in this shameful position. But weakness is an old friend whose company he's used to and bad judgment a mistress he picked up only recently but who now refuses to let him go. He slaps his cheeks with both hands and says to the same rhythm:

"The prostate is the size of a sweet potato . . ."

As she starts to wriggle among the dancers, the Owl responds, "And the hemorrhoids bite like nails . . ."

And the multi-headed single-voiced crowd chants:

"Hello, hello . . . bye-bye, bye-bye . . . .

Hello, hello . . . bye-bye, bye-bye . . . ."

331

The Tenth Strike

Three meters short of its objective, the broken vase vibrates in repeated spiral rotations, as though it too has been infected by the rowdy carnival dance. The human swarm has gushed through the staircase and out into the tower's expansive foyer, which is soon packed all the way to the main entrance. The musical band positions itself at the center of the foyer encircled by the dancing crowds and starts to splash out its crazy rhythms in every direction, like the sun's rays: generous to the point of burning.

Accompanied by one of her assistants, Lula Hamdi, the glittering belly dancer, climbs on top of the security clerk's desk. Together, they treat all eyes to their sizzling dance. The spotlights of the Japanese television crew target them, prompting them to boogie with redoubled energy. The photographer has managed to install his camera on a fully extended tripod and, standing on a small metallic platform he set up from elements crammed in his backpack, he devours all with a feverish lens: belly dancers, tenants, and of course the little Japanese presenter who politely squeezes herself among the revelers, simultaneously excusing herself and asking questions. Nobody pays her any attention, as though she were a phantom from another world. Eventually she gives up, then starts to sway, then to gyrate and sing along with the crowd in drunken delight:

"Hello, hello . . . bye-bye, bye-bye . . . .

Hello, hello . . . bye-bye, bye-bye . . . ."

The security clerk emerges through the side door that leads to the service room, with Hani, the plumber, at his heels. They slowly exhale smoke and, in intoxicated astonishment, contemplate the foyer's transformation. Then the plumber joins in the song:

"A thousand hellos to cool.

Welcome to globalization and business.

Mille au revoirs to geekiness,

to knowledge, thought, and reflection."

Sheikh Tamer, Karim Nafea's son, returning from late-night prayers, comes in through the main entrance. He is unable to grasp what his eyes are seeing. He averts his gaze whenever his eyes fall on one of the beautiful dancing women. Finally, he penetrates the philandering crowd with eyes firmly focused on the granite floor, all the time muttering prayers of repentance.

In his confusion, he collides with Islah, who, with tears swelling in her eyes, is struggling through the crowd but in the opposite direction. He pushes her away then they each continue along their course. After a period of time neither of them can determine, they simultaneously reach the main entrance on the one hand and the elevator on the other. Both manage to escape. As they disappear, neither can avoid the chanting bombardment:

"Hello, hello . . . bye-bye, bye-bye . . . .

 Hello, hello . . . bye-bye, bye-bye . . . ."

Abdallah Bassily rattles the cymbals, which look smaller than usual in the cushions of his gigantic fingers, and sings:

"From America's tits suckle the facts:

a country that has tasted McDonald's

will never resist again

and never run out of song."

The falling vase makes an extra few acrobatic summersaults, challenging the laws of nature—which have become a source of pride for the mortals who composed them. Dr. Mahgoub dances with the MP's wife, Sambo with Soad the maid, Mr. Kasseb with Zuzu the flirt, and the security clerk with the stocky police officer, while Antar runs around spanking the revelers on their bottoms.

The elevator doors slide open and deliver girls in revealing dresses pulling lipstick-smeared men by the ties. The girls start to ululate. Thousands of white doves flutter into the high-ceilinged foyer in what the revelers take for a gesture of welcome to the upcoming new millennium.

Outside, fireworks splash across the night sky and the Cairo heavens light up in green, red, white, and purple. Every single ray of light is reflected by the pinnacle they've installed atop Khufu's abused pyramid. Then—independent of the official celebrations—a white phosphorescent rose appears across the Egyptian sky, outshining all else. It lights up the world for a split second, then darkness prevails. Trapped in a party where he does not belong, Ashmouni starts to pull at his hair and chants in anguish, "The prostate is the size of a sweet potato . . ."

And as she boogies with the two men from the Lada, the Owl responds, "And the hemorrhoids bite like nails . . ."

And the crazy, debauched, amorphous mass repeats:

"Hello, hello . . . bye-bye, bye-bye . . . .

Hello, hello . . . bye-bye, bye-bye . . . ."

The Eleventh Strike

The Cadillac has been parked in front of the tower for over an hour. The chauffeur has quietly merged with the shadows. Ihsan, the bodyguard, looks about him in customary vigilance. Sensing no imminent threat, he allows himself to steal glances at the rose of light that decorates the tower's façade. Its beauty, visible miles away, must bestow joy in the hearts of Cairenes out for a promenade on the riverbanks or a trip in yachts and feluccas. The bodyguard is overtaken by a momentary feeling of calm, a false sense of security. From time to time, he observes the tower, smiling at the dancing human stream that continues to flow into the foyer from the stairs and elevators, transforming its elegant entrance into a cabaret. A cabaret united in a senseless drunken chant:

"Hello, hello . . . bye-bye, bye-bye."

His attention is drawn to a convertible parked in a dark spot close by. He cannot distinguish its color in the darkness of the night of a thousand years, yet he knows it is Shoukry Shaker's car. The sporty vehicle shakes from time to time, indicating the presence of passengers. He allows his imagination free reign and pictures what's going on inside the car's sensuous confines. In rehearsed decisiveness, he regains his alert posture and expels all daydreams.

Ihsan makes out the silhouette of a skinny young man in the distance. The figure carries a thick stick, which he uses to smash the windscreens and headlights of the parked cars. This is no doubt one of the lunatics of the Maadi gang, to which the newspapers have dedicated entire pages and headlines. He's surprised that the youth's hair is tied up in a ponytail that bounces as he moves. He decides that whatever happens to other people's cars is no concern of his. Still, he reaches inside his holster and grips his pistol, just in case.

At that moment—unseen by the bodyguard or anyone else—the falling vase is about to reach its predetermined destination. With the momentum of its extended fall, it slices the cold air. Shoukry, safe inside his convertible, is busy fondling a young girl in a scarlet evening dress with a fine wool shawl wrapped around her chest and shoulders to keep her warm. The vase's jagged edge pierces his lap. The spoiled millionaire cries out in a panic that soon turns into unbearable pain.

Pistol in hand, the bodyguard rushes to the sports car. The scab—slightly protruding as it heals—draws a dark line down the length of his face, giving him the look of an African warrior with a ritual tattoo or a Native American horseman in war paint. He yanks the car door open—almost pulling it off its hinges—and freezes before the red fountain erupting from the young billionaire's lap. His face and clothes are not spared its living spray. Then his eyes fall on the girl, her face illuminated by the glow of a street lamp. His gaze moves from her pale face to her rounded thighs exposed by her lifted dress.

"Zakia! What the hell are you doing here?" His ears no longer register Shoukry's hysterical shrieks or the drumbeats, trumpet wails, and non-chalant laughter. They no longer wish to hear any sound other than his sister's excuses. But Zakia has adopted the posture of a frightened kitten in the Ferrari seat. All she can manage is to pull down her dress to cover her knees.

He points his weapon at her. She shrinks in the car seat but doesn't look away. Instead, she returns his stare. The blood rushes inside his head, but the way she looks at him melts his heart. Who is he to judge her? He changes his mind and points the gun at Shoukry, drenched in his own impure blood. The young millionaire wriggles like a worm. Aren't

336

these the masters you've sold your soul for? What use are they to you now and you to them? But in the end who is he to judge Shoukry? Who is he to judge anyone? In his confusion, Ihsan positions the gun barrel inside his mouth. Traveling through its metallic tube, and in agonizing irony, the song penetrates the barrier of his suffering:

"Hello, hello . . . bye-bye, bye-bye."

He pulls the trigger.

The Twelfth Strike

The echoes of frantic screaming blend with the drumbeats and song, and reach the ears of the billionaire Abd al-Tawab, Tutu, in the Cadillac's solitude. Suffering from the chronic bewilderment characteristic of the buffer zone that separates sleep from awakening, he is unable to distinguish merrymaking from horror. Then the shock of certainty slices through the slowly brewing soup of sound. For a split second, he comes to. Then he returns to his wilderness. He sits cross-legged in front of a campfire in a distant desert. Abd al-Malak waves a red-hot copper mandal at him.

"All my wealth is legitimate. My word should be enough . . . I don't need to prove anything to anyone," Tutu replies in a cracked voice, but the false psychic is paying no attention.

He challenges him by slowly licking the ladle-like mandal himself, with the smooth, teasing delight of a girl licking an ice cream cone. Then he raises the mandal in Tutu's face. With the metallic ladle still a hand's width away, the billionaire feels his saliva turn to steam.

"I pay you to solve my problem. Not to judge me." Tutu's voice has acquired a feminine shrillness.

A shrillness that echoes the rising whistle of steam.

Tutu presses his palms against his ears. In his darkened corner of the car, he looks around him. Fragments of color have penetrated the tinted glass and now cover the white leather seats in a thick layer of phosphorescent light, a spectacle that is almost intentional.

Then that damned thought revisits him, to finally perfect its siege. Hundreds or thousands of years from now, when humanity has claimed its natural place in the dustbin of history, when another race, wiser and more benevolent will have taken control of life on earth, then—for reasons known only to them—they decide to erect a monument to humanity. That memorial shall take the form of a rectangular slab made of a gray translucent material. Tutu can see it clearly now, shining confidently through the Cadillac's windshield. It protrudes from the soil, unadorned by lights or flowers, graced by only two lines of writing.

The first line simply states, 'The Human Race.'

As for the second, he can almost extend his arm and pass a finger over it. He most certainly would have deciphered it, had it not been for the faint mist that keeps the words just beyond his reach.

Tutu fidgets in the Cadillac's rear seat. It is only a few words that bedevil him, one short sentence. But this is the sentence that summarizes thousands of years, millions of lives, monumental pyramids of love and hate, joy and cruelty, generosity and malice. One short, magical sentence can explain everything. And now it is out there, before his eyes. He can almost touch it with his fingertips, yet its knowledge is denied him. The sentence continues to nag and he's losing hope that his thirst will ever be quenched. His torment is aggravated by the rising whistle's shrill invasion.

Then he realizes that it is a phone ringing and reaches into his pocket for the cell phone. The nurse's voice is solemn, experienced.

"Thank you for your condolences," he replies calmly.

The edges of a crazy brazen song, emanating from somewhere in the background of his consciousness, keeps forcing itself upon him, penetrating his seclusion:

"Hello, hello . . . bye-bye, bye-bye."

He puts down the phone and instinctively checks his watch. The century's demise is a hair's width away but the clock's hand hasn't crossed the mark yet. To his grandmother, Amina Aboulgheit, the gift of life was both bequeathed and withdrawn in the twentieth century. She had not asked for more. Witnessing the new millennium had never made it on to her wish-list. She was not one to compromise.

Tutu rests his head on the upholstered car body and shrinks as far as he can into the Cadillac's dark corner. He extends an arm to Abd al-Malak. The spiritual medium raises the mandal from the embers and hands it over. Tutu holds the mandal in his hand. He contemplates the searing metallic hemisphere, takes pleasure in the heat it radiates to the world; the heat of truth; the heat of certainty. Then he extends his tongue and licks, allows himself to revel in the mandal's red glowing light and he feels pain as never before. The anguish of knowledge.

Now he's certain. He's suspected this for months. Now he knows he'll remain sleepless until the end. He will be granted no respite, no slumber, until—at an unspecified moment—his time runs out. No sooner has Tutu resigned himself to this truth than the Memorial for Humanity is exposed to him in its full glory: a rectangle embedded in the soil, created out of a metal yet to be discovered by science; a metal whose hardness is matched only by its translucence. Tutu is overtaken by tremors. He's laughing and crying in the same breath. Finally, the wisdom engraved in glowing letters is unmistakable. The eloquent synopsis of human history is, at last, legible:

The Human Race

I blew some air . . . so what?

Glossary

Abdelhalim Abdelhalim Hafez, an iconic song and movie star who rose to fame in the 1950s and 1960s, associated in many people's minds with the Nasser era.

Abdelrahman Elabnoudy a poet associated with the opposition to President Anwar Sadat's pro-western shift in the 1970s.

Abdelwahab Elbayaty an Iraqi poet who spent many years in exile.

Aboulahab, Abousoffian two leaders of Mecca in the seventh century who were fiercely opposed to the nascent religion of Islam.

Ahmed Zaki a movie star who rose to fame in the 1980s and 1990s.

Ahmed Zewail the Egyptian-American winner of the 1999 Nobel prize in chemistry.

Akhenaton an Egyptian pharaoh known as the first monotheist.

Albayan a tabloid subsequently shut down by the government.

Ali Kouta an active fan of the Zamalek soccer club.

Asalamu alaikum the traditional Islamic greeting, literally translated as 'Peace be upon you.'

Asbakia a square and park in downtown Cairo. The location of a large number of second-hand bookstalls, it constituted an informal cultural hub until the 1980s.

ashtatan ashtout words traditionally used to dispel—or appease—the spirits, meaningless in modern language, probably of ancient Egyptian origin.

'aysh saraya a rich and very sweet pastry, literally translated as 'palace bread.'

Azza Eid Abdelmawla a poet from an Egyptian oasis.

basboussa a rich and very sweet pastry.

Captain Zewar a soccer commentator in the 1970s.

Damietta a city on the Egyptian Mediterranean coast.

Daresalam a slum in southern Cairo, off the main road leading to the upper-class neighborhood of Maadi.

Eid a feast or festival, most commonly refers to either Eid al-Fitr at the end of Ramadan or Eid al-Adha when the pilgrimage to Mecca takes place.

El-Kosh a village in Upper Egypt that witnessed sectarian clashes between Muslims and Christians in the late 1990s.

Elsayeda Zeinab a popular neighborhood in central Cairo.

emma a traditional head cover for men, similar to a turban.

Falcao a Brazilian soccer star in the 1980s.

Farah Diba widow of the late Shah of Iran Mohammad Reza Pahlavi.

Fardous Abdelhamid an Egyptian actress.

Farid Alatrash a legendary song and movie star in the 1950s and 1960s, originally from Lebanon.

Farouk Elbaz an Egyptian-American geologist who became prominent for his work in planning the lunar landing sites for some of the Apollo missions.

Faten Hamama an iconic movie star who became known as the 'Lady of the Arab Screen.'

Gamil Batouti captain of EgyptAir flight 990 that crashed off the eastern coast of the United States in 1999. Information from the retrieved flight data recorder revealed him as saying, "I put my faith in God" immediately before the airplane's final plunge. This led US investigators to conclude he deliberately crashed the plane. The Egyptian investigative team, however, strongly contested this conclusion, pointing to mechanical failure. Egyptian public opinion regards this as further evidence of the spread of Islamophobia in the US. To this day, the findings of the official investigation have never been made public.

gelabia a traditional gown for both sexes.

Gihan Sadat widow of the late Egyptian president Anwar Sadat.

Hafr Elbaten an area in northeastern Saudi Arabia where Egyptian troops were stationed in 1991 in preparation for the liberation of Kuwait.

Hajj a term of address for those who have performed the pilgrimage to Mecca. It is commonly used to address older people as a sign of respect. The same word is used to describe the pilgrimage itself.

Hassanein Heikal Egypt's most prominent journalist for over half a century. Particularly known for his close association with President Gamal Abdel Nasser and clash with his successor, President Anwar Sadat.

Hussein Elsherbiny an Egyptian actor.

Ibn Khaldoun a famous Arab historian, Islamic theologian, social scientist, and statesman born in present-day Tunisia (1332–1406). He is sometimes called the "father" of the social sciences.

Ibrahim Nafea one of Hassanein Heikal's successors as editor in chief of *al-Ahram* newspaper.

jinn a kind of spirit. The traditional belief is that humans were created from clay, angels from light, and jinn from fire.

Kafr Shoukr a village in the Nile Delta.

Kamanana the meaningless title of a popular Egyptian song.

koshary a popular dish made of rice, noodles, lentils, chickpeas, fried onions, and various condiments.

Laila Mourad an iconic Egyptian song and movie star in the 1940s.

Maadi an upper-class suburb in the south of Cairo.

Magda an Egyptian movie star famous in the 1950s and 1960s.

millieme the smallest denomination of coin, no longer in use.

Mimi Elsherbini a soccer player turned commentator.

Mohamed Abdelwahab composer, singer, and movie star, a towering figure in modern Arab music.

Mohamed Heneidi a contemporary comedy film star.

Mohyiddin Ibn Arabi mystic, philosopher, poet, sage, he is one of the world's great spiritual teachers. Known as 'al-Shaykh al-Akbar' (the Greatest Master), he was born in 1165 into the Moorish culture of Andalusian Spain, the center of an extraordinary flourishing and cross-fertilization of Islamic, Christian, and Jewish thought.

Mourid Barghouti a Palestinian poet.

moussaka an eastern Mediterranean dish made from eggplant and sometimes mincemeat.

Omar Sharif an iconic Egyptian and international movie star.

Om Kolthoum possibly the most influential Egyptian singer of all time, she dominated Arab music for the greater part of the twentieth century.

Pope Shenouda patriarch of the Egyptian Coptic Church.

Qarun the prophet Moses's cousin, according to Islamic tradition. Endowed with immense wealth, he was known for his vanity and arrogance. In the end he faced God's wrath.

Rouka nickname of Farouk Gaafar, a famous Egyptian soccer player in the 1970s.

Salah Abdel-Sabour an Egyptian poet.

Salah Jahin an Egyptian poet and cartoonist, closely associated with the Nasser era.

Sharia the basic beliefs of Islam, commonly used to mean Islamic law.

Sheikh Sharawy an Islamic scholar and preacher who was the first to utilize television to spread his message and achieve tremendous popularity. He died in 1998.

shisha water pipe; hookah.

Shoubra a sprawling lower-middle class neighborhood in northern Cairo.

Shoubra Circle an intersection of tram lines at the heart of Shoubra.

Shouikar a famous comedienne and movie star for the past forty years or so.

Sokhna short for Ain al-Sokhna, translated 'the hot spring,' a reference to the hot spring that gushes beneath its seashore. It is located on the Gulf of Suez on the Red Sea, south of the city of Suez, on a narrow strip between the rocky mountain and the sea.

Suleiman Pasha Street a central street in downtown Cairo.

tarbush a red conical cap for men, no longer in common use.

Teleb nickname of Mohamed Abdelmoteleb, a popular singer in the 1950s and 1960s.

Yassine a brand of glassware that was particularly popular in the 1950s and 1960s.

Yousra a famous movie star since the 1980s.

Youssef Wahby one of the pioneers of Egyptian theater and cinema. Because of his formal style, he became associated with dramatic actions and statements.

Zafarana a small port south of Sokhna.

zar a voodoo-like ritual characterized by strong drumbeats and rhythmic dancing that usually ends in a trance.